2|19

DATE DUE

KW		
PD		
		PRINTED IN U.S.A.

Hayner PLD/Large Print
Overdues .10/day. Max fine cost of
item. Lost or damaged item: additional
$5 service charge.

Also by Jonathan Kellerman
Available from Random House Large Print

A Measure of Darkness (with Jesse Kellerman)

Night Moves

Crime Scene (with Jesse Kellerman)

Heartbreak Hotel

Breakdown

The Murderer's Daughter

Killer

THE WEDDING GUEST

JONATHAN KELLERMAN

THE WEDDING GUEST

AN ALEX DELAWARE NOVEL

RANDOM HOUSE
LARGE PRINT

Published in the United States of America by Random
House Large Print in association with Ballantine Books,
an imprint of Random House, a division of Penguin
Random House LLC, New York.

Cover design: Scott Biel
Cover images: Joerg Buschmann/
Millennium Images (beach), Silas
Manhood/Arcangel Images (man), Stephanie Haberl/
EyeEm/Getty Images (woman)

The Library of Congress has established a
Cataloging-in-Publication record for this title.

ISBN: 978-1-9848-8500-5

www.randomhouse.com/largeprint

FIRST LARGE PRINT EDITION

Printed in the United States of America

10 9 8 7 6 5 4 3 2 1

This Large Print edition published in accord
with the standards of the N.A.V.H.

To Teddy

THE
WEDDING
GUEST

CHAPTER

1

No Regrets.

Stupid name for a signature cocktail. Brears had found the recipe online, this tequila-Baileys thing. Seven shots plus the deejay speeding everything up plus the pink wine Leanza had drunk before the ceremony were killing her bladder.

When she got to the ladies' room, a line trailed out into the hall. Pathetic little ladies' room, like two stalls, because of what the venue had been before.

She took her place at the back. Her bladder felt like it was gonna explode.

No Regrets. As if.

Last week at the bachelorette in Vegas, Brears was all about regrets. After ten shots of her signature bachelorette cocktail, this rum and some sweet orange thing with bubbles in it. The week before there was a signature bridal shower cocktail, champagne and grapefruit soda and a toothpick with a little plastic bride on top.

Everything had to be "bespoke" for Brears, since she'd learned the word, she couldn't stop using it.

Once her mom or dad died there'd probably be a signature funeral cocktail.

At the bachelorette, Brears was throwing back shots faster than anyone while doing a man-spread on the sofa in the suite and letting out artisan shrimp pizza burps that smelled like the bottom of a fish tank.

Then she started talking, looking like she was gonna cry.

Plenty of regrets about Garrett, what the eff am I doing?

Everyone telling her what a great guy he was, she was doing the right thing.

Brears drinks, burps, looks like she's falling asleep but she isn't. Coupla more shots, she's all I love Garrett so so so so much.

I think.

Then she did cry.

But right then the hot-boy strippers came prancing in like ponies. Fireman / cop / cowboy / pool boy. Stripped naked in seconds.

Brears had no regrets about them.

Leanza was sure Garrett, who really was nice but

kind of smart-dumb pathetic, had no clue. His signature cocktail wasn't. Some kind of pale ale made
from oats? That is **not** a cocktail.

Leanza's stomach pressed down and moved
around weird. Like she'd swallowed a rat and it was
chewing on her bladder.

The line hadn't budged since she got there.

Two old women, had to be friends of Brears's or
Garrett's parents, got in line behind her and started
talking about what a lovely affair it was. Considering
the venue. Did you know? Giggle giggle.

Old bitches shouldn't giggle, they sounded like
maniac squirrels.

Maybe that was the problem with the ladies' room,
some grandma not able to get the plumbing going . . .
then oh, shit, there was Mom, barely able to walk,
her boobs hanging out as she wobbled toward the
line and Leanza knew she'd want to have one of those
girl-to-girl talks that proved to Mom she was still
young . . . oh, God, she was going to **explode**.

Then she remembered.

Upstairs, where she and the other bridesmaids
had sat in a crowded room and did their hair and
makeup—all by themselves, you'd think Brears
would share her stylists but no—upstairs there was
also a bathroom. Leanza hadn't used it but Teysa
had, Leanza remembered because Teysa came back
with the bottom of her dress all flipped up in
back and Leanza had joked you look like you just

took it in the backside and Teysa had laughed and Leanza had fixed her.

Problem was, the stairs were all the way on the other side of the building. Probably some office space for when it used to be a strip joint. Could she make it back there without totally exploding?

Would she get up there and then find someone else had figured it out first and then she'd have to come back here and go to the end of the line?

The only other choice was sneaking out into the back alley and squatting and just doing it. Some dude saw her, his lucky day, the way she felt, she could care less.

But the alley was even farther than upstairs and to get there she'd have to run all the way around the building and then out back.

No way, it was either stay where it wasn't moving or make a break for the stairs. And in a second Mom would see her.

Muttering, "Eff it," she ran.

The old ladies behind her said something rude.

Eff them, they were lucky they weren't getting sprayed.

Barely able to move her legs without leaking, Leanza climbed the shaky, creaky, dirty-looking stairs. What a dump, Brears's idea of creative.

Holding her breath and fighting to maintain control, she finally made it to the top and saw the door up ahead and to the right marked **Employees Only.**

No one waiting here, if she was lucky, no one inside. She charged the door.

Open! I am Warrior Princess!

Without bothering to close the door, she threw herself in.

Gross stinky place. No window, a gross stinky closet.

One urinal, one stall. Figures.

She yanked on the door of the stall, was already pulling down her pantyhose and her thong when she saw the girl.

Sitting on top of the lid of a closed toilet, her head dropped, dark hair falling to one side like a curtain. Dressed in a tight red dress and gold do-me sandals with heels as long and skinny as a lead pencil. Leanza hadn't seen her at the ceremony or the dancing, didn't recognize her, probably someone from Garrett's side.

Leanza said, "Excuuuse me."

The girl didn't answer. Or move. Or do anything.

Stupid bitch. How many No Regrets had she tossed back?

Eff her, this was a toilet not an armchair, do your stoner thing somewhere else.

Leanza took hold of the girl's bare arm.

Cold skin. Like not . . . human.

She said, "Hey!" really loud. Repeated it.

No answer.

Cupping the bottom of the girl's chin—it was

even colder than the arm—she lifted the drunk bitch's face, ready to slap her awake.

Brown eyes as expressionless as plastic buttons stared back at her.

The girl's face was a weird gray color.

So were her lips, gray with some blue around the edges, hanging loose, you could see some teeth. Dried drool trickled down both sides.

Then Leanza saw it: the circle around the girl's neck. Like a horrible red choker necklace but this was no jewelry, this cut into the skin, red and gritty around the edges.

Leanza knew she was being stupid but her mouth said, "Hey, c'mon, wake up."

She knew because she was the one who'd found her grandmother after the heart attack. Ten years old, a Sunday, walking into Grandma's bedroom wanting to show her a drawing she'd made.

Bottle of ginger beer spilled onto the comforter. The same plastic-button eyes.

The same gray skin.

Gripped by nausea, Leanza backed away from the girl. In the process, she kicked the girl's leg and the girl slid off the lid and down. Flopping as she continued to slide, her head making a weird thumpy noise as it hit the filthy floor.

Sliding toward Leanza.

Leanza scurried back.

Staring at the dead girl, she said, "Eff it," and let her bladder do whatever it felt like.

CHAPTER
2

Sometimes Milo briefs me before a crime scene, sometimes he waits until I get there.

This time he sent me an email attachment along with an address on Corner Avenue in West L.A.

This is for context; get here asap if you can.

His call had come in at ten oh five p.m. By ten fifteen, I was dressed and ready to go. Robin was reading in bed. I kissed her, didn't have to explain. Two minutes later, I was cruising south on Beverly Glen.

I turned west on Sunset, found the boulevard free and clear until a red light stopped me at Veteran near the northwestern edge of the U.'s campus. Activating my phone, I checked out the attachment.

E-vite. Gray lettering over a skin-rash-pink background.

The Thing: Brearely and Garrett are finally doing it!!!!!
Why You: Hey, they want you there!!!!!
The Place: The Aura
The Theme: Saints and Sinners
The Dress: Everyone needs to be hot!

I'd thrown on a navy turtleneck, jeans, and rubber-soled shoes that could tolerate bloodstains, wore my LAPD consultant badge on a chain. Dead bodies and the hubbub they attract call for unobtrusive, not hot.

I took Veteran south, drove through Westwood and into West L.A. Corner's not far from the West L.A. station, a stubby, easily overlooked street that paper-cuts Pico Boulevard as it hugs the 405 overpass. The address put the scene north of Pico, on a freeway-deafened strip of abused asphalt. Street lighting was irregular, creating leopard-spot shadows.

I passed a scrap yard specializing in English cars, a plumbing supply warehouse, a few auto mechanics, and an unmarked warehouse before reaching the final building, just short of a chain-link dead end.

Two-story stucco rectangle painted dark, maybe black, no windows.

A crudely painted sign topped a slab metal door. Thunderbolts above assertive lettering. Marquee bulbs rimmed the sign. Some were still working.

THE AURA

Alley to the left, parking lot to the right, now yellow-taped. Fifty or so vehicles sat behind the tape. Behind them was a generator-fed trailer that chuffed. Open door, a cook in a white tunic: pop-up kitchen.

Outside the tape was a smaller grouping of wheels: Milo's unmarked bronze Impala, a white Ford LTD that I recognized as Moe Reed's current ride, another Ford, maroon, that I couldn't identify, a gray Chevy.

Four detectives for this one. Plus the eight uniforms who'd arrived in a quartet of black-and-whites. Two of the squad cars were topped by clinking cherry bars.

Off to the right, the white vans, crime lab and coroner's, a pair of ominous twins.

No coroner's investigator car. Come and gone.

Easy identification or none at all.

Despite all the squad cars, the only uniform in sight rested her hip against the driver's door of a blinking cruiser. Working her phone, looking serene.

As I walked toward her, she gave me a glance. Usually I get stopped and have to show I.D. She said, "Hey, Dr. Delaware."

I'd seen her somewhere; the site of someone else's misfortune.

I said, "Hi, Officer . . . Stanhope."

Her phone screen was filled with kittens wearing funny hats. She clicked without self-consciousness. "Cute, huh? Around the back, Doc, it's pretty crazy."

Slowly spreading smile. "Guess that's why you're here."

The remaining seven uniforms were walking among the parked cars, copying license plates. Milo watched the process from a rear metal door. His arms were crossed atop the swell of his gut. His height, his bulk, and the scowl on his face fit the image of club bouncer. His droopy brown suit, tragic tie the color of pesto sauce, once-white wash-'n'-wear shirt, and tan desert boots didn't.

He lowered his arms. "Thanks for coming. Got a hundred people inside, a whole bunch of them boozed up. The plan is to settle them down, then Moe and Sean and Alicia Bogomil will try to get info. You get what I meant about context."

"A wedding?" I said. "I do."

He stared at me. Cracked up.

I said, "Interesting venue. Looks like a low-rent strip joint."

"That's 'cause it once was. Before that it was some kind of church."

"Saints and Sinners."

"Huh?"

"The wedding theme."

"Doubtful that's the reason, Alex. I've met the lovely couple, don't see them as that abstract. C'mon, let me show you where the big sin happened."

◆

A building-wide passageway carpeted in tomato-red low-pile took us past an open space. Parquet dance floor centering round tables for ten. Paper plates and a single scrawny sunflower on each table.

To the left were a long buffet table, three portable bars, a photo booth, and a bank of videogames. Empty red plastic cups dotted the floor along with crumbs and stains. Plastic streamers drooped from the ceiling. Four polyethylene columns attempting to look like plaster segmented the walk space from the party space. The remnants of a strip joint evoking Caligula.

The tables in the main room were occupied by sober-faced people dressed for celebration. Most were in their thirties, a few were old enough to be the parents of thirty-year-olds. A rear stage held a deejay setup. Obstructing a clear view of the stage were three chrome stripper poles, one bedecked with plastic sunflowers on unlikely vines. Lacking music and dim lighting, the room had the sad, rancid feel of every after-hours club. A bit of conversational hum drifted toward us, unable to compete with a heavy, gray silence.

Detective Moe Reed, with the powerlifter's build and youth of an actual bouncer, stood watch on a third of the tables. Detective Sean Binchy, tall, lanky, and baby-faced under ginger spiked hair, was in charge of the next group. Last was Alicia Bogomil, just turned forty, with gimlet eyes and knife-edged features. The ponytailed long hair I'd seen when I met her was replaced by a no-nonsense bun.

Milo and I had encountered Alicia when she worked private security at a hotel where a patient of mine had been murdered. She'd been a real cop in Albuquerque for seven years, moved to California for a romance that didn't work out, was languishing when she helped us with info.

She'd mentioned joining LAPD to Milo. I had no idea there'd been follow-through. No reason for me to know; for nearly three months, there hadn't been a murder where Milo felt I'd be useful.

As we passed the partygoers, a few looked up. The slumping posture and resigned eyes of passengers stranded in an airport.

I said, "How long ago did it happen?"

Milo said, "Victim was found at nine fifty, probably an hour before, give or take." He glanced at the crowd. A couple of people looked over hopefully. As Milo continued to walk, their heads drooped.

"Meet my new alter ego: Officer Buzzkill."

We continued to the end of the walkway, hooked left as if we were exiting through the front door, then he made another left and began trudging up a flight of grimy stairs.

I said, "Up to the VIP area?"

"Doesn't look like it ever was one, nothing pimped-up about the second floor."

"Maybe back in the day this place was a pioneer of income equality."

◆

He huffed and began climbing the stairs. At the top, a third left took us down a narrow, low-ceilinged hallway. Four doors, three of them closed.

A suited, gloved, and masked crime scene tech squatted near the open door. Beyond her was a small bathroom. Urinal and sink to the left, wooden stall straight ahead. The floor and walls were inlaid with yellowish tiles that had once been white.

Cramped, windowless space. A mélange of foul odors.

The stall door was propped open. A dark-haired young woman lay facing us on the floor. Late twenties to early thirties, wearing a blood-red, one-shoulder dress that had ridden up to mid-thigh. Pantyhose trailed up to what looked like red bicycle shorts.

She was diminished by death but still beautiful, with smooth skin and delicate features. Hints of cream in her skin where the terminal pallor hadn't set in.

Luxuriant wavy black hair fanned the dirty floor as if arranged that way.

I asked if it had been.

Milo said, "Nope, the girl who found her thought she was sleeping, poked her, and she slid and ended up like this."

The tech lowered her mask. "Hair falls that nicely, you've got a good cut." Young, Asian, serious. "I'm not being mean, she hasn't skimped. The dress is Fendi, the shoes are Manolo, and the hair is awesome."

Milo said, "Thanks for the tip."

I said, "The girl who found her, what was she doing up here?"

Milo said, "Trying to find a place to pee. She knew about this john because she'd been up here before the wedding. One of the bridesmaids. Those other rooms are where the wedding party got dressed and prepped."

The tech pointed to a yellow pool to the left of the body. "That's from the girl who found her, not the victim. Her bladder didn't hold out."

I said, "Where is she?"

"In Moe's group."

I studied the body. Didn't need to get close to see the ligature band on the dead girl's neck. Deep enough to cut into flesh and create a blood-flecked necklace.

"Garrote?"

The tech said, "Looks like something thin and strong, like a wire."

"Or a guitar string. Any musicians at the wedding?"

Milo said, "A maniac into real death metal, downstairs? I should be so lucky. Nah, just a deejay."

I said, "A bit more pressure and we'd have a near decapitation."

Both of them looked at me. "No insight, just an

observation." But I wondercd about the precise exertion of force.

I turned to the tech. "Strangulation but she didn't evacuate?"

The tech said, "She actually did a bit—there's a little mess under the dress but she's wearing a body shaper and it held stuff in."

She lifted the dress, pointed to the girl's inner thigh. The suggestions of a stain where the panty-hose met the shaper. "Not much from what I can see but we'll know more when she gets to the crypt."

She shrugged. "She doesn't look like she needs a shaper. Maybe she's a body perfectionist, didn't eat much beforehand 'cause she wanted to rock the dress and that's why there's not a whole lot of feces. Or she's just not a big evacuator, some people aren't."

Hearing the woman discussed that way, seeing her exposed, made my throat ache. I turned away and waited until the red dress was dropped back into place. "What makes you figure an hour ago?"

Milo said, "Leanza Cardell—girl who found her—said she was cold, so at least an hour."

The tech said, "Liver temp fits one to three hours, but you know how that is, this ain't TV."

I said, "When did the celebration start?"

Milo said, "Ceremony was at a Unitarian church in the Valley at five. Reception was called for seven but you know traffic, my guess would be seven thirty, eightish but I'll confirm."

"It couldn't have happened too early, with the rooms being used for the wedding party. So maybe closer to nine."

He thought about that. "Good point."

The tech nodded.

I said, "C.I.'s are gone already. Easy I.D. or none?"

Milo shook his head. "Zip. She's dressed for the wedding but Leanza doesn't know her and she claims to know everyone from the bride's side. Which is most of the crowd. I took a screen shot of her face, sent it to the Three Musketeers. Once you agree, they'll start showing it to the guests and the staff."

"Why wouldn't I agree?"

"I dunno, maybe you had some psychological thing in mind." He looked at the dead woman. "Poor thing—this is different, no? Talk about crowd control issues."

I said, "At least there are no kids. Not that I noticed downstairs."

"You know," he said, "that's true."

"Time to go for it."

"Hundred suspects," he muttered as he sent a text to Reed, Binchy, and Bogomil.

I said, "How many people on the staff?"

He checked his notepad. "Three bartenders, three cooks doubling as servers—which was just bringing chow from the trailer to the table. Three cocktail waitresses, two cleanup guys, the deejay, the photographer. Except for the cooks and the janitors, none of them are in uniform so they can't be distinguished from guests."

I said, "Per the invitation: Everyone has to look hot."

The tech said, "**She** certainly followed instructions." Smoothing the hem of the red dress, she stood. Five feet tall, maybe ninety pounds. Perfect for working in a cramped space.

I said, "I don't see a purse."

Milo said, "Nada."

The tech said, "The shoes probably won't help I.D. her, they look like a new model, you can get them anywhere. But the dress, maybe. If it's vintage, you could be dealing with upscale resale boutiques. On the other hand, there's online, so maybe not."

"You know your fashion, huh?"

"Sister wants to be a designer. She's obsessed."

"Maybe she can help with the age of the dress."

"She's sixteen, Lieutenant. My parents already hate that I do this, I was supposed to be a dentist. If I get Linda involved, they'll accuse me of being a bad influence."

Milo said, "Hey, that can be fun."

She grinned.

He edged closer to the corpse. "Dress doesn't look like it's been worn much."

The tech smiled. "Something nice and expensive, people tend to take care of it, Lieutenant. Could even be one of those runway things, worn once, then resold. The discount is huge."

"Killer couture," he said, shaking his head. "Thanks for all the input. Very helpful, CSI . . . Cho."

"Peggy," said the tech. She sighed. "For some reason this one seems especially sad to me. She took **so** much care to look her best."

I said, "Trying to impress someone."

Milo said, "Also easier to crash the party. If that's how it shakes out."

I said, "If she was a crasher, how would she know to come up here? Unless she's been here before. At another function. Or back when it was a club."

He eyed the body. "A dancer? Why not, nothing about her says she wouldn'ta been qualified. It's worth checking out if nothing downstairs pans out. God forbid."

Peggy Cho remasked. "If you don't mind, Lieutenant, I'm going to start printing the room. Place is gross. If my parents really understood what I do, they wouldn't let me in the house."

CHAPTER
3

Milo and I checked the other upstairs rooms. The first two were crammed with piles of female clothing, tubes, bottles, and jars of cosmetics, bobby pins, clips, hair dryers, curlers, and equipment I couldn't identify. The smallest space—probably a former closet—was a jumble of casual menswear that smelled like a locker room.

In all three rooms, windows were pebbled, painted shut, too small for an adult to crawl through.

Milo said, "Bad guy walked in just like anyone else."

I said, "How many points of access are there?"

"Front door, the rear where you came in, and on the north side where you drive through, there's what used to be a kitchen entry but is now used for storage. Next you're going to tell me you didn't notice any cameras and I'm going to nod my head mournfully. Place looks like no one takes care of it. Any other inspirations from what you've seen so far?"

"She could be a guest from the groom's side."

"Easy enough to check, not many people on his side."

"He from out of town?"

"Nope, local. They both are."

I said, "But it's her big day."

"From the few minutes I spent with them, all their days together are gonna be like that—want to meet the lucky couple?"

Before we descended the stairs, he put his phone on speaker, called Alicia Bogomil, and asked her to bring the bride and groom through the storage room and out to the north side of the building.

She said, "Got it, Loo."

"Any luck with an I.D.?"

"Not with my people, no one claims to know her."

"Claims," he said. "You're sensing evasiveness?"

"Nope," said Alicia. "No one seems squirrelly, the opposite, everyone's kinda numb, reminds me of when I worked a big fatal apartment fire in Albuquerque. Speaking of the bride, she seems pretty fragile. Emotionally speaking. I noticed you with Dr. Delaware. Good call, El Tee."

We left the building through the front door. Up close the signage was even shabbier, the stucco on the windowless front flaking off in patches. Hard to imagine this place as a church.

We turned right to the service driveway. Alicia stood midway up the wall, a few feet away from the couple of the moment.

From a distance, bride and groom were figurines lifted from a cake. They held hands and watched us, shrinking back like cornered prey.

Brearely "Brears" Burdette née Rapfogel wasn't much bigger than Peggy Cho. DMV put her at twenty-nine years old two months ago. Long black hair was twirled into sausage-like ringlets, trembling lips were glossed silver. A pug-nosed pixie face striped by mascara tear-tracks was veneered with too much pancake. Her gown was snow white, backless, sleeveless, semi-frontless, and decked out with seed pearls and lace. She dropped her new husband's hand and when he put his arm around her shoulder, she shrugged it off.

Garrett Burdette smiled weakly. Thirty-four, stooped and lanky in a gray suit, he had soft brown eyes already framed by crow's-feet. Even in heels, his bride reached only the middle of his chest. His license said he needed corrective lenses. The eyes were liquid. Contacts for the big day.

"Babe," he said.

Brears shook her head and sniffled.

"Want me to get you a tissue, Babe?"

"I want you to make this go **away**!"

Milo said, "Guys, we are so sorry this happened."

"You're not sorrier than **me**!"

"Of course not, ma'am."

His quick assent, combined with "ma'am," caused a pouting mouth to drop open, flashing teeth whiter than the gown.

What began as a smile quickly switched to a snarl. She turned her back on us, faced yellow-taped dumpsters and garbage cans.

"This is stressing me out!"

Garrett said, "It's horrendous, Babe."

Brears Burdette wheeled and looked at her brand-new husband. "Thank you, Mr. **Obvious**."

Garrett said, "Ba—"

She jazz-waved him off. "Just forget it."

His hands jammed into his pockets as he studied asphalt.

Milo said, "This has to be incredibly stressful, so we'll try to keep it brief. I know Detective Bogomil showed you a picture of—"

Brears said, "I **said** we don't know her and that's **not** gonna change. She's probably some slut who wanted to mess me up."

"Mess you up how, ma'am?"

"I'm not ma'am! My mother's ma'am! Everyone calls me what they call me, so just go with the program, okay? I'm **not** ma'am."

Garrett looked up, flushed. "Sir, everyone calls her Baby. Except me, I call her Babe—"

"Don't do their job for them, Garrett. Make

them do . . ." Another wave. "Whatever they do."
To Milo: "How would it mess me up? Like that's a
question? She shows up when she's not invited, the
party's going awesome and she turns it into shit?
What was it, an overdose?"

Garrett tugged his tie. "You're upset, sweetie." To
us: "Of course we feel bad for her."

The woman known as Baby growled.

Garrett said, "Right, Babe? We both feel upset
for her."

Bare arms folded across a lace-and-pearl bodice.
"Speak for yourself."

She turned again, took four steps toward the
trash bins, stopped. When she showed us her face,
it was crumpled and wet, mascara flow reactivated.

"I'm not mean. I really am not," she said. "It's
sad but I don't know her, okay? I really don't and
I'm so sorry it happened, I really am, no one wants
anyone to . . . all's I'm saying is . . ."

She threw up her arms. Jewelry clanked. "I **get** it,
it's terrible, worse than terrible, it's it's . . . tragic, I
shouldn't be bitching, it's tragic for her but it was
supposed to be **my** happy day!"

Garrett went to her and put his arm around her.
This time she accepted comfort, flopping her cheek
onto his chest and shutting her eyes.

He said, "It's okay, Babe. We'll get through this."

"I **know**, Gar. But why'd she have to do it at **my**
wedding?"

◆

As we walked them back inside, I said, "Can you think of anyone who'd want to mess you up?"

"No, sir," said Garrett.

Baby stared at me as if I was dense. "Everyone likes me," she said.

The couple returned to their table amid a scatter of dispirited applause. As they sat back down, Milo beckoned the three detectives out of the main room and over to the photo booth.

The looks on their faces made it obvious, but he asked anyway. "Any luck?"

Moe Reed was the first to shake his head, Sean following. Alicia Bogomil waited her turn. Still learning the ropes, making sure she knew her place.

"Unfortunately, nope," she said.

Milo said, "Any signs someone could be lying about not knowing her?"

"Not that I noticed, L.T.," said Reed.

"Same here," said Binchy.

Bogomil said, "A lot of them are intoxicated, so we could let them sober up and try again."

Milo said, "In a perfect world, great idea, Alicia. But we've already kept them here for a while and picking people out because they're tipsy is subjective and risky. We've got I.D.'s on everyone plus tags on the cars, will match that to the invitation list. Someone looks iffy, we'll find them."

Bogomil said, "Maybe the interesting list is folks who weren't invited. Like the killer and the victim."

Reed said, "You get snubbed so you strangle your date?"

"I know it sounds crazy, Moe, but people go psycho over weddings. Both my sisters morphed into evil space creatures and it caught on like a virus, everyone turned scary." She smiled. "Even me for a few seconds."

Binchy said, "You've got a point, Alicia. And maybe it was more than just a snub. What if it was a serious rejection? Like an ex of the groom. Or the bride."

"They both deny anything like that but it's an interesting thought, Sean," said Milo. "That said, this isn't the time to ask about it. They're not going on a honeymoon so I'll let them be and follow up in a few days. Alex, any psychological reason not to close this down right now?"

I said, "At the risk of adding to the buzzkill, I'd let most of the guests go but hold on to the staff, the woman who discovered the body, and the immediate family for a second go-round. Why no honeymoon?"

Alicia said, "His work, some sort of accounting thing. They've got a Maui trip planned for the summer. My group included the bridesmaids so I tried to encourage some girl talk. Leanza—the one who found the body—was in my section, too. That's her, the chunky redhead in the grayish-tan silk thing. She started off freaked out, had a couple Martinis and loosened up. So, yeah, she's a good candidate for follow-up. Why hold on to the family, Dr. Delaware?"

"Destroying a wedding has a personal feel." I picked a piece of paper from the floor. Printed account of the wedding procession. "This should help."

Milo took it and scanned. "Who's got the family?"

Reed said, "Me. Time to deliver the good news."

CHAPTER
4

Binchy went to corral the staff, Alicia beelined for Leanza Cardell, and Reed headed for a table just left of the dance floor where the family waited.

The chosen few; standby travelers watching morosely as everyone around them boarded the flight to freedom.

I took a look at the printed list. Flimsy white paper, computer-generated italics.

Marilee and Stuart Mastro, sister and brother-in-law of the groom.
Amanda Burdette, sister of the groom.
The groom accompanied by his parents, Sandra and Wilbur Burdette.

A bevy of bridesmaids. No ushers.

Then, in a darker, twice-as-large font:

**The bride, accompanied by her parents,
Corinne and Dennis Rapfogel.**

No kids meant no flower girl or ring bearer. Two sibs for the groom, none for the bride.

A woman everyone called Baby.

The only child.

Leanza Cardell was added to the family table, where no one greeted her. She brought a Martini glass with her, unpinned her red hair, shook it out, and turned her chair to face the stage.

Milo said, "We'll be taking people two at a time, any voluntee—"

"We're the bride's parents, we'll go first." A thin brunette around fifty stood and tugged at her dress. Everyone at the table stared at her, including her husband. She said, "Let's go, Denny."

Gold-chunk cuff links glinted as the father of the bride got to his feet, suppressing a burp. He followed his wife several paces behind, sat down leaving a chair between them.

Corinne Rapfogel was her daughter grown to sinewy middle age. The dress was a body-conscious black tulip. Spray-tanned and Botoxed as smooth as a freshly laundered bedsheet, she sported a diamond-and-gold mesh choker, four-inch gold hoop earrings, and a flower tattoo on her right wrist. Eyes under architecturally sculpted eyebrows were dark and guarded.

Some women seek mates who remind them of their fathers. If looks meant anything, Baby hadn't. "Denny" Rapfogel was bald, broad, and heavyset with a ruddy, meaty face that might've taken some college football punishment.

He said, "Helluva thing on a day like this. When Cor and I tied the knot, we had a nice ceremony, nothing crazy happened. But that's how it was back in the Jurassic era."

Corinne said, "You're making it sound ancient. Thirty-one years ago."

"Feels like ten minutes."

His wife nudged his arm. "Aww."

Denny Rapfogel winked at us. "Ten minutes with my hand held over a flame. Heh."

Corinne Rapfogel drew back. Had her husband been looking at her, he would've absorbed a nuclear-powered glare. "Let's get this show on the road, Dennis. I'm sure these nice policemen don't have time for your humor."

"Just trying to lighten things up," he said. To us: "This is pretty freaky, no? Even for you guys."

Milo and I said nothing.

Rapfogel tugged at his tie. "The girl who's dead, Baby and Gar say they don't know her and from what I've heard, no one else does. So it's obvious this was something bizarre that has nothing to do with us."

Milo said, "We'd still like to ask a few questions."

Rapfogel threw up his hands. "Sure, evening's blown to shit anyway, talk about money for nothing and chicks for free."

"Chicks?" said his wife.

"It's a song. **Dear.** The Stones."

Dire Straits, but why quibble?

Milo showed both of them the picture of the woman in red.

Corinne Rapfogel said, "We already saw it and told you and that hasn't changed, why would it?"

Denny Rapfogel said, "If you want to get a move on, cooperate, Cor."

She frowned.

Twin rapid head shakes. "No, I don't know her."

"Ditto," said Denny.

Milo said, "I'm sure this terrible thing has nothing to do with you but I have to ask: Can you think of anyone who'd want to harm you?"

Corinne Rapfogel said, "Why would you even ask that?"

"Disrupting a wedding seems like a personal thing, ma'am. So we need to—"

"Disrupting? That's an understatement. Baby's special day is **ruined.**" Sudden moisture in her eyes.

Denny said, "That's why they're here, they need to get to the bottom of it."

"Thank you, Mr. **Obvious.**"

Like mother . . .

Corinne looked over at her in-laws. "If it's anything personal, it has to be from their side. He's a veterinarian out in the sticks. You know what that's like."

Milo said, "I'm not sure I—"

"We're talking Hicksville," said Corinne. "Probably rubes like that movie . . . **Deliverance.** He doesn't even do dogs and cats, he does **farm** animals. Who knows what kind of people he gets involved with?"

Denny said, "Honey, I don't think a horse with the runs had anything to do with—"

"Oh, **shut** it, Denny."

Rapfogel colored, most intensely in the nose, now a cartoon thermometer bulb.

I said, "Dr. Burdette is a vet."

Corinne said, "A **farm** vet."

"What about his wife?"

"Housewife." As if that were a disease. "She says she works in his office part-time."

"Ah," I said. "So what do you guys do?"

"We run an agency," she said, sitting up higher. "VCR Staffing Specialists. The V's for Vanderbeek, that's my maiden name. The R's him."

Denny said, "The C's for cum. That's Roman for 'with,' not—"

His wife's throat clear stopped him.

I said, "Your agency manages . . ."

"Personal assistants for celebrities and people who matter," said Corinne. "Brett Stone and Kyla Berry have been our clients. They were supposed to be here but they got caught up in Europe. We booked both their P.A.'s two years ago and they say no one's ever been better."

Denny said, "Two years is like infinity for actors. They're—"

"Like everyone else, only prettier," said Corinne. To us: "Baby did some commercials when she was little. She was a **gorgeous** baby."

"Coupla diaper commercials," said Denny. "Kid gets paid for being a baby, we get to set up a college fund. Cool deal."

I said, "Where'd she go to college?"

Corinne said, "She considered **art** at Otis but decided on The Fashion Academy where she studied **marketing.** Sometimes she works with us. Consulting. It's helpful having someone in touch with her generation."

Denny said, "Millennials relating to millennials. We call that demographic synchrony—so do you guys have any clues, yet?"

Milo said, "It's early in the investigation, sir. With all those personalities you deal with at work, can you think of anyone who'd want to do damage to—"

"Definitely **not,** capital **N,**" said Corinne Rapfogel. "This has nothing to do with any aspect of our lives, our wheelhouse runs smoothly." She glanced at the dead woman's face. "She's cute, could be one of our clients but she's **not.** Okay?"

"Got it, ma'am. Sorry for—"

"I get it, you're doing your job. You catch the

m.f. who did this, I'll be in court when they sentence him to the gas chamber. After I collect on a massive lawsuit for pain, suffering, and emotional damages!"

Denny said, "They don't do gas, anymore. Right, guys?"

"Whatever. I want him caught. What he did was horrid—beyond horrid. He ruined this absolutely **glorious** day!"

The Rapfogels left the way they'd approached: she leading, he following.

Milo said, "And now, all you people watching at home, the parents of the groom."

Sandra and Wilbur Burdette walked together and sat next to each other. Both were tall, bulky, bespectacled, in their early sixties. Wilbur had yellow-white Carl Sandburg hair that flopped over a weather-beaten forehead. Sandra ("call me Sandy") had made no effort to hide the gray in a short, curly do. Her dress was bottle green, beautifully sewn, and floor-length, his suit, navy with single-needle stitching around the lapels. High-priced threads for both of them but they looked unaccustomed to formality.

I glanced over at the family table. With the Rapfogels gone, conversation between a couple I took to be the groom's sister and brother-in-law had animated a bit. Leanza Cardell drank, played with her hair, checked a clutch purse, drank some more.

Next to her but having nothing to do with her, a pallid, ponytailed young woman in a shapeless beige dress—a girl, really—read a book.

Milo said, "Thanks, folks."

Sandy Burdette smiled weakly. "Of course. This is so dreadful."

Wilbur said, "I tell you, it's the kids I feel sorry for. Anything we can do to help, Lieutenant, but I can't see what that might be."

"Appreciate the offer, Dr. Burdette."

Wilbur smiled. "Will's fine. I guess they told you what I do." He chuckled. "She—Baby's mother—probably made me out to be a clodhopper, right? Which is true, I guess. I'm an old Nebraska farm boy who never stopped liking critters."

Sandy Burdette said, "It is a bit of a culture clash."

I said, "Saints and Sinners."

"Well, yes, that, too," she said. "That kind of thing is foreign to us, I don't get it at all. But I suppose it's what's called edgy nowadays. What I was going to say, sirs, is that sure, people are different but the main thing is the kids love each other."

Not sounding convinced. She looked to her husband for confirmation. He missed the point and said, "Saints and Sinners, yeah, that is a hoot."

Sandy said, "In the end, it's all about compromise."

Will said, "So, guys, how can we help?"

Milo showed them the photo. Second time around for them, too, but no protest as they studied.

Will Burdette said, "Sorry, same thing I told the other detective. Never seen her. I'd expect her to be one of Brears's friends but Brears says no."

Sandy said, "Brears's friend was my first guess, too."

"Why's that, ma'am?" said Milo.

Deep-blue eyes rose and fell. "Well, you know. The age—the red dress, at least from what I can see it's pretty L.A.-girl, no? But Brears is absolutely at a loss—she's pretty much traumatized, the poor dear." Saying the right things but, again, without conviction.

Milo said, "You're from Calabasas."

Will Burdette said, "Since we moved from Nebraska thirty-two years ago. We have what I guess you'd call a mini-ranch."

"Working ranch?"

"Not hardly. My practice is farm critters, which means barn calls at all hours, no time to raise our own stock. We keep a few animals around because we love animals but mostly for the grandkids. Primarily rescues—dogs, a blind heifer, couple of goats, sheep, rabbits."

Sandy Burdette smiled. "Don't forget Glenn, dear." To us: "That's a desert tortoise we've had for God knows how long."

Will Burdette said, "Coming on twenty-two years. Healthy bugger, probably outlive us."

I said, "How many grandkids do you have?"

"Three boys," said Sandy. "Six, four, and three."

Her lips tightened. "A **decision** was made that they were too young to attend."

Will said, "Just as well, I suppose. Seeing as how it turned out."

I said, "Who made that decision?"

Sandy said, "Gar informed us but it was what she wanted. My poor son was really nervous, having to deliver the message. He would've wanted his nephews here but he goes with the flow." She pulled out a curl, tamped it back into place. "The wedding's basically been her thing. The rest of us are along for the ride."

Will said, "Saints and Sinners, still don't get that. I will tell you this: What I had to pay for a deejay and all those bartenders is a sin. We have a married daughter, her situation was a lot more normal. Church, pastor, the reception stayed at the church, sandwiches, soft drinks, and beer, now go off and be happy together."

He looked around the room. "They say this used to be some kind of church but to my eye you'd never know it."

Milo said, "Not hardly."

Sandy said, "Don't be coy, Will." To us: "Don't know if anyone told you guys this but before it became a rental venue, it was a burlesque joint."

"So we've heard."

"Ah." Disappointed. "Could that be related, Lieutenant? The kind of people a place like that would attract?"

"We're looking into everything, Mrs. Burdette."

"Those metal poles," she said, pointing. "I don't even want to **think**. But as I said, this is **her** big day."

"Was," said Will Burdette. "Best-laid plans and all that."

Older sister Marilee Mastro and her husband, Stuart, were M.D.'s around forty practicing family medicine. Enhanced by stilt heels, she topped his six feet by a couple of inches. Both Mastros were blond, blue-eyed, rosy-cheeked, and rangy. Long, grave faces gave them the look of an outtake from a Scandinavian travel poster.

I said, "Where do you practice?"

Stuart Mastro said, "That's in some way relevant?"

"Just collecting information, Doctor."

"We're both at Kaiser Murrieta."

Marilee Mastro said, "We live in Murrieta. Stu's full-time, I'm in the clinic twice a week so I can prioritize the kids."

"Three boys," I said. "Your mom told us."

Marilee nodded. "They weren't allowed to attend so we had to hire a hotel babysitter. In fact, I'd like to get back as soon as possible to see how they're doing."

"We'll get through this as fast as possible," said Milo. "Which hotel are you staying at?"

"Executive Suites on Santa Monica and Overland. We're all there, Amanda—my little sister—booked it. Correction: All of us are there **except** Amanda. She lives in L.A., goes to the U."

I said, "The girl with the book."

Marilee smiled. "Always. She's the big-brain in the family."

Stuart frowned. "Didn't see why the boys had to be excluded but now I'm glad. Not just what happened, the tacky ambience. This used to be a strip joint. Not exactly a wholesome environment."

Marilee stuck out her tongue. "It is kind of gross, thinking of what those poles went through, no? Can you imagine the germ cultures on them, hon? On the other hand, the boys would've had fun spinning around on them."

Stuart chuckled. "Kyle and Brendan would go nuts and Marston would be sitting in his stroller cheering them on. With our luck, they'd pull the darn things down."

"Reign of destruction," said Marilee.

"Boom," said Stuart.

I said, "Three boys."

"Oh, they're a trio of hellions," said Marilee, fully enjoying the thought. She crossed her fingers. Checked her phone. "So far, no calls from the babysitter."

"The boys being banished was the blushing bride's idea," said Stuart Mastro. "Garrett called to tell us but his heart wasn't in it. That's Garrett."

"Goes with the flow."

"That's one way to put it. He doesn't have strong

opinions on much except the Dodgers and the Lakers."

Marilee said, "You're making him sound insipid, hon." To us: "Garrett's smart and sweet but not a fighter."

Stuart said, "Goes along to get along."

I said, "That's not the bride."

A beat. Stuart shook his head.

Marilee said, "I'm sure she's a fine person. We don't really know her that well."

"Not a lot of contact before the wedding."

"The two of them visited my parents on Thanksgiving and Christmas and that was about it. Apparently her parents aren't big on family holidays, they were off on some sort of vacation."

I said, "So pretty limited contact."

Stuart said, "Never met her parents before today, only met **her** twice. Our conclusion was they're superficially a cute couple."

"Superficially."

"First impressions are by nature superficial," he said. "Now that I see them together, I'm assessing that they're totally different from each other. But maybe opposites can attract."

I said, "Can you think of anyone who'd want to destroy their wedding?"

"By murdering someone?" he said. "That's kind of flat-out insane, no?"

Milo said, "You heard there was a murder."

Stuart blinked. "Well, no, I didn't. What we were

told was someone died and then detectives showed us the photo of that girl. With all the police presence plus detectives it's pretty obvious this wasn't a slip-and-fall or a suicide, right?"

Milo said, "Mind taking another look at the photo?" He handed it to Mastro.

"Yup, that's the postmortem look. I know it because third year in med school I took an elective with the Riverside County coroner. Nope, same answer, never seen her."

He passed the shot to his wife. She said, "We were just discussing it before you called my parents over, and no one on our side has any idea who she is."

I said, "Should we concentrate on the bride's side?"

"I'm not saying that—actually, I guess I am. Simply on a probability basis. Nearly everyone here is from her side."

"What's the breakdown?"

"Our side is basically us and a few of Gar's college buddies." She looked at Stuart.

He said, "If there are a hundred people here, my off-the-cuff would be eighty-five to them, fifteen to us."

I said, "We noticed there were plenty of bridesmaids but no ushers."

Marilee Mastro said, "Another official policy, she thought it would take up too much time. Though to be fair, Garrett's never been real social. Maybe she'll draw him out."

"If opposites attract," said Stuart, "these two sure have a chance to prove it."

Marilee said, "Given how few of us are here and the fact that your victim's a young woman, wouldn't you say she's more likely to tie in with Brears? Not that I'm pointing fingers."

"At this point, Dr. Mastro, any information is welcome."

"I wish I could give you more, Lieutenant. It really is a horrible thing. Brears was so **into** it."

Stuart shook his head. "One day in their lives, it's the rest that count. If there's nothing else, Officers, can we find out how our little savages are doing?"

The table was down to Leanza Cardell still playing with her hair and studious Amanda Burdette, who'd produced a yellow felt-tipped marker and was underlining. As Milo got up to head there, he was distracted by something to his left.

CSI Peggy Cho, still suited and gloved, caught his attention with an upright index finger. We went over and she said, "A couple of things came up, probably better to talk up there."

We followed her out of the big room and up the stairs.

When she got to the landing, she said, "First

off, the prints. It's a mess, there are tons of latents, which isn't surprising considering it's a john. Don't imagine you have a list of candidates for comparison-elimination."

"If I need one," said Milo, "I'll recontact everyone who used those upstairs rooms. What I'm hoping is you'll find something that links to AFIS and we go after a nice convenient criminal."

"Wouldn't that be great," said Cho. "I'll do my best to lift everything but there's all sorts of overlays and smudges. Top of that, the analysis will be crazy. Lab's going to love you, Lieutenant. Even with scanning, it's going to take time. Now the main thing. I found what looks like a needle puncture on her."

"C.I.'s didn't say anything about that."

Cho shrugged. "Everyone misses stuff. Once I found it I looked for others. There aren't any on the rest of her unclothed skin, and this doesn't look self-administered. Unless you've heard of people shooting up back here."

Hooking her arm back, she pressed a spot at the base of her own skull.

Milo said, "Needle in the head?"

"Right where the spine enters the foramen magnum—that's a little passageway back here. I found it by accident, shifting her around so I could get prints from the walls of the cubicle. I was holding on to her shoulders trying to ease her down but my hand slipped and I reached out, got hold of her neck, and felt a bump. She's got thick hair, you wouldn't see it unless you parted the strands. Once they do a full autopsy at the crypt and shave her, it will be obvious. I just thought you'd want to know as soon as possible."

"Definitely, appreciate it, Peggy."

I said, "A bump could mean a fresh puncture. Incapacitated before she was strangled."

"That's what I was thinking," said Cho. "Because you know how long it takes to choke someone out, and especially with a wire cutting through flesh you'd expect to see signs of a struggle—lacerations on her hands as she fought to get loose. But there are none. I didn't even pick up any dirt under her nails, let alone skin."

Milo said, "Needle in the back of the neck. You ever seen that before, Peggy?"

"First time for everything."

He cracked a couple of bulky knuckles. "Killer dopes her, then takes time strangling her . . . show me."

CHAPTER

5

Two burly morgue drivers waited in the hallway facing the bathroom. One played with his phone, the other raised his eyebrows. "We good to go?"

Milo said, "Not yet," and followed Peggy Cho into the cramped fetid space. The body was prone on the floor.

Cho said, "Let me turn her."

"Want help?"

"No, I'm fine." She rotated the head gently, deftly parted the woman's dark mane, and revealed a bright-red dot on the nape of a long, graceful neck.

If the injection had pierced the spinal cord, the result would've been blindingly painful. A high-voltage shock.

I said, "No struggle says whatever she was injected with put her out quickly."

Cho said, "Maybe a fast-acting paralytic."

"Or a fast-acting opioid. Fentanyl comes to mind."

"You know, that makes sense," said Cho. "A proper dosage for pain can take only minutes, right? Squeeze in more and we could be talking seconds."

I said, "Margin of error's not that great. It could also be fatal."

"Oh, yeah, we're seeing tons of O.D.'s."

Milo said, "This shot probably wasn't fatal, at least not immediately." He pointed. "Look at all the blood around the ligature wound."

Cho said, "You're probably right and I don't want to be annoying, but that could be postmortem seepage. The things I've seen on the job, anything's possible."

Milo thanked her and we headed for the stairs.

The driver with the aerial eyebrows said, "We good now?"

Back on the ground floor, Milo said, "Fentanyl or something like it. The shit's all over the place, the Chinese are churning it out sending it to Mexico and the cartels are competing with Big Pharma. But there are still legit uses. Rick's aunt was on patches for chronic pain when she was dying. Wonder if Doctors Stu and Marilee find it useful in family practice." He blinked. "Wonder if there are veterinary applications."

I palmed my phone, ran a search. "There are,

same as for people. Chronic, intractable pain, surgical paralysis when appropriate."

"So I keep the Burdettes on the table. Okay, let's
do the little sister and Ms. Leanza. After we see how
Sean's doing with the staff."

Binchy was holding the attention of a table of people.
Doing a little dance-step, gesticulating with both
hands, adopting an air-guitar stance, keeping up a
smiling patter.

When he saw us, he stopped abruptly. But I'd
caught the tail end of his lecture.

"For my money, Rancid still rates as classic."

Mining the riches of his ska-punk former life.

Milo drew him aside. "Anything iffy from any of
them?"

"No tells that I picked up, Loot. Just the opposite, they're coming across salt-of-the-earth."

"Music fans."

Binchy colored around his freckles. "That, too,
but that's not why I'm saying—"

Milo slapped his back. "Rock on, kid, just giving
you a hard time. Got all their DMV data?"

"You bet." He showed Milo a piece of paper,
neatly hand-printed. "Surprisingly, every license is
current but I haven't had time to run any of them
through—"

"We'll do that later, Sean. Now I'm gonna
meet your campers and go over what you did. No
one blurts out a spontaneous, heartfelt confession,

they're free to go. Meanwhile, you go out back and collect all the auto data from the uniforms. Nothing iffy, you can head back to the office, leave all the info on my desk, and go home."

"You're sure, Loot?"

"Couldn't be surer, you deserve some free time," said Milo.

"I'm really okay, Loot."

"**Go,** Detective. Hearth, home, wife, adorable offspring—oh, yeah, pull out the Fender bass, do a Rancid ditty, show it on YouTube—just **kidding,** Sean."

The servers, bartenders, and janitors were Hispanic, except for the cocktail waitresses who were blond women around the same age as the bride. The deejay, a gaunt man in his twenties named Des Silver, wore a black velvet suit and a green porkpie hat. The photographer, a pudgy, patchily bearded young man in his twenties named Bradley Tomashev, wore an ill-fitting gray suit over a white T-shirt and cradled a Nikon.

No one unnecessarily avoiding eye contact or playing ocular pinball, no shaking legs, clenching and unclenching of fists, profuse sweating, tics, or other displays of undue anxiety.

That was just a spot evaluation and far from foolproof because psychopaths are better than most at staying calm under pressure and the more psychopathic, the colder their nervous systems. But you can't hold on to people without evidence and with the crime feeling personal, the chance of a woman dolling up to attend a party where her significant other was on the job seemed remote.

Milo let everyone go, except the photographer.

Bradley Tomashev said, "If Brears is okay with it, yeah I can send you the file once I put it together. It's going to take time, though. There's tons of images."

Milo said, "What we're most interested in are crowd shots. Coming, going, and during."

"Oh," said Tomashev. "There are some but not a lot, Brears didn't want that."

"What did she want?"

Tomashev shifted in his chair. "Brears is my friend and she's the bride."

"Same question, Bradley."

Tomashev sighed. "Don't tell her I told you, okay? I don't want to step in anything."

Milo crossed his heart.

"What she wanted was basically herself. Along with a little of the normal stuff. Like the procession, the vows back at the church."

"But otherwise, her."

"She's the bride, so whatever," said Tomashev.

I said, "Speaking of vows, was the clergyperson at the reception?"

"Uh-uh, the church was like a rented thing, some old guy showed up and read the vows Brears wrote."

Tomashev scratched his chin. Curly, rusty hairs rustled. "She wanted what she wanted, I tried to give it to her. I'm not really a wedding photographer, sirs, this is basically my first."

"Did you get paid?"

"No, sir. I was happy to do it."

Milo said, "Well, even a few crowd shots would help."

"I'll look for them, sir, but I didn't go out for those. Even with the dancing, she was always the focal point."

"All about Brears."

"She's the bride," said Bradley Tomashev. "My job was trying to make sure I honored that."

He trundled off, still holding his camera like an infant.

Milo said, "Unhealthy attachment to Ms. Rapfogel?"

I said, "He does seem enamored but I don't see that leading to murder. On the contrary, he'd want everything perfect for her."

He thought about that for a while. Hooked a thumb to the final table.

Leanza Cardell remained seated, still engrossed with her hair and the remains of a four-ounce Martini.

Amanda Burdette was up on her feet well before we arrived, hustling toward us swinging her book and her yellow marker. Rapid but stiff walk. The shapeless dress bagged on her.

I got close enough to read the book's title. **Meta-Communication in the Post-Modern Society: A Comprehensive Ethologic Approach.**

Milo muttered, "Beach read."

She flipped the book. A diagonal sticker on the back said **Thirsty.** Waving the marker, she said, "I've got a test tomorrow, I go first."

Milo glanced at Leanza. She drank and twirled, impervious.

"Sure."

We brought Amanda to the far right corner of the room and sat. Milo motioned her to an empty chair.

She said, "I'll stand. Been on my ass all day."

Small plain girl with dark eyes as animate as coffee beans and a husky, strangely flat voice that verged on electronically processed. She'd piled her ponytail into a careless top thatch. Errant brown hair frizzed like tungsten filament. No makeup, jewelry, nail polish.

No eye contact.

Milo pointed to the book. "The test is on that?"

"No-oh. It's on chemistry," said Amanda Burdette. "Chem for dummies but still."

"A challenge."

"Staying awake is a challenge because it's boring as fuck. Is any of this relevant? I don't see it fitting the narrative."

"What narrative is that?"

"Death at a wedding. I'm assuming unnatural

death. Everyone is because of all the time you're taking doing your police thing."

Milo smiled.

Amanda Burdette said, "I didn't realize I was being humorous."

He showed her the picture of the dead girl.

She said, "That's her."

"You know her?"

"Nope, just acknowledging it's her. Being phenomenological. As in you already showed me the same picture and I assume she hasn't morphed or otherwise altered her molecular status."

Milo looked at me.

I said, "You assume right. Any suggestions?"

"About?"

"The murder."

"Murder is bad," she said. "Unless it's justified. Like killing a Nazi. Or a molester."

"You're a communications major?"

"No."

I waited.

So did she.

I said, "What is your major?"

"I curate my own major."

"Really."

"Really," she mimicked. "As if you care."

Milo said, "Have we offended you, Ms. Burdette?"

"Your role offends me. The need for your services offends me."

"Crime—"

"Your presence means the world doesn't have its act together. By now, we should be more than rampaging baboons."

"You see the police—"

"Must we have a symposium?" said Amanda Burdette. "I see you as a prime symptom of a barbaric society. And yes, every society has needed people like you. Which is precisely my point: So-called humankind hasn't evolved."

I said, "The major you put together—"

"Cultural anthropology slash economic history slash—yes, communications, congratulations for being one-third correct."

"I went to the U., don't recall—"

"Obviously times have changed," said Amanda Burdette. "The powers that be deigned to allow me to construct a personal but informed narrative contingent on taking a certain amount of so-called science courses. Ergo chemistry for the mentally challenged, which ergo I need to pass. Which ergo requires staying awake and memorizing molecular structure so if you don't mind—"

I said, "Did you notice anything unusual during the wedding?"

"I noticed everything unusual. The phenomenon is by definition unusual. Two people wearing clown costumes and pretending they'll be able to avoid fucking other people for fifty years."

I said, "How about something specific to this wedding?"

"For starts she's retarded."

"Brears."

"Brears Brearely Brearissimo." She let out a metallic single-note laugh. "That sounds like a dog's name. Yes, **Brearely** is barely literate." Barest upturn of lips. "The image in my head is a pampered lapdog that gets its ass wiped by willing sycophants."

Milo said, "You don't like your new sister-in-law."

Amanda Burdette looked him up and down. Twenty years old but well schooled in the withering glance.

"It's not a matter of like. She's not worth thinking about."

"Your brother—"

"Gar's always been gullible."

"About?"

"Life. He's always blinded by something. At this moment it's alleged love."

"Alleged."

"I'm talking your language as a semantic shortcut," said Amanda Burdette. "Alleged perpetrator until proven otherwise?"

She undid the thatch, drew her hair forward, and played with it. "If it doesn't last, he'll be shattered, and she won't feel a thing because she'll have already fucked a bunch of other guys and planned her exit strategy. Will he learn? Probably not. Though life will eventually go on for him, too. And in answer to your probable next question, I can see someone hating her and wanting to fuck up her wedding. Could that entail killing this person?" Tapping the photo. "Why not? Depends on the narrative."

Milo said, "Whose narrative are we talking about now?"

"Obviously the alleged killer's."

"What exactly do you mean by narrative?"

Another dehydrating once-over. "I'll keep it simple. Every reality is tempered by innumerable bio-psycho-social constructs, contaminants, and other intervening variables. Everyone tells innumerable stories throughout their lives to themselves and others as well as to the greater external environment."

She engaged Milo's eyes with her own, smallish orbs. "And that means, Mr. Policeman, that your job will always be a giant pain in the ass for you because you will never spend your days dealing with honesty, nor will you ever reach the point where you feel you've accomplished anything. Because you haven't. Because people suck."

She hefted her book. "Anything else?"

Milo said, "Guess you've covered everything."

"I've covered nothing," said Amanda Burdette. "And by saying I have, you obviously don't get it."

She turned her back and walked away.

Milo said, "Did that just happen? Nasty little piece of work. Thinks she's brilliant but she just made me more interested in her."

"You've got your narrative, she's got hers."

"What's **yours**?"

"I'd like to talk to her." Eyeing Leanza Cardell.

This time, the unlucky bridesmaid got up as we approached. Wiggling to maintain balance and calling out, "My turn?"

Thickly built but shapely and blessed by a beautiful, clear-skinned face, she knew her flaming waist-length hair was an eye-catcher and used it like a prop, tossing and arranging and rearranging as she sashayed toward us in impossible heels. Her glossy satin dress shifted between gray and mocha depending on the light.

The garment looked tight enough to restrict respiration. One of those sadistic things brides pick for their supposed friends in order to look good in comparison. But Leanza seemed to enjoy working it, walking in a way that maximized gelatinous bounce. Her smile nearly bisected her face, her teeth whiter than fresh snow.

Milo led her to the area vacated by Sean's group.

She sat carefully, tugged her bodice down to expose an additional inch of bosoms.

"At your service, Lieutenant." A look at me. "Yours, too, sir." Tinkly, little-girl voice. Huge blue eyes awned by false lashes that could've been fashioned from tarantula legs.

Milo said, "Sorry for the wait, Ms. Cardell. Terrible thing you've been through."

"Call me Lee, Lieutenant. Yeah, it freaked me

out, I mean all I wanted was a place to . . . you know." Spidery flutter. "The little girls' room. But I'm fine now, had a Martini—that's okay, right? I mean I don't have to be totally sober to talk to you, do I?"

"What you endured, Lee, I can see booze helping."

Leanza Cardell laughed. "You sound kinda like a TV detective." Edging satin knees closer to Milo.

He said, "Columbo?"

"Who's that?"

"Historical figure."

"Huh?"

"Please run it by us again, Lee."

With her hair and chest as props, Leanza retold **her** narrative, creating a mini-drama in which her bladder starred.

"I mean, really, you go in to tinkle—that's what my grandma calls it, to tinkle—you go in to tinkle, are trying to pull down your panties, and you see that? I thought I'd lose it completely. So who is she?"

"That's what we're trying to find out, Lee."

"She was dressed to party, had to be on the invite list."

"She isn't and no one seems to know her."

"Really? I assumed she was from his side. I mean I knew she wasn't from Brears's side, I know everyone Brears knows."

"You and Brears go back?"

"High school, we were both cheerleaders."

"So your first impression was she was Gar's friend."

"Well," she said, "I just assumed. She's not? Wow, that's weird. You're sure she's not?"

I said, "No one from his side admits knowing her."

"Admits? You think they're lying?"

"Any reason they would be?"

"I'm not saying that—can I ask your name? So we can talk like people. You, too."

"Milo."

"Alex."

"Nice names for nice guys," she said, smiling crookedly. "All I mean, **Alex,** is that if she's not from Brears's side, she'd have to be from Gar's side, right? It's like, that's the whole thing, right? So if they don't admit—I mean it's the process of elimination, right? She has to come from **somewhere.**"

I nodded. "You were just sitting with Gar's family. Did anyone indicate they knew her?"

"Uh-uh. They weren't talking much. Pretending like it didn't happen, you know? Gar's dad did go on a bit about how much it cost and now look what happened, and Gar's sister—the married one—was saying she was pissed she couldn't bring her kids but now turned out that was a blessing."

We waited.

Leanza Cardell said, "That's it, really."

I said, "Did Amanda have anything to say?"

"Her? The freak? She **reads,**" said Leanza Cardell. "Brears warned me about her."

"Warned you about what?"

"Her being a psycho freak. Autistic like, what do they call it, spectral? You just met her, she's weird, right? Brears didn't want to invite her to the bachelorette in Vegas but she had to. Thank God she didn't come. Said she had a test. Wasn't nice about it."

"Rude."

"Not answering the e-vite, not answering Brears's calls. Finally, the day of she emails, like, 'got a test.' Every time I've seen her, she's **reading.** I mean come **on.**"

I said, "Speaking of the bachelorette, anything interesting happen?"

She flushed scarlet. "No, it was great." Loss of volume on the last two words. Her eyes slid to the right and back.

Milo said, "Lee, if there's something that could relate to this murder, we need to know."

Fingers knotted around flame-colored hair. Pale knuckles.

"Lee?"

"No, no, nothing like that, it was—the usual."

I smiled. "Never been to a bachelorette so don't know what the usual is."

She squirmed. Satin squeaked. "You know. We ate and drank and had . . . you know, male dancers."

"Any conflict—fights among the girls?"

"No, we were—it was all about the party."

White knuckles as her lips moved. Again, she glanced to the side.

I said, "Did Brears do anything that might've gotten her into trouble with someone?"

Leanza Cardell's head dipped toward her satin lap. "I really don't want to talk about this. It's not fair."

"To who?"

"Brears. She's entitled to her . . . time on the runway."

"Stardom."

"Yeah, it was supposed to be her big day."

I said, "So what, the party was an intro to the big day?"

"Well . . ." Grimace. "I don't want to talk about it."

Milo said, "Someone was murdered, Lee. If you know anything—"

"I don't. It had nothing to do with it."

"What's it, Lee?"

"Nothing."

"What happened?"

"Nothing," she repeated. "Dancers are nothing to anyone, they're like . . . they're . . . no one even knew anyone's name, okay? It's not like the two of them had an affair, just a quickie—"

She clamped her hand over her lips. "Omigod I'm such a . . ." Wet eyes.

Milo said, "There was some fooling around. A dancer and Brears."

"You never heard that from me. It's not impor-tant!" She began crying.

I said, "We're not here to judge." One of the baldest lies I've ever told.

"I've messed up everything!"

"You haven't, Lee. Really." I placed a hand on hers. Warm, slightly moist flesh. A body maintained on simmer.

She looked at me. "Really? You'll forget about it?"

"If there really was nothing more than some fooling around."

"There really wasn't, sir—Alex. I swear to you. We don't even know their names, everyone wears masks, no one knows anybody or **anything**." She looked around, panicked. Lowered her head again and said something inaudible.

"What's that, Lee?"

"Ma fau."

"Your fault?"

Mournful nod.

"For . . ."

"Not stopping it. He asked me first, picked me out and said I was hot, it would be fun. I said no way."

"You opted out. Nothing wrong with that, Lee."

"That's what I thought!" Squeezing my fingers.

I said, "Brears thought differently."

"It was supposed . . . I thought . . . I figured it would just be—" She stroked air. Placed a hand behind her head and pushed down. "I **should've** done it to **save** her. I just wanted to stay **classy**!"

I said, "You took care of yourself, Lee. Nothing to be ashamed of, just the opposite."

"But I should've **protected** her. She already had drank way way too much, she had these cocktails . . . I should've, I mean I tried, told her don't do it but she laughed and then she's getting up pulling her dress down so her you-knows are all exposed and then he's taking her hand . . ." More tears. "They actually did it. I couldn't believe it, they **did** it. And everyone's cheering."

"Then it was over," I said.

"**Don't** judge her. **Please.** That's how she **is.**"

"Determined."

She sniffed. "Yeah. She always gets her way. **Always.**"

Milo produced a tissue and Leanza dabbed her eyes. We questioned her gently, going over the same ground, probing for new info. She said, "Uh-uh, I swear that's everything. And no way the party is important."

I said, "How many girls were there?"

"Why? You're not going to talk to them—please, I don't want them to know I told!"

Milo looked at me. If we needed to find out, we could.

He said, "Sure. Big party?"

"No, just girls who're close. Four, okay? But no one would ever tell. Because . . . some of them also." Looking down. "Actually, everyone got into it. It was crazy. Except me." Looking down. "I had my period. Also, I didn't want to."

She ruffled her hair. "Totally crazy, we had masks. No one was themselves. Except me. And I was the one who felt weird."

She tottered as she stood. Milo said, "How're you getting home?"

"Uber."

"Okay, be careful."

"I will, sir."

Staggering off.

Milo rubbed his face. "Girls gone wild with a bunch of hired studs. The groom finds out, I can see an excellent motive for strangling the bride but not some third party. And there's no indication the groom did find out. From what I've seen he's still basking in the glow of oblivious love."

He laughed. "Poor sap. Probably happens more often than we think."

I said, "His family doesn't know, either. If they did, they'd have tried to stop the wedding."

"Mean Amanda would've loved **that** narrative."

"Amanda attending the bachelorette would probably have kept things tame."

"Chastity belt on legs?" He laughed. "I guess I could talk to the other girls at the party but if it turns out not to be relevant, I've made things even worse for these poor kids and their families."

"Agreed," I said. "At this point, best to be discreet."

He laughed. "Put otherwise, I remain stuck at ground zero."

We left the building and stepped out into cool night air soured by gasoline and garbage.

I said, "How long since this place was a strip club?"

"Back to the dancer thing?"

"She's a good-looking young woman who knew where the upstairs bathroom was."

"Or like Leanza she just had bladder issues, went looking, and lucked out."

"Leanza didn't luck out. She knew because she was a bridesmaid and had changed upstairs. The location's out of the way. My bet is Red Dress either was familiar with the layout or was meeting up with someone who was."

"Tryst in the loo?" he said.

"She may have been lured there for a hot time, but I don't see this as rough sex gone bad. Our bad guy came with a garrote and a shot of something nasty. She was brought upstairs to be killed."

"Bad guy's a wedding guest? Or he, too, knew the place from before? Why pick a stranger's wedding to kill your soon-to-be-ex?"

"Maybe some sort of fantasy—double-crashing and getting it on. Plus there'd be practical reasons.

When the building's not being used, it's locked, and noise from the party would be a great sound baffle."

"I guess so," he said. "But we're still talking high-risk, Alex. Anyone could've come up there at any time."

"Maybe danger was part of the fantasy. She was left to be found. Displayed in a demeaning way."

"Hypo full of dope," he said. "That takes me right back to Gar's clan with all their medical training."

I said, "Including the women. Sandy Burdette and Marilee Mastro are both tall, strong-looking women, and the injection would've reduced the need for physical control."

"Amanda isn't big but she's smart enough to plan and sweet as a wolverine. Now the big question for all of them: motive."

I shrugged. "We need to know more about the families—both sides."

"How kind of you," he said, patting my shoulder.

"What is?"

"The benevolent plural. We need to know."

"What are friends for?" I said.

"When it comes to our newlyweds, good question."

CHAPTER

6

A little after three p.m. the following day, Milo's office number flashed on my phone. I'd just gotten offline, researching The Aura. Party venue for a little over a year. Lackluster website, a few thumbnails of happy celebrants, most of which looked like canned archive shots.

He said, "Here's your daily recap, Doctor. Requested a high-priority autopsy but the crypt's so backlogged they're bringing in outside help. Pathologist I spoke to did think the fentanyl scenario or some drug like it made sense."

I said, "Working on Sunday?"

"The Lord's got job security, let Him rest. I also ran basic background on everyone at the wedding. Out of a hundred and three people, twenty-two have local arrest records. DUIs and penny-ante dope stuff except for one burglary—the deejay. That was fifteen years ago, it got pled down to trespassing and the details sound more like a landlord–tenant dispute. The families both look damnably law abiding but that's just surface stuff and I haven't checked the docs' civil records for malpractice."

I told him what I'd learned about The Aura.

He said, "Fits with what Sean turned up, I've had him looking at the place. He emailed their booking number and got a canned reply. Weddings, bar mitzvahs, anniversary parties, **quinceañeras.** The current owners bought it five months ago, a group from Hong Kong."

"Anyone mad at them?"

"Not that's turned up, so far. Making matters worse, no current lawsuits, no bitching on Yelp."

I said, "The last time girls danced around the pole was around a year and a half ago. Who owned it back then?"

"Guy named Ramzi Salawa, business address in Hollywood. Doesn't seem to be in the club biz anymore, his money comes from storefronts on the boulevard. I put a call in to Petra to see if anyone in her playground knows him, she poked around, nothing. I texted him and he surprised me by answering a few minutes ago. At LAX, clearing customs from an overseas trip. He sounded freaked about the murder, agreed to drive over on his way from the airport. Hour or so. You curious enough to want to observe?"

"Twitching with interest."

◆

When I arrived at the West L.A. station, a black-on-
black Mercedes 500 was parked illegally at the curb
and Milo was talking to a trim black-suited, black-
shirted, black-bearded man in his forties. The only
color relief, bright-red calfskin loafers.

Milo said, "This is Mr. Salawa."

"Ramzi, people call me Ron." Soft, mellow,
unaccented voice. I shook the hand he extended.
Pliable, warm, exerting the barest pressure.

"Nice to meet you, Ron."

"Yes, well . . . this is pretty shocking."

Milo said, "Turns out Mr. Salawa knows our
victim."

"I wouldn't say know, more like acquainted,"
said Salawa. "You can't tell me what happened,
Lieutenant?"

"Sorry, not yet."

"That place." Head shake. "Jinx from day one,
couldn't wait to get out of the business. Tried not to
get involved too much, period. That's why I didn't
really know her. Plus she was hired toward the end,
was maybe there for a couple months."

I said, "The club scene didn't work out for you."

"Disaster," said Salawa. "I'm a real estate guy,
never intended to get into entertainment. It was my
uncle's thing, he owed me money, gave me four crap
locations when he moved back to Dubai and The
Aura was one of them. It was supposed to be a great
deal. Maybe I'm just not cut out for it but my opin-

ion is what messed it up is internet porn. Why should guys bother to leave their houses when they can log on and get their jollies? So the ones who do show up are mostly losers without a lot of bank. We'd have them showing up already drunk, getting by with the cheapest two-drink minimum. They'd rarely spring for drinks for the girls and their tips sucked so we couldn't hold on to girls. Plus that type, you know. They can cause problems."

"What kind of problems?"

"Nothing serious, but still a pain."

"Meaning?"

"Drunk and disorderly. I didn't call you guys, didn't figure it was worth your time."

I said, "You solved your own problems."

"Bouncers," he said. "Cost me a big slice of overhead."

"So you sold out."

"To some Chinese," said Salawa. "Anyway, Kimby, I think that was her name, can't see why she'd want to go back there."

Milo said, "What's Kimby's last name?"

"Sorry, that's all I remember, sir. When you texted me I was totally thrown, wondered if someone would try to go after me civilly. Her family, you know?"

"You no longer own the place. Why would they do that, Ron?"

"'Cause of the way it is," said Salawa. "Bus-bench lawyers troll records. I know I sound paranoid but I already have a pain-in-the-ass time when I travel, getting hassled by customs at the airport, can't qualify for Global Entry."

Toothy smile. "They won't say why. As if. Anyway, I'm just finished closing my bags back up and you text me about this."

"Kimby," said Milo.

"I think." A red shoe tapped. "Sorry it happened to her but don't know her."

"Could you check her employment records so we can find out who she is?"

"I could if I had them," said Salawa. "Minute I closed with the Chinese I got rid of everything to do with that dump. There wasn't much records to be-gin with, the girls were independent contractors—that's how my uncle set it up. Less paperwork."

"Better for taxes."

Salawa blinked. Reaching into his jacket, he slipped on a pair of Maui Jim aviator shades. "He told me it was legal, sir. Whole deal was supposed to be turnkey. Later I found out he was in trouble—my uncle Moussa. Owed a lot of money to a lot of banks, going back to Dubai was an escape. My mom was ready to—she's totally pissed off, he's her brother, there's supposed to be family honor. I ended up with the club and three other parcels but every-thing had liens Moussa didn't tell me about."

I said, "Did Kimby know Moussa?"

"Maybe but he's not even in Dubai anymore, maybe Abu Dhabi, who knows? And to be honest, sirs, he's not the killer type, just a sneak. I only remember her because she was one of the better-looking girls. The situation Moussa put me in, I wasn't exactly getting supermodels."

Milo said, "Did you ever socialize with the girls?"

Salawa drew himself up. "I'm a married man." Small smile. "Not exactly a champ at it, this one's Number Three, but I don't play those games anymore. You ask anyone about me, they'll tell you the same."

I said, "Those problem customers, did any of them hassle Kimby?"

"Not that I heard. You'd have to ask the bouncers."

"Nothing you noticed yourself."

"I wasn't around much," said Salawa. "Less time I spent there, the better."

I said, "What can you tell us about Kimby's personality?"

Salawa let out an exasperated sigh. "These questions, sir. I didn't know her. Okay, it's a murder, I get it, you got to ask. But personality? I didn't give them psychiatric tests. What I can tell you is that when I interviewed her she seemed okay."

"Okay . . ."

"Quiet, polite, nothing weird. Not likely to be a pain." Salawa adjusted a lapel. "If they looked half decent I put some music on and tried them out."

"Kimby was a good dancer."

"Actually, sir, not really. She'd move back and

forth." Illustrating with his hands. "Like she was bored. But by that time I just wanted to fill the stage."

I said, "Did she hang out with any of the other girls?"

Salawa flicked the bottom of his beard. "Maybe I'm not getting it across: I wasn't involved with any of them."

Milo and I remained silent.

Salawa said, "I'm not trying to give you attitude, just telling you the truth. Can't believe she'd go back there. Why would she do that?"

Milo said, "That, Ron, is the question. So no stalkers you're aware of."

"No."

"What about a boyfriend?"

"For all I know," said Salawa, "she could've had a girlfriend. You'd be surprised how many of them swing that way. Wish I could tell you more, she seemed like a nice girl—oh, yeah, here's something. A couple of times I saw her doing a crossword. Or with a book. Does that help?"

"Everything helps, Ron."

"Then okay, I helped you. She's in her costume, waiting to go on, concentrating. Doing this." Salawa's upper teeth took hold of his lower lip.

"What was her costume?"

"What was available and fit. I wasn't exactly running a studio with a huge wardrobe allowance. So what was going on at the place when it happened?"

Milo said, "Wedding."

"Wow." Salawa grinned. "Should've happened at my first wedding. Bad omen to warn me off."

Out came Milo's pad. "The bouncers' names, please."

Salawa inhaled. "You guys are going to think I'm hiding something but I'm not. Like with the girls, they were independent, all I remember is first names."

"Then we'll take those."

"Okay . . . let me try to remember." Fingers tapped a temple. "The ones back then I **think** were James and Del . . . something. DelMar? DelMonte? Del something. You know how they get with their names."

"They?"

"Black guys. Okay, yeah, here's something: James had a common last name. Smith, Jones, Brown, whatever." Salawa shook his head. "Sorry—hey, I **can** tell you what they looked like. You want that?"

Milo gave him a thumbs-up.

"Okay," said Salawa. "James was totally bald, Del-whatever had the long stuff—dreds. **Big** black guys. I think one of them maybe played football. I think Del. Maybe both of them, not sure."

"Where'd they play?"

Shrug. "I can't even tell you why the football thing is in my head, maybe he mentioned it. Or someone did. Or I'm wrong. I must sound like an idiot."

I said, "How old are these guys?"

"Del was in his forties, James was younger—thirties. **Huge**—arms like a normal guy's legs. I think he might've been gay."

"Why's that?" said Milo.

"You know queers," said Salawa. "No matter how tough they are, sooner or later the way they move, the way they talk. I'm not saying he was a wimp. No way, José, someone messed with him good luck. I just got a feeling—the way he kind of . . . strutted? And sometimes he'd stand there and be doing this."

Dangling a limp wrist. "Maybe I'm wrong, but probably not. I've got a feel for people."

I said, "Your feel for Kimby was—"

"Nice girl, not much of a dancer, great looking. She didn't seem dumb. Can't say that for some of the other girls."

"The bouncers took care of problems. Did anyone mess with them and end up the worse for it?"

"No one got hurt," said Salawa. "I set rules: See them out and get them in their cars. If they weren't too drunk. If they were, we called them a cab. I lost plenty of money on cab fees. Trust me, **no** one got hurt, the proof is no one sued me."

Milo said, "Any idea how we can reach James and Del?"

"Hmm . . . I think James lived in the Valley—I'm saying that because sometimes he'd bitch about traffic coming over the hill. Del, I can't tell you."

"Independent contractors."

"That's how Moussa set it up," said Salawa. "I thought he knew what he was doing."

We watched him drive off in the Mercedes.

Milo said, "Let's take a walk."

"Food or peace and quiet?"

"Already ate." He hooked a thumb and we did our usual southward stroll into the working-class residential neighborhood that borders the station. Nothing fancy but maybe the safest blocks in L.A.

"So what do you think of Ron?"

I said, "Hard to tell. Anything in his background?"

"No criminal record but no angel. In frequent arrears for child support with the first two wives, they're always in court. Several convenient bankruptcies, and one fire at a warehouse he owned in East L.A. that looked suspicious but wasn't provable as arson. Unfortunately, when it comes to his club venture, he seems to be leveling. He got the properties because his uncle—who's a total deadbeat with a conviction for attempted bribery—owed him money on the sale of three apartment buildings they co-owned in Downey. Two of them Salawa unloaded at a loss, the other one and The Aura, he barely broke even."

"Struggling businessman," I said. "That could mean resentment and secrets."

"Sure, but he returns to a dump he hates on the

day of a stranger's wedding in order to kill a former employee? Can't see how that works."

"Maybe he lied and it was personal. He tried to impress us with how disengaged he was. But he did notice Kimby's looks and her dancing."

"Wouldn't any guy notice a girl like that?" he said. "Even guys who do this." Aping the limp-wristed dangle.

I laughed. "Maybe he's not as monogamous as he claims."

"Cuties on the side and she was one of them?"

"I keep coming back to the club layout. For all his claims about hating the place, meeting there could've been a turn-on. How about seeing if James and Del-whatever can elucidate."

"Common name," he said. "How about James Brown—wouldn't that be a hoot? Man's world and all that."

Half a block later, he stopped, found a panatela in a trouser pocket, rolled it between his fingers, and resumed walking. "Maybe I'm getting too far afield. I keep thinking about what Lee Cardell told us."

"Baby's wild ride in Vegas."

"A bride who fools with a male stripper, a few days later a dead female stripper? Do boys and girls in that world hang out?"

"No idea," I said. "It's been years since I experienced the joys of the skin trade."

He stopped again. "You've got a past?"

"Back when I was playing music the musicians spent after-hours at topless places."

"And you tagged along."

"I was eighteen and they paid for my illegal drinks."

"Bunch of hopheads out to corrupt you. Did it take?"

I smiled.

He said, "Dr. Enigma Within A Puzzle. I'm also still wondering about the injection, the whole medical thing, so while I waited for ol' Ronnie, I looked into the Mastros' civil status. Distressingly clean, not a single malpractice claim, which in these days is something. A few patients of Dr. Stuart Mastro do yelp at him for having a cold bedside manner. Dr. Marilee seems to be more popular."

"What about Dr. Wilbur?"

"No ratings at all. Maybe ranchers and farmers are too busy to spout off online. Okay, let's head back."

CHAPTER

7

As we neared the station, I said, "James the bouncer probably spends a lot of time in the gym. If he does live in the Valley, Moe might know him."

"The kid's Mr. Muscles but the Valley's a big place, Alex."

"It's a long shot but we're not talking Spinning classes. You want to get huge, you'd need serious iron."

"Optimism," he said. "Tsk, tsk, after all you've seen, you still won't change your ways."

Moe Reed was also working on Sunday, doing paperwork at his desk in the big detective room. The room was half empty and Reed wore a black T-shirt and sweats. Off-shift but wanting to tackle paper.

Milo beckoned him out to the corridor.

"Where does someone in the Valley go to look like Arnold? Or you?"

Reed stared at him. "You're considering an exercise plan, L.T.?"

"When swine aviate." Milo slapped the young D's massive left biceps. The resulting sound was cardboard on teak. "Where's your gym, kid?"

"I alternate," said Reed. "Got a pretty good setup in my spare bedroom but there's a limit to how much I can put in there, don't want the floor to cave. So for the big stuff, there's a place in Sherman Oaks—"

"Name."

"The Iron Cage. Can I ask why, L.T.?"

Milo explained.

Reed said, "Don't know of any Dels but there's a Jim sometimes spots me. And a James. And a Jameson, but none are bald. There are some bald guys whose names I don't know but the only black one's a little guy who deadlifts four hundred."

"Hair grows, Moses. Last names?"

Reed shook his head. "It's not at that level, we don't hang. Someone needs a spotter, it's a courtesy to do it. You're sure about the age?"

"That's what the club owner said."

"Then Jimmy's too young, more of a kid, maybe twenty. James and Jameson are both in their thirties. Also, they live together, L.T."

"A couple."

"I assume," said Reed.

"The club owner thought James was gay."

"Ah . . . I'm not sure I see either of them as bouncers. They're kind of . . . refined. Talk as if they're educated and drive a new Jag."

"All bouncers are apes?"

"When I did it, they were."

"When was that, kid?"

"After I graduated high school. Just for a month, I didn't like the atmosphere so I got a job driving a liquor delivery truck. Got to carry heavy boxes."

Milo looked at me. "First you, now him."

Reed said, "Pardon?"

"Apparently everyone's got a history, Moses. Alex will fill you in on his, if we ever get some spare time. Can you get me surnames on James and Jameson?"

"I'll give it my best, L.T." Reed turned back to the big room. Milo caught him by the elbow.

"Do it in my office, away from the riffraff."

Office in function, closet in size. The long-ago, vindictive decision of a corrupt police chief who'd retired under pressure and traded Milo for silence.

My friend's payoff was an evasion of departmental orthodoxy: instant promotion to lieutenant, normally an administrative rank. The big payoff: allowed to continue working cases rather than drive a desk.

Every succeeding chief eventually found out about the arrangement and like any other self-righteous cleric, began by setting out to annul it. Each backed down because Milo's close rate was even higher than the Robbery-Homicide honchos downtown, why mess with success.

The non-office stemmed from the hostile chief's conviction that solitary confinement in a window-less room off a grubby hallway would be cruel and inhuman punishment.

Milo took to it like a bear to a den.

Along the way, he developed a working relation-ship with other cops when necessary, had progressed to creating a mini-cadre composed of Binchy and Reed. But he'd never forget the time when LAPD claimed homosexual officers didn't exist and he'd endured isolation and worse and made solitude his thing.

He'd lasted long enough to see huge changes in the department's treatment of gays and everyone else, but continued to keep a low profile and avoid advocacy.

Sticking to his personal motto: Do The Damned Job.

As he and Reed lumbered up ahead, taking up nearly the width of the corridor, I wondered how the three of us would fit in what passed for his per-sonal space.

We wouldn't. Milo and I stood outside while Reed worked the phone.

It didn't take long, no ruse necessary. He simply began by asking the gym owner and got his answer.

Scrawling the info on a Post-it, he said, "Thanks, Rod, hoping to have time tomorrow—yeah, keeping the city safe."

Milo said, "At The Cage, you're a VIP."

Reed blushed and shrugged. "I've interceded in a few situations. Also, I pay my membership on time."

James Earl Johnson, Jameson Raymond Farquahar.

Milo called up the DMV shots.

"That's them," said Reed.

"Thanks. What were you doing when I interrupted you?"

"Robbery-assault, transcribing witness statements."

"Okay, back to reality."

"Happy to get away from it, L.T. Thanks for the break."

"Happy to distract you when there's something to do."

"Bring it on, you know how I feel about robbery," said Reed. "Assault I can deal with but the assault part on this one's wimpy—someone got slapped." Shaking his head and rolling massive back muscles, he trotted away.

Milo and I stepped back into the office, where he squeezed into his rolling desk chair and I stuck myself in my usual corner.

We examined the stats on both men. Johnson was six-four, two eighty-three, Farquahar six-five, two seventy-nine. The similarity ran beyond dimension: Birth dates put them a year apart—thirty-three and thirty-four—and they bore enough facial similarity to be fraternal twins.

I said so.

Milo said, "Brothers not boyfriends? You think Moe's gaydar's out of tune?"

"I think they look alike."

He grunted. "Whatever the story, they live together in Studio City."

He ran criminal searches, came up empty, checked vehicle regs and found a white Jag and a black Porsche Macan.

He logged onto a shared Facebook page filled with travel shots in Asia and Europe. James Johnson and Jameson Farquahar holding hands, embracing, and in a few pictures kissing. The rest of the photos were the men with two rescue dogs, a huge mastiff-type named Little and a miniature schnauzer named Biggs.

He scrolled. "Don't care about their taste in music or movies, let's check out their social life."

Active social life, a couple dozen male and female friends, plus sibs, nieces, nephews, and a pair of middle-aged mothers.

Jameson R. Farquahar was an associate at a law firm in Encino. James Johnson listed himself as a personal trainer.

That made Johnson more likely but close to a hundred men by that name lived in the Valley, so Milo switched his phone to speaker and tried Farquahar's office.

Closed on Sunday, nothing beyond general voicemail.

"Okay, tomorrow's a new day—uh-oh, the optimism flu must be catching. I'll find him one way or the other, starting with his true love—say ten a.m., here? I'm figuring to leave soon after."

Monday, I was back in my corner as he sat belly-to-desk and phoned the law firm.

Mr. Farquahar was in a meeting.

Identifying himself, he asked the secretary if she had a number for "Mr. Farquahar's friend, James Johnson."

"The police?" said the receptionist. "I can't believe James is in trouble."

"He's not in any sort of trouble but he may have information that can help us."

"Help you?" said the receptionist.

"A former friend is a victim."

"A victim?" said the receptionist.

Milo let his mouth go slack and his head go off-kilter. "Of a serious crime, ma'am."

"Serious?"

"It would be great to talk to James."

"Talk? I guess I can call him. Then he can decide. Let me call you back."

Click.

Moments later, Milo's desk phone rang. A soft, boyish voice said, "This is James."

"Lieutenant Sturgis, here. Thanks so much for getting back, Mr. Johnson. This is about a woman who danced at a club where you did security."

"Eileen—my husband's secretary—said someone's a victim."

"Unfortunately the woman was murdered."

"Oh, my God," said James Johnson. "Who?"

"A dancer named Kimby."

Silence.

"Mr. Johnson—"

"I don't believe I ever worked with someone named Kimmy. I used to do a lot of club security but not for a while."

"Kim-**bee**." Milo described the dead girl.

Johnson said, "What club are we talking about?"

"The Aura."

"Oh, that one. We're talking over a year ago, Lieutenant. Year and a half . . . Kim-**bee**? There might've been someone called Kim-**ba**."

"We were told Kimby but maybe."

"Told by who?"

"The owner of the club."

"The Egyptian . . . Ronny Salami," said James Johnson.

"Salawa."

"If you say so. He wasn't around much. I'm surprised he remembered my name."

"Actually, he wasn't clear on it."

"How'd you find me, then?"

"He called you Jimmy and described you as someone who probably lifted weights. Turns out one of our detectives thought he might know you from The Iron Cage."

"I'm never Jimmy, I'm James. We talking the Viking?"

"Pardon?"

"Moses the Viking," said Johnson. "Late twenties, blond, humongous lats, bi's, and tri's? He's the only cop I know of at The Cage."

"That's him."

"The Viking is a monster. One-handed pull-ups, when he two-hands he puts like a hundred fifty around his waist. I like him as a spotter because he can lift more than me, I feel safe."

"I hope you don't mind him telling us your name. This is an unsolved homicide and we're still working on identifying the victim."

"No, it's fine. The Viking's cool. The Aura, huh? I thought the place closed down."

"It did—it's complicated, sir. Any chance we could meet? At your convenience."

Silence.

"Sir?"

"Like an interrogation?" said James Johnson.

"Nothing like that, just a brief chat so I can learn as much as possible about my victim."

"Why would I know about her?"

"We're looking for everyone who worked with her."

"Kimba," said James Johnson. "Maybe Kim-bee but I'm still thinking Kim-ba . . . what I can tell you . . . if it's who I'm thinking of—she always seemed different."

"How so?"

"Like she felt she shouldn't have been there. That's about it."

"Could we meet anyway, sir?"

"What for?"

"Sometimes people's memories are jogged."

"I don't think mine will be."

"I'm sure you're right, Mr. Johnson, but this woman died in a particularly nasty way and unless we can identify her—"

"Fine, okay, if it's super quick. I just finished a client in Beverly Hills, got one coming up in Brentwood, I can give you a few minutes."

"If it's convenient for you to stop by, we're in West L.A. between Beverly Hills and Brentwood."

"Come to a police station? No, no, I don't think so. Last time I experienced a police station was when I was in college and went up to Bakersfield with the strength team for a competition and got picked up for walking while black."

"Sorry—"

"Not your fault, I'm just saying. You want to talk, you come to me."

Milo said, "Happy to, sir."

"Well," said Johnson, "there's a little park on the corner of Whittier Drive and Sunset, I was planning to have a snack, anyway. But I can't stay long."

"Thanks, sir."

"Kimba . . . I'm **pretty** sure that was her name."

The park was petite, lush, green, beautifully tended, maybe twice the size of nearby front lawns on Whittier Drive. Traffic on Sunset whizzed by. The air was warm and inviting. As we drove up, two squirrels stopped their frenzied mating and scampered off chittering.

Milo murmured, "Love abounds."

Several years ago a Hollywood publicist had been gunned down while waiting for a red light at the Whittier–Sunset intersection, the shooter a lunatic on a bicycle who'd botched robbing her and avoided capture by blowing his own brains out.

Other than that, a peaceful spot.

A black Porsche Macan was parked on the west side of Whittier. A huge man in a white tee, shorts, socks, and sneakers sat cross-legged on the grass drinking from a bottle of something opaque and brown. He noticed us right away and gave a hesitant wave. By the time we reached him, he was on his feet, a tower of toned, sculpted muscle. A shadow of dark hair sheathed his head, neat and clipped.

Milo extended his hand. James Johnson regarded it for a second before accepting. My hand is decent-sized, with long guitarist fingers. Johnson's grip was an enveloping blanket of warm meat that covered it completely. Soft, though. Aware of his own strength.

He settled back down on the grass. The brown stuff in the bottle looked like unfiltered apple juice.

Milo and I settled facing him.

James Johnson said, "Yoga class begins. Namaste. Actually, that's for the end."

Milo grinned. "Again, thanks for taking the time, Mr. Johnson."

"Wait before you thank me, Lieutenant, nothing in my memory has jogged. I didn't hang with any of the girls, it wasn't that kind of place. You did your job and went home."

I said, "As opposed to other clubs."

"Some places develop a—I guess you'd call it a social system. The ones that seem to last."

"Not The Aura."

Massive shoulders rose and fell. "Total dive, the Egyptian wouldn't spend a penny more than he had to. No benefits, everyone was an IC—independent contractor. You got paid in cash and not always on time. I didn't stay long. No one did."

"Including the girls?"

"Especially the girls," said Johnson. "The clientele was basically shabby old guys who didn't tip."

He uncapped his bottle and took a long swig. The look of apple juice but the aroma that filtered out was closer to vegetable soup.

I said, "Were there any problems with specific customers?"

"Nothing beyond a few harmless drunks. Overall boring, it was all I could do to stay awake," said Johnson. "I stood out in front and another guy did the back door and then we'd reverse. Front was losers arriving drunk, back was losers leaving drunk. If they were obviously impaired—falling over—we'd call them a cab, but mostly Salami told us to mind our own business. The guy just didn't care."

"No fights to break up?" said Milo.

"None that I had to deal with. We're talking sad wimpy guys who didn't even catch on to watered-down booze. It was **depressing**."

Milo said, "Who was the other bouncer?"

"I worked with a bunch of them," said James Johnson. "Like I said, people came and went. Good security's in demand, at solid places you get full benefits plus serious gratuity potential if there's people wanting you to VIP 'em. No way Salami could hold on to serious staff."

I said, "No VIP lounge at The Aura."

He laughed. "Not hardly."

"Salawa said there was a bouncer named Del something."

"DelRay Hutchins. You guys follow the Olympics?"

"Some of it."

"DR powerlifted on the 1990 team. Guy could dead close to eight hundred pounds, back in those days he could've qualified for one of those World's Strongest Man competitions. Not anymore, Eddie

Hall just went eleven hundred pounds. But Eddie's Eddie and who wants to bulk up to four-hundred-plus and wear a breathing machine?"

Milo said, "Del worked with you for how long?"

"Maybe the last couple weeks I was there," said Johnson. "Nice person. There were also some foreign guys—Russians, Finns, Croats, a massive dude from Morocco, an Israeli into that Krav Maga. Mostly older dudes, doing it part-time for a retirement gig, can't tell you their names. Soon as I found out the Roxy was hiring, I got the heck out of there. Door work wasn't my main focus, anyway. After a couple of years at Cal State L.A. and the weights team, I transferred to Tulane and got to defensive tackle. The NFL would've been nice but not with my injured ACL."

He massaged the back of one leg. "The goal was to get myself a high school coaching thing or build a career as trainer. I ended up with training, best thing ever happened."

He checked the time on his phone. "Five more minutes. Brentwood client's a producer's wife with an eating disorder. She is **not** into waiting."

Milo said, "What can you tell us about Kimba?"

"Good looking, quiet, like I said, not putting on any sexy moves onstage—basically she'd get up and fake it. Can't blame her, the losers coming in there weren't exactly stuffing Benjamins in g-strings."

I said, "Going through the motions."

"Minimal motions," said Johnson. He got to his feet with astonishing speed and grace, rounded his back. Letting his arms sag, he sidestepped to the right, the left, then back.

"The shuffle, you know? Like guys who can't dance but they're with a hot girl who can so they try to be part of it? That was her. Back and forth."

He sat back down and took another swig of vegetable matter.

I said, "Low-key and quiet."

James Johnson thought about that. "Not unfriendly-quiet. More like . . . reserved. She'd come in and say hi but she wasn't like the others."

"Not a lot of reserved dancers."

Johnson smiled. "I did it long enough so I can generalize. Girls like that, they're basically show-offs—exhibitionists. Same deal with actresses—some of the dancers still think they can **become** actresses."

I said, "Look at me, look at me, look at me."

"Exactly. Look at my body, look at my sexy face, look at my **moves.** Kimba wasn't into that—oh, yeah, she dressed different, too. I'm not talking her stage stuff. What she wore when she arrived."

He smiled. "Guess that's what you meant by jogging the memory."

I said, "What were her street clothes?"

"Baggy sweaters, jeans, running shoes. No makeup, hair in a high pony. Okay, here's something—another jog. She carried a backpack instead of one of those big fake designer things the other girls were into."

"Did her being different lead to conflict?"

"Not that I ever saw. But like I told you, I am **not** the expert, here. She definitely didn't hang with the other girls. In between shifts, the rest of them would be drinking or smoking or on the phone or doing their nails, whatever. Kimba would go into a corner, take a book out of her backpack, and read. Or she'd write something in a book, like a diary."

"Maybe a puzzle book?"

"Hmm," said Johnson. "Yeah could've been a Sudoku, crossword, word search, something like that. Jamie—my husband—gets into bed with one of those numbers thing and . . ." He mimed a giant yawn and grinned. "So, yeah, maybe. I wasn't paying close attention."

He took another look at his phone. "Two minutes."

I said, "What car did Kimba drive?"

"Some compact, Toyota, Honda, they all look the same to me. Gray, maybe? Or brown? Or blue? Honestly, I wasn't paying attention. Now I really have to go."

He stood, took car keys out of a pocket, and faced the Macan.

Milo said, "Just one more thing, sir. Do you have DelRay Hutchins's number handy?"

"No reason I would. What I can tell you is I think he moved to Lancaster. He **got** himself a high school football thing."

Milo thanked him again and handed over his

business card. "Anything else comes to mind, sir, please call."

"Sure. Kimba a victim. Man, that's sad. Where did it happen?"

"At The Aura."

"She went back there? Why the heck?"

"Good question, sir."

"Wow," said James Johnson. "Life's short, man, it's **short**."

CHAPTER
8

Three public high schools in Lancaster. DelRay Hutchins didn't work at Lancaster, Eastside, or Antelope Valley. Same for half a dozen religious academies in the area.

I said, "Maybe he didn't score a high school gig."

Milo nodded. "Time to dial down."

Moments later, the utterly uncurious receptionist at Piute Middle School said, "Coach? Let me try to find him."

A few beats later, Milo had finished a brief conversation with the fifty-three-year-old former powerlifter/AFL footballer/bouncer now training tweens in the fine art of collision.

No, Hutchins had never worked with a Kimba or a Kimby but **maybe** there was a girl named Kimmie-Lee who matched the victim's physical stats? Don't hold him to it.

Milo said, "Anything you remember would be useful."

"There's not much," said Hutchins.

His hazy recollections jibed with James Johnson's: quiet girl, stuck to herself, no problems with anyone he'd ever noticed, yeah, he'd heard The Aura closed down, why in the world would she return to "that trash dump"?

He was able to give Milo the numbers of two other dancers at The Aura ("friends of mine, no problem telling them I told you, they **love** me").

Anja "Catwoman" Przdowek and Brooklynne "Slinky" Baker roomed together on the western rim of Los Feliz. Both had arrests for minor drug possession and, in Slinky's case, for prostitution, twice.

They came on the phone simultaneously, giggling about being questioned by a "murder detective." Both proclaimed their "total adorable love" for Hutchins. "We don't see DR much since he moved but when he lived in Hollywood, he was kinda like a father to us."

Neither of them had other than a faint remembrance of the girl **they** recalled as Kimmy.

Quiet, stayed to herself.

Catwoman said, "Not mean-quiet, like shy-quiet."

Slinky did recall "two bizarre things." Kimmy didn't drink or smoke and she liked to read.

"Like a nerd," said Catwoman.

Milo said, "What did she read?"

"Like I'm gonna notice? You notice, honey?"

Slinky said, "Like **I'm** gonna notice? It's like she wasn't there, sir."

Milo said, "Staying in the background."

"Yeah," said Catwoman. "Not a star, that's for sure."

"Do you have numbers for any of the other girls who worked with her?"

"Negative," said Slinky. "Them bitches come and gone. Me and Cat are a couple."

"Got it."

"Hope you **do**. We're in **love**!"

Shared laughter.

Milo said, "You guys have been helpful. Anything else you want to say?"

"She had no chest," said Slinky. "Don't want to yelp her cold, not especially now with her all murdered, but to be honest, sir, she had **leetle** boobarellas and was a totally non-dancer. But I'm not saying she was nothing. Her butt was nice and her face was hot."

"Hot face," agreed Catwoman. "I am totally dis-amayed that anyone would hurt her."

"Find out who did it," said Slinky, "and fuck him **up**."

Milo hung up. The phone receiver landed with a horse-hoof clop. Out of a jacket pocket came another plastic-wrapped panatela. Again, he rolled it between his palms, creating tobacco dust. He does that more often, now, rarely smokes.

A wrist-snap lob landed the trashed brown cylinder in the wastebasket.

I said, "No net. Impressive."

"Huh." He crumpled a few departmental memos and shot them in, too.

A third cigar emerged. How many could he fit into a pocket?

He studied it, put it back. "So let's sum up blue Monday. Lotsa talk, no solid info."

I said, "Everyone gave a consistent picture of her."

"But they can't even agree on her name." He swiveled and faced me. "Any of them could be lying and what happened **is** related to the club and someone knows it. Or they're leveling and it's **still** related to the club. Or the wedding. Or the bachelorette party. Or something else completely. Why the hell **would** she go back there?"

He shot to his feet like a bottle rocket, leaving the chair creaking in relief. Stretching, he grazed his fingers on the ceiling. Sitting back down heavily, he set off a new chorus of squeaks and pressed a finger to his pocked brow.

"Know what's flashing in here? My two least favorite words: 'Anything's possible.' Tell me something that narrows it down. You can lie, too."

I said, "The description of her street clothes, her

backpack, and her books makes me wonder about a moonlighting student."

"Moonlighting coed? Kind of a cliché."

"Clichés endure because they're often based on truth."

"Using her spare time to catch up on classes," he said. "Or Johnson was right and she was doing puzzles."

"Maybe both," I said. "In any case, we just met another student who's sweet as a wolverine."

"Little Amanda. My my my." He sat back and grinned. "Could you lend me some neurons?"

He phoned the campus police at the U., spoke to a fellow lieutenant named Morales and asked about missing students.

Only one active case, a young man from Shanghai who'd taken a trip to San Diego a week ago and hadn't returned.

"If you can solve that, I'm your new BFF," said Morales. "Chinese consulate's calling me daily, along with various Feds and an intern for some assemblyman from San Gabriel. Like we control the brats when they're here, let alone when they leave. If your girl's not Chinese, please don't tell me she's some other kind of foreigner."

"Don't know what she is," said Milo. "Don't even have a name."

"Oh, man, you're at square minus one," said Morales. "Good luck."

Glib, no curiosity. Busy with his own problems.

Milo said, "I do have some possible names. Kimba, Kimby, Kimmie-Lee, Kimberly."

Morales said, "You're kidding, right?"

"Wish I was."

"Nah, none of those ticks any boxes here."

"One more: Amanda Burdette."

"Whole different name for the same girl?"

"Different girl and Burdette's definitely a student," said Milo. "It's possible she knew my vic."

Morales said, "Got forty-three thousand two hundred seventeen students to deal with—hey, here's a fun idea: Let's go down the list, one by one. By the time we're ten percent done, we'll be pension-eligible."

He laughed. "Not trying to make your life difficult, my friend, but no Kims or Amandas are on our radar and I can't help you. Unless your girls are part of that anti-fascist pain-in-the-dick bunch, likes to bust things up for stupid reasons. We got four of those idiots being naughty on CC last week. Breaking windows at a ninety-year-old professor's house because he brought some speaker to class they didn't approve of, thank God he didn't have a heart attack. Skinny little assholes in those Guy Fawkes masks, a couple move like they're probably females."

"Masks," said Milo. "Good luck on that one."

"Ha," said Morales. "Now you're getting even."

◆

During the conversation, I'd googled **missing u. student** and paired it with Kim-names.

Only one hit, on a crime history site: Twenty-two years ago, a local girl named Kimberly Vance had vanished. Not from the U., from the old school across town where I taught pediatric psych. Ancient history but I told Milo about it, anyway.

He said, "Guess what, I worked that one."

"That's Southwest Division."

"So it is."

"How'd it become a West L.A. homicide?"

"It became a West L.A. non-homicide. Rich sorority girl, ran off with a married professor, he took her to a free-love weekend up in Big Sur, got some weed in her, took her clothes off, and then she had second thoughts and hitchhiked back. Took her three days to reach L.A. Besides the prof, the biggest danger was getting run over by a semi."

"Same question: Why'd you work it?"

"Special request from above." He smiled. "You'll notice there was no follow-up story."

"Family with influence."

"Family who donated to the mayor's reelection committee."

"Too bad our girl has no obvious connections," I said.

"Our girl's business as usual," he said, loosening his tie. "Give me your tired, your poor, your dead."

CHAPTER
9

The ride from the station to my home in Beverly Glen ranges from fifteen minutes to an hour, depending on the whims of the commuting gods. This time I made it in twenty, snaking up the unmarked road on the west side of the canyon and hooking onto the former bridle path that sometimes turns to slush before connecting to my private road. All in a two-wheel-drive vehicle not meant for the ride. The Seville's been good to me; I reciprocate.

The house that Robin and I share is a crisp white piece of geometry surrounded by green. She designed it and contracted the build when the little wooden thing I bought soon after I began working was burned to the ground by a psychopath. The lot sits high, smaller than it looks but benefiting from the borrowed landscape of unseen neighbors. On clear days you can catch glimpses of ocean above the pine-tops. When the haze sets in, the contours of trees soften and that's not bad, either.

I parked next to Robin's truck and climbed to the entry terrace. We decided to under-furnish because stuff can get the best of you and neither of us likes to cull. Daylight is inevitably kind and the oak floors still echo, creating a comforting, musical prelude to solitude.

I called out Robin's name, got no reply. Changing into sweats, I sorted some mail in the kitchen and drank coffee from the pot she'd left. Walking out back through the kitchen door, I stopped by the rock edge of the fishpond, netted a few pine needles, tossed pellets to the koi, and enjoyed their conditional love. When the slurping ended and the fish began to meander, I continued to Robin's studio.

She stood over her bench, wearing magnifying eyeglasses and a shop apron with four front pockets. No music from hidden speakers this afternoon. Both of her hands were occupied and her greeting was a brief smile before she returned to the work at hand.

Special concentration required for delicate work: sealing a crack on the face of a 1938 Martin D-45 guitar. Three-hundred-thousand-dollar instrument. The man who'd owned it for seventy-two years had picked it up in a Bakersfield pawnshop and played it in cowboy bars running up and down California's interior spine. He'd died on stage, ninety years old, smoking Luckies and breathing through a tracheotomy hole. Rasping the first verse of "Amazing Grace" as his heart gave out.

His heirs couldn't wait to cash in.

The crack was long and threatening to open and not in a good location: treble side of the sound hole, trailing to the bridge, requiring a micro-surgical splice. Robin had spent a week locating the right sliver of Adirondack spruce in Nashville, giving the wood time to get used to L.A.

Today: the operation. I'd walked in at a crucial time.

I kept my distance from the bench and headed for the sagging brocade couch where Blanche—our little blond French bulldog—stretched, decorously inert. I sat down beside her, rubbed her knobby head. She rolled said cranium into my lap, gave my hand a single comprehensive lick, and molded her twenty-pound sausage body against mine.

Robin said, "Not only do you play around with another woman, you flaunt it?"

"What can I say? Charisma."

She allowed herself a pause for a laugh. Readjusted the magnifiers and peered at the splice. "I'd ask you about your day but I need to focus."

"Want more alone-time?"

"No, no, just . . . bear . . . with me . . . another . . . minute."

Ten minutes passed before she stepped back and

assessed the repair. I didn't mind the chance to decompress.

"Okay, so far so good." To the Martin: "You rest here and heal up, Daisy."

"It's got a name?"

"Orville christened all his instruments," she said. "His Broadcaster's named Molly. In the case was a cassette of him singing, back in the sixties. Buck Owens with more bottom. End of an era, none of the old guys are left. Remember how he used to bring her here in that Studebaker? The alleged case."

Pointing to a soft-shelled black thing held together with duct tape and decals from national parks.

Robin took off her glasses and wiped her eyes. "Somehow Daisy never got hurt."

I said, "What I remember is him spitting his chaw in the garden when he thought no one was looking."

"That, too." She inspected the guitar again. "Fingers crossed."

I walked over and had a look, trying to locate the repair. "Invisible."

"Oh, I see it, babe. But not bad." Removing her apron. "She's a supermodel, we can't be having scars. Know what he paid for her?"

"Couple of hundred?"

"Fifty bucks. Now his conspicuously unmusical offspring will profit and it'll probably go to some trophy hunter who keeps it in a vault." She wiped her face, then her hands, removed the bandanna from her head, and shook out a wealth of auburn curls. "I need coffee. How 'bout you?"

The three of us left the studio and crossed the garden. At the kitchen door, Robin stopped and kissed me. What began as a peck but ended up a serious lip-lock, her hand shifting from my waist to the back of my head.

When we broke, I looked at her.

"Yes, I can feel you-know-who. And the answer to your arched eyebrow is you bet," she said. "I need some relaxation and you're the sedative."

To Blanche: "Sorry, my little rival. You'll have to make do with a liver snap out in the hallway."

After sharing a shower, we went out to the terrace, ate Asian mix and peanuts, and drank. Sidecar for her ("don't skimp on the XO"), Chivas for me. The sun sank lazily. We stayed there, bathed in burgeoning blue darkness as the day eased offstage.

I'd given Robin the basics Saturday night, after returning from the scene.

She'd said, "Weddings. Everyone's at their worst. Amazing it doesn't happen more often."

I sipped scotch and reached for her hand. Our fingers fit like teeth in a cog. She lowered her head to my shoulder and I breathed in cinnamon and crème rinse and wood dust.

The two of us have been together forever, minus a couple of minor disconnects.

All these years, never formalized with paper.

The topic of marriage has never been taboo but it comes up less often as time stretches. Neither of us pushes the issue. I suppose that's a type of decision.

I don't wonder much why but sometimes the question mark slithers into my head.

The best I've come up with is we both endured miserable childhoods. Robin's an only child who needed to learn how to coexist with her mother; my father was a sometimes-vicious alcoholic, my mother chronically depressed, and my relationship with my older sister nonexistent.

Marriage aside, the topic of children **never** comes up. Despite working with kids my entire adult life, I'm happy the way things are.

Maybe I'm missing the paternity gene.

Maybe the status quo is working too well.

Maybe the reason will always elude me.

Despite my training, I'm not one for introspection. Working with other people's problems is a great time-filler.

Milo and Rick haven't tied the knot, either. Recently, they've had to deal with not-so-subtle pressure from those who believe the legalization of gay marriage confers obligation.

"Fuck that noise," Milo had pronounced a few months ago. The two of us at a tavern near the station, celebrating a vicious murderer's life sentence and booze-meandering to all sorts of topics.

I said, "Do what you want."

"Don't I always?" He tossed back his third shot, got to work on the accompanying beer. "Let me tell you about the crap I had to deal with last night. Boring-as-shit dinner party with some of the money people who help fund the E.R.—the things I do for love. We're talking one of those they tell you where to sit with goddamn place cards. Rick's like an acre away and I'm stuck with this heiress from Bel Air— 'scuse me, she's a social justice **activist**. Weighs around ninety pounds, apparently she substitutes opinions for eating. And one of them is that Rick and I are somehow **failing** in our social **obligation**."

I said, "And there you were thinking progress was about choice."

He called for a fourth Boilermaker. "Being told what to do is childhood. If my body's going to seed, least I can get are the benefits of adulthood, right?"

"Right."

"Not that I'm saying we'd **never** do it," he went on. "Maybe one day, for inheritance purposes. But hell, I'll be the first to go anyway, you know how long they live in his family, and it's not like he needs my goddamn pension. Which he can probably get hold of anyway, the department being so **progressive** and all that. According to the memos. Which I don't read."

Slamming his hand down on the bar. "**Fuck** that noise."

I said, "Amen."

He patted my shoulder. "I like that we're religious tonight."

Drinks finished, Robin said, "Okay, I'm sufficiently brandied to be civil. How was your day?"

"Not much to tell."

"Indulge me, baby. I like the sound of your voice."

I filled her in.

She said, "Anything's possible? Yeah, I can see that as terrifying for a detective. But your point about a student does make sense."

"Big Guy thought it was a cliché."

She laughed. "Fresh-faced Cindy working her way to summa cum laude by taking off her clothes? Yeah, I've seen that movie. It does happen, though. Remember those girls up at Berkeley—the little escort service they had going?"

"Sensual Seminar."

She elbowed my arm. "You remember at that level of detail, huh?"

"Vaguely."

"Ha. Now tell me the names of every seminarian."

"Fifi, Gigi, Mimi—"

She laughed and stood. "Want another drink?"

"Why not."

She paused to study the sky. Mauve and gray and wispy pink where daylight had resisted expulsion.

"Me, too, we've both earned our leisure. Not that we have to self-justify. But we always do, don't we? That's the way you and I are constructed."

"Want me to mix?"

"No, my turn." She stood and smiled down at Blanche, lying tummy-down, eyes shut, breathing slowly, chunky bod so flaccid she might as well be an invertebrate.

"You, on the other hand, little missy, are blessedly entitled."

CHAPTER

10

Milo phoned at ten a.m. Tuesday.

"Dug a little more on the families, dull shovel, hard clay. No hint of bad behavior for any of them. The only surprise is Amanda. Her age you'd expect some sort of social network presence. Zilch. Same for a driver's license, state I.D., or local address. She lives in L.A. but doesn't drive?"

I said, "It's happening more often. Driving used to be a symbol of freedom. Some kids today see it as a hassle."

"Ooh, traffic," he said. "Scawy-wawy invasion of safe space."

I laughed. "She goes to the U., probably lives in or near Westwood, maybe close enough to walk to campus. Longer journeys, she can bike or Uber."

"Jesus," he said. "A generation of fetuses."

"Hey," I said, "if they sit at home sucking their thumbs the crime rate could eventually drop."

"There goes my career. But not yours—don't gloat."

"In terms of her address, she could live in a dorm."

"Good luck prying that out of the U. I googled, looking for anything. Her name came up once: Two years ago she won an essay contest in high school sponsored by the Calabasas Chamber of Commerce. Patriotism and capitalism as bosom buddies. Different **narrative**, back then."

"Straight-arrow goes to college and turns all relativistic and postmodern."

"Oh, those big words, Doctor. Anyway, what I'm left with is a mouthy kid who reworked herself. Can't see how it relates to Kimby Red Dress."

"Unless Kimby was a student, like I suggested, and they knew each other."

"Backpack and books, yeah, I thought of that. That's another reason I checked Amanda's web presence. Best of all worlds, there'd be Instagram shots of both of them. Unfortunately."

Long breathy exhalation. "It is weird, though, Amanda being so covert. Who feeds the online beast? Egomaniacs, bigots, and millennials. Or is there another trend I missed?"

I said, "A few kids are withdrawing but not many. From what we saw, Amanda might have a stake in being different. Or relationships are problematic for her so she's withdrawn."

"Relationships with other women?"

"Her family's straitlaced. If her sexuality wouldn't fit in, she'd definitely want to keep it from them. That could be another reason she was so hostile."

"Amanda and Red Dress," he said. "Red Dress shows up to the wedding peeved because her girl-friend didn't invite her. Amanda needs to get her out of view, takes her upstairs to talk—she was a bridesmaid, she'd know about the bathroom. There's a confrontation and Red Dress gets the worst of it. Yeah, it's a great screenplay. Unfortunately logic doesn't touch it. If Amanda was caught off-guard, why would she be equipped with a syringe full of dope and a guitar string? Plus, she's small, hard to see her overpowering anyone. And she didn't have any scratches on her, any indication she'd been in a struggle."

I said, "Want me to play Devil's advocate?"

"What, you need permission? No, I don't. Yes, I do. Go."

"There was no struggle because the shot in the back of Red Dress's neck shocked her to the ground. Amanda had dope because she uses. Not necessarily a full-fledged junkie. She flirts with opioids—a little squirt here and there, lots of kids try it. That could explain her affect."

No answer.

I said, "You don't like it."

"I'm not feeling it, Alex. Yeah, she could be involved on some level. But managing to get away from the wedding party long enough to do all that, come back looking none the worse, and go back to her book? Now onward to the bride's family. **Lots** of litigation, there. The Rapfogels rent space in an office building, are tussling with their landlord—unpaid rent versus code violations. Even more interesting, five former employees are suing separately for back wages and 'workplace violations.'"

"Sexual harassment."

"Bingo. All five claimants are female, I managed to contact two. Neither was thrilled to talk to me and both said Red Dress's description didn't ring a bell. But one woman made it clear Denny Rapfogel was a pig. Took a while to pry it out of her, finally she said, 'You know. What's going around?' I say, 'Sounds like a disease.' She says, 'Exactly. The scrotal flu.' Then she hung up. Plenty of hostility potential, no? As in pissed-off husband or boyfriend. If Denny was the target, there'd be irony potential, too. You abused your wedding vows, asshole, now your little Baby won't enjoy hers."

I said, "That would fit getting rid of Denny. Killing an innocent woman doesn't. Red Dress wasn't an accidental victim. But now you've got **me** thinking. What if Amanda wasn't her lover, Denny was. Married guy dangles a woman on the side, promises to leave his wife but never does. Her frustration boils over, she shows up looking sexy and ready to humiliate him. Same scenario, different cast."

"He's big enough to pull it off but we've still got the problem of preparation. Who brings a syringe and guitar string to his daughter's wedding?"

"Someone who suspected what might happen," I said.

More silence.

Finally, he said, "No, I don't **don't** like it. Maybe, let's see what happens when I get more face-time with Denny . . . okay, last item: talked to Tomashev, the photographer. Still working on the images."

"Speaking of which, how come there was no videographer?"

"There was supposed to be. A studio gofer Tomashev works with. It fell through because she insisted on a deposit but never got one."

"Tight budget," I said. "That and the Rapfogels' unpaid rent says tough times. Another source of stress if Red Dress was tightening screws."

"Red Fendi," he said. "Alicia's checking to see if it's vintage. It is, she'll do a boutique crawl. And yes, I'm assuming a woman will do better at high-end dress shops, don't report me to the ACLU. Any suggestions beyond re-interviewing Amanda and the Rapfogels?"

"Maybe a follow-up with the bride and groom, because they could still be the primary targets. And pursue the strip-club angle. She worked The Aura, she likely had other gigs."

"Already assigned it to Moe."

"Time on for good behavior?"

He cracked up. "No address on Amanda so the Rapfogels come first. Think they're ready for my charm and charisma?"

"Undoubtedly."

"Even so," he said, "how about we toss in your therapeutic warmth, notable empathy, and all-around sensitivity?"

"Sure. When?"

"Now sounds about right. By the time you get here, I'll have a plan."

He was standing ten yards south of the station when I drove up. I cruised to the curb and he got in.

"What's the plan?"

"Improv. No one answered at their agency but it's ten minutes away, Wilshire near Barrington. I strike out, we had a nice breather."

As I shifted into Drive, the front door to the station opened and Alicia Bogomil came out wearing baggy gray sweats and white sneakers. In contrast, her long, butterscotch hair was combed out and glowing and she'd put on makeup and dangling earrings that flashed as she walked. Sashayed.

She saw us, immediately adjusted her gait to cop-march, and came over to the Seville.

"Hi, Doc. Off to explore the world of fashion, Loo. I figured I'd go home and dress up a bit." She plucked at the sweatshirt. White lettering exalted **The Albuquerque Isotopes.**

Milo said, "That a team or a chemistry lesson?"

"Minor-league baseball." Another pluck. "I Lysoled the locker they gave me five times but it still stinks of whoever, and now so does this. I'm figuring decent duds and a little perfume might not get me kicked out."

Milo said, "Hauting the couture? Go for it."

"Great," she said. "Nice seeing you, Doc. Think I'd look half decent in Fendi?"

Not waiting for a reply, she crossed to the staff parking lot. Back to loose limbs, hair swaying back and forth, in counterpoint to her rear end.

Milo said, "Good work ethic. She's doing okay, so far."

He read off the Rapfogels' business address.

I did a three-pointer using the staff parking lot and drove north.

He said, "I was gonna call the Burdettes and ask for Amanda's address, then I said maybe not. Overprotected youngest child, maybe with personality issues? Don't want her parents on edge this early. Make sense?"

"Perfect sense," I said. "And we could get the address from the U."

"You heard what the unicop said. They don't give out personal info."

"I'm thinking Maxine Driver."

"Ah," he said. "Think she'd do it?"

"If the incentive was there."

Driver was a history professor at the U., an elegant, erudite daughter of Korean immigrants with a special affection for freedom. Her academic interest was criminal life in prewar L.A. Last year, she'd provided information that had helped close the murder of a one-hundred-year-old woman. Her payback was access to a fat blue file that nourished four academic papers and a keynote presentation at an international criminology conference in Bonn.

I switched my cell to hands-off and called her campus extension.

She said, "Alex. Another juicy one?"

"Juicy but not historical."

I gave her the basics.

She hummed a few bars of "The Wedding March" and said, "Here comes the victim? Crazy—sure, why not, if you give me another murder book. Maybe I'll explore a new topic: the relationship between tribal rites of passage and violence."

"If Lieutenant Sturgis solves it, I'm sure that could be worked out."

"You're working with him again?" she said. "I like him. More sensitive than he lets on and over-whelmingly authentic."

"That he is."

Milo gave an aw-shucks pout.

Maxine Driver said, "So what exactly can I help you with?"

"The class schedule of a specific student."

"That's it?"

"So far."

"There'll be more?"

"Depends."

"Hmm," she said. "Divulging personal data is a big no-no, Alex. Privacy for the tots and all that."

"Just thought I'd ask."

She laughed. "Like I care? Name."

"Amanda Burdette. She's a sophomore, made her own major."

"Ah, one of those bullshit DIYs," she said. "Amanda Burdette . . . is she by any chance a rude little pretentious kind of spectrumy pain in the ass?"

I said, "That could describe her."

"Pale? Like one of those Victorian chicks who ate chalk? Arrogant mien utterly unjustified by reality?"

"Amazing, Maxine."

"What is?"

"Forty-three thousand students and you know the one we're looking at."

"I **know** her because I **had** her in one of my upper-division seminars. Twice-a-month spiel on social structure, the department stuck me with it. A dozen kids and she was conspicuous because of her attitude. She'd come in late, flounce to the back, and make a big show of ignoring me—head in a book that had nothing to do with the class. Always some dreary existential thing, Sartre and the like. If we made eye contact, she'd smirk and pull the book higher."

"Making a statement."

"Making a screw-**you** statement," she said. "I was so looking forward to flunking her but she had the gall to hand in a terrific finals bluebook, so what could I do? Little bitch can write and abstract. I could've downgraded her to B plus and gotten away with it, but who needs the headache? She got an A minus. So what'd she do to get Milo interested?"

"Maybe nothing, Maxine, and you know the drill."

"Yeah, yeah, the old cloak-and-dagger. Fine, last time it worked out great. I'll call my secret contact at a secret place to remain unnamed—nephew at the registrar's office, oops. Anything else?"

"A home address would be helpful."

"The police can't dig **that** up?"

"She's got no driver's license or social network presence."

"One of those," she said. "I call them burrowers. Little fanged shrews who bury themselves underground and emerge periodically to wax obnoxious. A lot of them seem to live with Mommy and Daddy and eschew motor vehicles."

"Her mommy and daddy are in Calabasas. I was figuring an address near campus, a bike and/or Uber."

"Makes sense, let me see what I can find."

"Thanks, Maxine."

"You can't tell me anything?"

"Sorry."

"Oh, well," she said. "I'll have to sustain myself

with fantasy. As in Milo ends up busting the little twit for something horrendous, she goes on trial, I'm in the courtroom the day she's sentenced, positioned where she has to look at me. She hears the bad news, we make eye contact, I hold up a Camille Paglia."

Academic's notion of revenge.

"A wedding," she said. "Obviously she's not the bride and I can't see her as a chirping bridesmaid."

I looked at Milo. He nodded.

"She's the groom's sister."

"The plot thickens," said Driver. "Okay, nice hearing from you, Alex. Tribal rituals gone bloody— weddings, bar mitzvahs—hey, circumcisions, my husband would love **that**."

CHAPTER
11

VCR Staffing Specialists occupied a ground-floor office in a squat two-story brick building. High-rises and strip malls abounded in East Brentwood. This building had been forgotten by time and developers. But maybe not for long: A **For Sale** sign was nailed to the brick, just right of a pebble-glass door.

A lobby floored in grimy fake terrazzo opened to a brown-carpeted hallway. VCR's suite was toward the back. Dead bolt below the doorknob but the knob turned.

Inside was an empty waiting room decorated with prints of Paris street scenes from the nineteenth century and the type of black-and-white celebrity photos you see in dry cleaners and other places celebrities never go.

Small desk, one chair. Hard gray tweed sofas said no one of import waited here.

Another wooden door centered the wall behind the desk. Voices filtered through. Muffled but not enough to conceal emotional tone.

Male voice, female voice, talking over each other.

Milo rapped hard and the conversation stopped.

The male voice said, "You hear something?"

The female voice shouted, "If you're so damn curious, go check."

Denny Rapfogel, flushed and sweaty and rolling a black plastic pen between his fingers, opened the door. He blurted, "What the?" then checked himself and offered a queasy smile.

His too-tight, green aloha shirt was patterned with Martini glasses and cocktail shakers. Off-white linen pants bagged to the floor, puddling over olive-green basket-weave loafers.

From behind him came a bark worthy of a watchdog: "**Who?**"

"The cops from the wedding."

"**Why?**"

"How the hell would I know?"

Corinne Rapfogel came into view, jostling past her husband. The impact jellied his jowls. The skin where his jaw met his earlobes reddened and his shoulders rose. Still, the seasick smile endured.

Corinne's smile was huge and white. "Oh, hi, guys." New voice, soft and kittenish.

Alicia Bogomil's plan was to doll up to get the job done. Corinne Rapfogel had dolled down for her work space, even accounting for wedding versus everyday.

She wore a blousy light-blue dress that hung past her knees, chipped white patent flats on her feet. Dark hair was tied back carelessly, with errant strands shooting out from the sides of her head, more than a few gray filaments glinting. Reading glasses perched atop a shiny nose. Like a lot of faces accustomed to heavy makeup, hers looked unformed and blurred without it.

Despite all that, she began vamping, working stubby eyelashes, cocking her head to one side, her hip to the other.

Milo said, "Ms. Rapfogel."

"Pu-leeze, we're old friends by now, right? Corinne." Taking hold of Milo's hand and holding on for too long.

Denny Rapfogel said, "They're not here to socialize, this is business." To us: "Hopefully good business—you solved it?"

Milo freed his hand. "I wish, sir. We're here for a follow-up, tried calling but no one answered so we thought we'd—"

Corinne Rapfogel said, "What can we follow you up **on**, guys?"

Milo said, "First off, has anything new occurred to you?"

"Occurred," she said, as if learning a foreign word on a self-teaching tape. Long, sweeping leftward movement of her eyes. "No, can't say that it has."

Denny said, "You're saying no progress at all? More I've been thinking about it, more pissed I get. They ruined our day."

Milo said, "The dead woman's day didn't go too well, either."

"The woman," said Denny. "You're not going to tell me you don't know who she is."

"Unfortunately—"

"Christ. What's the problem? With social media, who can't be identified?"

Corinne said, "Obviously some people can't."

Using the tone you employ for spelling simple things out to dullards. Denny knew it and glared. Corinne didn't notice, or chose not to. Her eyes made another sweep to the left. The fingers on her outthrust hip drummed.

She saw me looking. Smiled and nodded, as if we were sharing a secret.

I raised my eyebrows. She did the same.

Shall we dance?

Milo watched without expression. Denny Rapfogel, turning away from his wife, saw none of it. He shook his head. "Total disaster. That's what you came to tell us? Jesus H."

Corinne said, "It's **follow**-up."

"Whatever."

"They're doing their best. These are **honest** working guys."

Her turn to glare. The unspoken **as opposed to**.

The flush spread to Denny's cheeks. "It wasn't my dad who was an insurance dentist—"

"An **honest**, hardworking DDS," said Corinne. "You never knew him so don't be judging."

"Right." To us: "Her old man's face used to be on bus benches."

Corinne produced a rictal smile. "My dad grew up in the projects and earned his dental surgery degree from New York University. **Some** people take the initiative."

Denny muttered, "Bus benches."

Milo said, "So. Any new ideas?"

"Like what?" said Denny.

"Like whatever could help them, obviously," said Corinne. Another glance at me, followed by a conspiratorial nod.

I said, "Mr. Rapfogel, your comment about a ruined day is right on. I know you were asked this at the time but can you think of anyone who'd want to screw up the wedding?"

"From our side?" said Denny. "No freakin' way. Our side was mostly Brears's friends and obviously friends don't want to ruin anything."

Corinne said nothing.

I said, "Mrs. Rapfogel?"

She shook her head and said, "I can't think of

anyone," but the fingers on her hip had stilled and the index finger had extended. Keeping the gesture low and out of her husband's view, she curled the digit.

Come hither.

I returned her tiny nod.

She smiled.

Denny Rapfogel said, "Look, it's a bad time. The building just went up for sale and we need to do some contingency planning, okay?"

"Okay," said Milo. "Sorry for disturbing you, sir."

"If you ever actually solve it," said Denny, "any disturbance will be worth it. You find out who it is, I'll sue their ass."

Corinne said, "It's a criminal matter, not civil." That same patronizing tone.

He wheeled on her. "Like O.J.? Ever hear of that one? The cops fucked it up but the family got justice from the civil suit. Geez."

He stormed back into the rear office and slammed the door.

Corinne Rapfogel said, "Sorry, guys. I'll walk you out."

When we reached the sidewalk, she said, "Where's your police car?"

Milo pointed. "The green Seville."

"Ooh, plainclothes—I love that model. My dad had one, a white one with the designer gold plating. He used to loan it to me to go to the beach with my friends." Loosening her hair and shaking it out as she spoke.

I said, "A real classic."

"My dad was a classic," she said. "Unlike the junker I married." She edged closer. "Listen, guys, I'm leaving him but he doesn't know it. I just sat down with a lawyer."

"Guess I shouldn't say sorry to hear it?"

She laughed. "Hell, no." Another hip thrust. "Hell on **toast** no, it was long coming. I waited for the wedding to be over. Didn't want to spoil Baby's big day." Her eyes misted. "So much for that."

Milo said, "What an ordeal. Sorry. If you think of anything."

He and I turned toward the car.

Corinne Rapfogel said, "Hold on, guys." Her eyes flicked back to the office building. She walked several feet ahead of us and stopped.

"Look, I'm not saying this is anything relevant, but one of the reasons I'm leaving him is he can't keep it in his pants. That's why our business is sliding into the crapper. We've had a bunch of Me Too lawsuits and now we've got a poisonous reputation. He ruined the business, okay? He habitually pisses people off."

She paused, flipped her hair. "If there's anyone someone would want to mess up, it's him."

I said, "Is there a type of woman he goes after?"

"The type with a vagina." She looked ready to spit. Then she slumped.

"When I met him, he was good looking, believe it or not. Surfed, seemed nice, played tennis, kept in shape, I really thought he was the guy. The being buff lasted longer than the nice. By the time Baby was a toddler, he was cheating on me. Probably before, but that's when I found out about it. I threatened to leave him and he did the atonement bit and claimed it wouldn't happen again."

She middle-fingered the sky. "We've been to couples counseling with three different therapists, lot of good they do. He even spent some time in a ridiculous rehab place for sexual addiction. Like it's a disease, huh? Total bullshit, it's bad behavior. I asked **my** therapist and she agrees."

I said, "So he's pretty indiscriminate."

"The ones I **know** about were all too young for him." A beat. "Some were halfway cute. Like your victim, I guess. At least from that picture, she looked cute. Considering."

"But you don't recognize her."

"Nah," she said. "Except for the ones who worked for us, I never met any of them, he's a sneak, not a flaunter. Only reason I found out he was hitting on the staff is one quit and a year later she sued us and then came the others. Four others, can you believe that?"

Her turn to flush. "Bastard. Then I told a couple of my friends and boy did that open the valves. They started telling me about seeing him with bimbos, offering their husbands threesomes, all kinds of sleazy shit. You'd think they might've considered letting me know, right? They're ex-friends now, but that's okay, I don't need anyone."

The hip retracted. Her spine bowed. "I'm ready to strike out on my own, use the grit and initiative I learned from my daddy. He was poor, put himself through school—I might even go back to school, become a hygienist. I was in Daddy's office enough to know more about teeth than most dentists."

Milo and I both nodded.

I said, "Good luck, Corinne."

"Hopefully I won't need luck, just talent," she said. Another glance at the building. "If there's any-one who could inspire hate it's him."

Movement from the building. Denny Rapfogel lumbering toward us. He held out his hands, palms-up, in a what-the-hell gesture.

Corinne said, "Just saying goodbye."

"Can we get back to business? That rental agent just called back. There's a place on Olympic might work."

"Sure, Den," said Corinne. Under her breath, her lips out of view: "Motherfucker."

I drove west on Wilshire, turned south at the next light, and headed back toward the station.

"That was something," said Milo.

I said, "The ties that un-bind."

"Denny the dog, younger women. Looks alone, Red Dress would seem out of his class. But she took off her clothes for money. Maybe she thought he had enough so she could retire. But given Corinne's plans, you'd think she'd be watching him, might notice a hottie in Fendi. Even if she didn't, him slipping away long enough to strangle someone, tidy himself up, and return to the festivities woulda caught her attention."

"Maybe she's past the point of caring."

"Good point. There's also his role. My brother Patrick married off four daughters, told me father of the bride ranks right below janitor."

I said, "Any way to get Denny's phone records, maybe establish a link between him and Red Dress?"

"If it's a joint account and Corinne volunteers access . . . maybe. Lemme ask John."

He speed-dialed Deputy D.A. John Nguyen.

In place of Nguyen's usual wise-guy, baseball-reference-laced voicemail was a terse message. **I'm not in, leave a message.**

"Hmm." He phoned the main office, was informed D.A. Nguyen was out, no idea when he'd be back.

I said, "John sounds grumpy."

"That's because John's a rational human being—hold on." His cell chirped an excerpt from Handel's **Water Music**. "It's Reed." Click. "What's up, kiddo?"

"Struck out everywhere else but a bartender at The Booty Shop on Sunset says she used to dance there a couple of years ago. Not as Kim or Kimberly. He knew her as Sooze."

"Short for Susie?"

"When I suggested that to him, he got all puzzled, like I was talking in Afghani or something."

"Einstein."

"Old guy, probably been pickling himself for decades with well booze."

Milo said, "I'm not gonna ask your definition of old. Geezer was sure it's her."

"Says he is. And he described her the same way the bouncer did: lazy dancer, kept to herself. The backpack, too. She's the only one he's ever seen who did that, apparently dancers really do go for big designer purses. I asked him why he thought she acted different. He said she probably wanted to be different. I said maybe she's shy. He said, 'Shy people don't flash their pussies at perverts.' I kept that out of my notes."

"Does the place keep better employment records than The Aura?"

"Don't know, L.T., still trying to find out who owns it. Geezer gave me the name of what turned out to be a shell corporation, address near the docks in Wilmington that's now a parking lot. The manager's due in soon. I can wait around for her unless you need me somewhere else."

"Wait, kid. Have a Shirley Temple on me."

Reed chuckled. "You know me and sugar."

"Your loss," said Milo. "Female manager, huh?"

"How's that for cracking the glass ceiling?"

◆

Just as Milo pocketed the phone, it chirped again. Radical shift to something atonal—Schoenberg or the like.

John Nguyen said, "Finally, you ask me a no-brainer. With a joint account, you get permission from either account holder, it's legally obtained evidence."

"Even if the two of them end up in a nasty divorce."

"Do it before the divorce."

"Even with—"

"You want to debate? That's the law."

"Great. You okay, John?"

"I'm fantastic." Sounding anything but.

"What happened to the old voicemail?"

"New boss," said Nguyen. "Don't ask 'cause I won't tell, telling's what got me in the shit in the first place. Did you know baseball represents white male privilege and is an inappropriate intrusion on work-related communication? Bet you didn't. Bet you do whatever the hell you want over in Blue Land."

"You're white?" said Milo.

"When they want me to be I am."

Click.

Milo's lips fluttered, emitting a raspberry.

I said, "Good news on the phone."

"If it's in Corinne's name and she agrees. But probably a waste of time. What's the chance Denny would be stupid enough to phone his girlfriend when his wife has access to his call record?"

"Doesn't sound as if he's ever been discreet. Maybe part of the thrill is throwing it in her face."

"Okay, I'll try to get her permission. Maybe I'll stalk the office later this afternoon, get lucky and catch her by herself. Meanwhile, we've got another sighting of Red Dress but with a different name."

I said, "She's been working in L.A. for at least two years, has to have some kind of residence."

"It's a big county," he said, wheeling back and stretching his legs. "Kimby, Sooze. Backpack. Maybe you're right about her being a student. Or the barkeep's right and she was just putting on airs to stand out."

He looked at his phone again. "Nothing from Alicia on the dress, yet. Which I knew without checking because I already checked twenty seconds ago. What's the treatment for OCD?"

"It's anxiety-reducing behavior," I said.

"So?"

"Sometimes success does the trick."

He pretended to study the phone again. "Maybe if I stare at it long enough, something wonderful will take place."

"That happens," I said, "write a book and make millions."

CHAPTER
12

No word from Milo until Thursday, just after four p.m.

"Couldn't catch Corinne, office was locked. Headquarters for Rapfogel marital bliss is in Sherman Oaks. Couldn't see driving out there on the off-chance, so I left an ambiguous message on her cell, still waiting for a callback. Consistent with all that joy, the manager at The Booty Shop called in sick so Moe couldn't talk to her. Some of the dancers showed up, though, and he talked to them, the kid owes me. No one who works there now knew Sooze/Kim/whoever. The only remotely possible bright spot is the manager lives close to the station, I'm gonna try a drop-in. You free? Or just reasonable?"

Consuela Elena Baca lived in an aquamarine stucco ranch house near L.A.'s southern border with

Culver City. Neatly kept place, aloe and yucca and verbena in place of a slavering lawn, a copper-colored nineties Jaguar convertible in the driveway.

Decals on the house's front window touted the services of a security company. The door button elicited Westminster Abbey chimes.

From within, a nasal female voice: "Who is it?"

"Police, Ms. Baca."

"Not the alarm again!"

The door cracked but remained chained. Eyes so pale they verged on colorless took us in.

"Your I.D., please."

Milo gave her a look at his badge. Not his card; no sense beginning a conversation with "Homicide."

She undid the chain and appraised us again.

Tall woman in her forties wearing a clingy black rayon robe over something beige and lacy. Red nose, bloodshot eyes, white-blond hair bunched up atop her head.

"Yes, I'm Consuela." Sniffle, throat clear. A wadded tissue in her hand dabbed the nose. A droplet formed at the bottom of one nostril. She said, "Ugh," and caught it before it dropped.

"Listen, I really can't be paying any more false-alarm fines. It did **not** go off. Not once during the past twenty-four hours and I'm sure because I've been here all that time. Got this crud of a virus, okay? Haven't left the house. So whatever problem you think there is, it's not mine."

Name notwithstanding, Consuela Elena Baca

looked proto-Nordic, with milky skin, a high-bridged uptilted nose, and a firm, square chin. Leggy and full-breasted, close to six feet tall in fuzzy slippers.

Milo said, "This isn't about the alarm, ma'am."

"Then what?"

"May we come in?"

Consuela Baca thought. "Sure, but at your own risk. There's a gazillion obnoxious little germs floating around."

"We'll chance it," said Milo.

"Brave cops, huh?"

"Protect and serve."

She smiled. Coughed. Muttered "oops" and covered her mouth, bent over and coughed some more. When she stopped, her face was grave. "Is someone dangerous lurking around the neighborhood?"

"Not at all, ma'am. We're here to get some help."

"**I** can help **you**?" said Consuela Baca. A half shrug brought on more coughing. "Why not? There's been times you've helped me. At work, I run a night-club. Though it's inconsistent, sometimes you guys really know how to take your time—what the eff, c'mon in."

We followed her into a square white living room. A black sofa faced a red sofa. Both were shaped like dog bones. In between sat a chrome-and-glass table on a rug that looked stitched from white rags. On the table, a box of lotion-enhanced tissues. On the floor, a black plastic wastebasket overflowing with used paper.

Two walls were hung with half a dozen black-and-white photos, all featuring the moody chiaroscuro of prewar French camera work. Three depicted jazz combos playing in dim, smoky rooms. Spotlight on the leaders: Duke Ellington, Charlie Parker, Benny Goodman.

The remaining trio of images starred Consuela Elena Baca, naked, in her twenties. Darker shade of blond, a complex hairdo full of flips, shags, and layers, long smooth body adored by the camera.

She motioned us to the red sofa. Directly opposite her photo-memoir.

Ill but still able to choreograph.

"That was a long time ago," she said. "Great to be young, right, guys?"

Nowadays, even compliments can get you in trouble. We smiled.

She crossed her legs, allowing the robe to ride up to mid-thigh. "What kind of help do you think I can give you?"

Milo said, "If you know this woman, it would be a tremendous help," and handed her Red Dress's death shot.

She said, "Suzy Q? She's . . . oh, God, she **is**, isn't she."

"She's the victim of a homicide, ma'am."

Consuela Baca's right hand flew to her mouth. She reached for a fresh tissue, patted both eyes. "Poor Suzy. How? Who?"

Milo said, "Unfortunately, we can't get into how and we don't know who. That's why we're here. Anything you can tell us about her will be appreciated."

Pale eyes narrowed. "How'd you connect her to me?"

"One of our detectives visited The Booty Shop. We were told she danced there."

"That was a couple of years ago." She frowned. "They gave out my personal data?"

Milo smiled and took out his pad. "No, we detected and found out you managed the place. So you knew her as Suzy Q. Last name, please."

Consuela Baca kept studying the dead girl's image. "She's not someone I'd have thought would end up—I mean she never did anything high-risk. Not that I saw. If anything, she was kind of . . . buttoned-up—**restrained**, that's the word."

I said, "As opposed to other dancers?"

"Dancers," she said. "They teach you guys PC, huh? They're not ballerinas, they're strippers, and yes, a lot of them like to walk the edge. It's the nature of the business."

"What's the edge?"

"The wrong guys, the wrong drugs."

"Not Suzy," I said.

"Far as I knew. In terms of her last name, she

told me Smith. Susan Smith. I assumed it was phony."

"Because it was Smith?"

"That and fake names are also part of the biz. Girls do it for safety and security and because they like to create alter egos. When I worked in Vegas I was Brigitta. When I wasn't Ingrid. Or Helga. My Minnesota Swedish mother wasn't amused. My dad never said anything but when she started yelling at me, I caught him smiling."

The memory made her sigh. She took another look at the photo, shook her head, and returned it. "Poor Suzy."

Milo said, "When did Susan Smith become Suzy Q?"

"It wasn't a formal thing," said Baca. "She suggested it and I said okay. It's kind of a natural extension of Susan, no? Like Hannah becomes Honey Pie, Sarah's Sexy Sadie? I had one girl, her name was Dara, which was actually fine as a stage name. She thought becoming Drizella was a great idea. I told her that's one of the ugly sisters in 'Cinderella,' **bad** idea. So she became Dru. Is that better than Dara? But everyone has their own ideas. They do the job, I don't hassle them."

"Did you save Suzy's employment forms? Withholding, Social Security, that kind of thing?"

"Can't save what I don't have, guys. The only forms we keep are for the alcohol-license Nazis and the pests from the health department. The girls aren't employees, they're independent contractors. That's pretty much the industry standard."

"Did Suzy mention other places she'd worked?"

Consuela Baca got out a raspy fragment of laughter before being seized by a coughing fit. Another belated mouth-cover. "Sorry, sorry, don't want to infect you. No, she didn't mention because I didn't ask. It's not like we demand résumés. They prance in with no appointment, get naked, strut their stuff. They're up to our standards, we give them tryouts. They show up on time and stay sober, we give them time slots. Even the long-timers don't last. Suzy was a short-timer. Weeks, not months."

"How come?"

"Beats me," said Baca. "One day she just didn't show up. No big deal, there's never a shortage of product."

Milo slipped the photo back in his pocket. "What **can** you tell us about her?"

"Only my impression," said Consuela Baca. "Quiet girl, not much of a personality—oh, yeah, she claimed to be a student."

"Where?"

"She never said. And she could've been lying. That's what the girls do. They lie."

I said, "Another industry standard."

"You've got that right. We sell fantasy. Once it crosses over to reality—too many zits on an ass, too strung out to move right—it's goodbye, Cutie, because you've crossed over into honesty and honesty kills business. When the girls are up on stage, they're dream receptacles, not real people. I'm not going to sit here and tell you they're actresses—though some of them would like to think so. But we do run a show. Pretending for dollars. Good liars find it easier to pretend. I know my talent pool, guys. If we kept petty cash around, it wouldn't last a nanosecond."

"Sounds like you've got your hands full."

"Oh, do I," said Baca. "It's like juvenile hall. Someone willing to do the job isn't going to be a goody-two-shoes church virgin. Not that we haven't had some of those trying to break loose from Daddy and Mommy."

I said, "Free spirits."

"Girls gone wild or trying to." Tiny smile. "Like I used to be."

"Suzy didn't come across like that?"

"Hmm—you know, in her own way, maybe she did. Not a firecracker, a smolderer. That can be just as sexy."

She sniffled and dabbed, used her eyes to redirect us to her photos.

I said, "Those are pretty artistic."

"Thank you kindly, sir. The guy who took them **was** an artist. Did his main work for the studios back in the forties, got ripped off like everyone else who worked for the studios, not a penny in royalties. When he retired he freelanced. A customer who'd seen me on stage hooked him up with me.

George—George Grumann—was looking for a quote unquote 'ice goddess.' He took one look at me and said, 'The Valkyrie has arrived.' It was fun."

She gave herself another long look. "I think they came out quite well."

"Terrific."

She nodded, sneezed, coughed. "Sorry, I'm not used to having people over when I'm feeling shitty. I get that itchy throat, I usually take zinc right away and it kind of works. But it also makes me super nauseated and I just got over a stomach flu so I figured I'd muscle this one out."

She cleared her throat at high volume: grinding gears. "God, I sound like a wild pig."

I said, "Hope you feel better soon."

"That's sweet. Thank you."

"What did Susan say she was studying in school?"

"She never got that specific. Not to me, anyway. I don't encourage chitchat. Show up, look hot, do your thing, keep the alcohol flowing and the cocks hard."

"Was there another girl she might have confided in?"

"Not that I saw," said Baca. "She wasn't Miss Congenial, kind of kept to herself. I heard a couple of the other girls call her a snob. Actually, it was along the lines of 'what a cold bitch.'"

"Do you remember who said that?"

"You're kidding. We're talking two years ago, maybe more. No one around then is working for me now. Even if they have the attention span, they make bad choices and age fast."

Sliding a hand down her own sleek thigh, as if soliciting contradiction.

I said, "Did George Grumann ever take pictures of her?"

"Oh, no," said Baca, smiling. "George has been gone for—I'm not going to tell you how long on the grounds it might incriminate me." A beat. "He died twenty-two years ago. A year after he took my glams."

"What else can you tell us about her?"

She shrugged. "Her street presence was drab. She'd show up for work in clothes designed to **limpy-poo** a cock. First time, I said to myself, this one has the bone structure and the bod but no clue, it's not going to work out. But when she auditioned, she was tarted up the wazoo. Full-on makeup, smoky eyes, inch-long lashes, collection of not-bad wigs, fuck-me shoes, red micro-dress you could use for a handkerchief. When she got up on stage her dancing was different but actually pretty hot."

"Different how?"

She loosened her hair, freed a cascade of ice. "What I just told you, smoldering not burning."

"On the subtle side," I said. "Wouldn't think that would work."

Consuela Elena Baca sighed. "You're big boys so I'll explain it in big-boy terms. It's like with fucking, guys. You know how some women scream and thrash and make all those good noises, and others lie back with their eyes closed and this satisfied smile on their faces but they're both sexy? Suzy was the second type. She'd get up and do this little side-to-side shuffle, even look a little bored. She'd start off staring at the floor then slowly she'd raise her eyes and make contact with losers in the front row. Suddenly everyone's looking at her. Same thing with the pole. She'd take her sweet time getting with it and when she did, no acrobatics. More like she's hugging it romantically. Stroking it."

Licking her lips, she demonstrated. "Slo-ow. Not much in the way of calorie expenditure but there was something about her the clients dug. Maybe it was the holding back. Like in **their** monkey brains, pleasing her was some fantasy goal. That can be **real** sexy."

Recrossing her legs, she offered a view of the other thigh, Shifted a bit more. No underwear. "Whatever it was, it worked. She did okay on tips and the booze flowed."

Milo said, "She auditioned in a red dress."

"All she ever wore was red," said Baca. "It went great with her coloring, no argument from me. The bar bill's rocking, **you're** rocking."

"Any idea where she got her clothes?"

She laughed. "These questions. We're not talking designer stuff, guys. Probably Frederick's, Trashy, Next to Naked, Stage Hollywood, one of those. Or a vintage place that specializes in body-conscious. This town, there's no shortage of fuck-me rags."

Milo scrawled rapidly. "We're pretty ignorant about that stuff. Any other names you could give us?"

She rattled off several more shops. "You're writing it down? You're actually planning to visit each one of them?"

"All in the name of public service."

"Well, enjoy your work." She patted her nose. Cricked her neck and gave a low moan. "God, my joints—I need to rest, guys."

I said, "Sure—just a couple more questions? Did Suzy have any regulars?"

"She didn't stay long enough to build up a stable. We're talking two nights a week for what, six, seven weeks?"

"Any idea what she did the other nights?"

"Maybe crammed for exams?" She laughed. "Sorry, I'm not trying to make light of it, but she came and went. So what other clubs did you talk to?"

Milo said, "The Aura."

"That shit-pit? Hasn't been operative for years."

"It's a party venue now."

"Really," she said. "Did Suzy work there before us or after?"

"After."

"That's kind of nuts," said Consuela Baca. "If she needed money, why wouldn't she come back to us rather than waste time at a crap-dump like that? The

location's a loser and the owner, some Mideast type—
hey, **he's** someone you might want to look at."

"Why's that?"

"He's shifty. Tried to buy The Shop a few years
ago. His offer was ridiculous and it wasn't even real
money, just some complicated real estate swap. Suzy
did The Aura, huh? She must've slid way down. Was
she an addict?"

Milo said, "No evidence of that, so far."

"But maybe?" said Baca. "That could explain it.
Guys like the Mideaster will sell anything."

I said, "Who owns The Shop?"

"You don't know?" said Consuela Baca. "I do.
Family tradition, my grandpa and my great-uncle
ran clubs in Caracas then came to L.A. and opened
The Shop in the fifties. When they passed, my dad
took over. When he passed, my mom wanted nothing to do with it. She thinks she's a lady who lunches.
Daddy knew that and left it to me and I took over
and made it more profitable than ever. He knew I
could handle it because he saw how I handled Vegas."

"Congrats," said Milo.

"I accept your admiration. I deserve it."

We left her coughing and slapping her chest.

As I drove back to the station, Milo stared up at
the roof liner and blew out puffs of air. "The Valkyrie.
Lots of words but bottom line, no info. I keep
reminding myself about the tortoise and the hare."

I said, "Also, tortoises live longer."

"Probably 'cause they're too bored to die. Susan Smith. About as generic as it comes."

"You up for some positive psychology?"

"Don't know if I can handle it—what?"

"The Valkyrie wasn't totally useless, she firmed up the victim profile. Quiet girl, sticks to herself, plays herself down but transforms on stage. Wearing red. The Fendi might mean she came to the wedding to party. She was in work mode."

"What was the job?"

"A variant of what she did on stage. Using her looks to get money from an older man. Not a romantic thing with Denny, blackmail."

"Denny doesn't have enough dough to motivate blackmail."

"That's why he had to turn her down. But what if she didn't know that because he'd been leading her on? One of those gawker-turns-into-a-sugar-daddy things. Then his money dried up but her aspirations didn't. If she'd been leaning on him for a while, that would explain his being prepared with a hypo and a garrote."

"Dirty Denny," he said. "I can see him rubbing his crotch in the front row."

"Want me to turn around so you can show Baca his photo?"

He thought about that. "Nah, too risky. She didn't impress me as Ms. Discreet. For all we know, we just sat there and got played and sneezed on."

I said, "Pass the zinc."

◆

Back at his office, he tried Corinne Rapfogel's cell.

She said, "Twice in one day, Lieutenant? A girl could start to feel important."

"You are important," he said. "It was your big day that got ruined."

"No, it was Baby's day. My heart's really hurting for her. Are you calling because you just learned something?"

"Is your husband within earshot?"

"No, he's out. He's involved? Oh, God, I knew it! **Bastard!**"

"No, no, Corinne, but I did take you seriously and intend to dig around. I'm calling because I'm wondering if you'd consent to give me access to your phone records. Any cell or landline accounts at your business and your home. Unless there's an account that's solely Denny's. I'd need his permission for that."

"Records? What exactly are you after?"

"I'd like to find out who Denny communicates with."

"Well, I'm way ahead of you on that," said Corinne Rapfogel. "After you were here, I decided to take a look at exactly that. There's nothing weird on either the business landline or my line but guess what **wasn't** in the file?"

"His personal line."

"How's that for a clue, Lieutenant? We keep all our bills for a hundred and twenty days in an expense file. For tax deductions, we take off all our phones. Denny's bills are always in there. But now they're not. That's pretty suspicious, no? What's he trying to hide?"

"Good question," said Milo. "Problem is I can't access his line without his consent."

"Why don't you get a warrant?"

"It's not that simple."

"Not like on TV, huh?"

"I wish, Corinne. You checked out the bills because—"

"Did I actually suspect him of . . . you know? No, that was too horrible to think about. But you start wondering and stuff floats into your head. I've been totally traumatized. Can't sleep, can't eat, my mind's wandering all over the place but it always comes back to a bimbo crashing the wedding. Then I start thinking about all the other stress he's put me through with his pathetic little weenie. **Then** I flash back to something that happened when we were in Hawaii. Five years ago. What was **supposed** to be a romantic vacation, trying to supposedly heal our marriage. Everything was going fine. Until the second day when I caught him talking to some slut in a thong bikini out by the pool. It's not like I was snooping. I was trying to be hopeful."

Milo said, "Giving him a chance."

"Exactly. Again," said Corinne Rapfogel. "If I was Catholic, they'd make me a saint. Anyway, what happened was he got up early to take a swim. Our room had a view and I stepped out on the balcony to enjoy it. And there they were."

Her voice caught. "Total bimbo, not much older than Baby. They're standing real close to each other. Then their hips touch. Then he says something and all of a sudden she backs off and pushes him on his chest and stomps away. That's when she turned and I saw her piggy face. Fat porker way too flabbed out to wear that thong, she's literally falling out everywhere. I'm thinking he planned to bring her **here** on the Q.T.? To fuck her while I took naps or shopped?"

She growled.

Milo said, "You knew her."

"Stupid little cunt," said Corinne Rapfogel. "She put in an application with us to be a P.A. or an au pair, wanted to work with someone like Meryl Streep. As **if.** Denny interviewed her, said she was great, then I talked to her and saw she was a moron with no prior experience. Still, I scheduled a second interview but she never showed up. Now I get it: Why would she bother when he's probably paying her for other work."

"He's been known to do that?"

"Years ago. When Baby was a baby. I had post-partum, that was his excuse. I thought he'd changed. Stupid me."

"Oh, my," said Milo, giving me a thumbs-up.

Corinne said, "You're shocked because you're a decent moral person, Lieutenant. So what does he do when the slut piggies off? Takes a swim. Enjoys himself, he doesn't have normal feelings. He gets back to the room and I unload on him. He swears up and down it was just a coincidence, he had no idea she was in Hawaii, the only reason she got pissed was because she asked if she could apply again and he told her no."

Bitter laughter. "Can I sell you a bridge? But I let it go. I wanted it to be true. What can I say, stupidity on my part. Then we started getting sued and everything started coming out. That's his pattern: He takes advantage of stupid bimbos. Maybe your victim was one of those and he killed her to get rid of her."

"You see Denny as capable of murder."

A beat. "I don't know what I see, Lieutenant. Part of me wants to hate on him but part of me is terrified. Married to someone who'd do that? Baby having to live with that? One thing Denny's actually not bad at is being a father. Baby adores him."

She began to cry. "Excuse me. Hold on." Dead air for several seconds. "Sorry, it's just overwhelming. Why can't you get a warrant on him? Isn't what I just told you enough?"

"Unfortunately not, Corinne."

"Well, **that** sucks. The system **really** needs to change."

Milo said, "If Denny did spend significant money on other women, could he hide that from you?"

"I can't inspect every restaurant bill or every time

he dips into the petty cash. Which wasn't that petty, we used to keep five to ten grand around for incidentals. Back when we were raking it in—at the peak we were netting over four hundred K a year. Now it's down to nearly nothing. Could he support a bimbo full-time? Probably not, but he could give her toys. And with a skank whore, we're not talking suites at the Peninsula."

"Do you remember the name of the woman in Hawaii?"

"Marissa something."

"No last name?"

"Oh, God, this was years ago. Please don't go looking for her, it's not like she's the only one. He has no idea I've talked to a lawyer. I need time to get my financial ducks in a row, can't afford to tip my hand."

"Got it," said Milo. "But if her last name does come up and you're comfortable—"

"What would you tell her?"

"That someone ruined your daughter's wedding by murdering a young woman and we're looking at all former employees and anyone else associated with your business."

"Fine," she said. "I'm not going to remember, though. And you have to promise me you won't rat me out to him."

"Scout's honor."

"I was a Girl Scout," she said. "Back in the Ice Age."

"Let me ask you something, Corinne. Was there a point during the wedding when you and Denny weren't together for an extended time?"

I scribbled a note and handed it to him. He read, nodded, as Corinne answered.

"You mean could he have done it without my noticing? Sure. There were all kinds of points. At the church we were together from the procession until we left for the reception but once the party got going, it was chaos. I went circulating by myself to be friendly because he'd already been drinking and brushed me off when I suggested we do it together. For most of the time, everyone was on the dance floor or up at the bar. I can't tell you the longest period we were apart but I'm sure not going to give him an alibi."

"Okay, thanks."

"Working with the cops," said Corinne. "This is kind of an adventure."

He placed my note on the desk. "One more thing. Do you ever pay Denny's phone bill?"

"I always pay his phone bill," she said. "I handle all the bills."

"Is the number registered to the business?"

"Of course it is."

"And you're a partner in the business."

"I am—ah." She laughed. "I get where you're coming from. It's in his name but I actually share it. Yeah, you're right. You want me to ask Verizon for another copy of his bill."

"If you're okay with that."

"If he had something to do with wrecking Baby's big day, I'm **more** than okay. Minute I hang up, I'm on it. **Very** creative, Lieutenant. I can relate to that, I've always been the creative one. If we depended on **him** for ideas, we'd be living on Skid Row."

CHAPTER
13

I'd just left his office and was halfway down the corridor when he called me back.

Waving a sheaf of papers.

Back I went.

Summary of the autopsy results on Jane Doe #5 of this year composed by Acting Deputy Medical Examiner Basia Lopatinski, M.D. He'd printed two copies from his desktop. We read simultaneously.

Well-nourished white female, approximately twenty-five to thirty, in excellent health prior to death by asphyxiation due to ligature strangulation, "most probably by a metal filament." Tiny marks running diagonally along the neck wound suggested a wire topped by wound strands. Approximate gauge, making allowances for "skin compression

and atmospheric changes subsequent to death,"
.025 to .040 inch.

No alcohol or drugs in the decedent's system
but for a nonlethal dose of fentanyl mixed with
heroin. That, combined with the pain and shock of
the injection in a "nerve-rich site," could have
stunned the victim "possibly to the point of lost
consciousness."

I visualized it. Red Dress taken by surprise,
drugged into submission.

Leaving plenty of time to finish the job.

Why not simply O.D. her on fentanyl? The drug
was fast acting and easily lethal.

Why slow things down with heroin?

Fentanyl had begun as a Big Pharma profit well.
Drug companies touting it to doctors for conditions
far beyond its original use for intractable cancer pain.
Causing one of the worst addiction crises in history.

Cheap to produce. Maybe a mixture was what
you got on the street, nowadays.

Or someone had craved the prolonged minutes
it took to choke the life out of a human being.

Full-face, hands-on kill, a helpless victim.

Watching the lights go out.

I sent an email to Robin and resumed reading.

Stomach content analysis revealed partially di-
gested lettuce, corn, green beans, tuna fish, red
peppers, and an egg-based liquid, probably diluted
mayonnaise. All of that ingested approximately two
to three hours prior to death.

She hadn't intended to dine.

At the bottom of the report was a note by Dr. Lopatinski for Milo to call.

He complied, got voicemail, left a message.

I said, "The food's interesting."

"She had a tuna salad before showing up."

"What I mean is she ate before the wedding because she had no intention of enjoying the catering. Add that to no booze or self-administered dope in her system and the all-work-no-play scenario firms up."

My phone pinged a text.

Robin answering my question.

I sent her a **Thanks, hon,** and relayed the info to Milo: "At the low estimate, the gauge fits a wound guitar D-string, at the upper end, a light A-string."

He said, "So look for a killer with a Gibson. Hey, that would be a pretty good slogan."

I got home by four p.m. An hour later, Maxine Driver called me.

"Got Ms. Burdette's schedule such as it is, and guess what, an address."

She read off numbers on Strathmore Drive.

Walking distance from campus. "Thanks, Maxine. How'd you get it?"

"Don't ask," she said. "In terms of the schedule, there's not much. She takes one real class, chem for non-science-majors. The rest is independent study with no set time, her DIY is Multiverse Cultural

Aspects of Civilization. Part of a program the administration tried a couple of years ago but discontinued. Brainy little tots recommended by their high school counselors allowed the freedom to explore their inner whatevers."

"Why'd they drop it?"

"Word has it one of the kids committed suicide but I can't confirm and the official reason was attrition. As in too many of the geniacs dropped out. Not just from the program, from the U. I guess it makes sense, Alex. You're a precocious squirt, grow up hearing you're a god from helicopter parents who overstructure your life with one class after another. Then you leave home and all of a sudden you're expected to create your own structure. Poo-eh widdle tings pwobly withered."

"Not Amanda," I said. "She comes across assertive. To be charitable."

"Doesn't she. Survival of the rudest. That would explain politics."

I texted the address to Milo.

He phoned. "A student who lives near school. All that to get what DMV could've given me if she was normal—'scuse me, conventional. Thanks, so far it's the only scrap of good news. The pathologist is at some sort of convention and apparently San Diego's another planet. The big bad is Corinne's phone stalk of Denny turned up six months of his bills misfiled in another drawer, so he wasn't hiding anything. She recognized every number except twelve, took it upon herself to play amateur detective. Nine were legit prospective clients Denny was calling back. None of them ended up signing with the agency, which Corinne attributes to his 'Neanderthal conversational skills.' Another was a florist—'probably one of the times he was shitty to me.' The last was a condolence call to a cousin of his in Arizona who'd just lost a mother to cancer. 'Even though he never had the decency to phone all the time she was sick.'"

"True love," I said. "So she's probably telling the truth. Unless she's overacting because she's covering for him."

"I think she's righteous, Alex. She was clearly bummed about not digging up any dirt and when I hung up she was wondering about a secret phone account and saying she'd try to figure out who Marissa was."

"The game's not over. Denny could be using burners."

"If nothing else pans out, we'll do a loose surveillance on him. Meanwhile I'm learning about fashion. One of the boutiques Alicia visited didn't recognize Suzy/Kim but they were able to educate her about the dress: Three seasons ago an adorably pert actress wore it to the Golden Globes. Three years isn't that long, it coulda been bought new or online. I'm having her devote another half day to high-end places then switching her to stripper-equippers."

"Moe's being punished?"

"No, he's still got the gig but these places are all over town, with traffic it'll take forever. I'm figuring maybe tomorrow to visit the bride and groom . . . how'd Maxine score the info on Amanda?"

"Confidential source."

"She loves the intrigue."

"That she does." I told him about the disbanded program.

He said, "Suicide. Yeah, that would quash parental enthusiasm. But all Westside suicides go through us and I read every list. Kid at the U. doesn't ring a bell."

"Wouldn't the campus police handle it?"

"They'd be the primary if it happened in a dorm or some other campus facility and didn't end up complicated. But we're supposed to hear, anyway. So maybe Maxine's source isn't that golden. Not that it matters. Meanwhile, I'm sitting here still waiting for an image dump from snail-imitator and part-time photographer Bradley Tomashev. He says six-hundred-plus images. I'm ready to get my squint on."

I said, "Feel free to email a copy. Two sets of eyes and all that."

"Appreciate the offer," he said. "I'll prove it by accepting."

◆

An hour later, nothing new in my inbox.

I took Blanche for her brief afternoon walk, gave her fresh water, and waited as she lapped daintily. When she was through, we walked to Robin's studio. The Martin had been shipped and she'd moved on, a thick slab of spalted maple resting on her workbench. Her apron was flecked with snowy sawdust.

I said, "Beef. It could be what's for dinner."

"Perfect. All the heavy lifting, I could use the iron." She hefted the slab.

"Strat clone?"

"Les Paul clone, meaning more wood. This thing already weighs a ton, I was just about to shape it. Maybe ninety minutes?"

"Marinade is patient."

She offered her mouth for a kiss, gave Blanche a pat on the head, and began scrutinizing the wood.

In her own world, a beautiful place.

Back in the kitchen, Blanche promptly fell asleep on the floor.

I dry-rubbed a couple of rib eyes, which opened her eyes for a second.

"Not yet, Julia Child." She drifted back to dream-world.

After shucking two ears of corn, I made a no-frills romaine salad and rechecked my phone for the wedding photos.

Three new emails: a pair of lousy-syntax, huckster spams ("These stock is bounds to explode!") and a query from a judge regarding a recent custody report. The answers to the jurist's questions seemed self-evident but I responded as if they deserved contemplation. Then I ran a search on recent campus suicides at the U.

Not a word.

No surprise; colleges are known for keeping a lid on bad news. In the case of a young person's self-destruction, little chance of protest from the family.

I logged onto the L.A. **Times** homicide file, paged back to thirty months prior, and began scrolling forward.

The usual gang killings and domestics until a case that fit twenty-three months ago: Cassandra Michelette Booker, "a 19 year old white female," had died in Westwood twenty-five months ago, cause of death pending.

Googling **cassandra booker's death** pulled up nothing. So did substituting **suicide** or **murder** for **death** and pairing the deceased girl's name with **amanda burdette.** But **cassandra michelette booker** produced a five-year-old squib in **The Des Moines Register.**

Rotary Club award ceremony, three high school students earning trophies for essays on "Civic Responsibility: The Truest Freedom of All." Cassandra "Cassy" Michele Booker, a sixteen-year-old junior at Sandpoint High School, had scored second place.

An accompanying photo featured a pair of middle-aged, suit-and-tie Rotarians—a banker and an insurance broker—flanking three adolescents.

Two of the winners were boys, tall, bespectacled, and beaming. Between them stood Cassy Booker, small and thin and round-shouldered, blond hair plaited into pigtails.

Her long, pallid face hosted a tentative, off-center smile, as if she doubted her own merit.

Once you'd seen Amanda Burdette, the physical resemblance was inescapable.

Petite and fair wasn't an unusual look. But Amanda had also won an essay competition.

Writing prowess as a prerequisite for an honors program made sense. Or the ability to put words together convincingly was just another feather in a plume of precociousness.

I searched for more info on Cassy Booker, came up empty, and tried to learn about the make-your-own-major setup the U. had tried. Nothing. Getting up from my desk, I stretched and took **my** old Martin—by now a 50K instrument—out of its case. Just as I settled on my battered leather patient couch, Blanche padded in.

She stared at the guitar and jumped up beside me.

I said, "Where's your backstage pass?"

Batting her lashes, she looked up with big, soft brown eyes.

She favors mellow music so I tuned down to Hawaiian slack key and began fingerpicking slow and easy stuff. By the fourth note, she was back asleep and letting out volcanic snores.

I said, "Everyone's a critic," and threw in a few sixth chords to keep it evocative. **Let's hear it for Don Ho at the Islander.**

My fingers moved autonomously as my brain wondered about a mentally gifted young woman ending her own life. A beautiful young woman in a red dress having her life taken from her.

No link between the two that I could come up with. Just clammy, gray sadness.

I was finally able to steer my head away from all that, slow my fingers down even further, and visualize white sand and blue water.

Then, nothing but music.

CHAPTER
14

By the time Robin and I finished dinner, the photos from the wedding still hadn't come through.

She said, "That was delicious. Nice long bath fit your schedule?"

Slipping out of her clothes as she headed for the bedroom. I followed her. Blanche knew enough to stay in the kitchen.

Wet-haired and loose-limbed, in a T-shirt and shorts, I gave my phone a final look.

An email from Milo's home computer had arrived ten minutes ago. No heading. Text plus attachment.

A: technical problems on his end but finally. Not six hundred, seven fifty two.

Curse digital. Looking for a magnifying glass. M.

I wrote: **Deerstalker cap and calabash pipe, too?** and opened the file.

Page after page of postage-stamp images filled the screen, each enlargeable by keystroke. The first three hundred thirty-nine covered the processional and the ceremony.

Surprisingly traditional stuff. Color shots made it easier to look for Red Dress. Several other women had chosen variations on the color but she was nowhere in sight.

Next: four hundred thirteen photos from the reception. As Tomashev had said, the emphasis had been the bride. At least two-thirds of the images featured her in various degrees of close-up, maybe half in the company of her new husband.

Baby smiling.

Baby dancing by herself.

Baby doing jazz hands walking like an Egyptian trying on a variety of kittenish pouts sticking her tongue out curling it caressing her own chest gracing the camera with a dizzying collection of views of her butt.

When Garrett was in the frame, he alternated among an uneasy smile, the saucer-eyed bafflement of a tourist viewing a piece of unfathomable art, and an expression so blank he could've been a mannequin.

No sign of the girl in Fendi in any of those. Same for the few dance-floor photos that had managed to exclude the bride.

I kept scanning. Spotted her.

Image number five hundred eighty-three, the red dress bright as arterial blood.

She stood in a horde of celebrants crowding one of the bars at the front of the venue. Hanging back at the rear of the throng, a sober face among a sea of bleary grins and agape mouths.

Sober gorgeous face. The angle of her eyes suggested she was watching the entrance.

Waiting for someone?

I inspected the rest of the pictures, found nothing, and enlarged the image.

That blurred the details but clarified emotion. Serious bordering on grim. Definitely not a celebrant.

Waiting for something unpleasant. Having no idea.

I speed-dialed Milo's home number. The call got jammed up because he was trying to reach me at the same time.

Cellular version of the old Alphonse-Gaston-**after-you-no-after-you** routine.

I clicked off and then rang again.

He said, "See it?"

I said, "Oh, yeah. Are the shots in chronological order? If they are, she was killed toward the end of the party."

"I'm texting ol' Bradley right now to find out. Any other impressions?"

"She wasn't part of the festivities. She seems to be watching the front door."

"Waiting for someone she's pissed at. Or worried about."

"Exactly," I said.

"Fits your blackmail thing," he said. "Unless it **was** a date and she's peeved that he was late—hold on, Tomashev's texting me . . . some cameras have metadata, his doesn't, so no chronology. Also, he rearranged everything to prioritize Baby's photos. Has no idea when that one was taken."

"Going the extra mile even though he didn't get paid. Is she someone special to him?"

"I wondered the same thing and asked him and indeed she is. But nothing romantic, the two of them go back to middle school. He's chubby and gay and used to get bullied a lot. She stuck up for him when no one else did."

I said, "Nice to hear something positive about her."

"Tomashev says she's a 'cool girl' when she's not uptight. I asked him if he'd come up with any new ideas about who'd want to mess up her big day. He said he'd been thinking about it and could only come up with two possibilities that probably weren't true. Obviously, I pushed him. First, maybe another girl. In school, lots of them were jealous of Baby because she was cute, athletic, and popular, but he had no specific candidates among her current friends."

"What's the second?"

"The second made him really nervous, I had to pry it out of him. He remembers Denny Rapfogel being tense when he posed. Which was different from Denny's usual demeanor, Tomashev had always seen him as a friendly, maybe too-friendly guy. I asked him to pick out a few images to illustrate. He's got a point, Alex. Check out two fifty-nine and six eighty-three."

Both were family shots: bride, groom, two sets of parents. In the first, taken in the church, Denny Rapfogel hovered behind his wife, slit-eyed and wearing a smile forced beyond any hope of mirth. In the second image, at the reception, his face had gone blank and he'd put space between himself and Corinne.

I said, "Distant and preoccupied."

"If he just choked a girl out, he'd have good reason. I'd love to be getting that feeling, Alex— everything jelling. But I'm not there yet. With his marriage and his business falling apart, there'd be all kinds of reasons not to smile."

"Time for surveillance."

"You read my mind," he said. "Then again, they sent you to school for that. I'm gonna do it myself, wanna take a look at where and how these people live. Any other ideas?"

"Still wary of the Valkyrie?"

"Depends on what's at stake."

"You could show her Denny's photo and ask if he was a customer. Or take advantage of her flu and show it to the bartender. Same for other strip joints if you've got the personnel."

"Good idea. The baby D's don't have time, I'll do **that** myself, too."

CHAPTER
15

Surveillance is a mind-numbing, often fruitless process that can go on for days. I didn't expect to hear from Milo for a while.

He knocked on my door at eight a.m. the following day.

"You're an early riser, right?" he said, stooping to pet Blanche and marching to the kitchen.

"Good morning."

He stopped just short of the fridge. "These are your breakfast options: I take you out for a hearty repast or I whip us up something here, your provisions, my labor."

His face was grizzled, his hair greasy. Sagging, food-specked sweats screamed all-night ordeal.

But his eyes, though bloodshot, were active and his expression was toys-under-the-Christmas-tree.

I said, "How about I cook and you show-and-tell."

He plopped down at the kitchen table. "Eggs, **por favor,** I'll take four. Throw stuff in, max protein would be welcome. Also, toast, doesn't matter what kind but pile it up. That coffee fresh?"

I poured him a cup, brought it over with heavy cream.

"You're pretty good at this," he said. "You sure you never wanted to be an actor?"

"What's the happy occasion?"

"New info on Denny Rapfogel. Remember how I told you NCIC and the department had nothing on him? I decided to give it another try, found out his Social and got all his previous addresses. California boy all the way, he's originally from Fresno, moved to Clovis when he was a teenager. Between the ages of eighteen and twenty-two, he was known to local law enforcement. DUIs, drunk and disorderly, couple of burglaries from commercial establishments, receiving stolen property. Looks like no punishment beyond a bit of local jail time, then probation, which he served without violation."

I said, "Wild oats eluding the Feds."

"You know how it is, cities don't always report. Anyway, Mr. R was a certified bad boy."

"Nothing since then?"

"Unfortunately not. Maybe he changed his ways, maybe he just got careful. To me the bottom line is he's shown himself capable of antisocial behavior. It feels like a few more bricks in the foundation, no?"

Long-ago youthful crimes were a long way from calculated murder. It felt like a reach.

I nodded.

"There's more," he said. "I watched his and Corinne's house from seven p.m. on. Nice two-story, south of the boulevard—what're you putting in there?"

"Onions, tomatoes, spinach, Jack cheese, leftover steak."

"Ahh, you're a prince—no, you're better, you're one of those Venice guys who ruled city-states—a doge . . . I like my eggs easy, Lord Alessandro."

He swigged coffee, ran a hand over his hair. Bent low and stage-whispered to Blanche, "When the doge isn't looking I'll slip you something."

I said, "Surveillance paid off?"

"You be the judge. Both of them got home soon after I arrived. Same office but separate cars. Which tells us something about that thing you talk about—their psychodynamics. Around eight thirty, Corinne leaves wearing exercise clothes and a gym bag. A few minutes after that, Denny comes out in a black suit and T-shirt. He goes to his car while talking on the phone. Cheap-looking flipper, could be that burner we wondered about. Conversation over, he gives a big smile, gets in, and drives off."

"None of that wedding grumpiness."

"Just the opposite, little bounce in his step. He drives higher up in the hills, stops at a cute little cottagey house a quarter of a mile away. Hillside lot, one those aerobic driveways. Gated, but you can see through and there's outdoor lighting. He punches in a code, the gate opens, he speeds up to the front of the house and parks. By the time he's out of his car, a redhead in white short-shorts and tank top is outside greeting him."

He laughed. "If you call a long, soulful kiss and a crotch tweak a greeting—those eggs aren't getting too firm?"

I emptied the pan onto his plate.

He filled his mouth. Chewed like an industrial combine and swallowed. "Tastes like rib eye."

"Good call."

"That, Doge Mio, is the essence of friendship. Okay, so Denny and the redhead head to her house. She puts her hand on his ass. They're both bouncing now, like a couple of bungee jumpers. He stays in there for an hour and a quarter, leaves by himself, cruises down to Ventura, drives to a bar in Studio City. I took a risk and peeked. He's by himself with a beer. I go back to the car, he comes out twenty minutes later and goes home. Corinne's car is back. I watched for a while to see if any sparks would fly but nothing."

I said, "Maybe he drank to put booze on his breath as a cover. I've been downing shots by my lonesome, honey."

"You're a devious lad. Anyway, lights go out around eleven, I leave. But here's the interesting part. While I'm sitting out there, I'm running a check on the girlfriend's house and it's owned by a woman named Sliva Cardell."

"Relative of Leanza."

"Close relative, Leanza's mommy as verified by Leanza's Facebook. Her and three brothers, no daddy of note. On Sliva's page, there are old bikini shots that she posts as if they're current. Googling her name pulls up real estate ads—she's a broker."

"Was she at the wedding?"

"Yup, her car shows up in the list from the parking lot and when I got home I found her in a few of the wedding photos. Including the one with Red Dress."

He took another bite, wiped his hands, drew out his phone, and began typing.

I said, "Two girlfriends in one frame. Any eye contact between them?"

"Nope, my luck doesn't extend that far. Sliva's closer to the front, like she's waiting to get to the bar and tank up. She's putting on a little show for a bunch of younger guys surrounding her. Blue dress, super low-cut, bending and offering them a view of her maternal instincts."

He pulled up an image on his phone, enlarged a section, and pointed. "This is Saucy Sliva."

Still too small for me to catch subtle details. But nothing subtle about bright-orange hair cut in a short glossy cap, an electric-blue off-the-shoulder, low-cut piece of satin, and cleavage that could hide a paperback book.

Strong-shouldered woman, thick arms, white flash of smile. "Analysis?"

I said, "Obviously, Denny goes for the mousy type."

Milo's eyebrows shot up as he barked laughter. Chewing frantically, he pounded his chest, swallowed with a gulp, coughed, drank coffee. "Don't do that while I'm eating."

I thought: **That limits me.**

I said: "The doge obeys rules?"

"Everyone obeys rules. I can't see any obvious link between shtupping a bridesmaid's mom and Red Dress. Except what it confirms about Denny. This is a guy ruled by his gonads who's been known to break the law. Like I said, brick by brick."

He finished the omelet, examined the toast. "Whole wheat, fine, why not?"

I poured myself my fourth cup of coffee and sat down across from him. "I still think the method exhibits rage or sadism. Using dope to be able to look into her eyes. But there'd be another advantage to knocking her out first. Physical strength wouldn't be a factor."

"A woman."

"There seem to be a few of them in Mr. Rapfogel's life."

"Hell hath no fury," he said, pushing away the toast.

I said, "The obvious angry woman is Corinne but she'd be the last person to trash her daughter's wedding and she'd be too conspicuous to slip away. Sliva, on the other hand, wouldn't be missed. Does she look as sturdy in real life as in the pictures?"

"She's no bikini model but she ain't flabby, so sure, sturdy enough. Especially with a fentanyl backup."

He pulled up Sliva Cardell's image again. "Not much fabric to damage, here. And yeah, those arms are pretty substantial, no?"

He logged onto a Facebook page. Sliva in her thirties wearing a flesh-colored thong bikini that created a first impression of nudity. Voluptuous and hard-bodied, topped by shagged yellow hair that approached the crack of her buttocks. "Definitely not a wimp. So what, getting rid of the competition?"

I said, "The motivation seems lacking. We're talking cold brutality in order to win a broke guy never known to be faithful. Unless she's got some serious pathology going on."

"Last night, she looked pretty enthusiastic about ol' Denny. Maybe a younger, hotter rival tipped the scales. As far as kinks in her psyche, no past criminal record and I can't exactly show up and ask to interview her."

"Can you put a separate watch on her?"

"Depends if any of the baby D's are available and that's looking weak because all of a sudden, there's flak from above." He cleared his throat. "Apparently, I've been co-opting staff for non-essential assignments." Laughing. "Like I actually read the memo."

He phoned Reed. Voicemail. Same for Binchy and Bogomil.

I said, "The kids leave, they don't write, they don't call."

"Moses called last night. No one at any of the other strip clubs knows Red Dress. Same response to Denny Rapfogel's DMV photo, including the barkeep at The Booty Shop. I emailed the shot to James Johnson and got the same answer."

He laid his phone on the table. Two swallows of coffee later, it played Beethoven and began jumping. He glanced at the screen, said, "The crypt," and switched to speaker.

"Lieutenant Sturgis, this is Basia Lopatinski." Mellow voice, Slavic accent.

"Thanks for calling back, Doctor."

"Of course, I initiated the correspondence. As I said, I think it's good to speak with you about your Jane Doe but maybe not over the phone?"

"I'll come over there when it's good for you."

"I have just completed a two-day seminar on splenic abnormalities in Santa Monica and am about to have lunch nearby. Could you come to the Ostrich Café on Wilshire Boulevard? The internet says slow service but good food. I'm hoping they don't cook big birds."

I found the address and showed it to him. Just west of Tenth Street.

"See you in twenty or so minutes, Doctor. I might be bringing our consulting psychologist."

"Very good, Lieutenant," said Basia Lopatinski. "I may be how you say—spinning wheels—but I think it will be interesting."

"Something not in the autopsy report?"

"I tell you when I see you."

CHAPTER
16

Le Ostrich Café shared a block with a vegan restaurant, a high-end butcher shop, and a fish market. Nothing about the place stood out. A general practitioner among specialists.

Cramped, crowded interior with a take-out counter and a coffee bar. The fare on the chalkboard was pastries and salads. As Milo and I looked around, a woman in an oversized gray sweater and black jeggings stood up and waved.

Forties, leggy, model-thin, but half a foot short of model height. Short, wispy ash-blond hair topped a triangular face marked by a strong nose and an unusually broad, full-lipped mouth. One of those mouths that enjoys smiling and was having a grand time proving it.

Milo made the introductions, calling her "Doctor" and doing the same for me.

She said, "Basia," and smiled even wider. Her barely touched meal was sourdough bread, cold string beans topped by sesame seeds, and a discouraged green salad.

She said, "I made an unfortunate choice. The only protein they have is chicken breast and that's like blank white paper."

Milo said, "We can go over to the butcher shop and get you some charcuterie."

"It is tempting, Lieutenant. Please sit. Unless you want something here. Then you have to go there for order and pickup."

Milo pointed to a jar on the counter. "And they expect tips."

"Ha," said Basia Lopatinski. "It's better than Soviet Poland but not as good as America should be. Do you want something?"

"No, thanks, Doctor. We're intrigued by your call."

"I am intrigued as well, by your strangled Jane Doe. I requested to meet you away from the crypt and didn't put what I'm going to tell you in the report, because recently we have instructions to adhere to observed facts and avoid theory. I, especially, need to behave myself because I am not full-time staff."

"Freelancing?"

"That's one way to put it, but really probation," she said. "In Warsaw, I was a professor of forensic pathology. Here, I'm considered barely out of training. I just took my California and national boards." She crossed her fingers. "Meanwhile, I am supervised and my current supervisor is the guy who wrote the no-theorizing rule."

"Who's that?"

"I'd rather not say, Lieutenant. Not that what I have to tell you is controversial. It's merely outside the scope of my job description."

"Got it."

"Okay, then." Another generous smile. "Initially, there were three things about your Jane Doe that stood out to me. First of all, the use of what was most probably a wire garrote in such an unusual manner. As you know, ligature strangulation is a comparatively rare cause of death. Even then, most ligatures are cloth—rope, shoelaces, clothing. A garrote fits more with a gangster execution—I saw a few when I did some training in Italy. In those cases, a strong, thin, band of metal was used and the wound was far deeper, generally close to complete decapitation. What we have here is basically a subcutaneous wound that only grazes underlying muscle. Yet enough pressure was exerted to bring about asphyxiation."

I said, "Someone taking their time."

"Someone exercising precise control," said Basia Lopatinski. "If this was a musical matter, we might say a virtuoso performance in lento tempo."

"That's interesting. Maybe we're dealing with a musician." I told her about the guitar string gauges.

"Yes, I thought of that as well. But as I said, theory is not encouraged."

She buttered a slice of bread, nibbled a corner. "The second initial point of interest is consistent with the first. As I'm sure you know, fentanyl is fatal in extremely small doses. I know you policemen wear gloves because even a subcutaneous dose can be dangerous. And when combined with heroin, the danger of a lethal overdose is significant. And yet we don't have that. Not close. We have a cocktail with just enough to incapacitate, perhaps to the point of unconsciousness, perhaps only to the point of semiconsciousness."

Milo said, "A sadist prolonging the process."

Lopatinski took three more bites. "Yes, sadism makes sense. The third factor isn't supposition, it's correlation. Whether or not it's a causal correlation—I'm being too abstract, sorry."

She took a sip of tea. "The third factor is another homicide. A case I handled in Warsaw."

Milo sat forward. "Unsolved?"

"No, solved. That's what makes it even more interesting. I'll summarize. Eight years ago I was a professor of pathology and deputy chief medical examiner at the Warsaw morgue. A victim came in, a prostitute dumped in a public latrine in a bad part of town. The murderer was caught—a career criminal who also played folk music on the street for gullible tourists. Ignacy Skiwski. I will spell that for you."

Milo copied. "A latrine."

Basia Lopatinski said, "Exactly, the first similarity. The others involved modus. Pre-injection—with heroin alone, fentanyl was not widely available then. Initially, the injection was believed to be in the antecubital fossa where an addict would inject."

She patted the inner crook of her arm. "This victim **was** an addict, no one thought anything of it. But then we shaved her head and found the wound in the neck and I realized the arm puncture had already begun to scab so it was older. I informed my superior and he told me to concentrate on the strangulation because it was the true cause of death. I did, but what stood out to me was exactly the same as your case. No deep wound, just enough pressure with a metal garrote to cut off oxygen fatally."

I said, "Folk music. A guitar string."

She nodded. "The police recovered a cheap instrument from Skiwski's room that was missing a string—I don't remember which one. I termed the gauge consistent with the wound. As I wrote in your report, skin is not static, it moves around, so one can never be sure."

I smiled. "That theory made it into Jane Doe's summary."

"Ah! You have found me out, Dr. Delaware. Yes, I slipped it by. In any event, Skiwski was apprehended and bound over for trial."

Milo said, "How'd he get caught?"

"Another prostitute saw him leaving with the victim and the victim's blood was recovered from his clothing. He never confessed but he had no alibi or explanation. Also, he had a criminal record."

"For what?"

"Theft, drunkenness. More important, aggressions on women."

"What kind of aggressions?"

"Beatings, intimidation."

I said, "Sounds like low impulse control. When he graduated to murder he got sophisticated?"

"All I know is what I saw on the table. In any event, a month or so after Skiwski's arrest, he hung himself in his cell."

"Did he use another guitar string?"

"Towels," she said. "For himself, he was gentler."

I said, "How old was he?"

"Thirties—late thirties if I recall correctly. Why do you ask?"

Milo understood the question. "That's old enough to have done it before."

Lopatinski's eyes rounded. Soft, golden brown. A woman who saw death daily but hadn't been twisted into something dry and acrid. "You think it was a serial?"

I said, "It's the kind of crime you see in serials."

Basia Lopatinski thought about that. "Yes, you're making sense. I don't believe the police found any matching crimes. Did they look for any?"

World-weary shrug.

She picked up the gnawed slice of bread. "Even had I thought of it, I'm not sure I would have suggested it. We were liberated in 1992 but attitudes persisted. Don't rock boats."

"And now you've got no theorizing."

"What can I say, Dr. Delaware? One gets used to cognitive limits but the imagination persists." Another three nibbles washed down by tea. "Eight years ago, and then it turns up again, here. You see why I wanted to let you know."

Milo said, "Deeply appreciated, Doctor. Was Skiwski's case publicized?"

I got on my phone.

Basia Lopatinski said, "In local papers, of course."

"Including the details—the guitar string?"

"Including that."

"What about international exposure?"

"Did someone in L.A. read about it and decide to imitate? I have no idea how widely the story circulated."

I held up my phone. "Nothing comes up here."

Lopatinski said, "Perhaps it was covered in a Polish American paper. I will check, if you'd like."

Milo said, "We'd definitely like."

An expansive grin seemed to bisect her face. "May I assume you won't—how do you say—rat me out?"

"To Eschermann? God forbid," said Milo.

Lopatinski stared at him, then laughed. "You must be a detective."

"On good days."

I said, "An alternative to international coverage is someone living in Poland back then who moved here. Or corresponding with someone in Poland."

"And then they decide to imitate? Psychopathic contagion?" said Lopatinski. "I had a case when I was in medical school in Poznan. Teenage girls coming down with what looked like bedbug bites that turned out to be psychosomatic eczema. One after the other, they'd break out into lesions. An entire school was quarantined before the truth emerged. But that is far from imitative murder."

"Not contagion," I said. "Just someone seeing possibilities."

Lopatinski's mouth narrowed as if yanked by a drawstring. First time she'd displayed anything other than cheer. "I reported all of my observations to a detective and he passed them along to a reporter as his own insight. I would hate to think that my communication was in any way responsible for a copycat."

Milo said, "You did what you were supposed to, some idiot blabbed to the press. It's always gonna happen. Unless no one ever talks to anyone about anything and that kinda sounds like the bad old days in Poland, no?"

"A detective **and** a psychologist?" said Lopatinski. To me: "Your good influence?"

Milo said, "What, I can't be warm and fuzzy on my own? Bottom line, Doc, you've really helped, here. Thanks for going the extra mile. So was this piece of shit a decent musician?"

"Quite the contrary, Lieutenant," said Basia Lopatinski. "Everyone said he played out of tune."

He renewed his offer of indulgences from the butcher and when Lopatinski turned him down with a demure head shake, he thanked her again. As we headed for the door, he veered to the display counter.

"Pastries actually look pretty okay."

He bought two dozen mixed, returned to Lopatinski's table, and put the box down.

She said, "What's this?"

"Thanks from the department."

"Really—"

"No argument, Doc. You go beyond the call of duty, you get refined sugar."

Outside the restaurant, he eyed the butcher shop for a moment, walked on by. "Now what? I subtly ask everyone at the wedding if they've ever been to Poland?"

"It's the age of self-advertisement," I said. "People put their vacations online. Why not start with Corinne and Denny. Maybe they like to travel."

In the car, he punched numbers on a phone.

A subdued Corinne said, "VCR Staffing."

"Hi, it's Milo Sturgis. That story about Denny in Hawaii. Is that the only place he's done it?"

"Probably. He just got caught that time."

"Where have you guys traveled?"

"Why're you asking this?"

"Trying to get to know him."

"I've told you everything you need to know: He's an asshole."

"So no European—"

"Of course we've been to Europe." A beat. "Not for a while—at least ten years ago . . . no, thirteen. Baby was in high school, off on a senior trip. I'd travel all over the place but **he** likes the sun so it's Costa Rica, Mexico, Belize, all that. He spends his time cooking his skin and checking out bikinis. Maybe I'll get lucky and he'll contract melanoma or something."

"Europe's too cold."

"Depends when you go. I used to like it in Paris. I mean no matter the weather, how bad can Paris be?"

"Paris, Rome, it's all good. Heard Prague's nice. Hungary, Poland, also, nowadays."

"One of my friends told me Prague's gorgeous," said Corinne. "Maybe I'll go by myself." Her voice caught. "Maybe Paris wasn't as good as I'm remembering. Maybe every time he went off on his own to take a walk he was doing something gross, I don't know what to believe anymore."

"Sorry," said Milo.

"No sorrier than me. This call, is he actually a suspect? I mean do I need to move out for my personal safety?"

Milo said, "He's not, Corinne, and I couldn't advise you to do that unless he's been violent to you or threatened to be."

"Never lifted a finger, Lieutenant. Rarely raises his voice, he just . . . makes me feel alone. I've always thought of him as a coward. Except when he used to surf. He was brave about tackling big waves—God, this is depressing, I really don't like talking about it."

Click.

Milo shook his head. "Your local constabulary, spreading good cheer."

While I drove back to the station, he got back on his phone and checked the Rapfogels' social network to verify what Corinne had said. Only one trip memorialized. Instagram posting of the couple eating gigantic lobsters in what looked like a rain forest. She, bored, looking to the side, he hunched over his meal, a bib full of stains.

He said, "Denny's as red as the crustaceans, she just might get her wish."

In the time it took us to get back, he'd run similar searches on the Burdettes and the Mastros. "Nope, they keep it domestic. Nebraska and national parks."

Up in his office, he said, "Last try: the happy couple . . . here we go . . . Tahoe . . . San Francisco . . . Two Bunch Palms out in the desert . . . apparently no one's into pierogi."

I said, "Speaking of the happy couple."

"You think it's time?"

"They were the primary victims and Red Dress is closer to their age than to their parents'."

He scrolled and found the address Garrett had listed. "East of here, near La Cienega and Olympic. Be a few hours until he's off work."

"Why not talk to Baby alone?"

"Yeah, might be interesting. If she talks."

"Why wouldn't she?"

"I'm a bad memory—hell, why not try a solo. But I want to be there when Garrett arrives, kill two birds, and that's still a way off. You know what? I'm gonna sit here and go through the whole damn list of names from the invite list and search for a magical Slavic connection. I don't want to keep you, go home and be normal."

"And have to drive back for Baby and Garrett?"

"I was hoping you'd say that."

We took the list to a deli near the station, ordered a pot of coffee, and reserved a corner booth courtesy Milo's usual extravagant cop tip.

His phone, my phone, both of us squinting and delving into the travel habits of total strangers.

Two hours later, not a single reference to Poland though a few people had been to Prague and one couple had thought Budapest interesting.

He said, "Gotta talk to the Polish tourist bureau, they're falling down on the job. Okay, my head hurts, let's see if Baby's in her crib."

CHAPTER
17

The newlyweds lived on the ground floor of a twenties, white stucco Spanish fourplex on Holt Avenue just south of Olympic.

Garrett Burdette answered the bell-ring. Home early.

"Lieutenant," he said.

He wore black horn-rimmed glasses, a blue oxford cloth button-down, gray wool slacks, black loafers. In L.A., CPA work clothes.

From behind him: "Who is it, honey?"

He kept his eyes on us. "She's not feeling well."

Milo said, "Sorry 'bout that, if it's a bad time—"

"Who **is** it, Gar?"

He frowned and swung the door wide. Baby's small body was curled on a pale-blue sofa, a bag of corn chips in her lap. She wore a black tank top and white yoga pants. No tissues, no blanket, no cup of hot tea. Maybe she was tougher than the Valkyrie.

She said, "Oh, hi, guys." Brightly, no trace of nasal congestion. Or resentment. "Don't let them stand there, honey."

Garrett stepped aside. The apartment was barely furnished but for the couch and two folding chairs. Cardboard boxes were lined up against a wall along with stacks of wrapped gifts. The air smelled of ripe fruit and petrochemicals, the source of the aroma a pear-shaped room deodorizer plugged into a corner socket.

Freshly painted walls were bare except for a large, framed color photo of Brearely Rapfogel in a filmy white dress. Sitting in a field of lupine, looking like something from Renoir.

Kindred spirit of the Valkyrie?

She waved at us. Her hair was loose, her eyes clear. A lovely young woman. The absence of makeup made her prettier.

"Would you like something to drink. Or some of these? I've got another bag." Holding out the chips.

"No, thanks, Ms.—is it Burdette or Rapfogel, now?"

"It's **Mrs.** Burdette," she said. "I decided I'm traditional."

She smiled at her husband of six days and extended a languid hand. He took it and she tugged him down gently beside her. Holding on to his fingers, she leaned a head on his shoulder, placed her other hand on his knee.

Garrett's expression was that of a kid who'd been given an expensive violin and had no idea how to play it.

Baby began stroking the top of his hand. He lowered his attention to his lap. Crossed his legs protectively.

Milo said, "Sorry you're not feeling well, Mrs. Burdette."

"Oh, it's nothing," she said. "A little tummy upset when I woke up. I told Gar he didn't need to come home but he's my super sweetie and insisted. **Thank** you, honey."

Garrett shrugged. "Easy day."

"That's because you're so smart." She kissed his cheek. "I'm actually feeling better, honey. Maybe we can go out and find a food truck or something? I could really go for a street taco."

"Sure."

"Awesome." She smiled at us. "You're probably thinking this chick is nuts—bipolar or something. The last time you saw me I was like a total bitchzilla."

"No, you weren't," said Garrett.

"Not in the least," said Milo. "What a terrible thing to go through."

"It was," said Baby Burdette, "it really was. But I didn't show my best side." She shuddered, like a puppy shedding water. "But that's all in the past, the future's what counts. And the present. Our present is awesome, I've got the **best** guy."

Garrett mumbled, "Thanks, Baby."

"I mean it, honey." She sat up straight. "So. Are you guys here to give us the good news that you solved it? I keep thinking about that poor, poor, poor girl. I know when you talked to me it was like I didn't care. Honestly, I probably didn't, not then, I was so . . . I couldn't focus. But now I can. And I keep thinking about her. Who is she?"

Her cheeks puffed and she exhaled.

Milo said, "Afraid we still don't know."

Both newlyweds stared at us.

"So why are you here?" said Garrett.

"You can't find out anything?" said Baby.

Milo said, "Unfortunately, she had no I.D. and no one at the wedding seems to know her."

"Can't you just go on—I don't know—a missing persons site or something?"

Milo smiled. "We have."

"Oh. Sorry. Don't mean to say you're not doing your job, it's just, how can someone be . . . like a ghost? Especially with computers."

Garrett said, "If people want to get lost, it's easy."

His wife turned, seemed to study him. "What does that mean?"

"Computers go both ways," he said. "People think the internet has opened up the world and that's true to an extent. But it's also closed it, because people can hide behind fictitious identities. Right, Lieutenant?"

Baby continued to look at him, baffled. "But can't you just . . . hack them?"

"Sometimes. But there's always a struggle between the hiders and finders." To us: "My firm had a client with an employee who absconded with funds. She prepared for it by laying down a misleading cyber-trail. They still haven't recovered the money."

"You do stuff like that?" said Baby. "Detection?"

Garrett's smile hovered between affection and condescension. "No, I just handle tax returns, Baby. The client is looking for the maximal write-off so I had to know the details."

"Wow."

"No big deal."

"It's a **huge** deal, honey. I'm so **proud** of you. So why **are** you here, guys?"

Milo said, "Follow-up. Looking to see if you've thought of anything."

"I tried to think," said Baby. "I really wanted to figure it out. But I couldn't."

We turned to Garrett.

He said, "If I had to guess, I'd say she was a crasher."

Milo said, "Why's that?"

"No one knows her."

"Did you have any other crashers?"

"Not that I know."

"Not that **I** know, either," said Baby. "But that

movie—the two guys who crash all the time? Owen Wilson—obviously, it happens."

Garrett said, "Maybe it got out that we were going to have an awesome party and she figured she'd mooch but someone followed her."

"Followed her," said Milo.

"Well, yeah. We don't know people like that."

"For sure," said Baby. "I like your theory, honey. Just a crazy thing. What do you think, Lieutenant?"

"It's certainly possible."

Looking satisfied, Baby Burdette ate corn chips.

Milo gave me a whenever-you're-ready look. The dialogue we'd prepped.

I said, "So when are you guys going on your honeymoon?"

"We were gonna do it in a month, now we're hoping for a couple of months," said Baby. "It's a little mixed up. I want to get a job but I don't want to start something and then ask for time off. We're still trying to figure it out."

"What kind of job are you interested in?"

"Fashion marketing. That's always been my passion."

I said, "Speaking of fashion, the victim's dress was Fendi."

Milo smiled. Improvisation.

"Really," said Baby. "That's horrible."

Garrett said, "That it was Fendi?"

"That it mattered enough to her to **wear** Fendi. I mean something that awesome, you don't just throw it on. Even if you are crashing. You're . . . appreciating."

Her eyes clouded. "Even if she was crashing, she was respecting us, honey. It wouldn't have even hurt us, one more person, some drinks, guacamole. Right?"

"Right," said Garrett without conviction.

"Really, honey. What's the big deal? I'm feeling so, so sorry for her."

She returned her head to his shoulder.

I said, "When you find time to honeymoon, where you planning on going?"

Baby said, "Some island, maybe the Grand Caymans. My dad told me there's a beach you can play with stingrays, they're super sweet."

Garrett said, "Supposedly."

"They **are**, honey. I saw a video, they're like these big portobello mushrooms and you can hold them and pet them."

I said, "Sounds fantastic."

"I think so, too."

Garrett said, "Long as you stay safe."

"Don't worry, silly—and it's us, not me. You're going to try it, too."

No answer.

"**Ho**-ney."

Garrett removed his glasses and sighted through them. "Okay."

She kissed his cheek. "My **brave** man."

He recrossed his legs.

I said, "So no plans to go to Europe."

"That would be awesome, maybe one day," said Baby. "It's far and there's not always sun and I **need** sun."

"Ever been there?"

Dual head shakes.

I said, "Paris is pretty great."

"You get to go to Paris?" said Baby. "On like an international case?"

"Just a vacation."

"Well, lucky you, Mr. Policeman. Yeah, my mom says the same thing. About Paris. She's always trying to get my dad to go back, they haven't been in a long time, he just wants sunny places."

Garrett allowed himself a half smile. "Hence, the Grand Caymans."

"I know, hon, I just love it when the sun touches my skin." Drawing a palm down a sleek arm. "When it first hits you, it's so—it's like a big . . . golden kiss. 'Course you have to wear sunscreen, my dad doesn't, one day he's going to get something."

She gave Garrett's arm a gentle punch. "You're going to wear sunscreen, Mr. Forgetful. I don't want that big brain of yours cooking."

"I'll do my best."

"I'll do it," said Baby. "I'll slather you." Tweaking his chin.

Garrett's attention to his lap took on renewed intensity.

"Sweetie," said his wife.

He fidgeted, made a grab for her hand, held it tight.

I said, "I've also heard Eastern Europe's pretty good."

Garrett blinked. Twice.

Baby said, "How far east? Like . . . Muslim places?"

"Czechoslovakia, Hungary. I've heard Poland's great."

Tight jaw and three more blinks from the groom.

The bride said, "Have you heard that, honey?"

"No. Never heard that." Letting go of her hand, he stood and fooled with the placket of his shirt. "Got to wash up."

"Sure, honey."

He headed toward the rear of the apartment. Dark hallway, more wrapped gifts.

When he was gone, Baby said, "Washing up means he needs to pee. He's like that, a real gentleman."

CHAPTER 18

I drove to Pico, hooked a right, and drove west.

Milo said, "Ol' Gar tightened up when you mentioned Poland."

"He did, indeed. Where'd he go to college?"

He checked his notes. "Berkeley."

"Eight years ago, he would've been twenty-one, twenty-two and still enrolled. Maybe they had a Warsaw exchange program."

He googled. "They have one now—the history department . . . contours of existence . . . otherness . . . Europeanness . . . Jesus, when did they stop using English? I'll try to find out if the same deal was going on eight years ago."

He made a call. "Voicemail, but they're always switching on and off, some sort of safety thing."

"Who?"

"Little birdies." Closing his eyes, he sat back.

A mile later: "How far east, Muslim places? She's cute but no genius. And I got the feeling ol' Gar knows it. Think it'll last?"

"Who knows?"

He laughed. "Another classic evasion from the master. What about her bipolar comment? She **was** a different person, just now."

I said, "Everyone tosses out diagnoses with no clue, blame talk shows. What I saw at the wedding was a young woman traumatized by having her dream day blown to bits. The stress level drops, she relaxes."

"Baby's really a sweetheart?" he said. "Guess it fits what Tomashev said, her standing up for him in school . . . okay, another try at the avians. I'll switch to speaker but don't let on you're here."

A sleepy-sounding male voice that I recognized said, "Yeah." His unnamed source at Homeland Security. For years he and Milo had been trading info, each of them claiming outstanding debt.

"Sturgis."

"I can read."

"I need a—"

"Obviously. What?"

Milo read off Garrett Burdette's name and birth date.

"What's he suspected of?"

"Nothing unless he was in Poland eight years ago."

"Something's going on there? We haven't heard that."

"Nothing political. A murder."

"You think he did it in Poland eight years ago."

"He might've gotten ideas from a psycho named Skiwski who did it eight years ago."

"Don't spell that, I've already got a migraine."

"Taking a sick day?"

"Poland," said Sleepy. "Brace yourself: This is going to be heading in another direction. Soon."

"What do you need?"

"Don't talk about need, your account is far from paid up."

"So you say. What?"

"M-13 psychos, we'll be needing addresses. Your brain-dead state legislature says you can't cooperate with us on illegals."

"You want me to apologize?" said Milo.

"A little genuflection wouldn't hurt. I'll let you know when I find out about Poland but get ready to cough up."

"I learn something, it's yours. Long as you're being saintly, run the same check for a Dennis Rapfogel. Here's his DOB."

"Twofer?" said Sleepy.

"We talking only one M-13er?"

Click.

Moments after we arrived at his office, an email came in from Dr. Basia Lopatinski. Her personal account, not the crypt.

She hadn't found any California coverage of the Skiwski case but asked us to check out the attachment.

Fuzzy photocopy of a Polish newspaper article. Incomprehensible Slavic prose, small photo in the center of the story. Lopatinski had drawn an arrow in red marker and written, **This is him.**

The arrow tip ended at the shaved head of a gaunt, hollow-cheeked, stubble-faced man, sitting cross-legged on cobblestones, hunched over a cheap round-hole guitar. The spidery fingers of his left hand pretended to form chords. The right dangled uselessly. At that point, six strings on the instrument.

An open cardboard case sat in front of Ignacy Skiwski. A group of young people sat and stood around him. Males, females, jeans and long hair.

Students or pretending to be.

None of them were Garrett Burdette.

Milo said, "A bargain-basement Manson?"

"The power of song."

"You recognize any of them?"

"No."

"Me, neither. On that cheerful note, it is time for you to be normal. Have a nice rest of the day."

Nothing from him on Saturday. A full week had passed since the wedding murder.

A lot of noise has been made about a crucial, near-mystical forty-eight-hour period for closing homicides. Miss that deadline and the chances of a solve plummet.

The truth is, there's nothing magical about two

days. Most murders lack mystery because they're committed by stupid, impulsive people who make no attempt to conceal: domestics, bar fights, walk-ups and drive-bys in front of crowds of witnesses.

Toss in stupid impulsive bragging leading to anonymous tips and the detective's job is to observe, make notes, obtain warrants, arrest and interview obvious perpetrators, all the while trying not to do anything that screws up the evidence chain.

But when a murder is preceded by thought and misdirection, actual detection is called for. Those are the ones that baffle, stretch past forty-eight and beyond, and often freeze up.

They're the killings Milo loves, though he'd never admit it. Complaining all the way, he usually manages to slog through and attain clarity.

That and my basic makeup generally lead me to be optimistic. But this one, an entire week with possibilities widening rather than narrowing, a victim still defying identification . . .

By ten a.m., continued radio silence and Sunday was shaping up the same way as Saturday.

Robin and I are both designed for work so stepping away from obligation takes a conscious effort and a conversation.

Sunday, eleven a.m., she initiated both and I agreed and we set out for a drive up the coast highway, the glorious Pacific to the west, the fire-ravaged foothills of Santa Barbara County to the east.

The Thomas blaze of a few months ago, followed

by mudslides churned by a worst-time rain, had been hellish for thousands of people, lives, livestock, the material accumulation of lifetimes demolished in vicious flashes. Months later, Nature had decided to reverse her curse, kissing the gently rising slopes and drawing forth greening and blooming. Still, it felt like a party hat at a funeral.

We drove half an hour beyond the Santa Barbara city limits and pulled over in Solvang, craving Danish pancakes at a touristy place that was always bustling. Hipster snobbery aside, there really **is** no difference between tourists and travelers and sometimes foot traffic is the ultimate vote.

The wait for a table was extended by holding out for a spot on the patio where Blanche was welcome. She'd enjoyed the drive from the cushy, leather perspective of the Seville's backseat, serene and observant as ever.

While we feasted, she contented herself with a chlorophyll-laced treat that supposedly helps with dog breath. Plus the occasional "accidentally" fallen shred of hotcake.

The restaurant was situated in a too-cute shopping center that could've been designed by Hans Christian Andersen stoned on aquavit. Plenty of cellular interruption but Robin and I didn't contribute; we'd agreed to switch off for the day.

I'd pretended to embrace the idea but wasn't fooling Robin. As we got back in the car for a return trip, she grinned and said, "Go ahead."

"With what?"

"Hey, Blanchie, he thinks he's being subtle."

Both of the females in my life grinned. I switched on my phone.

Nothing from Milo.

Good. Bad.

On the return trip we hit the inevitable jams on the 101 when underpowered cars confront the rising grade and start wheezing. Just past Ventura—the origin of the fire—Robin fell asleep and Blanche followed soon after.

I tuned the radio to KJazz. A blues show was on, some high-powered Chicago stuff that felt too upbeat this close to a disaster zone. But then on came Houston Boines's "Crying in the Courthouse." Boines had lived to ninety-nine but his wail sounded authentic.

This song, about losing everything, fit just fine.

When we got home, I looked at my phone.

Still nothing.

Crying in the police station.

He called at ten forty p.m.

"Been normal?" he said.

"Better." I told him about the pancakes.

He growled. "Sadist. For two nights I've been eating crap while watching Denny Rapfogel's house. Nothing happened the first night but on the second his car was gone so I tried Sliva Cardell's place. No

Denny, but another guy showed up, black Bentley convertible. Ran his plates, hotshot mortgage broker. He cruised through the gate just like Denny had, got the same welcome from La Sliva, this time in a filmy nightgown. Maybe even more groin calisthenics than with Denny. So much for true love making her a suspect. Wanna lay odds I keep watching her and other guys don't show up?"

"Think she's a pro?"

"Selling another type of real estate? Could be. Anyway, thought you'd want to know. Now I'm heading out for pancakes."

CHAPTER

19

Monday at eight, just as I was gearing up for a run, my phone rang.

My most frequent caller. "Never got 'em."

"What?"

"What do you think? Flapjackos con jarabe. The plan was to try this morning, that place near Rancho Park, but something just came up. I'm scanning the daily death list and one from last night caught my eye. Strathmore Drive in Westwood."

"Amanda's street."

"Amanda's **address.** DB's a white male, forty-three years old, named Michael Lotz. No detectives were called so it wasn't flagged as suspicious. But still. Waiting for a callback from the uniform sergeant who took charge. Figured I'd shortcut it with the coroner by going through our new buddy

Lopatinski but she was out . . . one sec . . . okay, hold on, that's her."

I waited, stretching hamstrings and quads, followed by a couple of deep bends and some work on the hips and the heels. Blanche padded in and I bent again to pet her. She rubbed her head against my ankles. I sat down on the battered leather patient couch, Blanche jumped up beside me and curled close to my chest.

Several more minutes before Milo came back on. "Lotz was sent to the crypt tagged as an O.D. No signs of foul play, paraphernalia near the body. He's currently stacked in one of those fridge closets they use, Dr. Basia went and had a look. Guy's arms are a mess of old scars and newer punctures. If nothing iffy comes up, they're not planning on an autopsy."

"The same address as Amanda doesn't qualify as iffy to them. But to you . . ."

"Maybe it's nothing but I can't ignore it. After I talk to Dobbs—the sergeant—I'm taking a look at the scene."

Two hours and ten minutes later, a text: **Going over there. Ten thirty work ok?**

I sent him a **See you there,** got out of my running clothes, took a quick shower, gulped coffee, and left.

Strathmore Drive is a short hilly side street that diagonals toward the U. One end dies at the campus's western rim; the other bottoms at the shaggy eucalyptus windbreak, manicured grass, and neatly arranged headstones of a vast veterans' cemetery.

The block was lined with multiple dwellings ranging from apartment buildings dubiously maintained because they housed students so-why-bother? and newer, larger structures.

I arrived before Milo, found the address, and scored the last parking spot, directly across the street.

Amanda Burdette lived in the largest building, a four-story mass that stretched to the sidewalk without aid of landscaping and took up a sizable chunk of the block. The slope of the street created the illusion of a behemoth on the verge of toppling. The complex was gray stucco except where occasional balconies painted blue-black jutted like bruises. Subterranean parking made up the entire ground floor. Three mesh-gated driveways with call boxes, each topped by a CC camera and an equal number of pedestrian doors, unmonitored.

As I sat there, a woman in a sari exited one of the doors pushing a twin stroller. Moments later, an adolescent in a U. sweater, fixated on his phone, stumbled downhill toward the village. Next: a girl in short-shorts distracted by earbuds, wheeling a bike out of one of the pedestrian doors. Then the far door opened and an older, bearded man in a tweed jacket, cardinal-red pants, white socks, and sandals shuffled by.

Not much auto traffic until Milo's unmarked sped up from the direction of the cemetery. He stopped at the Seville, held up an index finger, and pulled into the nearest of the three driveways. Punching a button on a call box led to metal mesh sliding open. He drove through.

I got out and jogged across the road but didn't make it before the gate closed. Through the mesh I could see diminishing taillights.

From the far end: "Hold on, I'll get you in."

The gate reopened. Passing a **No Walking on the Ramp** sign, I did just that.

The unmarked was parked in a **Reserved for Management** slot. Milo stood at the car's rear end next to a man in dark-blue work clothes.

"This is Mr. Bob Pena," he said. "He's the day manager and the guy who runs everything. We've already had a nice phone conversation and he's supplied a photo of last night's victim for us. Bob, Alex Delaware."

Pena was slight, fiftyish, and droopy-eyed. The work set was starched and pressed, the pants cuffed and tumbling over polished bubble-toed shoes. The oval patch on his breast pocket was embroidered **Robert P.**

He said, "If I ran everything, this wouldn't happen."

I said, "The overdose last night."

"Someone dying, it's not a thing for us," said Pena. To Milo: "Like I said, we don't get that, here."

Milo handed me a black-and-white photocopied license.

Michael Wayne Lotz had died three months after his forty-third birthday. Five-ten, one fifty-two, brown, brown. The photo showed a balding, dark-stubbled, blade-faced man with uncertain eyes.

Pena said, "I mean, once in a blue moon you get a student gets stupid, takes something, the ambulance drives 'em right across the street to the med center. It's close, so they don't die."

I said, "Mr. Lotz wasn't a student."

"It's crazy," said Pena. "How could I know about him?"

Milo said, "By that Mr. Pena means Mr. Lotz worked for him."

"His sleeves were always down," said Pena. "Even when it was hot. What do I know about addicts? If I wanted to deal with addicts, I'd work one of those Section Eight dumps downtown. He did his job, stayed in his hole, made no problems."

"By hole Mr. Pena means Mr. Lotz's room here on the ground floor." Milo's long arm stretched to the left, behind Pena's back. Directing me to a fenced-off section, mesh like the gates. **High Voltage. HVAC. No Entry.**

Bob Pena said, "It was part of his employment package."

I said, "What was his job?"

"Cleanup, odd jobs, gofer-stuff," said Pena. Head shake. "Owners aren't going to like this."

I said, "Who are the owners?"

"Academo, Inc. Big company in Ohio. He came through their human resources, they send me someone, I don't argue. Like with cleaning companies, electricians, all that good stuff. They send, I take."

"Academo," I said. "They specialize in off-campus housing?"

"That and some Section Eight and maybe other stuff, I don't know," said Pena. "It's a good business, big schools, you get too many students for the dorms. The U. refers them over here when they're full up. Also, some of the rich kids don't want to live in dorms. We're a lot nicer than a dorm."

I said, "Does the company gets subsidized by the U.?"

Pena frowned. "I don't know the details, my job is to take care of the physical plant, fix problems. Not problems like this. This is like . . . I don't know **what** it's like."

Milo said, "Where's Lotz's car?"

"I'll take you," said Pena, pointing to a far corner. We followed him across the garage to a twenty-year-old gray Volvo squeezed into a space marked **No Parking**. Dusty, rusted in spots, the tags four years old.

Milo looked inside the car, walked back to Pena. "Okay, let's have a look at his place."

"I kept it locked for you," said Pena. Eager to take credit for something.

"Appreciate it, Bob."

"Whatever helps. No one's been in there since the other cops last night and the EMTs and then the morgue guys. So what was it, heroin?"

"We don't know yet, Bob."

"Probably heroin," said Pena. "That needle and spoon next to him?" Head shake. "Go know. You do your best to run a tight ship—I was on a dry cargo in the navy. I know what tight ship really means."

"Could we see the hole, Bob?"

"Yeah, yeah, sorry, I'll let you in. Then I got to send an email to Ohio."

Selecting a key from a clattering ring, Pena unlocked the mesh fence and led us into a dim concrete area half filled with stacks of labeled boxes. Bulbs. Hoses. Filters. Pipes. Fittings.

A slab-metal door led to a larger storage space throbbing with pneumatic and electric noise. Both side walls hosted equipment: a bank of water heaters, another of A.C. condensers. Electrical panels, a spaghetti snarl of phone hookups, overhead conduits, pipes, insulated ducts.

Past all that, a wooden door with a cheap lock opened to a windowless afterthought. Michael Lotz's domicile was ripe with body odor and the vinegary reek of heroin, the walls barely plastered drywall. Generous for a jail cell; as a dwelling, sad.

A doorway to the left led to a prefab fiberglass bathroom. Toilet, sink, prefab shower, all in need of cleaning. I thought about Red Dress's final moments.

In the main room, a single-sized mattress sat on a sagging box spring, next to a fake-wood dresser and chair and a black plastic lamp. Black sheet, purple-and-black quilted covers pushed toward the foot of the bed, much of the cloth dripping onto a vinyl floor. Two pillows bent into kidney-bean shapes, one black, one yellow, leaned against the wall.

Curling, Scotch-taped posters abounded: naked women, women in bikinis, high-octane race cars and homologated street versions. Grown man living in the fantasy world of a teenage boy.

On the dresser, a hotplate, a six-pack of Bud Lite, an almost empty bottle of Jose Cuervo, a dozen candy bars, plastic dishes and pot-metal utensils for one. Nearby, tucked in a corner near the entrance to the bathroom, a brown mini-fridge burped and wheezed.

The room was pleasantly cool, the beneficiary of being belowground plus an industrial-strength ventilation system. Trade-off for the wasp-drone coursing through the walls, bottoming the refrigerator's percussion.

Pena pointed to the hotplate. "He's not allowed to have that."

Milo said, "How was he supposed to eat?"

Pena appeared surprised by the question. "No cooking in here, he knew the rules."

Milo sniffed the air, walked to the corner across from the fridge, sighted down at the floor, and pointed. Granules of white powder specked the concrete an inch from the bed. A few inches away, an empty mini-baggie.

"Don't imagine rules were that important to him." He checked his phone. "No reception down here?"

"Uh-uh," said Pena. "Sorry."

"I'm asking because I'm waiting on a warrant to search this place."

"You can try in the garage but it comes and goes there. Best to go outside."

Milo said, "We'll go up to the lobby until the warrant comes in, then come back here."

"How long's that going to take?"

"Hopefully it'll be soon."

"Okay, I guess," said Pena. "No offense, but you guys just standing around could make people nervous."

"The police make your residents nervous?"

"You know students, everything bothers them."

"Don't imagine someone dying here last night's gonna comfort them, Bob."

Pena licked his lips. "I was hoping to keep that kind of quiet."

"Sirens last night didn't give it away?"

"Not really, sir. There's always ambulance sirens—like I said, we're close to the med center. 'Specially at night. And when I found him, I opened that gate for them and they rolled right in."

"Ten fifteen p.m.," said Milo. "How'd you come to find him?"

"I took off to go to the doctor, made up by

working late. I came back, checked around, he was supposed to bring the extra garbage to the dumpsters out back and didn't. I went to talk to him."

"You let yourself in here?"

Pena blinked. "I'm allowed."

"All the doors were locked?"

"The mesh and the metal. The wood one wasn't. I knocked first. He didn't answer so I opened it. I needed to talk to him."

"He always leave his door unlocked?"

"Wouldn't know," said Pena.

"You didn't have a lot of meetings with him down here."

"Right, mostly during the day," said Pena. "After the doctor, I went out to dinner with my wife, then like I said I came back to check and found the extra garbage. She was waiting in the car, I told her I'd be right out." Long exhalation. "I couldn't believe it. I told her to go home, I'd be tied up. Had to take an Uber home."

"What a thing, Bob."

"A big thing."

"So you knocked, he didn't answer—"

"There was a light on—down there, a crack under the door. I figured he fell asleep. I wanted him to take care of the garbage. So I go in, and he's there." Pointing to the bed, then the floor. "Half on, half off, he's all blue, his mouth's hanging open. Then I see the spoon and the needle. I couldn't believe it. I called 911. Not from here, like I said no reception, and like I said the garage isn't great so I went outside. Saw my wife in the car, to be honest I'd forgot about her, she says you okay, I say no, tell her what happened, tell her to go home."

Pena sucked saliva through his teeth. "What do you need a warrant for? He's dead. And it was an accident, right?"

"We like to be careful, Bob. If Mr. Lotz was a longtime user, it could be an accident."

"Could be?" said Pena. He gave a sick smile. "Okay, I get it, you guys take all kinds of flak."

"Part of the job, Bob. So Mr. Lotz hid his secrets pretty well."

"Too well."

"Other than that, did he do his job okay?"

"It's not rocket science," said Pena. "Pickup janitorial, odds and ends. Not much heavy lifting, the main cleanup is done by a service. He was quiet—like a loner."

"Hired by Academo and sent to you."

Pena nodded.

"Residents pretty happy, overall?"

Pena's eyes rounded. "Why wouldn't they be?"

"What you said about students," said Milo.

"Oh, yeah. What I meant was they got their needs. Got to have the Wi-Fi working, the A.C. going all the time, got to be able to watch their shows and listen to their music."

"And no cops. Like the one's who'd come if there was a noise complaint."

Pena shifted his feet. "We don't have that. We talk to them, it works out."

Milo pulled out a photo of Amanda Burdette taken from one of the wedding shots. "This resident happy?"

Pena squinted. "Left my glasses up in the office."

Milo drew the photo back to give him more distance.

"Her?" said Pena. "Yeah, she's here. Why're you asking about her? She in some sort of trouble?"

"Not at all, Bob. She just happened to be involved in another case—not as a suspect, a witness."

"Witness to what?"

Milo waved off the question. "That's actually what got me curious about what happened here. I saw the address in Lotz's file and remembered it from her witness statement. I'm sure it's nothing. Big city, big building, all kinds of things happen."

"Exactly," said Pena.

"Long as I'm here, though, I might as well touch base with her. Where's her unit?"

"You need to do that? Fine, she's in C. The third building."

I said, "There are two other buildings?"

Pena smiled like a kid delivering a secret. "It's one of those optical illusions. From the outside it looks like one building with three entries but it's really three separates. When they built them, they put on a big front to cut costs. This one's A, the others are B and C."

"Any passage from one building to another?"

"Nope, structural walls between them."

"Did Lotz work in all three buildings?"

"Yup."

"Who lives in the other basement rooms?"

"No one, they're storage."

Milo tapped Amanda's photo. "Building C. What unit?"

"She's really not in trouble?" said Pena. "That's all I need, more trouble."

Milo said, "Perish the thought, Bob. By the way, how many units are there, total?"

"Thirty-one times three. Ninety-three total."

"Amanda's been no problem."

"That's her name?" said Pena. "I know it sounds weird but I don't bother with the names because they come and go. To me she's C-four-eighteen. Fourth floor."

"Do you know if she's in?"

"Not a clue, don't pay attention unless they call with a problem."

"No calls from Amanda."

"Nothing," said Pena. "I don't keep tabs on them, sir. It's not like they work regular jobs, keep regular hours."

"Got it, Bob. Where's the mailroom?"

"Downstairs in B. We got a service, delivers to each unit."

"Nice."

"That's what they pay for."

"Okay, we'll pay Amanda a visit while we're waiting for the warrant."

"Sure," said Pena, sounding anything but. He rubbed the top of his head and screwed up his lips.

"Is there a problem, Bob?"

"No, no problem—the company likes privacy for the residents, that's all. It's like a thing for them."

"Privacy."

"We need to be better than a dorm."

"Don't worry, we're not gonna break down her door, Bob. Just a gentle knock."

"Sure," Pena repeated. "And yeah, I never hear from her. To me that's a good resident."

The three of us walked outside and over to Building C. Milo pointed to a closed-circuit camera above the door. "Saw that at A. Need the tapes, Bob."

"No tapes," said Pena. "Direct feed to the company computer."

"You don't have a copy?"

"Nope. There's a problem, I email them, they look for it and mail it back."

"What kind of problem?"

"Stolen bike, that kind of thing. Doesn't happen a lot."

"Okay," said Milo. "Email the company and get me the past twenty-four hours on all three buildings."

"I need to get authorization from one person before I ask another person."

"How long will that take?"

"I can try today, sir."

"You do that, Bob. Tell all the persons to hurry so we can keep things simple and assure privacy."

"I'll do it but it's up to the company."

"Be convincing, Bob. Now unlock that door. Please."

Building C's lobby was pale green, undersized, and unfurnished, lit by LED ceiling cans and carpeted in sand-colored Berber showing its age. At the rear, two elevators.

Pena said, "I don't need to come up with you, right?"

Milo had been working his cell, adding Michael Lotz's Volvo to his warrant application. He looked up and gave one of his unsettling smiles: timber wolf baring its teeth just before feasting. "Actually, we'd rather you didn't come up, Bob. In terms of the CCTV, best thing would be the company emails it to me directly."

"I don't know, sir. Never had to do this before."

"Thanks for your help, Bob."

Pena looked alarmed. "I didn't really do any-thing."

Milo's smile held. Pena scurried off, exited back to the street, and turned right.

Milo said, "Being helpful seems to bother him."

I said, "Company man. If things get complicated, he doesn't want to be seen as allied with you."

"Meaning he'd lie to keep his job."

"Good bet. You see anything to lie about?"

"After I toss Lotz's place, I'll let you know."

I said, "Didn't see a phone or a laptop in there. No Wi-Fi could explain the computer, but everyone has a phone."

"Guy living like that, there's a good case for burners."

"Maybe, but if you need dope, you keep an active phone."

"Point made. It's a hole, all right. What a way to live."

I said, "Float away on a heroin cloud and not much matters."

He frowned, glanced at his cell. "Judge Klee promised A-sap but nothing yet. Then again, **his** loyalties are to himself."

Sluggish elevators, both reluctant to leave the third floor. Finally, they arrived simultaneously. Empty.

Milo said, "Eenie meenie," and stepped into the left-hand lift. We took a slow, grinding ride to the fourth floor, stepped out to a hallway crowded with chain-locked bicycles and scooters.

More Berber, scuffed and stained and fraying around the seams. The walls were milky gray, the doors deep gray, each furnished with a black button to the right.

Muffled voices and too-loud music, most of it hip-hop, leaked from behind some of the doors.

At the far end of the corridor, a scatter of empty beer cans.

Behind the door of unit 418, silence. No bike or scooter but something had deposited a strip of tarry grit that ran to the door. Transportation kept inside.

Milo put his ear up against the door.

"Someone in there," he whispered.

His knock went unanswered.

Pushing the black button evoked an insectoid buzz—fatigued cicadas.

No response.

A door five units down opened and a heavyset girl with yellow cornrows dangling past her waist emerged, stared at us for a moment, then headed for the elevators.

Milo repeated the knock-and-buzz.

Nothing.

He put his ear to the door again, backed away, and talked softly. "She stopped moving around."

"Not in a social mood."

"Big surprise." He got close to the door. Cleared his throat and said, "Amanda?" at medium volume.

Silence.

We returned to the elevators. Both were lolling on the ground floor. When they didn't respond, he said, "Let's take the stairs—no cracks about aerobics."

I said, "What aerobics? We're climbing down."

"Everything's relative."

◆

Lots of trash in the stairwells, along with a scatter of dead roaches, spiders, and the desiccated remains of other six-legged things.

I followed as Milo thumped down. He moved stiffly, grunting every third or fourth step, a resentful rhino. Just as we reached the second floor, his cell chirped and he stopped. "Sturgis . . . oh, hi, Judge Klee . . . sure, no prob. Sure. Appreciate it . . . yes, that, too . . . yes I realize I should've included it . . . got it, thanks, Judge."

We resumed our descent. His stride was looser. Happy ungulate.

I said, "Good news on the warrant."

"Telephonic approval's in place contingent on my filling out the papers perfectly when I get back to the office and don't add anything. Let's take a closer look at Mr. Lotz's manse."

CHAPTER
20

At the door to building A, he phoned Pena and got voicemail. Muttering, "Not a promising start to our relationship, Bob," he tried again with the same result. Glaring, he said, "One more time . . . there you are, Bob. We're ready to get into Lotz's place. Like now . . . yes, I have a warrant . . . see you out front."

Whatever Pena said made him smile.

I said, "Penitence?"

"More like terror. He impresses me as a guy who'll always be afraid of something." He tapped his foot and scrolled through his email. "Crap . . . crap . . . crap . . . all crap. The disinformation age."

The door opened and Pena came out. "I called the company about the feed. Person in charge was out."

"Who's that?"

"Sandra Masio."

"What's her number?"

"Got it on speed dial, don't know it by heart."

"Where's your phone?"

"Back in my office."

"Where's that?"

"Ground floor of B," said Pena. "So I can be in the center of things."

"Here's my card, Bob. Find the number and email it to me while we look over Mr. Lotz's grand palace."

"He never complained about living there." Pena licked his lips. "Nothing like this ever happened."

I said, "How long have you been working here?"

"Four years."

A year and a half before Cassy Booker's death. "How many deaths have there been during that time?"

Pena blinked twice. "Why would there be deaths, sir?"

"Four years, lots of people," I said. "Things happen."

"What I meant was no employees ever"—Pena looked at the floor—"did what he did."

I said, "What about resident deaths?"

A beat. "There was a professor—an old guy, visiting from somewhere, U. put him up here for a year. Right after I started he had a heart attack. He was old."

His eyes raced to the left, faltered, reversed direction, and slid past my scrutiny.

Milo said, "What else, Bob?"

"A little later there was one other one."

"A professor?"

Head shake. "A student, don't know exactly what happened. The EMTs took her away, later the family came and took her stuff without talking to me. Company didn't hold her to the lease."

"Big of them," said Milo. "How'd she die?"

"No one told me, sir," said Pena. "They took her in an ambulance and she never came back."

"You weren't curious."

Pena tried out a smile, ended with a queasy parting of lips. "You know what they say about the cat."

I said, "Did this girl die two and a half years ago?"

Milo's eyebrows rose.

Pena chewed his lips. "That sounds about right. I wasn't here, someone else did the 911."

"Who was that?"

"I had an assistant."

"You don't anymore?"

"Not necessary."

"Corporate downsizing."

"I don't know what it was, but he's gone and I don't need it," said Pena.

"He met the parents."

"Don't know what he did, just the 911. Back

then I was also supervising some Section Eights the company has downtown."

Something he'd just said he'd avoided.

Milo said, "What's your former assistant's name?"

"Kramer."

"First name."

"Pete. He was part-time."

I said, "What was the girl's name?"

"It's important?" said Pena.

Milo said, "Maybe, maybe not. We can check county records, but it'd be easier if you just told us."

"Yeah, yeah, sure, but like I said, don't know their names, even the ones living here now. Unless they cause big problems, there was this kid, son of an ambassador. Long name I couldn't pronounce, called himself Tim. Him I remember, nothing but problems. We finally expelled him."

"When was that?"

"When I started."

Clear memory of four years ago.

I said, "The girl who died, which building and unit did she live in?"

"Building B," said Pena. "The unit I can't tell you. Don't even remember the floor—it wasn't One, that I **can** tell you, my office is on One, she wasn't near there. Maybe Two. Probably Three. I'm pretty sure not Four." He scratched beneath his lower lip. "I want to say Two or Three."

Another failed smile. "It was a long time ago."

"Was her name Cassandra or Cassy?"

Milo's eyes widened.

Robert Pena said, "Like I said . . . maybe. Could be, sounds right. Like **you** said, you can check records."

"Right," said Milo. "And what you can do is unlock that gate and the metal door and give the company another call about the camera feed."

"Yes, sir."

Pena trudged off.

Milo turned to me. "What was that all about?"

"Maxine told me a girl in the same program as Amanda had committed suicide. I ran some searches and found her name. Cassy Booker. Pena seemed evasive about other deaths, so I gave it a shot."

"Same program as Amanda. She write an essay, too?"

"As a matter of fact, she did."

He folded his arms across his barrel chest. "You didn't think to say anything because . . ."

"The case was going in a lot of directions and at the time it didn't seem to clarify anything."

"Protecting my feeble brain from too much input?"

"Trying to be efficient, Big Guy."

"Hmph."

"I'm still not sure it's relevant. College student suicide isn't all that rare—five to ten per hundred thousand, meaning two to four a year on a campus the size of the U."

"But now you're asking Pena about it."

"Long as we had him, I figured why not."

He stared at me. "You don't see Amanda as Princess of Doom."

"I was actually wondering if she's a potential suicide."

"Why? The program's too much stress?"

"Her affect's off—flat, withdrawn. At her brother's wedding she opted out emotionally. You could see it as hostility but it could be serious depression."

"Or she's just got a weird personality."

"Weird people can get depressed."

His arms tightened, bunching his jacket sleeves. "Sad, not a brat, huh?"

"It's a possibility."

"You took your cautious pills today."

"Take 'em every day."

He freed his arms, began finger-counting. "On the other hand, her brother's wedding is totally ruined by a murder involving heroin and fentanyl and she doesn't appear to give a damn. A few days later a junkie who just happens to clean up her building spikes himself to death. If we find Lotz died from the same cocktail as Red Dress, I'm breathing hard. We find out so did this Cassy Booker, I'm hyperventilating."

"You see Amanda as a dope dealer?"

"I don't see anything, I'm just feeling weird." He slipped on rubber gloves. "You're obviously not, good for you. I'm gonna go excavate."

"Want help?"

"No, too cramped in there."

I get paid irregularly and stingily by LAPD but refuse to go on the department payroll because it would kill my spirit and radically slash my income. The uncharted arrangement Milo and I have makes a lot of what I do—driving him around, questioning witnesses, inspecting crime scenes—a potential violation. That's never caused a problem because Milo's solve rate is astonishing and the chief thinks I'm part of that—he's the one who tried to lure me into civil servitude.

On top of that, for all its paramilitary stance, LAPD flexibility is commonplace even when there's scant benefit to the department. A glaring example is celebrities swapping ride-alongs for autographs and selfies cops can show their kids.

Back in 1991, a charming, good-looking Austrian writer named Jack Unterweger came to L.A. on a magazine assignment about international law enforcement and got chauffeured around the downtown red-light district by veteran detectives. Unterweger turned out to be a sexual sadist who'd strangled seven women in Europe and he used what he'd been shown to savage three additional victims.

Despite that, no change in policy resulted, because L.A. is Improv City: Reinvent yourself, make up the rules as you go along, all the while inhaling whatever whiff of fame you can suck from your aspirational bong.

I'm fully at ease tossing victims' residences, not so much standing around and doing nothing as Milo pulled a peeved solo.

No problem, it would pass.

I walked around the parking garage until I snagged some bars on my phone, checked my mail and my messages, wrote a few replies. Then I looked up Academo, Inc.

Closely held corporation in Columbus, Ohio. Scant info beyond a couple of articles in business magazines that specialized in financial porn.

The forty-five-year-old brainchild of an Ohio State alum and benefactor named Anthony Nobach, the company was presented as a model of entrepreneurial spirit. Born to humble beginnings, Nobach had earned spending cash as a freshman by charging fellow students modest fees for locating cheap housing. The following year he created a moving company named Cheap Tony's with rates tailored for students.

By the time Nobach graduated, he'd amassed several parcels of depressed real estate near campus and was converting slums and tear-downs to low-rent student rentals. His next step was rehabbing a failed government housing project bought on the cheap and creating a private student dorm, with much of the cost absorbed by the university and a federal housing grant.

Academo now owned and operated mega-structures in Boston, Cleveland, Syracuse, Rochester, Bloomington, Salt Lake City, Tucson, L.A., and San Diego. Anthony Nobach, described as "religious and a model of mid-Western probity," remained as CEO. A younger brother, Marden, was the chief operational officer.

Online consumer ratings were the predictably meaningless mix of adoration and excoriation. Overall grade: 3.5 stars.

Keywording **academo inc** and **death** produced nothing. So did substituting **suicide** and **murder** for **death**. An image search pulled up shots of other properties. The company favored character-less structures with the same unbroken façade as the building we were in.

I called Maxine Driver and asked her if the students in the DIY program knew one another.

She said, "No idea. What's cooking?"

"Nothing yet."

"When dinner's ready you'll ring the bell?"

"Your reservation has been duly noted."

With Milo already cranky, I figured an overstep wouldn't make much difference and phoned Basia Lopatinski at the coroner. Away from her desk, voicemail. I asked her to look up Cassy Booker's file.

Heading back to Michael Lotz's room, I entered the utility area and came face-to-face with Milo, flush-faced, waving a piece of paper.

"Where'd you go? Look at this!"

CHAPTER
21

Memo paper torn from an **ACADEMO, INC.,** pad.

The logo a Greek Revival building fit for the Ivy League, below that: **We house the leaders of tomorrow.**

Below that, clumsy block lettering in red ball-point.

An address on Corner Avenue.

Then: **aura 8–10 Sat pm.**

I said, "Lotz's handwriting?"

Milo said, "Matches his DMV signature and the ink's the same as an Academo pen in one of his drawers."

He shook the paper, green eyes incandescent. "You still feeling cautious? What this look like to you?"

"A game plan."

He crossed himself. "Hell, yeah. Unless Lotz was on the invite list, he was a **very** bad boy. And he doesn't sound like some homicidal mastermind. More like the type who could be bought. Maybe by a resident who does have a high IQ."

"Amanda commissioned a hit on Red Dress?"

"She'd have the opportunity to know Lotz. Yeah, she's young, but she's also a brain with abnormal emotions, so why not? It makes other stuff fall into place. Like Garrett's squirrelly look when we mentioned Poland. That coulda been him knowing something nasty about baby sis. Or he's involved more directly. As in Red Dress is a girl from his past who threatened to embarrass him on his big day. For all his Joe Nerd thing, maybe he's got some bigger secrets than his wife's Vegas fling."

He took the paper back. "I got sidetracked to the Rapfogels because Denny's a dog and Corinne pointed me toward him. But looks like it's the wholesome Burdettes I need to focus on. As in back to Pa Walton and his farm animals. Because vets use fentanyl, easy enough for Amanda to waltz into a barn, lift what she needs, and pass it along to Lotz. Maybe he kept some for himself and that's how he ended up dead. Or she hot-shotted him to clear her tracks."

He took a breath, flapped the paper against his thigh. "I'm not making sense?"

"You're making a lot of sense."

"But?"

"No buts."

"This is a game changer, Alex. I find out any of the Burdettes visited Warsaw—hell, if they like to **polka** I'm on them."

"Anything else come up in Lotz's room?"

"His wallet had an expired Discover card and I found five fifties behind a bunch of underwear."

"Lots of cash for a junkie to keep around."

"Exactly, money's like water to them. So it had to be a recent cash infusion. Everything else I found is: stash of baggies, two dozen disposable hypos, another scorched spoon, collection of disposable lighters, more candy and cookies, also with his skivvies. All I've got left is pawing under the bed, then looking at the bathroom. I find a guitar string, I'm Nirvana-bound."

"Good luck."

"You're not coming?"

"For what?"

"You don't mind getting dusty, you can do the bed. Bathroom's too gross, I'll do that."

"All is forgiven?"

"What the hell's that supposed to mean?"

"Slip of the tongue." As we returned to Lotz's hole, I told him about calling Lopatinski.

He said, "**Great** idea!"

That level of glee, I kept one thought to myself: **Still no I.D. on the victim.**

I followed his lope back to the room. In the doorway, he said, "I'm having second thoughts about you getting under the bed, amigo. Those are nice pants."

"Protect and serve. As in you," I said. "Give me gloves."

Everything he'd found was tagged and bagged and arrayed neatly in a corner of the cramped room.

I said, "Have you flipped the mattress?"

"Yeah, but not the spring. Sure you want to do it?"

The "nice pants" were black jeans. My shirt was ash-colored chambray. Both would dust off.

"No prob."

He went into the bathroom and I pushed the mattress half off the box spring. Lifting one side revealed a partial view of dust motes and a trio of dead roaches, maybe cousins of the tribe in the stairwell.

From the bathroom, Milo said, "Gimme a break. Old junkie and his cabinet's got nothing but aspirin and shaving stuff and a stick of Mennen . . . okay, **here** we go, conveniently behind the stick. Ciprofloxacin, prescribed last year at a clinic in Venice. What's that, Alex? Like methadone?"

I said, "Antibiotic."

"What do the pills look like?"

"Round, white, a number on one side."

"Hmm . . . maybe they're real, I'll have the lab verify . . . looks like Lotz was old-school, didn't get into the prescription game."

I said, "Heroin's relatively cheap nowadays. If he's got a reliable supplier, why mess with anything new?"

"A stodgy type, huh? Okay, time to check the toilet tank . . . nothing. You finished?"

"Halfway there." I walked around to the other side of the bed, lifted the mattress on a notably more generous supply of motes, along with woolly swirls of dirt, six dead roaches, three dehydrated M&M's—orange, blue, brown—and an errant baggie.

Right half of the bed, if you were lying down. If Lotz was right-handed like ninety percent of the population, the side he'd favor.

I began probing the dirt, found nothing in the first couple of piles. But as I nudged the third, a sharp white corner asserted itself like a tiny shark fin.

I tweezed it out, setting off a tiny dust storm.

Another remnant from an Academo notepad, folded in half.

Black-and-white photocopy of a six-month-old California driver's license issued to Suzanne Kimberlee DaCosta. Thirty-one years old, five-seven, one twenty-four, black, brown, address on Amadeo Drive in Studio City.

Familiar face, pretty even under heartless DMV lighting.

Now Red Dress had a name.

I said, "No protection but I've definitely served."

Milo stepped out of the bathroom. I showed him the license.

He put his palms together. "Thank you, God. And your personal assistant, **this** guy."

He turned away quickly but I'm pretty sure his eyes were wet.

CHAPTER
22

What's in a name? Plenty.

I sat in the passenger seat of the unmarked as Milo worked his department-issue laptop.

Within seconds he had Suzanne DaCosta's criminal record at hand, a puny archive consisting of two marijuana busts seven years ago in Denver and a public indecency arrest pled down to misdemeanor nuisance three years after that in Oceanside. No jail time.

One registered vehicle, a six-year-old gray Honda Civic. He put out BOLOs on the car.

Suzanne DaCosta's social network was almost as thin as Amanda Burdette's: no accounts on Facebook, Instagram, Snapchat, or Twitter, no narcissistic display of pseudo-talent on YouTube. But a LinkedIn page advertised her availability as a "research assistant" and offered up an 818 landline.

He said, "Guess it depends what you're researching," and punched in the number. Disconnected.

The reverse directory offered up the same landline and Studio City residence. An image search pulled up no pictures of Suzanne DaCosta but it did flag the address as a one-story ranch house south of Ventura and west of Laurel Canyon.

Milo plugged in his GPS and shifted into Drive. "Ready for the Valley?"

"Got my car here, I'll follow you."

"Better yet, I follow you to your place and then we go over the hill in one set of wheels. Fuel conservation, as in mine. Also, A.C. in this thing sucks."

We got to my house in ten minutes, took a moment to check in with Robin. She was making deft circular motions on the bowl back of an old Venetian mandola with a pad of cotton. French polishing. She held up a wait-a-sec finger.

Taking over the social obligations, Blanche toddled up with a chew stick in her mouth and got petted by both of us. Her smile said everything was right in the world.

Milo said, "Ah, yes, the sun is shining, Pooch."

Robin put down her polishing pad, came over and kissed me on the lips, Milo on the cheek. "You're looking rather pleased, Big Guy."

"I see you, I'm full of glee."

She flashed a gorgeous smile. "Flattered, but something tells me it's more than that."

Milo looked at me. "Smart girl, that where you get your insights? Yeah, I finally identified my victim. And Romeo found the crucial evidence."

He summed up.

She said, "Dirt pile under the bed. In those nice jeans I bought you."

She brushed something off my left leg. Everyone laughed and we left.

I drove north on the Glen while Milo looked up Michael Lotz's criminal record.

The screen filled. "Oh, you've been a bad boy, Mikey . . . bunch of assaults from age eighteen on, probably has a sealed juvie record, too . . . looks like he started out in Pittsburgh . . . then over to Harrisburg . . . Philly . . . Akron, malicious mayhem in Patterson, New Jersey, couple of batteries in Newark."

I slowed as a truck snail-crawled across two lanes and attempted a right turn. Milo showed me a page of mugshots. In most of them Lotz's hair was long and unruly, his unremarkable face covered by a beard. Old eyes, slackening skin, deteriorating confidence.

I said, "Transient addict, maybe homeless."

"Plenty of those . . . okay, here we **go.** He stabbed someone to death eighteen years ago, back in

Akron . . . sounds like a bar brawl, voluntary man-slaughter pled down to involuntary, he served five out of ten in Youngstown, Ohio . . . suspected prison gang involvement, probably has tattoos, need to see his corpse."

He phoned the crypt, talked to an attendant named Pedro, and asked which pathologist would be doing Lotz's autopsy.

"I don't see any autopsy on the schedule, Lieutenant."

"Big backlog."

"Yeah," said Pedro. "But that's not it. He's marked for X-ray and an exterior only. You know how it is with O.D. suicides."

"This one might not **be** suicide."

"Oh? How come?"

"He's related to a homicide I'm working. If there was an autopsy, who'd be doing it?"

"Dr. Rosen filled out the forms. She's out right now, teaching at the med school."

"Don't know her. New?"

"Yup," said Pedro. "She's part-time, we got a bunch of those."

"Do me a favor. Ask Dr. Lopatinski if she can do the autopsy. If she can't, have Dr. Rosen call me. Whoever does it, make sure every bit of body ink is logged."

"He's ganged up?"

"Good chance of that. More important, I need a tox screen A-sap."

"Hold on," said Pedro. "I'm writing it all down."

"You're a gentleman and a scholar."

"Don't know about scholar," said Pedro, "but my mama raised me right."

Milo returned to Michael Lotz's criminal résumé. "So he's capable of killing . . . okay, what's next?" He frowned. "Nothing's next, just a bunch of possessions for personal use . . . starting in Philly after his release. Straight release, no parole . . . now he's heading west . . . west: Omaha, Tulsa . . . a second one in Tulsa five years ago . . . and a third. Then it stops. All of a sudden he switches from bruising to using?"

I said, "If you don't need to mug someone to get heroin, it's a great pacifier. Maybe he found himself that reliable supplier. Or began trading dope for favors."

"Hit man for hire," he said. "Stalking Suzanne to that bathroom, shooting her up, and garroting her doesn't sound like a rookie move. So why's he dead? I'm not thinking suicide due to guilt."

"Unlikely," I said. "He O.D.'d accidentally or someone made sure he O.D.'d."

"Another fentanyl cocktail."

"Or just purer heroin. If whoever hired him was also his supplier, it would be easy. Not hard to see a motive: He outlived his usefulness and his addiction made him unreliable. With the gang thing—three busts in Tulsa—maybe someone at their PD will know him."

He pulled out his pad and scrawled. Laughed. "All these parents paying for their kids to have a safe space, this asshole's lurking in the basement."

"Pena said he came through Academo's HR. The company's headquartered in Columbus. Lotz has no record there but he did spend time in Ohio—Akron and then the prison time in Youngstown."

"Long-term relationship with someone in the company?"

"Someone who also knew Suzanne. Lotz didn't get a repro of her license by himself. Whoever hired him was close enough to her to get hold of the real one and photocopy. That fits with the personal nature of the crime."

"Hostile boyfriend, maybe living right where we're headed," he said, tightening his jaw and patting his jacket where his gun bulged. "Or a girlfriend, God forbid I of all people should assume."

Half a mile later, he frowned: "Lotz having the notes on the wedding and the photo says he's involved but what if he was just a go-between who hired some other scrote to actually do the deed?"

I said, "Another reason to get rid of him."

"But a complication. I need to trace his movements that day, see if he left the building at the right time." He sent a text to Robert Pena about the CCTV feed. Waited for a reply, got none, and cursed.

I said, "Let's take another look at Tomashev's photos, see if Lotz shows up."

"Good idea, soon as we check out Suzanne's digs.

I snag a shot of Lotz with Amanda, I don't need any mood-elevating substance."

"You see her as hiring a hit man."

He swiveled away from the screen and toward me. "Why the hell not? She lives where Lotz works, easy for them to have contact."

"In addition to her age and lack of criminal experience, she's socially inept. Big leap from passing someone in the hall to contracting murder. You ask the wrong person, you put yourself at risk. How would she be able to sense Lotz was a good candidate?"

"Maybe she's not as nerdy as you think."

"Maybe but what's her motive?"

"How 'bout one of the usuals: Romance gone wrong, Suzanne threatened to show up and embarrass her. You figured Suzanne for a student. They met on campus, had a thing, Amanda ended it."

I said nothing.

He said, "Impossible?"

"Nothing is."

"Hmph."

Several silent miles zipped by. Lovely day in the Santa Monica Mountains, trees and shrubs and grass and sky offering thanks for being placed in California. We hit the peak at Mulholland and began the descent to the Valley. Half a mile from Ventura Boulevard, Milo rubbed his face and scratched the side of his nose and drummed the laptop.

"Maybe Amanda didn't hire Lotz, Garrett did. He's no Rico Suave but he comes across as more normal than his sister, right? And for a newly married guy, a jilted stripper girlfriend threatening to blow up his wedding would be plenty of motive. Plus he **was** the one got hinky about Poland. What if he spent time there, heard about Skiwski, got ideas about guitar strings. How'd he meet Lotz? Simple. He's visiting Amanda, sees Lotz doing his janitor thing, they talk, something clicks. And in terms of access to dope, same deal as with Amanda: Daddy's stash in the barn."

He held out a palm. "No need to say it, I'm a long way from evidence. But at least I know who my victim is. Let's see where and how she lived. I find any sign Garrett's been there, he's toast."

CHAPTER

23

The computer had offered a spot-on image of the house on Amadeo Drive. What it hadn't provided was tone and nuance.

Suzanne DaCosta's last known residence was a sixties box marred by signs of neglect: cracking and flaking at the corners, ragged window sashes, missing roof shingles. All-concrete frontage killed any notion of landscaping.

Milo pointed.

DaCosta's gray Honda Civic nosed a dented metal garage door. Behind it sat a pair of eighties Corvettes, one white with a red interior, the other white and beige.

All three vehicles were dusty.

Milo said, "White Vettes. That remind you of anything?"

I said, "Your basic call-girl ride back when hotels pretended not to notice."

"Oh, yeah. Nowadays it's SUVS and hatchbacks. The girls carry massage tables to get past the desk."

"Maybe Suzanne sidelined."

He visored his eyes with a hand and peered into the Honda. "Laundry on the passenger seat . . . bottled water . . . jogging shoes. Poor kid, she was living her usual life."

Back to the Vettes. "Two cars for one girl I can see, not three. Maybe Lover Boy's into velocity."

"His and hers," I said. "Romantic. Until it wasn't."

He looked the house up and down, gave his gun another pat, and approached the front door.

The bell sounded a three-note chime.

A chirpy female voice called out, "Who is it?"

Before Milo could answer, a second female voice echoed the question. The result was an out-of-sync duet, like a poorly dubbed film.

Milo said, "Police."

The first voice said, "Really?"

"Yes, ma'am."

The second voice said, "Hold your I.D. up."

Milo showed the peephole his badge.

"Hold on, I'm turning off the alarm."

A bolt slid, then another, and the door opened on two twenty-something blond stunners in bikini bras and Daisy Dukes.

Black top for the taller girl, emerald green for her shorter, bustier friend. Moisture beaded on toned bronze bodies but dry hair. Soaking, not swimming.

"Welcome, Police," said Black, flashing perfect teeth. Soft honey curls ended at her shoulders. Emerald's hair was dyed nearly white and hung to her waist.

Milo introduced us.

"Milo and Alex. Sounds like a cutie cartoon." She giggled. "Sorry. I'm Serena, she's Claire. It sure took long."

"What did?"

"The noise up there," said Claire, curling a silver-nailed thumb backward.

"Up where?" said Milo.

"Where? You're kidding."

Milo smiled.

"Oh, wow." Claire flipped her hair, adjusted a bra cup, and rolled her eyes. Huge black irises were a counterpoint to Serena's icy blues. Dramatic contrast, as if both women had been sent by a casting agent. "Where? Really? The hills up there. We complained to you guys like"—to her friend—"four times?"

"At least," said Serena. "Loma Bruna Circle, crazy big party house. You can't see it 'cause of the trees but you sure hear it. Every week it's a techno shit-storm."

Claire said, "We work, we need our sleep."

Serena said, "You guys don't know about it? Oh,

man. Everyone else does. The neighborhood com-
plains, you guys don't do squat."

Claire said, "What we heard, the A-H who owns
it is related to the mayor."

Serena said, "Money lucks, everyone else sucks."

Twin glares from lovely eyes, followed by pouts.

Milo said, "I'm sorry for the hassle, ladies.
Unfortunately, we're not here for that."

"Then what, garbage cans or something else stupid?" said Serena. She ran a slender finger under the
sodden waistband of her short-shorts, shoulder-
nudged her friend. "We got out of the pool for
nothing, girl."

Milo said, "We're here about Suzanne DaCosta."

"Kimbee?"

"When's the last time you saw her?"

Eye-consultation between the women. Serena
said, "Like a week and a half?"

Claire said, "We don't keep watch on her.
What's up?"

"Unfortunately, she's deceased."

Black saucers, blue saucers. Four hands leaped to
finely molded lips.

Serena was the first to allow her arms to drop.
She shook her head. "No freakin' way."

"I'm afraid so."

Claire's right hand dropped and began clawing
under her waistband. Frantically as if something
beneath the denim was attacking her. Her mouth
expanded and became a maw. She bent double.

"No no no no, not that, not again, no no no no no."

Letting out a gagging noise, she ran into the house.

Milo said, "Again?"

Serena said, "Her mom died like four months ago. Something just blew up in her brain, she was beautiful and super fit, also a model, didn't deserve that. To make it worse, her dad died when she was a little kid. She **hates** death."

"So do we, Serena. That's why—"

"Kimbee's really . . . ?" She began crying and shook her head some more. "I guess our noise thing is pretty bullshit to you."

"It sounds like a super hassle," said Milo. "I'll make a call and see what I can do. Meanwhile, can we come in and talk about Kimbee?"

"Yeah, yeah, sure, of course, sure. Let me go calm Cee down, you guys sit wherever."

CHAPTER
24

"**W**herever" was a limited choice: a sun-cracked black leather sofa or a floor carpeted in grubby green. No other furniture in the low, shallow living room. The house's interior matched its dermis: unadorned, pallid, shabby.

We took the couch and waited while female conversation filtered from the left. A box of bottled water sat near a glass slider that opened to the rear of the property. Where the yard wasn't swimming pool it was scarred pebbled decking and discouraged wooden fencing. Power lines ruled on a blue paper sky. The pool was small, a remnant of the time when aquatic design was dominated by the mystique of the kidney. Robes and towels were piled on a pair of mismatched lounge chairs. A brick incinerator sat in a far corner, souvenir of a time when creating smog was a civic duty.

The lack of furniture in the living room wasn't due to minimalism. Most of the space was taken up by wheeled, tubular racks of women's clothing.

Gowns, dresses, bathing suits, blouses, slacks. At least a third of the floor space was taken up by shoes. Scores of them, unpaired and bunched into piles like leather mulch.

Milo said, "Not much in the way of ambience. If they are pulling tricks, it's outcall not in-call."

I said, "Serena said Claire's mother was 'also a model.' Maybe these are work duds."

"Maybe," he said. "Or it's the euphemism of the month. Like 'dancing' for Ms. Kimbee."

Wincing as he mentioned the name. For over a week, he'd been living with his victim as a wisp. Now she had an identity and a home and the pain of her murder was seeping into his bones the way it always did.

Faint padding footsteps previewed the women's reappearance. Both had removed their bras and put on gauzy midriff tops that proved more revealing. Black tights, green tights.

The two of them folded lithe bodies, graceful as origami, and settled on the carpet. Exemplary posture, legs folded yoga-like, hands on firm thighs.

They closed their eyes, breathed a couple of times, looked straight at us.

"Okay," said Serena. "We're ready."

Claire sniffed and poked at a corner of her eye and looked doubtful.

Milo said, "Sorry to drop it on you like this. Unfortunately there's no good way to deliver bad news."

"Ain't that the truth," said Claire. "My insides are pretty much filled up with bad news."

Serena said, "I told them about your mom."

Milo said, "So sorry."

Claire said, "Aneurysm, she's doing her Pilates and it just . . ." She lowered her head, let it dangle.

Serena put her arm around her friend and drew her near. "Hey, girl."

Claire looked up. "I'm fine."

I said, "It's great that you're here for each other."

Serena said, "We go back to elementary. I was in fifth, she moved from Boise, was in fourth—can I tell them the story, Cee?"

"Uh-huh."

"You're sure?"

Nod.

"Okay," said Serena. "She's super hot now but back then she was kind of short and kind of a little chubby and she got ragged on."

Claire said, "I was a fat nerd, mean bitches tortured me." Slowly spreading smile. "You kicked some butt, girl."

Serena grinned. "Four brothers, you learn to take care of yourself." She held up a fist and growled.

Claire giggled. "Warrior Princess **kicks** it."

I said, "Where'd you guys grow up?"

"Spokane," said Serena. "I was always there, like I said, she moved."

"How long have you been in L.A.?"

"Two years. No work in Spokane so first we moved to the west side—Seattle, then down to Portland. Then we learned if you're serious about working, it needs to be here or New York or someplace like that."

I said, "Modeling."

"Not the skinny-ass fashion bullshit," said Serena. "We're not seven feet tall and we have real boobs and booties." Running her hands over said assets. "We're **not** gonna starve and smoke ourselves into cancer."

Claire said, "You could be tall enough."

"Five-six?" said Serena. "No way, baby girl." She laughed. "She thinks I'm giant because she's an elf—five-two."

"And a half," said Claire.

Serena smirked. "Right. She's a toon but she's got the bod. A lot of the jobs, she gets them first and then she brings me in."

"You do fine by yourself," said Claire. "You got the NAMM."

I said, "You guys do trade shows?"

Serena said, "That's our specialty. We straight model, which is basically standing around being hot, or we're brand ambassadors, which is we do demos while being hot. Like the auto show, we did it this year, I got Subaru, she got Kia. You open and close doors, get inside with the geeks, show them what buttons do what."

Milo said, "What's NAMM?"

I said, "National Association of Music Merchants."

He looked at me.

I played a couple seconds of air guitar.

Claire's black eyes sparked. "You're a musician?"

"Amateur."

"Oh."

Serena said, "NAMM's huge and crazy loud. When we do it next year, we're bringing earplugs."

Claire said, "Loud and boring but we made serious brass."

"**Serious**," said Serena. To us. "We're saving up to own a ranch." Big grin. "Then we get our cowboys, hey?"

"Hey."

"We'll need them because we are **not** going to shovel horseshit, they want to get with us, they're paying dues."

Milo grinned. "Sounds like a plan."

"It's an **awesome** plan," said Serena. "Rabbits, little ponies, baby goats—they're friendly like dogs. And they'll be safe forever, we're vegan."

Claire said, "We **love** animals but we can't keep a single pet here. Not even a friggin' turtle."

Serena said, "Landlord's a dick."

I said, "Did Kimbee like animals?"

Smiles died, eyes dropped. "She never said she didn't."

"Where'd you guys meet her?"

Serena said, "At NAMM."

I'd been to the show with Robin a few times, knew the scheduling. "Last January."

Serena said, "Not last, the one before that."

"What was she doing there?"

"Same as us, some guitar thing," said Serena. "It's all mostly guitar. You wear a bikini and move a little while these old rockers play."

"Mummy Boys," said Claire, laughing.

Milo said, "That's a band?"

Serena said, "Uh-uh, that's a description. They have leather skin and wear leather. Their hair extensions do **not** work. We call 'em Mummy Boys."

Claire said, "We like guys clean and lean. Like a military dude."

"Your boyfriends are military?"

"We don't have boyfriends," said Serena. "We're picky."

"Mummy Boys hit on us whenever we do NAMM," said Claire. She stuck out her tongue.

"Doing it with King Tut?" said Serena. "I don't think so."

I said, "NAMM's huge. How'd you meet Kimbee?"

Serena said, "In the lounge, taking a break. I saw her before that. Up on this revolving platform, wearing this leopard thong bikini you needed an excellent wax for and red five-inchers. They put tons of bronzer on her and did like half her head in corn-rows. She said it gave her a headache."

"What company hired her?"

"No idea."

Claire said, "She didn't have to move much 'cause of the revolving stage. A real **old** Mummy's thrashing and she's going round and round."

"Excellent balance," said Serena. "Long as you work the legs, they always want the leg thing."

I said, "What's that?"

Springing up, she set her feet several feet apart. Solemnity gave way to a sexy pout that bordered on hostility, followed by an exuberant hair toss and the lowering of eyelids. Bending her left leg, she put her weight into the stretch.

"Good for the quads," said Claire, "but after a while it starts to hurt."

Serena said, "You're making like you're a cat." Purring in illustration.

Claire said, "A wildcat. Like you're ready to spring and jump on any guy."

"Got it," I said. "So Kimbee was good at the leg thing."

"We all are, it's part of the job."

She rose with identical grace and assumed the same pose, her back to her friend. Feline bookends.

"It's no big deal," said Serena. "Not like ballet where you're torturing yourself. That's what Kimbee studied."

Claire bit her lip. "You're police so the way it happened—it was bad, huh?"

Milo said, "Unfortunately, you're right. This is a homicide investigation."

She sighed. Both women seemed to wither. They settled back down on the floor.

"It's crazy," said Claire. "Why would anyone hurt her? She was easy, real nice."

I said, "Good roommate."

"She was cool," said Serena.

Milo took out his pad. "Where'd she study ballet?"

"New York, that place—Juilliard."

"When?"

"She didn't say. Just that it was crazy hard. And painful."

"Where else did she live besides New York?"

Claire said, "All she mentioned was Vegas."

"What'd she do in Vegas?"

"Dancing."

Milo said, "Any idea where in Vegas?"

Shrugs and head shakes.

Serena said, "We didn't talk about it much. She didn't talk much, period."

Milo gave me eye-encouragement.

I said, "So you met her at NAMM and decided to live together."

Serena said, "Not then. She didn't need a place, then. Around a year later."

Claire said, "We didn't need a roommate. We

didn't have a real bedroom, just the garage. The landlord converted it but it's kind of . . . not gross, but it's . . ."

Serena said, "Totally ghetto. We told her before she saw it. She said no problem, she needed somewhere quick, would take a look. She did and said, Perfect. We only charged her a hundred a month, we even paid the utilities because you can't separate it from the house."

I said, "What was Kimbee's rush?"

"Bad boyfriend," said Claire.

"Domestic violence?"

"Nah," said Serena. "More like they were over and she needed a place. But sometimes she'd be gone, so maybe she went back to him, like off and on?"

Milo said, "Did she write you rent checks?"

"Nope, cash. Five twenties."

"Did she have her own mailing address?"

"Nope, we get all the mail. If there was something for her, we gave it to her."

Claire said, "She didn't get anything, really. We don't, either, except catalogs. Everything important's online."

Serena said, "Once in a blue moon she'd get clothing catalogs. Like what we get."

"No personal mail."

"Nope."

"You think she might've gone back and forth to her boyfriend."

"Or got herself another," said Serena.

Milo began working his phone.

Claire said, "She didn't want to work NAMM the second time, said it gave her a headache, she had another gig. A couple of times we told her about conventions she said the same thing."

"She asked us if we ever wanted to do Vegas. We said no, thanks. We get enough work in California."

Claire said, "We don't travel. In Portland we had to do sci-fi conventions, putting on space alien costumes and smiling at geeks." She nudged Serena. "Remember the one, the green body paint didn't want to come off?"

"Green with plastic scales. Gross. Smelled like hot glue."

I said, "Anything else you can tell us about Kimbee?"

Claire said, "When she was here she liked the pool."

"Her car's here."

"She didn't drive it much."

"How'd she get around?"

"Probably like everyone. Uber, Lyft, whatever."

Serena fluffed her curls. "That worked out good because if she wanted to pull out, we'd have to move the '82 Vette—the red insides, that one starts."

Claire said, "We don't like to drive, either. The Vettes burn gas. We only registered the '82. The '81 needs an ass-load of work."

Milo typed away. I said, "What made you guys decide to buy both?"

"We didn't buy either," said Serena. "My stepdad gave them to me and whatever I have is **hers.**"

"Nice gift."

"He owns a used-car lot and needed a tax write-off or something. We drove the '82 down from Spokane, it broke down twice. We didn't want the '81 but he flat-bedded it to us anyway. The deal was we find out what it needs and he pays for it, if it's reasonable. We've been too busy to hassle with it. We'll sell both of them for our ranch."

She smiled. "Want to buy it?"

"Tempting but no, thanks."

"Greg's an okay stepdad. He was Number Four and my mom screwed up by divorcing him. Now she's on Number Five, he's a **total** dick."

Claire had spaced out during the car talk. She refocused and said, "How did she—how did it happen?"

Milo said, "It took place at a wedding."

"No **way.** Like at the **ceremony?**"

"At the reception."

"Wow. That's crazy. Someone shot her in the middle of a party and you still don't know who?"

"It's a little more complicated, Serena. It happened last Saturday. You said the last time you saw her was a week and a half ago. Any idea what she was doing the few days before Sunday?"

"Nope. We can't even say she was or wasn't here, just that we didn't see her. She could come and go without us seeing her."

Milo's phone buzzed a text. He read the screen.

I said, "Did she talk to you guys about going to a wedding?"

Head shakes.

"Can you think of anyone who'd want to hurt her? Anyone at all?"

"I can't, sorry, sir," said Claire. Glancing at Serena.

Serena said, "We didn't talk about personal stuff. Cee and me only do that with ourselves."

I said, "She did tell you she needed to get away from her boyfriend."

"Because she was looking for a place."

"Did she seem at all afraid of her boyfriend?"

"You think he did it?"

"We need to look at everything."

"Who is he?"

Milo said, "We were hoping you could tell us."

"You don't know anything?" said Serena.

"It's a tough one, guys."

"Wish we could help you. I mean that. A friend of ours, Kevin, he got shot over a meth thing in Spokane. They never found out who did that and it ate up his parents. How are Kimbee's parents doing?"

"Wish we could tell you. What did she say about her boyfriend other than needing to get away from him?"

Claire said, "Nothing. Except she called him a brain."

"The Brain," said Serena. "She was living with The Brain, needed a change."

I said, "Did she ever bring anyone home?"

Serena said, "Not that I saw."

Claire said, "Me, neither."

"No one was stalking her," said Serena, "if that's what you mean. We look around all the time, we're careful because both of us had stalkers. Cee had two."

"Here in L.A.?"

"Uh-uh, Spokane. High school. So now we look out, someone was hanging around anyone, we'd know. That's why we like it here, weird stuff sticks out, it's quiet. Until the A-H on Loma Bruna bought that place."

Milo stood. "I'll see what I can do about him."

Claire said, "Hey. I just thought of something. Sometimes she said she was going to the library to read."

"Was she in school?"

Both girls shrugged.

"Out by the pool," said Claire, "we'd sometimes see her with books."

I said, "Books about what?"

"Big ones."

"Which library did she go to?"

Claire said, "It wasn't like a big conversation, look at me, I'm so smart I'm going to the library. It's just once, I went out to move the '82 'cause she did want to use her car. She said the library."

Serena said, "Another time, I saw her walking and I'm like, Hi, wassup and she points to her backpack and is like, I'm going to the library. I thought it was cute."

"That she liked to read?"

"That she'd admit it."

Claire placed a hand on her belly. "I don't like the way I'm feeling. I'm going to miss her."

"Aw, girl," said Serena.

"I need to go to the bathroom."

Claire left.

Serena said, "She's going in there to cry. This reminds her of her mom. I better go in and help her."

Milo said, "Sure. Thanks for your time. We're going to check out her place. You guys have an alarm. Did she?"

"Nope."

"Didn't see a lock on the garage door."

"There isn't one because it's not a real door," said Serena. "You slide it up **then** there's a wall with a regular door and that one has a lock. The landlord did it to hide turning it into an illegal dwelling. That's why he doesn't charge us for a two-bedroom. If he could, he would, he's a total dick."

"Who's the landlord?"

"Dr. McClurg, he's a dentist." She shifted bare feet. "Do you have to tell him about Kimbee? He doesn't exactly know about her."

Milo said, "If he had nothing to do with her, don't see why we'd need to tell him anything."

"He didn't. Promise."

"No prob. So it's okay for us to look in the garage?"

The question surprised her. "Sure, of course."

"How about a key?"

"It's easier to use the back door, same key, I'll get it for you."

She hurried off, filmy top billowing over coltish legs.

I said, "All that phone work was getting the victim warrant?"

"Judge Klee, God bless him."

"You asked Serena permission because with one address, technically you need her or Claire's approval."

"Which I just obtained smoothly and unobtrusively."

"Crafty devil."

"Charm," he said. "Everything I know, I learned from you."

CHAPTER

25

Serena returned with a hot-pink key on a matching chain.

Milo said, "Very cool."

She said, "So we can see it easily." Small smile. "Also, style's the thing, we try to put style into everything. When we own goats on our ranch, they're going to get groomed like show dogs. Can you guys go out by yourself? Cee's pretty sad, I want to stay here for her."

The garage's rear door was approached via a narrow strip where the fencing was blanketed by clematis. Two plastic garbage cans sat a few feet away. Milo gloved up and checked them. Force of habit.

He headed for the door.

I said, "Nothing interesting."

"Gluten-free imitation something and enough bottled water to hydrate South Africa."

He inserted the key. I stood back as he stepped inside.

Seconds later: "C'mon in."

Suzanne "Kimbee" DaCosta's hundred bucks a month had bought her two hundred square feet of whitewashed drywall, plywood ceiling, and concrete floor glossed by translucent spray-on coating. Where the gloss wasn't covered by a fake Persian rug, structural cracks were suspended, like gristle in aspic.

One corner was hidden by two walls of plastic shower curtains. Behind the curtains were a prefab shower, a mirrored medicine cabinet bottomed by a glass shelf, a small sink, and a toilet. A freestanding full-length mirror took up the opposite corner. A red silk scarf had been draped over one side.

Sleep came by way of a bright-blue futon against the wall. Perpendicular to the mattress was the same kind of portable clothes rack as in the main house. Seven red dresses hung neatly from padded black silk hangers. Orderly color progression: arterial blood to maroon. An equal number of tops in the same color progression was followed by a dozen pairs of blue, black, and gray skinny jeans and leggings.

Light from a dormer in the roof cast a fog-colored beam rife with dancing dust.

Across the room were shoe boxes stacked three-high, a pair of brown metal four-door cabinets, and a collection of orange cardboard box-files laid horizontally. Bottles of cosmetics and perfume sat on one of the cabinets.

First Lotz's hole, now this.

Milo spent a while snapping photos with his phone, then handed me gloves and pointed to the shoes. "Do me a favor."

I checked each box. Size eight and a half, a few hotshot designer labels, others I hadn't heard of. Stilettos, pumps, sandals, spangled sneakers, all blood red.

I said, "Nothing but footwear."

"Hmph." He'd moved on to the orange files. Opened the first and said, "What?" Then: "That's a first," as all the boxes gave up their contents.

Precisely folded thong underwear, socks, and pantyhose. Red and black.

At the bottom of the last box were three pairs of body shapers like the one Kimbee DaCosta had worn the last day of her life.

"Why the hell would she need these?" he said.

I figured that as rhetorical and didn't answer.

"No, I mean it, Alex. She had a dancer's bod, what the hell was she covering up? Give me something psychological. I need to understand this girl."

I said, "She made her living from her looks. Maybe she saw it as maintenance."

He grumbled again. "She was sure maintaining at the wedding. To me that says she figured to meet someone who mattered."

I thought: **Or just force of habit.**

I said, "The Brain?"

"Garrett Burdette's pretty smart and he makes decent money. They break up a year ago but maybe library time means she was still trying to impress him."

"She told Serena and Claire she'd ended the relationship. Why crash his wedding?"

"She was the one who got dumped and was saving face."

"You're figuring she was planning to humiliate him."

"I'm figuring she pressured him with some sort of ultimatum and deadline **before** the wedding and he didn't give her satisfaction. Best guess is the 'or else' involved either coming back to her or money."

"Pay me to keep quiet about the affair."

"Look at this place. Better than Lotz's hole but that's all you can say about it. She wasn't exactly raking it in."

He rearranged the orange boxes, walked over to the brown metal cabinets and tried a drawer.

No give. Same for all of them.

"Locked. Good. We'll save the best for last."

He inspected the makeshift bathroom.

Liquid soap and four types of expensive shampoo on the floor of the shower. The mirrored cabinet held analgesics, lotions, additional cosmetics and their applicators, shampoo, brushes, combs. A small bottle of Windex explained the spotless mirror.

On the floor were a hair dryer, a curling iron, and a box of rollers.

"Not a single damn narcotic," he said. "Where are the weak-willed victims when you need them."

I took a look at the interior of the medicine cabinet. "No birth control, either."

"Autopsy said she wasn't pregnant, never had been. Maybe after a few interesting years she decided to try celibacy."

He eyed the locked cabinets. "Gimme your car keys."

He returned with the crowbar I keep in my trunk. Took photos of the brown cabinets, muttering, "Chain of evidence," then nosed the tip of the bar into the seam between the top drawer of the right-hand cabinet and the frame. One hard move and flimsy metal surrendered. Releasing the top drawer triggered some kind of latch and all six slid open. He looked inside.

"Undies in a box-file, now this?"

Emptying every drawer, he placed the contents on the floor.

Books.

Nothing but.

Hardcovers and large-format paperbacks, all with bland covers.

Upending every volume, he flipped pages and checked endpapers. "Introductory sociology? Western philosophy? Why the hell would she lock these up?"

"Maybe she's saying, **This is important to me.**"

"A dedicated intellectual who models and strips." **Why not?**

I said, "It's consistent with what the Valkyrie and the bouncers told us. In her spare time, she read. And once upon a time she did ballet, so maybe she had a taste for the classics."

"You know anyone at Juilliard?"

"Robin probably does."

"Por favor?"

Robin said, "Just Sharon Isbin, she's head of the guitar department. If all you're after is enrollment, why doesn't Milo just call the ballet department?"

"Higher-education folk tend to distrust the police and if they tell him no, it could take weeks."

"Okay, I'll see if Sharon can point him in the right direction. Too late to try now, tomorrow morning."

"Thanks, hon."

Milo called out, "Thanks, **darling!**"

Robin said, "Someone's in a good mood. Progress?"

I said, "Small steps."

"Like most things that matter." I clicked off.

Milo fished out another book and shook it. "Here's a racy one, **Civilization and Power** . . . nothing personal in this whole damn place."

As he made a second circuit of the garage, I had my own look at the volumes Kimbee DaCosta had sequestered.

Textbooks and nonfiction for the educated layperson. A sprinkle of yellow **Used** stickers brought back my starving student days. But no inscriptions, stamps from campus stores, or indication where any of the books had been sold or resold.

Still, the collection felt like college reading material and I said so. "Maybe we'll get lucky and it was the U. and Maxine can snoop around."

"How about getting telephonic with her again?"

Voicemail at "Professor Driver's" office and personal cell. I asked her to call.

Milo said, "Here's another possibility: Amanda knew Kimbee from school and fixed her up with Garrett. Because she thought Baby was a dolt and figured one brain deserved another."

I said, "Do we know for a fact that The Brain was male?"

"The girls just referred to him as a boyfriend."

"Maybe they were assuming. A girlfriend would explain no birth control."

"You just turned up the spotlight on Amanda. Talk about a juicy motive, Alex. Being exposed as gay at her brother's nuptials."

He pushed the brown cabinets back in place. "Time to get this place dusted for prints and DNA."

I said, "There goes the neighborhood."

"What does that mean?"

"Like the girls said, this is quiet suburbia. The tech van will attract attention. You ready to go public on a street where neighbors are used to complaining?"

He tapped a foot. "Let's see if the lab can give me one tech in a low-profile car."

"Peggy Cho might welcome the opportunity."

He phoned Cho, hung up smiling.

"Inspired, Alex. She's finishing up a robbery in Granada Hills, is thrilled to go quote unquote 'longitudinal,' can be here in twenty. Meanwhile, let's see if I can do something about the A-H up on Loma Bruna."

A phone chat with a North Hollywood lieutenant named Atkins elicited a promise to crack down on the party house.

I said, "That was easy."

"Uniforms have been going out there for months. Each time, there's immediate compliance so they don't push it."

"Now there's a change in policy?"

"Now there's a change in Ben Atkins's consciousness. He just remembered a favor I did him, don't ask."

"The power and the glory."

"The first is useful, the second is bullshit."

We returned to the main house. Serena and Claire were back on the floor drinking apricot-colored smoothies.

Milo told them about Peggy Cho's impending arrival.

Serena said, "CSI? Can we watch?"

Milo said, "Only one tech's coming and she likes to work alone. We'd actually like to avoid being noticed, period. So no one else in the neighborhood will know."

"A girl CSI, cool," said Serena. "So only us is in on it."

"If that's okay."

"Sure—Cee?"

Claire said, "I can keep secrets. Been doing it my whole life."

We waited outside for Cho. When she arrived, a drape on a front window lifted and Serena gave a thumbs-up.

When we got inside, Cho's nose wrinkled. "My brother rented something like this. Chemical john, not too hygienic."

She began to work and we returned outside where Milo slim-jimmed the Honda and used an internal lever to pop the trunk.

Flares, a spare tire, a jack, a wrench.

He said, "And here I was expecting the **Oxford English Dictionary**."

Back to the car's interior. The clothing on the backseat was more casual than the duds in the garage. One pair of jeans; one pair of slim-cut sweats—black, not red; a red sports bra, a red baseball cap with no insignia, white athletic socks banded with red at the top, red-and-white Nikes.

I pictured Kimbee DaCosta taking a run. Exhilirated by a balmy evening breeze.

The glove compartment gave up a pair of Ray-Ban aviators in a soft case, a registration slip listing the same address, and one shred of possibility: proof of insurance, a company named BeSure.com.

Milo closed the car, googled, found the company had gone out of business last year. We returned to the garage.

Peggy Cho said, "Not much by way of prints, so far, just what look like the same set in the logical places. I can tell because the thumb's distinctive and I remember it from Saturday."

"My victim."

Nod. "But not much of her," said Cho. "Like she was here but she really wasn't."

We returned to the Seville. I said, "Where to?"

He said, "The world of ideas."

CHAPTER
26

The nearest public library was the Studio City branch on Moorpark, white stucco under a swooping half dome of pale blue. Airy inside, gray carpeting and golden wood furniture and shelves.

We walked past a sandwich board advertising upcoming events.

L'Ecole French Conversation Group; Laughter Yoga; Rolfian Deep Tissue Massage as a Pathway to the Center of Consciousness; Baby & Toddler Story-Time.

Milo said, "Yoga can make you laugh? Yeah, probably, if you saw me in yoga pants."

A sprinkle of people sat at tables working laptops and phones. One woman read a book: S&M porn for the middle-aged.

A single librarian, thin, brunette, around thirty,

with sleeve tattoos and black, dime-sized gauges in her elongated earlobes. A slide-in sign in a slotted holder said **Stevie L. Dent.**

She'd watched us since we stepped in. When Milo introduced himself, her eyes narrowed. When he showed her Kimbee DaCosta's photo she shook her head, primed to respond.

"We don't give out information on patrons."

"As well you shouldn't. However, this patron is dead."

Stevie Dent's mouth dropped open. "You're serious."

"Nothing but serious. We're trying to learn what we can about her."

"I see . . . well, I guess you'll need to prove she's deceased, Officer. We're a primary community data hub and our strict policy is guarding against unauthorized release of personal information."

"Good policy," said Milo. "And no problem proving it to you. How about we take you to the morgue? You won't be allowed to view her body but you can examine her paperwork."

Stevie Dent gulped. "Who murdered her?"

"That's what we're trying to figure out. We've been told by her friends that she used the library. Was it here?"

Hesitation. Minimal nod. "She came here to read." As if clarification was necessary. Maybe, in a world of deep tissue massage and hilarious Eastern exercise, it was.

"How often?"

"Maybe once a week," said Dent. "Sometimes less, sometimes more? I really can't say."

"Any particular day or time?"

"The afternoon. I figured she had a flex job, maybe an actress. Because of how she looked and dressed. All in red."

Milo said, "A little theatrical?"

Stevie Dent shifted in her chair. "That's an adjective. I'm not judging. All I'm saying is she was possibly used to being noticed. I had a roommate in college who majored in theater and she was like that. Clothes you'd notice."

I said, "Did you ever see anyone noticing her?"

"Never. She sat over there and read and minded her own business." Pointing to the farthest corner of the main room. Close to the stacks but visible from the desk.

I said, "What contact did you have with her?"

"Just to see her come and go."

I said, "She didn't check out books?"

"No, she just took them from the stacks and put them back. We don't encourage that, volumes get misfiled, but as far as I know she never caused problems."

"What kind of books did she go for?"

Dent shook her head. "Couldn't tell you."

"Was she ever with someone?"

"Always by herself."

"How long would she stay?"

"An hour, maybe two?" said Dent. "I wasn't spying on her. She was upright."

Milo said, "In what way?"

"Sometimes she'd bring her own books and she'd make sure to show them to me inside her backpack. So I'd know she wasn't stealing."

Milo said, "Books to the library, coals to Newcastle."

"Pardon?"

"Did you find that unusual? Bringing her own reading material?"

"Not at all," said Dent. "People come with laptops and devices, everyone's welcome, we want to satisfy a diversity of needs—we just installed a charging station outside for hybrids and electrics."

"Making yourselves relevant," I said.

"We've always been relevant, sir. We just need to market our brand."

"Got it. Anything else you can tell us about Kimbee?"

"That's her name?"

"Suzanne Kimberlee DaCosta. Her friends call her Kimbee."

"Cute name," said Dent. "Sweet, fits. She seemed like a sweet girl."

We waited.

She said, "That's it."

Milo said, "Thanks. How's your Hardy Boys selection?"

"What's that?" said Stevie Dent.

I took Moorpark to Van Nuys, headed south, and merged onto the Glen. As we began climbing, Milo sent a long text.

When he was finished, he said, "Today's bucket list."

"What comes after scaling Everest with no supplemental oxygen?"

"The really challenging stuff," he said. "Looking for Kimbee's relatives, following up with Homeland on Garrett, then, depending on what I find, maybe another chat with Garrett when his wife's not around. That I could use you for. How's your schedule?"

"Late afternoon would work best."

"Let's see how it shakes out." He sat back, stretched his long legs, closed his eyes.

I said, "If COD on Cassy Booker's suicide turns out to be heroin and fentanyl, it might bear a closer look."

"You called Lopatinski. Any reason for me to take over?"

"Only if you have a problem with me following up."

"None whatsoever, amigo." His eyes shut again. "While you're talking chemistry, ask her about Lotz's—anything on the bloods, has she been able to change their mind about the autopsy."

"Will do. I'd also like to look into Pena's assistant, Pete Kramer. He handled the situation with Booker before he was made redundant."

"You think there's a connection?"

"I think former employees can be helpful same as exes."

"Ah, the fine art of cultivating hostility. Sure, delve."

Then he slept.

I dropped him at the station, took Pico to Westwood Boulevard, where I sat in burgeoning traffic that lasted well into the Village. Students jaywalking obliviously didn't help. Neither did random road work. Trailing the lower rim of the U.'s city-sized campus, I continued the northward trek onto Hilgard and hooked east on Sunset. Every turn slowed the mph, as if some sadistic traffic Satan were churning chrome butter, and by the time I entered the Glen, the trip was long stretches of inertia peppered by momentary spurts of forward movement.

Faster to walk the three miles to my house, but I was stuck with a combustion engine. I never use the phone while driving but this was driving like prison's a hotel. I began the search for Peter Kramer.

Common name spanning multiple continents. I added **property manager** and got hits in Brooklyn, Fort Lauderdale, and Silver Spring, Maryland. Images accompanied the last two: a thirtysomething condo superintendent in Florida, a seventysomething, yarmulke-wearing nonspecified in Maryland.

The car in front of me moved a few inches. Before I did the same, the driver behind me leaned on the horn. I checked the rearview. Young woman, maybe a student, in a VW Bug. Bouncing in her seat and waving a phone and flipping me off.

Another half-foot roll, then a total stop. The ranting behind me persisted.

The car stuck in the southbound lane opposite me was a Tesla driven by a black-T-shirted, white-haired man with flabby, crepe-laced arms unimproved by a barbed-wire biceps tattoo. He looked at me and shook his head.

Appreciating the empathy, I shrugged.

His face darkened. "You don't fucking get it. If you didn't use your fucking phone, we could all fucking go home."

A woman in an open-air Fiat behind him raised her eyebrows and did a he's-nuts corkscrew motion with her index finger.

Hoping she meant him, not me, I smiled at her, rolled up my window, turned on the radio. Given the miasma of the moment, the blues seemed about right. Anything but the news.

CHAPTER
27

I got home nearly forty minutes later. Robin had left me a note in her fine calligraphic hand. **Left a message with Sharon I., went to Trader Joe's, Blanche snoozing.**

Dogs' natural routine is to sleep most of the day but they wake easily. Maybe it's a self-protective throwback to their wolf origins a zillion years ago. Maybe they're just curious about the baffling world people have created.

In the service porch behind the kitchen, my dog lay curled in her crate, soft brown eyes wide open.

We use the crate because denning's another natural dog thing. Some pooches don't like it but Blanche does, savoring her space the way a kid enjoys a tree house. But we don't lock it and when I said, "Hey, gorgeous," she yawned and smiled, nudged the grate open with her nose, and padded out. Rubbing her knobby head against my leg, she told me about her day, an oration of grunts, beeps, and snuffles.

When she finished, I said, "Sounds like you had more fun than I did," refilled her water bowl, gave her a liver snap that she mouthed daintily, and brewed a half pot of coffee. My cup filled, we headed for my office.

She lay at my feet as I called Younger Peter Kramer in Florida. Disconnected number. Older, skullcapped Peter in Maryland answered in a hoarse, husky voice. "Kray-mer."

Fudging my qualifications, I asked if he'd ever worked in L.A.

"Why do you want to know?"

"It's related to a case, here. A property manager with your name worked in Westwood—"

"I don't know any Westwood," he said. "Police? I take care of buildings in Baltimore, near the race course."

"Pimlico."

"You been there."

I lied, "Long time ago."

"It's the same dump, things happen, try to get cops to show up. California? Haven't been out there in twenty years. Good luck."

I ran another Peter Kramer search using **real estate management, building supervisor, dormitory, dorm,** and **private dorm.**

Nothing.

Back to the name by itself, unlimited. Two and a half million hits.

Logging off, I tried Basia Lopatinski's number at the crypt and lucked out.

She said, "Alex. Something new?"

"We got an I.D. on the wedding victim."

"Good! Who is she?"

I gave her the basics.

"Studio City," she said. "I will put this in the file. Thanks for letting me know."

"Anything on Michael Lotz's tox screen and autopsy?"

"The bloods aren't back, yet, but he shows all the external signs of an opioid O.D. His body's a pin-cushion and he's got all sorts of Nazi-type tattoos. No decision on an autopsy, they're having a sched-uling meeting tomorrow. I'm hoping they'll take my recommendation to cut him open. Why didn't Milo call himself?"

"He's swamped so I volunteered."

"Nice of you," she said. "It's an interesting thing the two of you have. I've heard some other detec-tives are jealous."

"And others have nothing good to say about it."

She laughed. "So you know. Okay, check back with me by the end of tomorrow on the autopsy. Maybe the tox will also be back."

"One more thing. I was wondering if you could

look up an old case. Suicide a couple of years ago in Westwood. A student at the U. named Cassandra Booker."

A pen scratched. "What would you like to know about her?"

"Cause of death."

"This has something to do with Ms. DaCosta?"

"Same address as the building where Lotz worked."

"Hold on." A series of keyboard clicks. "Heroin and fentanyl, but a lot more fentanyl than DaCosta. Without an immediate shpritz of naloxone, this would've been rapidly fatal. It's listed as undetermined not suicide. We do that for the family's sake when an accidental O.D. is a reasonable possibility."

Maxine Driver had heard differently. School gossip?

I said, "Any psychiatric data in the file?"

"Let me see . . . no, sorry."

"Any way to ask the pathologist?"

"That was Doctor . . . Fawzi. He's not with us anymore, somewhere in the Mideast, no idea where, and there's no guarantee he'd remember."

"Where did she die?"

"Says . . . in her room on her bed," said Lopatinski. "Not the bathroom like DaCosta if that's what you're getting at. That, the dosage, no garrote, I have to say I'm seeing more discrepancies than similarities, Alex. To either Ms. DaCosta or

Mr. Lotz—no needle marks on Ms. Booker, new or old."

"She snorted."

"A lot of kids do it that way. They don't like pain but aren't afraid of long-term consequences. That's the definition of youth, right, Alex?"

I returned to the Peter Kramer search, using **Los Angeles** as a limiter. Still well over a hundred possibilities. Of those, only a handful of commercial sites included phone numbers, a good portion of which were inoperative or linked to clickbait or other nonsense. That's the internet: an ocean of quantity, droplets of quality.

The Kramers I was able to reach were baffled by my questions; a few grew irritated.

What could Bob Pena's assistant tell me, anyway? The facts of Cassy Booker's death were sad but non-probative. The poor kid had died alone on a bed in a private dorm, the victim of the same cocktail that had created a national scourge.

Fentanyl, cheap, fast acting, turbocharged, and snortable, was **the** current rock star of brain poisons, and people of Cassy Booker's age were a prime audience. Combine that with the discrepancies Basia Lopatinski had noted and there wasn't much to work with.

Except.

Suzanne had been murdered at the wedding of Amanda Burdette's brother and Cassy had lived in the same complex as Amanda and been part of the same academic program as Amanda. The girls were close in age, physically similar.

The few leads we had pointed to Suzanne's murder as a contract killing at the hands of Michael Lotz. But when it came to his own violent appetites, did Michael Lotz go for a whole other type of victim?

Had Amanda been pegged as a victim, only to be saved by Lotz's inadvertent overdose? Turning it another way, had **Suzanne** been slaughtered because of a relationship with Amanda?

The Brain.

A mean-spirited, antisocial young woman colluding with the addict in the basement to get rid of an inconvenience?

I tossed that around for a while, decided I had nothing to offer Milo that couldn't wait until morning.

But he couldn't.

CHAPTER
28

At nine thirty p.m., I'd just picked up my old Martin and was settling down to play. Robin was showering. While shopping for groceries, she'd gotten an away-from-the-office reply from Sharon Isbin at Juilliard.

Blanche sat at my feet, waiting for her favorite fingerpick, "Windy and Warm." When I placed the guitar back in its case and reached for the phone, she let out a deep sigh.

I consoled her with a neck rub and clicked on. "Working late?"

Milo said, "Time is an abstract concept." Lightness in his voice. "The bad news is I can't find any info on Suzanne DaCosta and her license is only half a year old, so I'm thinking it might be an alias. To balance that out, two big good things: First, I spotted Lotz in one of the wedding photos,

I'll show you when we get together. Second, just heard from Homeland. Garrett B. hadn't been to Europe. Until today. Not Poland, Italy. He and La Bambina took an Alitalia flight that landed in Rome this morning. Sleepy tried getting their whereabouts from Italian immigration, don't ask. I'm having Moe, Sean, and Alicia call every goddamn hotel in the city."

I said, "Accelerated schedule on the honeymoon."

"Right after we talk to him about Poland. Funny thing 'bout that, huh? And during that period Lotz dies. You talk to Basia, yet?"

"She'll know more about the autopsy after a meeting tomorrow. Lotz's bloods aren't back but the signs of an O.D. are obvious, including lots of track marks. He's also got what sound like prison tattoos. My big thing is Cassy Booker died of a heroin-fentanyl overdose. Not suicide, undetermined. Basia says without a no-alternative suicide, they do that for the family."

"I know," he said. "Either way, Alex, it's not murder, just a college kid O.D.'ing on the poison du jour."

I said, "True, but Amanda and Cassie being enrolled in the same program and living in the same complex bugs me."

"Garrett and little sis are both involved in very bad stuff? Sure, why not? Get me word from Maxine that the girls actually hung out, Amanda goes on the radar. Meanwhile, it's her suddenly rabbiting brother who interests me."

"Anything come up on him?"

A beat. "I was afraid you'd ask that. If you must know, he appears annoyingly spotless. Eagle Scout, high school salutatorian, graduated with honors from UC Irvine, got hired by the numbers-crunchers he still works for. I'm gonna drop in at his folks' place tomorrow, see if we can pry something out of them. Maybe also get a look at Pa Walton's barn where the animal dope is stored."

"Calabasas," I said. "Back to the Valley."

"That appears to be my current karma. I'm figuring let the traffic fade, we leave around nine. This time I'll drive."

We. Assuming I'd never turn down the opportunity.

Ace detective.

CHAPTER
29

In L.A., twenty miles from city center can take you to a world apart.

Calabasas, spilling into the Santa Monica Mountains on the western edge of the San Fernando Valley, used to be a low-key pocket of rustic, horsey serenity. That's been altered by an influx of retired athletes and celebrities who've achieved fame for merely existing, along with the metastatic palaces they erect and businesses that cater to self-love and shallow notoriety.

A few of the old-timers gripe. But real estate prices have skyrocketed and the heirs of ranchers, fruit farmers, and horse breeders are often thrilled to trade acreage for passive wealth.

On a good day, Calabasas is a half-hour drive from my house, and this was a great day. Traffic on the 101 was sparse and rage-free, the air warm and dry and redolent of old wood and new grass, the blue of the sky so brilliant it verged on unlikely.

Surrounding the freeway, russet and olive rolling hills aimed skyward, gilded by splashes of egg-yolk sunlight.

Milo had picked me up five to nine, mumbling something that might've been "Good morning," and handing me a photograph.

The same crowd shot near the bar where we'd spotted Suzanne DaCosta in her red dress. Lots of small heads. Milo had used a black grease pencil to circle one of them.

A man standing to her right, a few feet behind. Nondescript, Caucasian, middle-aged, clean-shaven, wearing a dark suit, white shirt, and dark tie.

Mr. Blend-In. A face you'd never notice unless you knew who you were looking for.

The same went for the trajectory of Michael Lotz's droopy eyes. Objectively, it was impossible to peg him as watching his victim. But given what he'd done, impossible to think otherwise.

Milo said, "That clinches it, as if it needed clinching," gunned the unmarked's engine, and raced toward my gate. I clicked it open just in time for him to speed through. As we sped north on the Glen, I studied the photo some more then put it aside.

A woman, unmindful.

Prey. Predator.

◆

Twenty-eight minutes later, we were exiting the freeway at Los Virgenes Road and driving through a swath of luxury car dealerships, upscale coffee bars and restaurants, plastic surgery practices, day spas, faux-western-wear boutiques, and realtors peddling gated enclaves. Also fast-food joints and gas stations; everyone needs quick fuel from time to time.

It took several miles of climbing the southern foothills to get past that.

First came clumps of the type of house you get near the freeway. Then the terrain unfolded and began to breathe and we were coursing past pastures and soft hills studded with ranch houses, outbuildings, and corrals.

Milo said, "No pumpkins in sight."

I knew what he was talking about. "So much for the Halloween trade."

Some people believe Calabasas was named to commemorate a two-hundred-year-old accidental dumping of squash seeds from a Basque farmer's horse cart. Others are convinced the name honors a Chumash Indian word describing the flight plan of geese. No one really knows the truth but like most California controversies, that doesn't inhibit strong opinions and the shaming of dissidence.

Currently, squash was winning out.

We rode a ribbon of two-lane highway into the mountains for another quarter hour before reaching the Wagon Lane address of Sandra and Wilbur Burdette.

Easy to spot because a sign on a post featured their name over large reflective numbers. No house visible, just a copse of California oaks and a sinuous dusty drive.

The oaks, gnarled and evergreen, are survivors adapted to drought that predate anyone's settlement by millennia. During the boom days of West Valley development, entire groves were destroyed without a blink. Nowadays, master planners transplant the trees to golf courses.

Milo said, "Here goes," and turned onto the snaky road. The curves kept his speed low. A second sign twenty feet in proclaimed: **Wilbur A. Burdette, DVM. Ride-ins Welcome.**

I said, "No gate. Friendly folk."

Milo said, "At least for the next couple of minutes."

Four twists of asphalt later we arrived at a flat pad housing three burgundy clapboard structures, an empty corral, and a smaller fenced-in area holding miniature goats and sheep. More oaks to the left, fencing a grove of olive and citrus trees in full fruit. The tail end of the drive was lined with yucca, aloe, and ground-hugging thatches of creeping bougainvillea.

All of that backed by two or three acres of tall grass followed by pink and gray granite mountainside.

The front structure was a one-story house. To the right stood a cabin of the same style and composition. Abutting the corral and the pen was the largest building, low-pitched and windowless. Bringing a knowing smile to Milo's glare-ravaged face.

The barn.

I said, "You're looking like a narc."

"Whatever it takes."

He rolled toward a carport created by screwing together steel pipes, covered by white canvas, and housing a white Ford F-150 pickup, a coffee-colored Mercedes diesel station wagon, and a white Toyota Supra.

I kept up with Milo's eager lope. A rubber welcome mat said **Welcome!!!!**

Another staked sign to the left of the door: **For patient calls, please ring in at Dr. Burdette's office right behind the house.**

The cabin.

Milo said, "I've been called beastly but let's start with being human."

His bell-ring caused a dog to bark. Then another. Then, a canine chorus.

From within came a whooshing noise. Paws scratching the other side of the door, an opera of howls, growls, yips.

A woman called out, "Quiet, guys!"

Immediate silence.

The same voice said, "It's open, come in."

Milo turned the knob and we faced a convocation of dogs self-arranged in height order, like schoolkids in a class photo.

In front, two unalike brown terrier mixes looked up at us wide-eyed, quivering and breathing hard, fighting the desire to express themselves vocally. Behind them stood a slightly larger, curly-coated, bluish-gray poodlish thing with world-weary eyes and a huge drooping tongue. Occupying the next tier was what looked like a purebred white greyhound with a missing ear that did nothing to diminish its aristocratic air and a colossal black, white, and tan bearish creation with some Newfoundland in it, panting.

Sandra Burdette stood behind the largest dog, her hand resting on its withers.

She said, "Excellent listening, guys. Now you get **treats**."

The dogs turned in unison, precise as an honor guard, and faced her. She lowered the hand. They sat. She said, "You are **so** good," and, beginning with the terriers, now nearly apoplectic from immobility, offered each eager mouth something bone-shaped and green.

"Enjoy!"

Treats in-jaw, the party dispersed without a glance at us, revealing all of Sandra Burdette.

She wore a pink gingham western shirt with pearl snaps, untucked over baggy jeans. Face scrubbed and sunburned at the edges, gray hair tied up loosely, a bag of green treats in one hand, dish towel in the other.

While dealing with the dogs, she hadn't paid much attention to us. Now she did and her eyes narrowed.

Milo said, "Lieutenant Sturgis—"

"Yes, I remember. How could I forget? This **is** a surprise. I left the door open because I'm expecting a FedEx with some horse meds for Will. This evening he'll be tending to a pregnant mare in Santa Paula."

Milo said, "Is Dr. Burdette here now?"

Head shake. "Ojai. Amiatina donkeys. What did you need to talk to him about?"

"Just following up, ma'am. Happy to talk to you."

"To me? About what?"

"We just learned the identity of the victim."

"Oh. It took this long?"

"Her name's Suzanne DaCosta. Sometimes she went by Kimbee."

Blank face.

Milo said, "So you don't know her."

"Me? I didn't know anyone at the wedding except for our few friends. Have you talked to the other side?"

"Everyone's being contacted," said Milo. Artful dodge. "We actually wanted to speak to the newly-weds because she's closer in age to them but apparently they've decided to take an early honeymoon."

"Yes, they have." Sandy Burdette squinted. "I'm confused. Hasn't this already been covered? When you spoke to all of us and no one knew her?"

"We always follow up, Mrs. Burdette. Things can slip people's minds. May we come in?"

"I suppose so—sorry, you've driven all the way, sure. I've got a fresh pot of coffee."

The house was open and spacious, with honey-colored, tongue-and-groove pine walls and a peaked open-beam ceiling of the same wood. Meticulous maintenance, everything aligned at precise angles. Despite the dog battalion, now out of sight, and three cats that seemed to materialize out of nowhere before padding off, not a trace of animal odor.

My eyes traveled to the rear beyond a knotty-pine kitchen, where glass sliders offered a view of a second pen enclosed on all sides with chicken wire.

An enormous tortoise had all that space to itself.

I said, "Glenn."

Sandra Burdette said, "You remember." Genuinely pleased.

I said, "We saw the goats and the sheep coming in. Where's the blind heifer?"

The smile vanished. "Unfortunately Candace left us four days ago, a sudden internal bleed. She was never a healthy girl—not just the eyes, her limbs weren't as strong as they should've been. Will feels terrible. There was nothing he could do but he hates losing anyone."

She motioned us toward the center of the living room.

Given the setting and Sandra Burdette's clothing, you'd be forgiven expecting a western motif, but the Burdettes had opted for French Provincial: stiff brocade chairs, curvy silk couches, gilt-edged case goods, crystal vases stuffed with silk flowers.

On the walls, lots of family photos, amateur quality, including two blond boys who'd been excluded from the wedding.

The remaining space was taken up by photographs of a smiling Wilbur Burdette posing with ribbon-winning farm animals and their owners. A hand-stitched sampler read: **THANKS DR. WILL. THE NEWBERRY PARK 4-H CLUB.**

Sandra said, "Make yourselves comfortable."

Not easy with the hard-pack furniture but we faked it and she headed for the kitchen, returning with a black lacquer tray. Thermal pitcher, three mugs, milk and sugar.

"How do you take your coffee?"

Milo said, "Black's fine."

I said, "Same here."

"Tough guys, huh?" Sandra Burdette smiled and turned younger. Mischievous eyes hinted at the apple-cheeked, robust girl she'd once been. She whitened her coffee and dropped in two sugar cubes.

Milo smiled back. "This is great coffee, ma'am."

"Learned from the best. My dad was a short-order cook in Omaha. Worked double shifts so I could go to college. I studied nursing—human, not critters—worked as an army RN before I met Will."

We nodded and drank and pretended this was a social visit.

Milo was the first to speak. "Please excuse the question but has anything else come to mind?"

"About the horror?—that's how I think of it. No, not a single thing. To be honest, I'm trying to forget."

She set her mug down. "My assumption's been if it has to do with anyone, and I'm not saying it does, it's their side."

"Is there something about them that makes you say that?"

"Logic," she said. "I know it's not **our** side, so who does that leave?" Looking away. "They're different from us. A little more **colorful**."

I said, "Did it surprise you that Garrett went for someone colorful?"

She blinked. "I suppose it did. But with kids you get used to things. You'd better or you'll always be losing sleep and beating yourself up. Will and I have always been about independence. Respecting the kids' individuality."

"Makes sense."

"It makes **perfect** sense," she said. "Trust me, it's the only way." Her eyelids lowered. "Kids are a challenge."

I said, "We didn't get a good feel for Amanda."

"In what way?"

"She didn't want to talk to us."

"My Amanda." Long sigh. "She's over-the-top smart, always was. I suppose with that comes . . .

some quirks. She marches to her own drummer and sometimes I'm not sure what the beat is. Garrett and Marilee are more conventional, the two of them were always close. Amanda's considerably younger. They were always nice to her but I think she felt like an outsider." A beat. "Amanda's always been a bit of a nonconformist but I wouldn't have it any other way."

I said, "A real individual."

"As real as it gets."

As she'd talked, I'd studied the family photos. Not close enough to see details but a pattern: Amanda standing a foot or so apart.

Sandra Burdette said, "Anyway, that poor girl. I don't know her from Adam."

"Her name's Suzanne DaCosta."

Head shake.

Milo got up and handed her the picture.

She winced. "She is—was—a pretty thing. You're sure she's not one of Brears's friends?"

Milo took the snap and sat back down. "Doesn't seem to be."

"Then I don't know what to tell you. And in answer to your question, yes, I was surprised when Garrett chose Brearely. But she's been good for Garrett. Brought him out."

I said, "He's shy?"

"He was **super** shy as a kid, then he got more social, had friends. He's never going to be a party type. He's studious, earnest. Finds satisfaction in doing things well and that requires time and hard work. Now that he's settled in a fantastic career, it won't hurt him to be with a girl like Brearely."

Trying to sound convinced.

I said, "Getting him out in the world, like the trip to Rome."

"Yes, exactly."

"Is this Garrett's first time abroad?"

Milo shot me a sidelong smile. **Smooooth.**

Sandy Burdette said, "If you don't count Canada or Mexico. Back when we took family vacations, we went to Lake Louise once and Puerto Vallarta once. Then everyone got serious about school and work and we just stayed here and had barbecues."

"No European trips for you and Dr. Burdette?"

"Not our thing, that probably makes me sound like a hick. I know it's beautiful over there, the history, the culture. I'm looking forward to seeing the kids' pictures when they get back. But with Will's schedule and, besides, there's so much of America to see . . ."

I said, "When we spoke to Garrett and Brearely they talked about an island honeymoon in a few months."

"They surprised us, too. All of a sudden we get a text from the airport from Brearely—I'm sure the whole thing was her idea, Garrett's not one for impulsiveness. But like I said, that's not bad, right?"

Milo said, "Right." Time for his mug to lower. "Mrs. Burdette, this may sound strange but do you know anyone who's been to Poland?"

"Poland? Why in the world?"

Trying to sound surprised but not quite getting there. Her eyes slid to the left. Locked. Two brief inhalations, then a return trip. Avoiding looking at us. The knuckles around her mug handle were smooth and pale.

Milo said, "Our job, we have to ask all kinds of questions." **Including one you've just answered.**

"Poland?" said Sandra Burdette. "The girl was Polish? What was her name—DaCosta? That doesn't sound Polish."

"I wish I could say more, ma'am."

"**None** of us have ever been to Poland, Lieutenant. The only ones who've been to Europe, period, are Marilee and Stu. They went to Portugal on their honeymoon but only because they could combine it with a summer fellowship at the Lisbon school of medicine. But Poland? Never."

Too long an oration. Her face had flushed.

"Okay, thanks, ma'am."

Sandra stood. "Is there anything else? I do have some chores."

"Love to look at that tortoise, you don't see those too often."

She frowned. "Sorry, no-can-do. Glenn's endangered and just getting over a virus. The state brought him to Will for treatment and when Will got him better, they gave us a special permit to keep him. We don't let people get close to him."

"Aha. Well, good for you."

Automotive rumbling followed by the thump of a vehicle door shutting drew everyone's attention to the front door. Moments later, Will Burdette, clad in a western shirt that matched his wife's, khaki cargo pants, and dusty cowboy boots, stepped in and set down a hard case with a Red Cross sticker on the side while looking at us quizzically.

Pushing white hair off his forehead, he pulled out a Wash'n Dri, wiped his hands, rolled up the wipe, pocketed it. "I figured that Chevy for a cop car. What's up, guys?"

Before we could answer, a loud drum paradiddle rocked the floor and the dog horde thundered in, swamping him. His grin was instantaneous and broad as he patted and mussed fur, rubbed behind ears, allowed himself to be licked. "They okay for T-R-E-A-T-S, sweetheart?"

Sandra said, "Already gave them Greenies."

"Well," said Will, "a few of the organic jerkies shouldn't hurt."

"You're spoiling them, honey."

"Someone has to." Out of a pocket came a plastic bag stocked with small brown strips. Just as his wife had, Will Burdette gave the sit command before administering canapés to each animal.

"Be off and enjoy, my friends." A hand waved and the celebrants raced away.

Milo and I had gotten up to shake Will Burdette's hand. Huge mitts with the texture of seasoned hardwood.

I said, "Impressive training."

Will Burdette said, "Sandy's got the knack. So, what's the story?"

Sandra said, "They're following up. About Poland, of all things."

"Poland?" Eye-tennis between the two of them.

Will squinted. "That's kind of out of the blue. What's the relevance?"

"Can't get into it right now, Doctor. It's just something we're asking everyone."

"Okay. Well, my answer is, it's a country in East Europe, used to be communist."

Another grin but none of the warmth he'd shown the dogs.

Sandra said, "They wanted to know if we've ever been there."

Will laughed. "Our descent's English and Scots-Irish, if I'd go anywhere it'd be the UK. Poland? Heh. That's a little eastern for our taste. Although I have taken care of Malopolskis. That's a horse with Polish and Arabian mixed lineage, gorgeous things. Had a client in Camarillo years ago, she kept a couple. Great temperament, really sweet eyes. But that's about it Polish-wise."

Another protracted speech.

Sandra said, "There's some coffee left, hon."

Will said, "Sure," and took a couple of steps forward. Rolling gait worthy of a cinema cowboy.

As his wife headed for the kitchen, she said, "How're the donkeys, Will?"

"For the most part thriving, one's a little smaller than I'd like but supplements should help."

"They come from Italy, caught colds on the trip over. Will got them better."

He said, "They got themselves better, I just guided the process. Tough little buggers."

Milo and I sat back down. Will Burdette cocked a shaggy eyebrow and remained on his feet. Finally, he placed himself on an absurdly small rococo chair, fingered a pearl snap on his shirt, and man-spread.

Milo said, "As I told Mrs. Burdette, we have identified the victim. Suzanne DaCosta."

Will shook his head. "Doesn't ring a bell. Did you ask the other side?"

"We're asking everyone."

"What's it been, week and a half? Took a while."

"That's the way it sometimes goes, Doctor. In addition to updating you, we came here to see if either of you knew her."

"Then I guess you came for nothing. Sorry, guys."

Sandra returned with a significantly larger mug—beer-stein-plus—and handed it to her husband. Shifting behind him, the way she'd done with the dogs, she placed her hands on his shoulders. "Three cubes, hon. These guys take it black."

"Do they? Tougher than me." Will smiled, sipped. "Delish, sweetheart. So, is there anything else?"

Milo crossed his legs. **I'm in no hurry to leave.**

The movement brought Will's eyes to his own widely splayed limbs. Like an architect's compass contracting, he put his knees together, placed his boots square on the floor, pitched forward, squinting and setting his jaw. **I'd prefer you get the hell out of here.**

Not much coffee left in Milo's cup but he nursed it, letting the silence congeal.

Will Burdette said, "Don't want to rude, guys, but I've got a load of paperwork."

Milo said, "Just a few more questions, Doctor. I'm sorry if this offends you but in tough cases we need to be thorough. Do you use fentanyl in your practice?"

Sandra's eyes widened.

Will's tightened. "You bet I do. It can be very effective with animals. You guys ever read Herriot?"

I said, "The Yorkshire vet."

"You've read him?"

I shook my head.

Will Burdette said, "Great writer, I started off wanting to do human medicine, his books changed my mind. He's got a thing in one of them about sick animals he thought were terminal being revived just by relaxing them and controlling their pain. You deal with the pain and it stops this self-destructive cycle that leads them to give up."

I said, "Stress reduction. Giving the body a rest."

"The body **and** the soul because let me tell you, guys, animals have souls. I know fentanyl gets a bad rap because the Chinese are cranking it out and pushing it over here and people have weak wills so they're dying all over the place. But animals don't get addicted, they just get better. So if I can save a sheep or a cow with fentanyl or any other drug, I'm going to use it. I'm assuming you're asking me because fentanyl had something to do with that poor girl's death."

"It may be a factor."

"I'll take that as a yes," said Will Burdette. "So you're wondering if this country vet took dope from his own heavily documented supply of controlled substances and it somehow ended up in a stranger who crashed his son's wedding. No offense, but that's some fantasy."

"Unbelievable," said Sandy, kneading her husband's shoulders.

He said, "Mmm, feels good."

Milo said, "Like I said, tough questions, Doctor. If you don't mind, we'd like to know who has access to your controlled substances and could you please show us where you keep them?"

"I don't have to show you, right?" said Will. "You'd need a search warrant or something along those lines."

"We sure would."

"The Constitution, Lieutenant. It's a wonderful thing." He stood, handed his coffee to his wife, and said, "C'mon, nothing to hide. But let's make it snappy."

CHAPTER
30

Sandra remained in the house as we followed Will outside. Next to the unmarked was another Ford pickup, blue with an extended cab, big mag wheels, and a sign on the door advertising his practice.

He veered toward the small pen, where the goats and sheep clamored to greet him. Petting and nuzzling, he laughed and said, "Catch you later, kids, pun intended," and continued to the mini-me cabin.

Up close it was a solidly built little structure, the red clapboard smooth and freshly painted, a sliding white barn door in perfect plumb and secured with a dead bolt and a beefy brass padlock.

"This secure enough for you?" Pulling out a big chromium key ring, he used one key to spring the lock, another to release the bolt. Then he slid the door to the right, reached in and flipped a light switch, and stood aside.

"After you."

The interior was larger than Suzanne DaCosta's garage but not by much, white-walled with a drop ceiling and a black linoleum floor.

No office equipment, just tools for the art of healing animals.

The largest fixture was a steel-topped examining table with a green, triangular base. Growing up in the Midwest, I'd seen a lot of that green: John Deere tractors. Protruding from the base was a steel tilt level and a red foot pedal. At the head of the table stood a surgical lamp; off to the side were two forbidding metal chairs.

The facing walls housed unoccupied wire kennels. The wall perpendicular to the cages was a white metal floor-to-ceiling cabinet with side-by-side doors each sporting a Red Cross decal.

Another pair of locks. Medecos; serious hardware. Will Burdette rotated his key ring and opened them.

Inside were metal shelves holding bottles and boxes neatly stacked and arranged. Rubber gloves, IV setups, disposable surgical tools, syringes of varying size, pills, powders, liquids.

He drew out a box at the top of the pile and another sitting next to it.

"This one's fentanyl patches and this is the liquid we use for infusions. There are also inhalers available—that's what screws up a lot of human addicts, too easy to get high. But I've found them tough to use on horses and cows."

Replacing the boxes, he brought out two others. "These are my other narcotics. Hydromorphone and good old morphine. Fentanyl's a whole bunch stronger and if it gets into your skin you can get sick or even worse. But it works fast, so if you're careful it can be a wonder drug for an acutely ill animal. Not that I use a lot. If euthanasia's called for, I over-tranquilize them. It's safer, easier, more humane. All these agents are for serious pain. Don't imagine you've ever seen a two-ton bull brought to its knees by agony."

Milo said, "Fortunately not, Doctor."

"The bigger they are, the more pathetic it is. Gets you right here." Will Burdette grabbed a handful of shirt above his belt buckle. "**Your** clients are already out of their misery. I see more than my share of suffering and I do what I can to eliminate or allevi-ate it. In terms of who has access to this cabinet, you're looking at him. Now you're going to ask me is there a spare set of keys and the answer is yes. In the house. So theoretically Sandra could get hold of it and steal dope. You know those dope-fiend wives."

He slapped his thigh and laughed.

Milo said, "Sorry—"

"Forget it. Like you said, you need to ask."

Keeping his voice low and smiling. Both lent him an air of menace.

Milo said, "No offense, Doctor."

"None taken, Lieutenant. You're doing your job. If everyone did theirs, we'd have a better country. Anything else?"

"No, sir."

Back outside, he stopped to play some more with the goats and sheep. "They're as human-friendly as dogs. The goats especially. These are dwarf Nubians. My grandsons love 'em."

I said, "Nice setup."

"To me it's Eden. I came here from Nebraska because a group in Canoga Park offered me a job. But it didn't work out, so I tried to go it alone and started with a fair share of small-animal work. Then the city folk moved in with their dogs and cats so there was too much competition. Top of that, I like the big critters and don't mind making house calls. So I concentrated on building that up. I still occasionally get a small patient. Mostly calls from neighbors and shelters. Had a seventy-pound pit bull couple of weeks ago, rose thorn in its paw, terrific animal."

For all his wanting to get rid of us, another long response to a brief question. People get like that when they're nervous.

We said our goodbyes and got into the unmarked. Morning was departing, some cloud cover was drifting in, cooling the air.

But as we drove away, the sweat on Will Burdette's forehead beaded like glycerine.

◆

Once we were off the property, Milo said, "You feel like I do?"

I said, "The Poland thing got to both of them."

"Both of them gabbing—see that flop sweat on him? The way she cued him in before we had a chance to speak? They're hiding **something**."

"And trying to direct us to the Rapfogels."

"No love lost. Sounds like the start of a great marriage."

My cell beeped. Robin. I switched to speaker.

She said, "Hi, sweetie. Sharon's touring but took the time to call back, how's that for a gracious virtuosa? She didn't think giving out the information would be a problem seeing as we're talking about a murder victim so she texted the head of dance and just got back to me. Your Ms. DaCosta has never attended Juilliard under that name or anything close to it. They did have a ballet teacher, pretty famous, Madame Beatrice Da Costa. The dance head wondered if someone was using her name—like a wannabe composer claiming to be a Mozart."

"How long ago was Madame at the school?"

"She arrived in 1952, a year after the dance division was established. She was already old and died five years later. So if she's some kind of a relative, there are multiple generations in between. My bet is Suzanne was just pretending, poor thing."

"Okay, thanks for taking the time, hon."

"If not for you, who?"

I told her I loved her and clicked off.

Milo said, "Hmph," and headed back toward the freeway. Speeding up the way he often does when his head knots up with question marks.

As we neared the on-ramp, he said, "So I've got a phantom who reinvented herself aka just plain lied. Which explains why I haven't been able to trace her before she got the driver's license. Meaning the goddamn I.D. could be useless along with everything she told her roommates, the Valkyrie, and the bouncers."

The heel of his hand pounded the steering wheel hard enough to make it hum. His other hand ran over his face, like washing without water.

"One step forward," he said. "A hundred thousand backward."

I waited awhile before saying, "Maybe we should concentrate on what we do know—rework it."

"What, she liked to read?"

"She liked to read academic material. Hunkered down in a corner of the library by herself. In that regard, we're not talking pretension, she had serious intellectual aspirations. If she wasn't enrolled at some sort of college, she may have planned to be. And that brings us right back to the brainy lover."

"Going to school to impress him."

"Not the kind of thing you make up randomly. My bet is he's real. Another thing that's stuck with me: that body shaper. Again, why would a woman with an ideal build bother with that?"

"This is L.A., Alex. Twenty-year-olds get Botox."

"Maybe so. But it could also be something she did for him."

"The Brain has a thing for tight undergarments?"

"The Brain has a thing for control. If he played up her flaws, he'd gain more upper hand. Or it's just a bondage fetish. Which is also about control."

"Keeping her tight and unavailable."

"Easier if you're dealing with someone socially and intellectually beneath you. Her wearing the shaper to the wedding says she expected him to be there."

"Which brings **me** back to Garrett, who sure **was** there. It's starting to add up, Alex: Guy cuts out right after we talk to him about the Land of Pierogi and his parents get squirrelly about the same topic. Baby probably thinks she's turned him into a spontaneous, lovey-dovey swain. Talk about 'that's amore.' "

"True love," I said. "Of himself."

He phoned Moe Reed. Nothing on his end about the newlyweds' hotel accommodations; same for Sean and Alicia.

Milo said, "Keep trying," and clicked off. He put his weight on the accelerator.

At Reseda, I said, "I'm thinking to call Basia again."

"About what?"

I told him.

He said, "You really see a connection?"

"Depends on what she tells me."

Lopatinski was at her desk. "Hello, I was just about to call you—Milo, actually."

"He's right here, driving."

"Hi, Milo."

"Basia."

"There will be an autopsy on Mr. Lotz within the next few days but I don't expect it to reveal much. His bloods likely tell the story: heroin plus fentanyl **plus** diazepam. A lot of diazepam."

I said, "A Valium appetizer followed by an opioid entrée? Or everything mixed together?"

"No way to tell, Alex."

"Was there enough Valium to put him under before the hot-shot?"

"You're wondering if it's the same process as DaCosta: Immobilize then strike."

"Exactly."

"Unfortunately, with a long-term addict it's hard to say what does what. They build up tolerances, the brain changes, they can handle dosages that would kill you and me. All I can tell you is the three drugs combined were far more than needed to stop his heart."

Milo said, "Ever see a mixture like that before?"

"I have seen accidental overdoses in polydrug users but not a premixed cocktail. None of the other pathologists around here have seen it, either. I believe it makes homicide likely. For an addict, adding a tranq to a fix would be a needless expense and distraction. One more thing: Mr. Lotz's insides haven't been explored yet but his outsides do tell a story. Eight tattoos, six of them conforming to samples in our prison-gang photo file. Two are typical of the Scottish Clansters, they're active in southern Ohio and Kentucky. Four are your basic neo-Nazi garbage."

"Nasty stuff."

"A good candidate for someone looking to hire out for a nasty job."

I thought: **living beneath all those students.**

Milo said, "What about the other two tattoos?"

"**Mother** in a heart with an arrow through it and a cartoon wolf."

"The world of fine art."

"I prefer Monet. Anything that I should know from **you**?"

Milo said, "Not yet."

I said, "Did you have time to check Cassandra Booker's file?"

"Not yet but it's unlikely anything in the autopsy's going to add clarity."

"I'm not interested in her organs, just what she was wearing when she came in."

I told her why.

She said, "Something a psychologist would think of . . . I'll take a look and text you."

◆

Five minutes later, I was reading her message aloud to Milo.

"Pale-blue cotton dress, size six, Miss Bluebell label; blue-and-green-checked sneakers, size seven and a half, Vans; white cotton panties, size S, Young and Free label."

The best saved for last. Basia's sense of drama:

"White mid-thigh tights, size S, Tone-Upp label."

I looked up the company. One product: "invisible body shapers."

Milo didn't respond.

I said, "Not impressed?"

"**Unpleasantly** impressed, life just got more complicated. If my damn head explodes, duck."

Dealing with my best friend can be like doing therapy. What you don't say matters more than what you do so I kept my mouth shut.

We'd just merged onto the 405 South before he spoke again, droning at a low volume.

"The kid's from Iowa. So what, I talk to the parents? It's telephonic, talk about hampering my charm. Even if I **could** fly out there and meet them face-to-face, what the hell would I **say**? The daughter who destroyed your lives by ending hers— **accidentally**—was maybe spurred on to shoot herself up, or better yet **murdered** by some power-hungry psychopath who'd already had his way with her and convinced her to wear Lycra? Not that I know this for a fact or have anything resembling evidence in that regard, Mr. and Mrs Booker. It's just one of those **detective** feelings. So I thought I'd **share**."

I said nothing.

He said, "You're the shrink. Can it be done with greater sensitivity?"

"Not that I can see."

"So I just stash this morsel away."

I said, "I'd look for a link between Suzanne and Cassy."

"A habitually lying stripper and a nineteen-year-old Iowa girl? Only link I can see is The Brain somehow knew both of them and right now, he's arm in arm with his honey sucking on a cone of gelato."

"I'll keep trying with Maxine, see if she can learn more about the DIY program, even confirm a relationship between Cassy and Amanda. You were talking about surveilling Amanda. Maybe now would be a good time."

"Maybe," he said. "Definitely."

CHAPTER
31

He stopped in front of my house, keeping the engine running. "Gonna set up the watch schedule for tonight, maybe I'll get lucky and catch Mandy doing something bad. Have a nice rest-of-the-day."

Before I could answer, he'd sped away.

Robin's Post-it was stuck to the inside of the front door. Out delivering a Baroque lute to a rock musician in Pacific Palisades who didn't play Baroque music or the lute. ("Took Blanchie. I need intelligent conversation.")

I went to my office and tried Maxine Driver again.

She said, "You **are** persistent. I was just about to text you, good, this saves my fingernails. Unfortunately, I don't have much to report. I made all the calls I could think of without arousing suspicion. Got a general sense that no one wants to talk about the program."

"The suicide?"

"I was told it just didn't work, kids dropped out. What I did manage to pry out is that it wasn't a touchie-feelie group thing. No meetings of all the kids, just individual mentoring when requested."

I said, "When requested. Sounds like a loose setup."

"That was the point, another do-your-own-thing. That's the way it is nowadays, Alex. Too much structure's a no-no because if you offend the little bastards they slime you on Yelp, you might as well be a sushi bar or a shoe store. You'd expect administration to back up the faculty. You'd be wrong. They read the ratings and get all antsy about fewer applications leading to a lower rating in U.S. News leading to Academic Armageddon."

I said, "Toddlers running the nursery."

"Except toddlers are cute. Or so I've heard."

"Who mentored these tots?"

"Outside advisors."

"Not regular faculty?"

"Nope."

"Academics from other colleges?"

"No idea, Alex. For all I know they used volunteer alumni. The program only lasted two quarters, which in postmodern, ADHD college terms means it never happened."

I said, "Poor you, Maxine. Short attention spans must be tough for a historian."

"It's death on wheels. I mention Darfur I get blank looks. I talk about socialism and the little darlings think it means a lot of likes on Facebook and Instagram."

"Thanks, Maxine."

"Wish there was something to thank me for. Any progress at your end?"

"We got a victim I.D. but it could be false. Suzanne DaCosta. Please tell me she sat in your class next to Amanda."

She laughed. "Want me to see if she was ever enrolled here?"

"If you could."

"Easy-peasy," she said. "Compared with all that CIA attitude I get when I ask about that stupid program."

I phoned Robin.

She said, "On the way home, sitting on Sunset near the Archer School. Two blocked lanes, guys in orange vests and hard hats standing around near big machines looking way too mellow."

A couple of miles west of the Glen. "ETA?"

"At least half an hour."

I groaned.

She said, "Exactly. I thought I'd cook but now I don't feel like it. Let's go out."

"You bet. Where?"

"Anywhere away from idlers in orange vests."

I checked my notes for direction.

One source I hadn't gotten close to: Peter Kramer, assistant manager of the apartment complex when Cassy Booker had died.

I searched some more, came up empty. Lots of reasons for that. Given the building on Strathmore, one stuck in my head. Unlikely, but . . .

I looked at my watch. Unfair to Basia?

Then again, if she was still in the office, she was working.

She answered, sounded tired. "I'm on my way out, Alex."

"Sorry. Forget it."

"Very clever, making me curious. What?"

"I was wondering if you could look up one more name to see if he ever checked into your hotel."

"Hotel," she said, laughing. "Morbid. I like that. Who's the potential guest?"

"Peter Kramer. To be relevant, his death would have to occur no later than two years ago, February."

"After the Booker girl died. You think he's connected to her?"

"Probably not but he worked at her building and disappeared shortly after she died."

"Hold on."

Click click click.

Her breath caught.

"Oh, Alex. The body of a man by that name came to us on March seventh. He was found in an alley off East Fourth Street."

"Skid Row."

"Right in the center of Skid Row. Would you care to guess COD?"

"Heroin with a fentanyl chaser."

"No, just heroin," she said. "We termed it accidental . . . well-nourished Caucasian male, thirty-four years of age . . . et cetera, et cetera, et cetera . . . **this** is interesting: one fresh puncture mark in the right cubital fossa but no sign externally or internally of addiction."

"A virgin?" I said. "A serious shot of heroin alone would do it."

"Based on his blood chemistry, a very serious shot. Twice the estimated lethal dosage."

"Any family contacts listed?"

"Father," said Basia. "Milo needs to officially ask for the infor—oh, forget it. Do you have a pen?"

CHAPTER
32

Paul Kramer, M.D., office on Wilshire Boulevard in Beverly Hills, residence on South Camden Drive in the same city.

Sixty-nine years old, board-certified in orthopedic surgery, M.D. from Tufts, internship and residency at Mass General in Boston.

I texted the information to Milo along with what it meant.

My phone pinged an incoming text. Not his reply, Robin letting me know she was hung up in another clot on the western edge of the U., figure at least another fifteen minutes.

So near, yet . . . Blanche is serene. Good influence on me, I'm deep-breathing.

I answered: **Poor you. Bel-Air tonight? It's still Sunset but later should be okay.**

Let me think. OK, thought: Yum!! Give me forty-five to clean up.

No need but sure.

Shameless flatterer. AKA good relationship.

My phone pinged an incoming call.

Milo said, "Kramer. How'd you find all this out?"

"Bothered Basia. Maxine couldn't tell me much—no evidence of any group meetings—so I tried another avenue."

"God bless you," he said. "This is getting interesting in a bad way."

I said, "Maybe a visit to Dr. Kramer can clarify."

"Let's try for tomorrow. Meanwhile I'm watching Amanda and she's not obliging by doing anything iffy. One short bike ride to get a burger in the Village, then back inside the building. I'm going to wrap it up in another hour and take the chance nothing happens before Alicia's on shift tomorrow morning. What time would you be up for Kramer's dad?"

"Whenever he's available."

"I'll call his home at seven a.m., surgeons are early risers." The sound of chewing intruded on his speech. "Street taco, in case you're curious. Okay, thanks again for being curious and obsessive. Maybe I'll sleep tonight, maybe abject terror will keep me up."

"What are you scared of?"

"That damn building," he said. "Something's obviously going on there. What if we're totally wrong about Garrett and it's some twisted troll we don't know about? Lives quietly in one of those units, gets off on sadistic pharmacology? How the hell am I going to pry **that** out."

I said, "Ergo following Amanda, persisting with Mr. Pena, and trying Dr. Kramer."

"Went to parochial school. Latin doesn't calm me down, just the opposite."

Robin was home ten minutes later. Forty-five minutes of "cleanup" distilled to half that time, the result an hourglass body in a clinging navy dress set off by quiet but strategic jewelry. Auburn curls fluffed and nearly wild, shining, brown almond eyes huge and clear.

Some perfume I'd never smelled before.

I kissed her long and hard. She pressed against me.

"Ooh. **Someone's** got a healthy appetite."

"For food, as well."

"Hah." Taking me by the hand, she led me out of the house and down to the Seville. "Looking forward to a bit of luxe, been a while. And we always get priority parking 'cause the attendants love the car."

"Blast from the past."

"Oh, no, sweetheart. They really **love** it. It says

you're someone who prizes loyalty and takes care of what he adores."

The Bel-Air was redone a few years ago, a smart rehab that managed to hold on to what mattered at the loveliest hotel in L.A. while freshening up. As the attendant who took the Seville whistled and said, "Nice, sir," Robin winked. Maybe he phoned the restaurant because we scored a quiet outdoor booth that looked out to the swan pond.

Great food, great booze, great service.

More important: We turned off our phones and kept them silent.

As we left, Robin hummed sweetly, her arm locked in mine, her heels clacking on the stone pathway.

Dessert was enjoyed at home.

Flopping against the pillow, the color still rising from her sternum to her chin, she said, "There's got to be a better word than **appetite**."

CHAPTER
33

forgot to turn the phone back on and when I remembered the following morning at seven thirty, there were five messages from Milo, all variations on the same theme: Dr. Paul Kramer was expecting us at his house at eight a.m.

I took a quick shower, got dressed, tossed down coffee, toasted a jalapeño bagel, and chewed on it as I drove to Beverly Hills.

The two hundred block of South Camden Drive sits prettily between Wilshire and Olympic. Two-story prewar homes nice enough to evade teardown mania are arrayed along a quiet, sycamore-lined street. Beverly Hills began as a meticulously planned city, and this district was created in the twenties for prosperous merchants and professionals. If Paul Kramer, M.D., had bought his cream-colored

Spanish in the seventies, he'd paid around a hundred grand for a fifth-acre lot now worth four million.

Milo had just pulled up as I parked. He waited and we approached the house. A white Maserati new enough to sport paper plates rested on a brick driveway bordered by white azaleas. The lawn was impossibly emerald, backed by boxwood hedges, birds of paradise, and some sort of lily blossoming butter yellow.

"Morning." We approached the house and he stopped at a low iron gate leading to a courtyard. "Didn't know if you'd make it."

"Dinner last night with Robin. We went for quiet."

"The ultimate privilege. You guys score up some good grub?"

"The Bel-Air."

He let out a low moan. "Too early in the day to weep."

The gate was unlocked, more design element than security. The courtyard was paved with gray gravel and centered by a burbling blue-tiled Moorish fountain. Loggia to the right, carved oak door dead ahead.

Milo said, "Nice place. Nice guy, too, Dr. Kramer. At least on the phone."

"How'd he react to talking about his son?"

"Surprisingly calm. Like it was logical."

We climbed three steps to the door. As he raised a fist to knock, it opened on a white-haired man around eighty.

Small, stooped, smiling but without enthusiasm, he wore a Palm Springs tan, a powder-blue cardigan, a white polo shirt, and navy slacks that matched suede loafers.

"Lieutenant? Paul Kramer."

"Thanks for meeting us, Doctor."

"Of course."

Handshakes all around. I said, "Alex Delaware."

Dr. Paul Kramer squinted. "Why is that name familiar?"

Milo said, "Dr. Delaware's our psychological consultant."

"Is he? Does that have to do with questions about Peter's mental status?"

"No, sir. It has to do with a complex case."

"Complex," said Kramer. "That could mean anything . . . please."

We entered a two-story foyer floored in glossy, red Mexican tile.

Kramer said, "This way," and led us two steps down to a large living room set up with overstuffed couches and weathered Mexican colonial furniture. Grand piano in one corner, hand-plastered walls bare but for two muddy landscapes and two over-sized photographs.

One photo featured Paul Kramer twenty years younger with a blond woman his age, both in formal wear. Next to that, three young, dark-haired late adolescents, sitting shoulder-to-shoulder, beaming.

"Something to drink?"

"No, thanks, Doctor."

"Then, please."

We took the couch he'd indicated and he lowered himself into a red leather chair.

"So," he said, resting a hand on each knee. "What has changed in regard to Peter's death?"

Milo said, "Can't answer that yet, Doctor. We're making initial inquiries."

"Hmm. All right, I won't press. I'm not totally in the dark, Lieutenant. I looked you up. You're a homicide detective. I'm assuming you suspect something nefarious, rather than the accident the coroner said it was."

"We're here to learn more about Peter."

Paul Kramer tugged at his lower lip. "The accidental thing was . . ." Head shake. "I'm happy to tell you about Peter. So you'll know him as more than a victim."

He pointed to the picture of the three young men. "That was taken the day we took our boat to Catalina. On the left is my oldest son, Barton. He's a professor of neurobiology at MIT. On the right is my youngest son, Josh. He's a Harvard MBA who moved to Israel to work in technology. For fun, he joined the Israeli judo team and won a bronze medal at the Olympics."

Brief intake of breath. Paul Kramer rubbed a knuckle with a thumb. "In the middle is Peter. My wife—she died ten years ago—contended he was the handsomest. As a man, I don't pick up on that kind of thing so I'll defer to her judgment."

I said, "Handsome but not a student?"

Paul Kramer turned to me. "Now I know why your name's familiar. When I was in full-time practice I sometimes consulted on pediatric cases due to my specialty—the spine. An orthopod at Western Pediatric asked me to look at a case. A boy with osteogenesis imperfecta, the question was, Would surgery help? I read the chart and came across a psychologist's notes. I was impressed because there was none of the usual jargon and a healthy dose of logical suggestion. You, right?"

I smiled.

Kramer's nutmeg face creased in confusion then relaxed. "Of course, confidentiality. I'll take that as a yes. So now you work for the police."

Milo said, "With the police."

"Ah," said Kramer. "Part-time?

I nodded.

"You're right, Dr. Delaware. Anything academic was painful for Peter. Perhaps we shouldn't have been surprised. His milestones were always considerably slower than his brothers', he never learned to read with ease, and math baffled him. We received the usual diagnoses. Learning disability, ADHD, some nonsense about optometric asynchrony from a quack the school recommended. We tried medication, tutors, special education, nothing worked. In fact—and this is going to sound cruel—Peter was a sweet boy but there was absolutely nothing he was especially good at. So we probably weren't the best family for him."

His eyes moistened as they aimed at the piano. "I once played at concert level, Barton still does. He won a Westinghouse science award as a Harvard-Westlake sophomore. Lenore had a law degree and an MBA, painted wonderfully, produced exquisite bonsai trees, and sewed her own evening wear. Josh taught himself to read at four, was always straight A's, lettered in three sports at Harvard-Westlake, and wrestled at Harvard College."

He threw up his hands. "Life's not fair, right? Not that anyone in the family ever disparaged Peter. He was cherished by all of us. But . . ."

"It was tough for him," I said.

"Painful. He **was** handsome. And charming, girls liked him. But by his junior year at alternative school they were the wrong type of girls. That was his last year of formal education and most of it was spent playing hooky. The school was designed for students with special needs so they would've kept him in no matter what he did. But he refused, said he was sick of feeling retarded. Lenore and I went round and round with him on that and finally gave in on condition that he'd home-study and earn a GED. You can guess how that turned out. He did get a job, I'll grant him that. Construction assistant on a development downtown. One of my friends was the general contractor."

"How did that go?"

Paul Kramer said, "It didn't. A few months in, Peter stopped showing up at work and before we knew it, he'd packed a few things and was gone from here. For over two years, he cut us off, we had no idea where he was living, Lenore cried at night. He didn't come begging for money, I'll give him that. Then one Mother's Day, he showed up wearing a full beard and hair to his shoulders and told us he'd been working on a sportfishing boat in Florida. Assisting the captain, which I took to mean some sort of scut work. Meanwhile, Barton's off researching the brain and Josh is investing and amassing trophies."

I got up and took a closer look at the shot of the brothers.

Hair tousled and windblown, so close in age they could've been triplets. No wattage variation in their perfect smiles.

A knife-blade of gray sea in the background.

Paul Kramer said, "That was a good day. When you're sailing, you don't need a Ph.D. Peter did okay when he was able to pay attention."

I said, "Was the Mother's Day visit a drop-in or did he stay?"

"He stayed. Lenore was thrilled. Even though Peter stayed up in his room, didn't clean up after himself, and we rarely saw him. He'd sleep during the day, go out at night, come home at all hours. Sometimes there'd be money missing from Lenore's purse or my wallet. Friends advised us to use tough love but we didn't want a confrontation."

He dabbed at his eyes and cheeks. "I might've tried getting tough but Lenore had the softest heart in the Western Hemisphere. Plus when Peter felt social, he'd go shopping with her, they'd lunch, have a grand time. I found the situation distressing so I upped my work hours. It put a strain on my relationship with Lenore but we resolved that."

Paul Kramer laughed. "By that I mean Peter and Lenore did their thing and I got used to it. Finally, he left, just shy of his twenty-third birthday. By leaving I mean I paid for an apartment in Hollywood and set up a trust fund that gave him enough money to live on for five years with me controlling the payouts. Lenore was dead-set against it. She'd never admit it but I think part of her enjoyed having Peter as a perpetual child. The apartment was my idea. I subverted her and essentially bribed Peter to get the hell out of here. Lenore figured it out. There were some cold nights."

He shook his head. "She said she forgave me but I'm not sure she ever completely did. I tried to get Peter another construction job but he said he'd do his own thing and ended up working as a busboy in various restaurants. We'd see him spottily, though Lenore and he talked on the phone. Then she developed a brain tumor and our life became a nightmare for the eighteen months she hung on. Bart and Josh flew in as frequently as their situations permitted but Peter was the star. He was at his mother's side continually, totally devoted. That was when I learned to admire him. I saw the goodness in him that I'd been blinded to because I'm a conventional man."

I said, "After your wife's death—"

"I fell apart and paid no attention to any of the boys, least of all Peter. I dated, got married again— we won't discuss that, it lasted five months. Peter was close to his mother, he had to be devastated. But I wasn't there for him and when he told me he was moving back to Florida, I wished him luck."

He leaned forward. "I saw it as one less complication in my life."

"Before he left, were drugs—"

"A factor in his life? Definitely. The ones I know about are marijuana, Ecstasy, quaaludes, cocaine, and alcohol. I know because Peter was open about his drug use. Basically, he'd brag and dare us to do something about it. He knew his mother was a soft touch so he—but that's water under the bridge. And despite all that, Dr. Delaware, I never picked up **anything** to do with heroin. Peter had been terrified of needles since childhood. Even when getting a tattoo became the thing, he said he'd never get one. **Not into pain** was the phrase he used."

Milo said, "Nowadays people snort and smoke heroin."

"So I was told," said Kramer, "by the coroner who did his autopsy."

He looked down, hands knitted and twitching.

"Second worst day of my life, the first was when Lenore was diagnosed. I suppose I went into denial about the heroin aspect, asked the coroner if he'd found any needle marks. He said he hadn't but that didn't prove anything—what you just said, people inhale. I demanded to know if Peter's autopsy revealed any signs of long-term opiate use. I'd done some research, knew the signs: pulmonary hyperplasia, micro-hemorrhages of the brain, inflammatory heart tissue, liver disease. He admitted Peter's body showed none of that. But his interpretation was Peter, being a novice, had snorted far too much. Still, accidental never sat right with me. And now you're here."

I said, "Peter was thirty-four when he died. What do you know about his life between the time he returned to Florida and then?"

"The second time, he was gone for seven years. I'd get emails two, three times a year, mostly when he needed me to wire cash. Which I did, he didn't request much. But we were essentially out of touch."

"Emails from where?"

"Obviously Florida—the Gulf Coast, the fishing thing. Then Texas, he'd gone back to restaurant work in Austin and later the same in San Antonio. Then it was fishing again, back to Florida, he claimed he'd been promoted to first mate or something along those lines. Whatever it was, it didn't last long. He went down to Mexico—Cabo San Lucas. Then Panama and Costa Rica. He asked for money and informed me he was working at a zip-line outfit in some Costa Rican jungle, had discovered he wasn't afraid of heights. How do you respond to something like that? Congratulations, you can hang from a wire? I sent him half of what he requested."

He glanced at the piano, unlaced and fluttered his fingers. "Was I an S.O.B.? Certainly. Widowhood and a disastrous second marriage took it out of me. I wound down my practice, played more golf, tried to get back to music and found I'd lost my flair. I'd visit Barton and his wife in Boston twice a year. Every eighteen months or so I'd endure a sixteen-hour trek and see Josh and his girlfriend in Tel Aviv. I was just back from Israel when Peter showed up here. Unannounced, just like the first time. He was thirty but already had gray hair. He said he needed temporary lodgings so I took him in, we went to dinner, he talked, I listened. Apparently after Costa Rica he'd gone back to Panama City where he'd worked at a hotel. First in the dining room, then the front desk. He said he'd discovered hotel management was his passion and he'd come back to 'develop himself.' He also had a girlfriend he'd met there. A dancer at a club, she'd be arriving soon and they'd be living together, could I advance him on the rent? I gave him enough for six months."

"Generous," said Milo.

"You think so?" said Kramer. "More like go-away

money." His lips folded inward. "I was an S.O.B. in general and a rotten dad, specifically. And then he died. And now you're digging it all up."

I said, "You do know about his last job."

"Assistant manager at some apartment building. It depressed him, he'd hoped for hotel work but his résumé didn't cut it. Was his death somehow connected to that?"

Milo said, "We're curious about the building."

"In what way?"

"There may be things going on there."

"It's a dope den? Westwood Village?" said Kramer. "I guess that's not so far-fetched. Students, the weirdos who hang around students."

"Did Peter talk about that?"

"Not to me, Lieutenant, but I used to attend at the health center, I know what I saw."

I said, "How much contact did you have with Peter when he worked there?"

Kramer ran a hand along the top of neat, white hair. No strands out of place but that didn't stop him from patting. "I wish I could say we grew closer but we didn't. I'm assuming Peter didn't need money because he stopped contacting me. The only reason I found out about his death was he'd listed me in his phone contacts and the coroner's investigator found me."

Milo said, "Do you have that phone, Doctor?"

"No. I told them to dispose of all of Peter's effects.

It was hard enough cleaning out Lenore's closet. I didn't need to go through that again."

I said, "Did you ever meet the girlfriend from Panama?"

"Once. I took them to dinner at Spago and she seemed very pleasant. Far better behaved than Peter, who drank too much wine and got loopy and started talking about his mother. I didn't appreciate hearing Lenore described in a drunk's slurry voice. The girl could tell, she managed to calm Peter down. Nice young lady. Good looking, too. Peter always had a way with the girls."

I pulled out the photo of Suzanne DaCosta.

Paul Kramer said, "Yes, that's her. Are you telling me she was involved in Peter's death?"

Milo said, "Part of what we're dealing with is her murder."

Kramer's eyes popped. "Murder? She was also a junkie? **She's** the one who gave Peter heroin?"

"There's absolutely no evidence of that, Dr. Kramer. Ms. DaCosta is our primary case and she led us to Peter."

The fingers of Kramer's right hand flew to his cheek and drummed the skin lightly. Large fingers for a small man. Expressive, a surgeon's source of grace and authority. "DaCosta? That's not the name I was given."

"Suzanne Kimberlee DaCosta. Sometimes she called herself Kimbee."

"Not to me, she didn't," said Paul Kramer, returning the photo. "I have a good memory for names—most of my age peers don't—and I remember **distinctly** that Peter introduced her as Susan Koster. And **she** said, 'Call me Susie.'"

CHAPTER

34

We left Kramer's house and rode a block before Milo pulled to the curb and began working his mobile computer.

Detective work is like building a suspension bridge: No matter how precise the engineering or elegant the architecture, nothing matters until the last gap is closed.

Armed with Susan Koster's true identity, Milo began piling up facts like a spoiled kid hoarding Christmas gifts.

Within seconds he'd called up Susan Katherine Koster's DMV records: first license at eighteen, two renewals followed by a two-year gap consistent with working in Panama. After that, nothing until she materialized as Suzanne Kimberlee DaCosta.

No paper trail in Nevada. If her story about

working in Vegas was true, she hadn't put down roots in the Silver State.

That was consistent with the type of short-term gig that brought some attractive young women in and out of Vegas. Working in the brothels of Nye and other counties with legalized prostitution would've resulted in some sort of registration. But illegality raises the price of goods and services and if she'd gone for the big bucks in Sin City and had never been arrested, no record.

One consistency on every Susan Koster license, an address on Mentor Place in North Hollywood.

The online map kicked out the image of a boxy green bungalow east of Laurel Canyon and two miles north of Ventura Boulevard.

A hop from the Studio City garage she'd sublet from Serena and Claire.

As Milo continued to type away, I logged onto a pay site I'd used before. PayPalling a few bucks hooked me into thousands of high school yearbooks. Knowing the age and address of my subject sped up the process and within seconds I had a North Hollywood High senior photo, taken twelve years ago.

The same pretty face, a bit fuller and less defined, obscured by bangs that hung to her eyebrows and curtained by long dark hair ironed straight. Her eyes were wary, heavily shadowed, her mouth sour and downturned.

Photo shoot on a bad day or high school hadn't been her thing.

Maybe the second because she'd listed no achievements, academic or athletic, nor any extracurricular interests.

A dancer who'd failed to make the pep squad? Or an outsider who hadn't regarded applying as worthwhile?

That set my mind racing but I kept my thoughts to myself and showed the thumbnail to Milo. He gave the V-sign and returned to his keyboard, pulling up the reverse directory and identifying the occupant of the house on Mentor Place.

Dorothy Maria Koster.

County tax files listed her as the owner and sole occupant and the house as nine hundred thirty-eight square feet sharing a four-thousand-foot lot with two equally petite residences. DMV made her forty-eight years old and served up a thin face topped by a curly blond bob. Blue eyes, five-four, one hundred eighteen pounds, corrective lenses required.

One registered vehicle: a ten-year-old blue Buick LaCrosse.

Impeccable driving record, not a trace of any sort of questionable activity.

Milo said, "Law-abiding citizen. Time to meet Mom and ruin today and every day that follows."

He called the landline listed on the directory, held on for six rings, got a robotic male away-message and left his name, rank, and cell number.

Then he sat back, closed his eyes, rubbed the lids, and rested his head against the seat. "I'll try her again in an hour. What do you suggest, in the meantime?"

I said, "Not a bad time to theorize."

"About?"

"Susan's death."

"Don't make me beg. What?"

"She was with Peter Kramer for a while but he clearly wasn't The Brain."

"Maybe I should be looking into his genius brothers." He opened his eyes and pivoted toward me. "Sad, kid like that in the wrong family."

"Poor fit," I said. "I see it all the time."

"It causes problems all the time?"

"It can be worked with."

He nodded. "My brother Brendan. The rest of us are built like beer kegs with legs. Football, weight lifting, wrestling. Then we get **this** when we turn thirty." Patting the bulge of his gut. "Believe it or not, I'm not the tonnage champ in the family. My brother Mel beats me by at least thirty pounds, my brother Will's six-five, gotta be three fifty minimum. **Brendan,** on the other hand, is not only the smartest, he takes after my mother's side, a bunch of leprechauns. Five-seven, one thirty on a good day. The rest of us could bench-press him and not breathe hard. He became a graphic artist, moved to Pittsburgh, owns his own ad company."

Abrupt laughter, bassoon-pitched, gushed from

between his lips. Someone else might've thought he was smiling. I knew he was remembering.

"Little Brendan was the one everyone suspected was gay. He ended up married to a beauty queen and has five terrific kids."

I said, "Keeps life interesting."

"What does?"

"When order is disrupted."

"Hah. I sure disrupted **my** family. When I finally snuck out of the closet, Dad came close to stroking out . . . so ol' Peter wasn't up to Suzy's intellectual aspirations and she tossed him over for someone who was?"

"That's the bet I'd take. He got replaced **and** eliminated."

"By Susie and The Brain, or just The Brain?"

"Nothing suggests she was violent."

"If she had no beef with Kramer, why would The Brain bother? Didn't sound like he was serious competition."

"Not for the time being," I said.

"The Brain worried she might change her mind and took out death insurance? That's pretty savage."

"Or he's got over-the-top dominance needs and decided to get rid of a complication."

"And then **Susie** became a complication? What, she failed an achievement test? Forgot to put on her body shaper?"

"Or he simply got bored with her," I said. "He was ready to end it but she wasn't, because to her

the relationship was more than romance. It repre-
sented what she thought was a new life. Feeling
smart. That garage doesn't look like full-time lodgings. She probably drifted back and forth between
it and The Brain's place. But then he kicked her out
permanently. She found out he was going to the
wedding and decided to confront him—"

"Or he was part of the wedding party."

"Garrett?" I said. "Fine, either way. She threatened
to show up, he said, No prob, see you there, wear that
sexy red dress, we'll have fun, discuss our issues.
Instead, he sent Mike Lotz to take care of her. A
junkie who **also** ended up replacing Pete Kramer.
That can't be coincidence, Big Guy. Maybe The Brain
had something to do with Lotz being hired."

"What kind of influence would he have?"

"He could be a longtime resident, comfy cozy in
a penthouse, with access to vulnerable students like
Cassy Booker."

Maybe Amanda Burdette; I kept that to myself.

Milo said, "Older guy, gets all intellectual with
younger women, gets into their pants . . . until he
ditches them."

"Easy to see why Lotz had to die. Addicts aren't
known for discretion so once he carried out his mission, he became a liability."

"Or Mr. Cerebral just gets off on killing people."

"They're not separate issues," I said. "View the
world as your solo stage, everyone else becomes a
prop."

He returned to staring at the street. "Goddamn building. That obsequious little bastard Pena still isn't returning calls. Same for the woman he gave me in Columbus—Masio—and everyone else I've tried at Academo. CCTV's rarely a big deal. These people are starting to smell bad."

Turning the ignition key violently, he revved the unmarked's engine. "What to do before I get to death-knock poor Mrs. Koster has just made itself obvious."

"Onward to the wilds of Westwood Village."

"You are quite the brain, yourself."

CHAPTER

35

Staying on the Glen to Wilshire, he headed west, gliding along the Wilshire Corridor, a stretch of wannabe New Yorkish high-rises between Comstock and Westwood Boulevard.

As he entered the Village, he said, "The way you put it before, housecleaning. That's cold, kiddo. You're supposed to be the sensitive guy but you talk about the worst stuff like it's business as usual."

Interesting point. Working with him had probably armored me with a carapace of sorts.

I said, "If you'd prefer, I can dredge up a pout and some tears."

He laughed again, softer, less corrosive, covered the distance to the Strathmore complex far too quickly.

Parking illegally across the street, he said, "You're

getting one more chance to do this politely, Bob," and tried Pena's number. No answer.

I said, "Maybe he's on vacation. Enforced or otherwise."

"Or worse." He groaned and put his palms together. "Merciful God, please don't tell me Bob's also been housecleaned by The Phantom of Westwood."

We got out and headed for Building B. Just as we arrived, the doors opened and two girls emerged.

U. sweatshirts, short-shorts, lace-up boots, long hair swinging in rhythm with spangled smartphones.

"I'll be penniless in New York," said one. Enjoying the notion.

"I'll be penniless in Los Gatos," said her friend, equally buoyant.

They hurried off, laughing. Milo shook his head and reached for the door.

I was closer and caught it.

He muttered, "Reflexes," strode past me, crossed the entry, and beelined to a ground-floor door marked **Manager.**

No resistance from the knob. He stormed in, leaving me to catch the door.

Bob Pena was sitting at an ugly woodite-and-chrome desk, eating a sandwich. As Milo charged toward him, his eyes bugged.

"Bon appétit, Bob. Don't choke. Yet."

Pena put down the sandwich and gaped. Home-made meal resting on a bed of waxed paper: bologna on white, sliced carrots, potato chips, plastic-wrapped cheese saltines, a cluster of green grapes. Can of Fresca to wash it down, the top not yet popped.

"I—how'd you—"

"Get in here? Obviously your security leaves much to be desired. Why haven't you returned my calls, Bob?"

Pena shrank back. Atop the desk was a black-bound ledger, a copy of **Sports Illustrated**, and a standing calendar in a cheap turquoise plastic frame. Soft-focus photo of Academo's home office in Columbus, a columned heap of colonial bricks fit for a mortuary.

Milo said, "That was a real question. Bob."

"I—I—I had nothing to tell you."

Milo cracked his knuckles and settled a haunch on a corner of Pena's desk. Brushing aside the ledger and the magazine, he studied Pena the way a snake examines a mouse. Pena scooted his chair backward but there wasn't much by way of escape space before he collided with a metal file cabinet.

Milo said, "I'm genuinely puzzled, Bob. CCTV footage comes up all the time when we're working cases and everyone we ask is happy to help."

Pena looked at his lap. "I'd like to help."

"But?"

"The decision isn't mine."

"The company has a problem cooperating with law enforcement."

"I gave you the name of someone—"

"Yeah, yeah, Sandra Masio. Problem is, she doesn't answer my calls, either. No one at Academo does."

"I'm sorry," said Pena, sounding as if he meant it.

"I mean it's not a controversial thing. Bob. All we want to know is did the late Mike Lotz leave the building on a certain day. We're talking a dead junkie janitor. I can't imagine why the company would give a shit."

Pena's arms stretched forward, hands braced along the edge of the desk. His cheek muscles twitched and one eye sagged.

Milo inched closer and drew himself up. Beer keg with legs tilting forward, about to topple.

Pena's knuckles blanched. "I'm really sorry."

"A junkie janitor. So it makes us wonder. Maybe someone else is being protected."

Pena blinked.

"Is that it, Bob? Someone who lives here? A VIP tenant—smart guy, a professor type?"

Three more blinks. Frantic head shake. "I don't know about that."

"You're sure?"

"I don't know anything about what you're talking about. I just do my job." Pena's voice had weakened. Trying to muster indignation and failing pathetically.

I pointed to the ledger. "Does that list all the tenants?"

"No, no, expenses." Wheeling forward, Pena flipped the book open, showed us columns of numbers. "For taxes."

I eased the ledger out of his hand and turned other pages. Itemized costs, no names.

Milo said, "Okay, show us the book that does list the tenants."

"Can't do that," said Pena.

"Can't or won't?"

"Can't. Company policy. If it was up to me, honest, I'd—"

"What's the big secret?"

"Privacy," said Pena. "It's what sets us apart."

"From?"

"Regular dorms. You got to understand the situation."

"Educate us."

"We've got rich folk wanting something different for their brat—their kids."

I said, "Nowadays, brats don't care much about privacy."

"Not them, who cares about them?" said Pena, volume rising, sparked by an upsurge of confidence. Quoting policy does that for some people. "It's the parents. They're paying the bills, they want their babies protected."

Milo said, "Then maybe they should find out that people seem to like this place for dying."

Pena made a gagging noise. "That's . . . not true."

"No? Cassy Booker, Lotz—and, oh yeah, your old buddy Peter Kramer."

Pena's mouth dropped open. "What?"

"Kramer's dead."

"**What?**" Pena's right hand began clawing behind his ear.

"You didn't know?"

"Why the heck would I **know**?"

"He worked for you, then all of a sudden he's not here."

Pena shook his head violently. "What I **know** is one day he didn't show up. I called him, he didn't call me back. I figured another flake, it's L.A. He was always a little spacey."

I said, "How so?"

"Spacey, you know—spaced out. I'd ask him to do something, sometimes he'd hear me, sometimes he wouldn't. He wasn't any great shakes—don't want to bad-mouth him if he's dead but it wasn't a big loss. What happened to him?"

Milo said, "He stopped living, Bob."

"I mean—was it . . . **bad**?"

"Haven't heard of too many fun deaths, lately."

"Oh, God." Pena slumped, shook his head.

"So," said Milo. "How 'bout that CCTV footage?"

"I told you, it's not here. Goes directly to the company."

"Kind of a screwy system, Bob. What if you have an incident here—armed terrorists shoot the place up, serial killer goes from room to room and cannibalizes brats—hell, what if North Korea drops a bomb on your roof? You'd want to look at footage pretty quickly, no?"

Silence.

"Bob?"

Pena's response floated above whisper-level. "That happened, I'd ask the company."

"Well," said Milo, "any of that ever happens, I hope Sandra or whoever does a better job than they're doing now. And you know what, we're going to take the burden of decision off your shoulders, Bob. With all the people dying here, getting a court order to search your tenant rolls will be a snap."

He patted Pena's shoulder with terrifying gentleness. "One other thing. Bob. If I suspect you've concealed or monkeyed with those rolls before I get access to them, I'll have you cuffed, booked, and sitting in a cell faster than you can say **obstruction of justice.**"

Pena's shoulders sagged. "Okay."

"Okay, what?"

"Do what you gotta do." Smiling wanly, Pena picked up his sandwich. Held it out. "Want it? Lost my appetite."

"Tsk," said Milo.

"Do what you gotta do," Pena repeated. "Free country."

◆

We returned to the unmarked where Milo put his cell on speaker and speed-dialed Assistant D.A. John Nguyen.

Nguyen listened to the specifics. "So the company's either hiding something or they're just bureaucratic assholes. Unfortunately, either way, you've got no grounds to pry their cold, dead fingers from their corporate info."

"C'mon, John."

"Being a shithead isn't a crime, Milo. If it was, both state legislatures and the governor would be eating jail food." Nguyen laughed. "Which is a cool fantasy, no? You can try getting paper from one of your sap judges but don't hope for much. Problem is, you're not dealing with a specific suspect. This is a civil matter, judges don't want to wade in that septic tank."

"I'm gonna go for it."

"It's your time and effort. Don't call me up and bitch, 'cause I'm gonna say—"

"I told you so."

"Toi da noi voi anh roi."

"What's that?"

"I told you so in Vietnamese."

"Sounds nicer."

"Not when my mother says it—tell you what I'll do. I'll check out this company, see if they've got any local liabilities—not just a few people croaking on dope. The kind of civil stuff certain judges will take on."

"Such as?"

"High rate of tenant complaints, poor maintenance, rent gouging, lax payment of property taxes and utilities, failure to comply with inspections. Something serious comes up, leveraging a bit of stupid footage shouldn't be a problem."

"Thanks, John. How do you say it in Vietnamese?"

"No idea, Mom never thanks me." Nguyen laughed. "Oh, yeah. **Kam ung.**"

CHAPTER
36

Phone back in pocket, Milo consulted his Timex. "Still early. Not that I've accomplished anything. You up for another try with Susie's mom or should I drop you at home?"

I said, "I'm free."

He said, "If that's a statement of spiritual and emotional well-being, I find it offensively smug."

We were back in the Valley half an hour later. Focusing the online map revealed Mentor Place as a twig in a bramble of side streets. Milo GPS'd and followed the directions of a sultry female robot. Three brief twists off Laurel followed by two equally stunted straightaways and a surprise right turn finally got us there.

The kind of place where GPS made a difference:

a stunted, two-block afterthought, narrower than any other in the neighborhood.

Probably a converted back alley from the Valley's postwar boom, when ranches and citrus groves buckled before an influx of sun-seekers, G.I.'s at loose ends, industrious optimists, and self-inventors of varying morality. A human tsunami, flooding the region with hope and recklessness and avarice, every inch of loam up for bid.

The houses lining Mentor Place fit the notion of barrel-bottom: old, small, undistinguished, and from the frequent cracks and skewing, structurally iffy.

The street merited even more than L.A.'s usual level of municipal neglect. The road was puckered and potholed, curbs had crumbled, fissured side-walks shrugged upward where burrowing tree roots had triumphed. The trees were a random assortment placed at irregular intervals and in need of grooming. Some of them—carobs and jacarandas and orchids—had dropped blossoms and branches and pollen that collected in heaps of unexploited mulch. A few were dead and listed ominously.

The house where Susie Koster had lived as a teen was still green—one tone lighter than lime—and scraped yellow in spots. As promised by the assessor, the squat box shared an unfenced lot with three identical bungalows, two painted white, one daring to be mauve. A few geraniums ran along the front of one of the white houses. Otherwise, the entire property was flat brown dirt backed by twenty dense feet of eugenia hedge.

Decades ago, a parasite had killed off acres of estate-concealing eugenia on the Westside, the pests hopping from mansion to mansion. Maybe isolation and neglect had its advantages.

No cars in any of the driveways. Working people.

Milo looked at his watch again. "No way I want to leave her a note, might as well kill some time."

He spent the next forty minutes judge-shopping. No one was willing to give him access to the Strathmore resident files. Several normally cooperative jurists expressed doubts he'd proven the occurrence of any crime.

I ignored his grumbling and used the time to pull up a custody report due in a week. Reading and re-reading my findings, then creating a separate file for the revisions I needed to make. I was nearly done when Milo said, "Action."

Two cars had driven onto the property, a mini-convoy of sorts. The first, a squat black Fiat 500, rolled up in front of the mauve house. A young blue-haired woman in all-black spandex got out, arms filled by three squirrel-sized black Chihuahuas. Black Goth lips parted as she smiled and waved at the driver of the second car.

Blue Buick LaCrosse, freshly waxed but some of the paint had surrendered to age and sunlight. Dorothy Koster gave Chihuahua Girl a return wave and a warm smile. Both of them unaware of our presence across the street.

Susan Koster's mother wore a pink-and-white waitress uniform and white flats and clutched a bag of groceries. She said something pleasant sounding to her neighbor.

The younger woman laughed and let loose the dogs. They scampered up to Dorothy, who knelt, put down her bag, and was ready when one of the tiny pooches jumped into her arms. Full-on mouth kiss. Same for the other two.

I thought of Will Burdette's canine battalion. Blanche, always happy to see me.

Milo said, "Enjoy these few minutes, Dorothy."

All three dogs continued to dance around the woman in pink. After a few moments she threw back her head in laughter and wiggled her fingers and the trio raced back to their owner.

Milo sighed. "Let's give her a chance to get settled."

And then we'll unsettle her.

Five minutes later, he was letting a pitted brass knocker fall on a catch plate.

Within seconds, Dorothy Koster had opened the door. Still in her uniform, **Dotty** embroidered above the right breast pocket.

Smiling, but surprise killed that. "Yes?"

Milo introduced himself.

She said, "Police? What's going on?"

Milo said, "Ma'am, I'm sorry—"

Dorothy Koster didn't need a reply. "Susie?" She gasped and swayed and her head began lolling from side to side.

Milo said, "Ma'am—"

Dorothy's eyes rolled back in her head. Then her knees gave way.

We both shot forward but I got there first and caught her around the waist. Small-boned woman, limp as week-old salad. "Ms. Koster?"

Out cold.

Turning cold.

I got her inside, propped her in a tweedy recliner, checked her pulse and her pupils.

Milo said, "She's breathing."

"Steadily," I said. "Probably a vasovagal faint."

"Jesus."

"Water will help."

Four of his long strides took him across a diminutive living room overly furnished with more tweed pieces and white-painted rococo tables. He stepped into a minimal kitchen, filled a glass from the tap, and studied the bag of groceries. Folded neatly on the counter, its contents arranged precisely. Fresh produce, cans of soup, bread.

"Here we go." He handed me the glass. I patted Dorothy Koster's cheek lightly, uttered her name a couple of times, wet my fingertip with water and ran it over her lips.

Nothing happened for a few seconds, then she purred, eyes fluttering. Opening. Pupils constricting as they gazed up at a ceiling light, then dilating as she lowered her attention to me.

"Huh?"

"You fainted, Ms. Koster."

She continued to study me, puzzled.

"How about some water?" I held the glass to her lips but she rejected the offer, sharply turning her head to the side.

I said, "Take your time."

She whirled back to me. Stared up, tight-eyed and tight-lipped.

"Uh," she said. Her arms straightened as her hands slapped flat against my chest. She shoved. Not much force to it but I retreated and let her sit by herself.

She continued to stare at me, then her eyes rotated to Milo. Her groceries. Back to Milo. Crumpling like crepe, she sat back.

"Susie."

We said nothing.

Dorothy Koster looked at me. "Sorry . . . did I hurt you?"

"Not at all."

"Really sorry . . . I'll take that water."

Two glasses and a wad of tissues later, she was ready to talk. Like most people in her situation, she craved details. As he always does at the beginning, Milo avoided specifics and parceled out the basics. Managing to make them sound like much more.

Some people see through that and press. Dorothy Koster seemed satisfied.

"Again, so sorry for your loss, ma'am."

"My poor baby girl." Hands covered her face. "Oh, God, I can't believe this is happening."

More time; more tissues. She balled them in one hand. Grimaced. "When you came to the door, I **knew** it."

Milo said, "Why's that, ma'am?"

"Because I lead a boring life, Lieutenant. Boring is safe, I like boring, everything goes along just fine." Deep breath. "So it had to be something to do with Susie. She's always been . . . she's a wonderful girl, the biggest heart, smart—a lot smarter than she realized . . . but . . ."

She shook her head.

I said, "She wasn't into boring."

"Not by a mile. So I knew, I just knew. If there's going to be a . . . a . . . a shakeup, it's going to come from Susie . . . at a wedding? Of someone she didn't know? That's crazy."

Milo said, "We're still trying to make sense of it."

"You have no idea who did it?"

"Not yet, ma'am. It took a while just to identify Susie. She was using a driver's license listing her as Suzanne DaCosta."

"That's a new one." Dorothy Koster smiled.

"How exotic. She was always reaching. For what I don't know. Restless. The problem is she didn't want to do the things that might've actually . . . forget that, I am **not** talking bad about my precious precious baby girl."

We let that settle for a while. Milo looked at me.

I said, "The more we know about Susie, the better chance there is of finding out who did it."

Dorothy Koster said, "What kind of things do you think you should know about her?"

"The kind of person she was, who she hung out with."

"She was a **good** person. **Big** heart. Who she hung out with? I have no idea. Even when she lived here I had no idea. And that was a long time ago."

I said, "How long?"

"She left after she graduated high school. So . . . twelve years. She didn't cut me off. I'd get postcards. **I'm here, Mom. Everything's going great.**"

"Postcards from where?"

"Everywhere—up north—San Francisco, Oakland. Even wine country—Napa, Sonoma. Nevada was a big one—Reno, Las Vegas, Tahoe. Once Nashville. Memphis. Then she went out of the country. Mexico, Costa Rica, Panama. She was a dancer. She always supported herself. She danced in shows."

Higher pitch on the last word. Not quite believing her daughter's explanations. Her eyes got steely as she folded her arms across her chest.

Back away from this topic.

I said, "What was she like growing up?"

"Gorgeous," said Dorothy Koster. "Beautiful child right from the start, everyone noticed, everyone said she was stunning. People asked if I was going to put her in pageants. As if I would. Putting a child through **that.** I know about that kind of thing because my mother did it to me and I hated it. That was down south. Louisville." Sigh. "I ran away, too. At the same age—eighteen. I guess history has to repeat itself."

"Does Susie have siblings?"

"No, it was just we two." Her arms tightened across her narrow frame, reaching around to her back. "I could use more water. Must've dehydrated myself, too much coffee at work. I get it free, sometimes I overdo."

Milo filled another glass. She said, "Thanks," took one sip, put it down. Her arms began the journey of folding again. Midway there, she changed her mind and threw them up.

"In answer to your next question, she doesn't have a dad."

We said nothing.

"I mean obviously she **has** one. But she never knew who he was. I knew but I told her I didn't. I don't feel bad about lying, trust me, he was a bad person. I didn't want her going on one of those look-for-your-roots things, you know? She wouldn't have liked what she found. And don't you ask me for a name, either. He doesn't know and I'm sure he couldn't care less."

I said, "Understood."

She frowned. "He would **not** care."

We waited.

"Here's the thing," she finally said, "it was a one-time deal, stupidest mistake I've ever made except for it produced Susie." Her laughter was frightful. "Now there's not even that. So it was just stupid. Like I've lived my life for **nothing.**"

More crying before she looked up, eerily smooth-faced. "Do you think God's punishing me?"

I said, "I'm sure not."

"Then **why** did it happen?"

"I wish we could answer that."

"I wish you could, too," she said. "But you can't, no one but God can . . . I mean I don't think a punishment that big would fit a one-night stand. That would be some kind of God, right? All the rest of the time, I led a good life. Got married legally when Susie was two, he was a nice one, worked at the sausage plant in Vernon. Died ten months later. Work accident, you don't want to know. I got his pension, it wasn't much but I got to buy this place. Susie was too young to realize. After that, I said **enough**, don't rely on men or anyone. I didn't **want** to date. I'm not a spirited person, anyway, don't have a taste for going out. So it was just we two."

One hand gripped the other. "I can't believe this is happening."

I said, "Susie was a beautiful child."

"Beautiful **and** smart. Smarter than she realized," said Dorothy Koster. "Smart enough to figure out her own way of reading. Because the regular way, that phonics thing, wouldn't work for her, the teachers thought she was dumb. She was eight, they kept holding her back, you'd think someone would try to help. They didn't. So she went and did it her own way. Memorizing words. How's that for smart? I mean you have to think and remember all those words? They—the school system called her LD."

"Learning disabled."

"Learning disabled, perceptual issues, special needs, you name it, they're great with labels. Once she taught herself to read she did okay. Except math, math wasn't her thing, period, but so what? You don't need fancy numbers to get through life, if you showed me an algebra book, it would be like reading Egyptian or something and I've made my way just fine."

"Did she have any particular interests?"

"Dance was her thing. She was graceful. When she was little I spent you don't want to know how much on ballet and tap lessons. Then she said she'd be fine on her own, she didn't need all those teachers telling her what to do. Which made sense to me. You're born with that, right? You can't teach a big fat ape to be graceful, right?"

Milo smiled.

Dorothy Koster said, "I swear there were times

she could **float.** Now you're telling me she's gone. It makes no sense."

He said, "When's the last time you heard from Susie?"

"The last time was . . . a while ago. She called me, she was happy. New boyfriend. The boyfriend before that she was happy, too. I said why'd you end that one? She laughed, she'd never really let on about personal stuff. The boyfriend before she found in Panama. If you're going to ask me, don't know his name—just that she said he was smart and good looking and Jewish. I've got nothing against Jewish people, my boss at The Kitchen is Jewish, Andy Streit, treats me well, treats everyone well."

I said, "What else did she tell you about the boyfriend from Panama?"

"Not **from** Panama. She met him **in** Panama, he was American. She was dancing at a hotel, he worked there. He was going to run his own hotel one day."

Milo said, "No name, huh?"

"You think he did it?"

"Not at all, ma'am, just trying to collect information."

"Well," said Dorothy Koster, "she did have a nickname for him. Handsome Hilton. Like the hotel, but he wasn't a real Hilton. It was like she was making fun of him. In a nice way. Susie could get like that. Liking someone but still playing around with them. She teased me. But in a nice way. My name, Dorothy, she was always trying **Wizard of**

Oz jokes. Like I should get a dog named Toto, that kind of thing."

I said, "No problems with Handsome Hilton but she moved on."

"The new one was supposedly brilliant, she called him The Brain. Which reminded me of a science-fiction movie that scared me when I was a girl. This brain, separated from a body, sitting there in a glass jar, bubbling and buzzing."

She shuddered. "Anyway, she said this one had taken her to a new level. Opened her mind to books, theories, stuff she'd never thought about. It made her want to try harder. I said, See, I always said you were smart but me you didn't believe. Usually, when I tried to make a point, she'd change the subject. This time she said, You know, Mom, I think you're right."

Dorothy Koster's face crumpled. "Finally I get some credit, huh?"

I said, "How much schooling did she have?"

"She finished high school, had to repeat a bunch of summers but finally, yeah, they graduated her. I said how about junior college, you've got what it takes. Instead, she left. Just packed her bags while I was at work and left me a note to say she was traveling and **poof**. Maybe if she went to junior college like I said . . . God wouldn't just do that. So I guess there really is the Devil."

◆

Milo asked if she had photos of Susie, anything at all that could be helpful. Her answer spoke volumes.

"I've got photos from when she was little, elementary school. Once she hit junior high, she refused to let me take any."

"Why's that?"

"She said she was ugly, she didn't want a record of it. I said, that's the craziest thing I've ever heard of—oh, yeah, I did sneak one in. When she was at dance class, she was probably fifteen—no, sixteen, hold on."

She stood up, tottering, but avoided my supporting hand. "I'm fine, that was just a weird thing." Walking to the left, she was gone for a few moments, returned with a color snapshot.

Lovely, lithe girl in a pink tutu and white tights. Toe-pointing on pink ballet shoes, arms outstretched gracefully.

I said, "Gorgeous," and meant it.

Milo said, "Really lovely."

"She was, she was," said Dorothy Koster. "Now—when can I come get her, sirs?"

"Soon as you're able, ma'am."

"I've got the money. Harry's pension fills in the gaps. Who do I talk to?"

He gave her his card, one from the coroner's administrative office, and three from mortuaries that work smoothly with the crypt. Some people carry spare change and gum. His pockets are a bit different.

Dorothy Koster said, "Okay, thanks."

"Is there anything you can think of that might help us, ma'am?"

"Nope." She waved his card. "If that changes, I know how to reach you."

She accompanied us to the door. "I won't say nice meeting you, but you did a good job, it's got to be tough."

"Thanks so much, ma'am."

"That's part of it," said Dorothy Koster. "The way you call me ma'am."

CHAPTER
37

As he had following the visit with Paul Kramer, Milo drove a bit and pulled over. "You're thinking what I am, right?"

I said, "Same story as Peter Kramer."

"It's like they were on the same path." He sucked in his breath. "Ended up in the same place."

"By the same hand."

"Like you said, the fucking Brain cleaning house."

"Susie would've been ripe for a Pygmalion thing," I said. "Convinced she was stupid, finally someone tells her different."

"Trips to the library, goddamn textbooks. Not for her sake. He was out to control and manipulate her. Offs her boyfriend, plays with her for a while, she outlives her usefulness, he gets Lotz to drive a spike into her head and choke her out."

"You see Garrett as capable of all that?"

"Because he comes across as a wimp? Why not? If he fooled Susie and maybe the Booker girl, why the hell couldn't he put on an act for us?"

"Kramer and Lotz had a link to the building. The only connection Garrett has is his sister lives there."

"Maybe that's enough. He visits, notices things. Collects people like a serious psychopath."

"You know what I'm going to say."

He waved a big hand. "Anything's possible **but.** What's the but?"

"All we really have on him is that he's bright."

"Plus that look he gave when Poland came up, same for his parents. Plus, the goddamn wedding was **his,** who better to need damage control—hold on."

He reached for a buzzing jacket pocket, removed his phone, went on speaker. "Alicia . . . what's up, kid?"

Bogomil said, "Something to report on Amanda, Loo. Finally she left and went somewhere other than to campus or to get food in the Village. Got on her trusty little bike and pedaled past the Village—sketchily, I might add. She spaces out, doesn't look where she's going, drifts in front of cars. Couple of times she got honked, didn't even react."

"Lost in thought," said Milo.

"Lost in something," said Alicia. "Anyway, this time she kept going east and crossed Hilgard into the residential streets. Then over to Wilshire at Selby where there's a light. She crosses, bikes a couple of blocks west nearly getting pulverized, then turns off at one of the fancy high-rises and rolls down into the sub-lot."

Milo copied the address she recited. "The gate was open?"

"No, there's a call box. She knows the combination. Interesting, no?"

"Very."

"It's a high-end place, Loo, even for the Corridor. Valets out front, working with the level of chrome you'd expect. I considered asking the staff if they knew her but the heap I got from the impound lot and the way I'm dressed they'd probably call the station on me. Plus I wanted to check with you first."

"Good thinking, kid. Let's hold off for the time being. Where are you?"

"Back at my desk. I watched the place for a couple hours but it's tough, no parking on either side of Wilshire and I couldn't exactly slide the heap in with Bentleys and Mercedeses. So I just kept circling and passing. No sight of her since, sorry."

"Nothing to apologize for, getting that address is a big step."

"Hopefully it's not her rich grandma's crib."

"There was no grandma at the wedding."

"Oh, yeah. So maybe it was some kind of tryst. Though it's hard to see her having a thing with the kind of guy who'd live there. Not only is she weird, she's dowdy. Today she rode her bike in this ugly, flimsy gray dress, it's billowing and blowing up like an umbrella, her legs are spread open from here to Arizona and she's totally unaware. If she wasn't wearing a shaper, she'd have given Westwood quite a show."

"A shaper."

"It's a girl thing, Loo. Tights you put on under other clothes, they end above the knees and take care of bulges you don't want to advertise. Not that this one has any bulges. Skinny and straight up and down as a boy. Why'd she wear a shaper? Maybe she's got a twisted body image, maybe it's for biking. Or like I said, she's just weird."

"Maybe," said Milo. "Okay, take the rest of the day off."

"Why?"

"Your watch on her went way past the call, even with the overtime I'm gonna write up. This is good work, I want you rested."

"Really?" said Bogomil. Softer voice. "That's totally nice. Maybe I found my niche."

He hung up, pocketed his phone, stared out the windshield. "Don't say it."

I said, "Say what?" But I knew what he was getting at.

He ticked a finger. "A, unless Garrett has millions no one knows about, he doesn't have a place in a Corridor high-rise. B, he's in Italy so it can't be him

Amanda just went to see. Let alone wearing a body shaper for."

My mind raced, what-ifs tumbling in. I kept silent.

He drummed the dashboard, produced a panatela that he quickly replaced with a chocolate lollipop. "Sugarless, got it at the dentist."

I smiled.

"Hey. I didn't mean no talk for the rest of the day. I wanted a Trappist monk for a buddy, I'd write the ad differently."

That broke me up. When I recovered, I said, "The Corridor's fine for luxury housing but you'd still need somewhere to shop and recreate."

"So?"

"The nearest place for that is the Village. If The Brain spends time there, he'd have ample opportunity to come across the building on Strathmore, maybe meet a vulnerable young female. And/or a vulnerable addict like Lotz. Alternatively, he learned about the building from Susie Koster through her relationship with Peter Kramer."

He kept working on the lollipop, jaw tightening, eyes compressing.

I said, "That doesn't work for you?"

"It works. Go on."

"What makes you think there's more?"

He grinned.

"Okay," I said, "third possibility is that The Brain is rich enough to keep two places—Wilshire for his main crib and Strathmore for finding his prey. Or sticking with the affluence angle, he's familiar with the building because he's got a financial interest in it."

"A honcho at Academo."

"Not necessarily. When outfits like Academo build, they don't put up all of the money, they go to outside investors and syndicates. The Brain being a serious investor would explain Pena getting squirrelly."

He held up a hand in mock self-defense. "I ask for a breeze and get a hurricane. Okay, so we could be looking for an intellectual type with big bucks, maybe with a link to Poland. How about we take a look at Wilshire, we get lucky some prancing Slavic popinjay in a monocle will just happen to strut out to his Rolls."

CHAPTER
38

Traffic back to the city was less obliging. Fifty-three minutes after leaving Dorothy Koster's North Hollywood hideaway, we were coasting the eastbound lanes on Wilshire just past Westwood Boulevard.

A red light at Selby gave us the chance to idle in front of the address given by Alicia. Towering above a copper-roofed porte cochere paved in gray slate was a sharp-edged obelisk clad in pink granite and trimmed with more copper. Glass doors offered a coy hint of crystal chandelier. Twenty-four stories, generous windows offering views to everywhere.

Three maroon-clad valets hustled to accommodate a queue of vehicles. As Bogomil had promised, high-end horsepower: Porsche, Mercedes, Mercedes, Bentley, Range Rover, Mercedes. Every set of wheels black or white.

Milo found a parking spot three blocks north of Wilshire and we headed back to the tower. Not much foot traffic on the Corridor and walking in L.A. can generate suspicion if you don't look like you belong. Milo had on one of his fossilized gray suits, a white wash-'n'-wear shirt, and a skinny brown tie. Respectable enough if you didn't get too close. I'd thrown a blue blazer over a gray polo and jeans, which could mean anything from tourist to movie mogul.

As we neared the building, another white Mercedes pulled in. Moments later, engine hum was drowned out by a roar of anger.

We slowed our stride, ready to spy while looking apathetic.

The choler was coming from a middle-aged woman in total pink Chanel. Including inflated lips. Her target was one of the valets, a thin red-haired kid no older than twenty. The other two valets, older men, stood by as Red weathered the blast, grinding his jaws.

The gist of the rage was Chanel's conviction that "five minutes, thirty-eight seconds, I've been tim-ing," was too long to wait for her car to come up from the sub-lot.

The kid looked at his feet. Chanel's botulin eyes managed to move a smidge. "That's **it**? You have nothing to **say**? You're a fucking **idiot**!"

One of the older valets, beefy and gray-haired, hurried over. "Ma'am, so sorry."

"That's not enough! I want to hear it from **him**! It's **him** I gave my keys." The immobile orbs tugged themselves down to a diamond-bracelet watch. "**Six** minutes, forty-eight seconds!"

The kid hung his head.

"Pea-brain—what, you don't understand English?"

The older man said, "I'll get your car. Jeremy, take a break."

Chanel said, "A break from what? He's not **doing** anything."

"Jeremy." Waving his fingers. "Ma'am, I'm getting your car right now."

"Not the Escalade, the Mercedes."

Jeremy shuffled off, exiting the porte cochere and walking west.

Milo looked at Chanel, stamping her foot and patting blond meringue hair. "Classy."

I said, "She did us a favor."

"How?"

"I'll explain while we walk."

We followed Jeremy's slouch up Wilshire, hanging half a block behind. Nowadays, a lot of people seem incapable of moving their feet without consulting their phones. Jeremy jammed his hands in his pockets and kept up a slow but steady pace.

When he crossed Malcolm Avenue, we closed the gap and Milo said, "Jeremy?"

The kid stopped, turned slowly, head protruding

like that of a turtle inspecting a fly egg. Milo walked up to him, card out. Jeremy scanned but didn't react.

"Lieutenant," he said, sounding amused. Up close, his skin was pallid where buttermilk freckles didn't intrude. Pinkish eyelashes lowered and rose, exposing stolid, hazel eyes. "My dad's checking up on me?"

A smile full of braces.

Milo said, "Your dad?"

"Captain Karl Jacobs."

"Pacific Division."

Jeremy's grin was all-knowing. "What, he thinks I'm screwing up?" Shrug. "Maybe I am. Maybe it's breathing toxic fumes from the cars, like poison in my brain, or something. Still, shouldn't detectives be chasing crime or something?"

I said, "Why would you think you're screwing up?"

"I just got my ass reamed by some rich lady."

"We saw. Not your fault she's a total bitch."

Jeremy's smile withered. "You saw it?" He studied me, unsure how to respond.

Milo said, "We were interested in the building and happened to walk by. Man, you've got a talent for cool. That was me?" He blew out air. "My partner's right. They gave Oscars for bitchdom she goes home with a big, ugly statue."

Jeremy's analysis shifted to him. Hazel eyes sharpened. "Why are you talking to me?"

"Like I said, the building. We saw you and thought you might know stuff that could help us. I'm serious, man. You've got nerves of steel."

Jeremy shrugged, working hard at not being pleased by the compliment. The flush under his ears gave him away. "Yeah, I'm chill. It's like the way my brain works. My dad thinks it means I don't give a rat." Soft titter. "Usually, I don't."

Milo said, "Your dad got you the job at the building?"

Jeremy tweaked a lapel. "You really don't know?"

"We really don't."

"More like forced me to do the job. Now I got to wear this shit." Tweezing a maroon lapel between his fingers and grimacing.

"Why that building?"

"One of the other valets is one of you, retired, used to work for Dad. Dad called Rudy, Rudy fixed it, Dad said I had no choice if I wanted to live at home." Another rueful touch of the lapel.

Milo said, "Rudy's the one who just told you to take a stroll?"

"Yeah. He makes like he's on my side but I think he narcs me to Dad regularly 'cause when I get home Dad has all these questions, it's like he knows what happened. Tonight'll probably be like that. Like it's my fault things jam up and it takes time."

Steady eyes. Every word spoken in an even tone. "Dad didn't send you to narc me some more?"

Milo crossed his heart. "We're West L.A., never met your dad. I mean, I've seen him, it's obvious where you got the hair—"

"Yeah. Gee, thanks, Karl."

"We're totally leveling with you, Jeremy. It's the building that interests us."

"There's criminal shit going on there?"

"Sorry, can't get into details, but if you could answer a couple of questions it would be a huge help."

"Doubt it, I don't know shit," said Jeremy. "I been working there for two months. Part-time."

Milo said, "How part-time?"

"Two days a week."

"What do you do when you're not there?"

"Chill. Play bass with my band." A beat. "Three times a week, I do the counter at Burger King in Venice."

"Pico or Sepulveda?"

"Pico," said Jeremy, smiling. "Sorry, no donuts."

I said, "Sounds like a busy schedule."

"They're forcing me to do shit jobs so I'll quit and go to college."

"Mom and Dad."

"**She** didn't go to college and she became a dispatcher. **He** didn't and he became a captain."

Milo said, "Interested in police work?"

Jeremy stared at him as if he'd disrobed in public.

I said, "Music's your thing."

"I like it." Shrug of narrow shoulders. "I'm not that good."

Milo said, "Practice, practice, practice."

"Huh?"

Milo showed him a picture of Susan Koster. "This girl. Recognize her?"

"Yeah," said Jeremy. "I saw her a few times. Going in but not coming out. Not for a while. She's a hooker?"

"She seemed like a hooker?"

"I dunno. You guys are cops, you don't look for legal stuff." Jeremey studied the picture. "She's super hot, tight red dress showing off this killer bod, big heels. Who's her john?"

I said, "Coming in but not going out?"

"Not during my shift," said Jeremy.

"Day shift?"

"Yeah. You get them during the day."

"Hookers."

"Hookers, girlfriends of rich guys," said Jeremy. "It's the same thing. Pay for play." He studied the traffic on Wilshire. "There is **so** much pussy around but you got to have the ess-cee."

Milo said, "Ess—"

"Spending cash." Orthodonture flashed. Another look at the photo before he returned it with reluctance. "So what'd she do? Rip off some rich dude?"

"No idea who she came to see?"

"How would I know? I'm stuck breathing in gas fumes, rich people throw me their keys or yell at me."

"Is there a front desk inside?"

"Yeah, but there's no one usually there. The management changed, they're not putting any ess-cee out, people are pissed."

"Like the bitch."

"She's always that way," said Jeremy. "Husband produced stupid shit on TV, he kicks it, she gets the dough, thinks she's a queen or something."

Milo said, "Rest of the building like that? Showbiz types?"

"Showbiz." Jeremy's lips formed around the word as if it were a punch line. "I don't know who they are except they're all rich. I know her because she acts like that, Rudy gave me her story." A beat. "She's got a stupid name. **Taffy.**"

I said, "Do you know any of the tenants?"

"Not tenants, you can't call them that, they're owners. Why would I know them."

"They treat you like shit."

"A couple are nice. These two doctors, the Haleys, they're like a hundred years old, get picked up by a chauffeur in an old Rolls."

"Speaking of wheels, what did the girl in the red dress drive?"

"Hmm . . . you know, I never saw her drive anything, she'd just walk past looking hot."

I said, "No taxi drop-off? Uber?"

"Probably," said Jeremy. "Never noticed. Why would I?"

Milo said, "An hour or so ago a girl in a gray dress rode in on a bicycle and rolled into the sub-lot. About your age."

"You say so."

"You didn't see her?"

"Like I said, I'm busy with the cars."

"We thought you might notice a girl on a bicycle. Or just the bicycle parked down in the sub-lot."

"There's no bike down there now," said Jeremy. "She probably took it on the elevator. She a hooker, too?"

Milo smiled. "Would you be willing to help us?"

"Like what?"

"Keep your eyes open for a girl on a bicycle. You see her, this is my number." Handing his card over.

Jeremy pocketed it without reading. "That's it?"

"You see her with someone, that would be even better, Jeremy. But whatever we can get is great."

"Great," said Jeremy. "That's like an alien . . ." His lips moved. "An alien conception. I'm going back. I don't, Rudy'll narc me."

"What's Rudy's last name?"

The kid stiffened. "What, you're going to talk to him about me?"

"Not a chance," said Milo. "We'll maybe eventually talk to him about the building but your name won't come up."

"Yeah, right."

"Scout's honor."

"What's that?"

"An ancient ritual. Rudy . . ."

"Galloway. He used to give traffic tickets. He's a total dick."

We waited until he'd passed under the port cochere before retracing our steps and passing the building a second time. Things had quieted. Only two cars. Rudy and the other valet lolled near a phone-booth-sized structure and smoked cigarettes. Off to the side, Jeremy stood motionless, studying slate.

Milo said, "Twenty-four stories of people with fuck-you money. Try prying info out of the staff."

I said, "One thing in your favor: The residents are owners, not tenants. Meaning they pay property tax and are on the assessor rolls."

He stopped short. "Plug in the address, see who's divvying up to the county . . . there's got to be what, sixty units, seventy units, maybe more . . . cross off Taffy, the old doctors, look for a single guy or one whose wife travels . . . hell, yeah." Slapping my back. "Muchas gracias."

CHAPTER

39

Back at Milo's office, he began researching the pink obelisk.

Completed in 1984, before the city imposed height restrictions. Ninety-four units.

The roster the assessor kicked out made him groan.

Fewer than half the owners were cataloged as individuals; the majority had shielded themselves behind ambiguously named trusts, holding companies, and limited liability corporations.

Milo said, "No one's listed as Homicidal Asshole, aw shucks."

He phoned Binchy and Reed, asked them to keep up the watch on Amanda Burdette, adding the details of the pink tower.

Just as he'd turned away from his computer screen an incoming email caught his attention.

As he read, his lower jaw dropped. Inching closer to the message as if he'd missed something, he rubbed his face. Sat back and pointed.

From: GB2341@cirrusfactor.com
To: MBSturgis@LAPD.org
Topic: Meeting possible?
Lieutenant Sturgis: Brearely and I are leaving Rome and will be back in the US tonight. We'd like to meet with you as soon as possible, even tomorrow. Best, Garrett Burdette

Milo said, "Would 'hell, yeah' be over-eager?"

Hi, Garrett: Sure, no prob. Hope you had a good time. How about 10 a.m., tomorrow my office?

Robin put down her fork.

Dinner had been a surprise greeting, fragrant and just-plated as I got home. Grilled cumin-rubbed lamb chops, hummus, spicy carrots, and tomato-based Turkish salad. She'd cooked the meat. The sides had come from a take-out place in Pico-Robertson, not far from the run-down studio apartment of a ninety-three-year-old Spanish guitarist who could no longer drive and whose fingers failed at restringing his '46 Santos Hernandez.

Robin had been servicing Juan's prize instrument for a long time and considered her visits welfare checks.

I said, "This is delicious. So how's he doing?"

"Such a sweet man, it's sad. While I was working, he tried to show off with some Villa-Lobos on his other guitar, the cheapie. He managed to hit a few good notes that reminded me he was one of the best. But mostly . . ." She shook her head. "Anyway, you can thank him for dinner. I brought him a sandwich from the old deli and noticed a new place nearby. Kosher Tunisian. Smelled great, so I figured why not? What do you think?"

"Terrific. I'll clear and wash."

She smiled. "I'll accept that offer unless Big Guy calls and you need to run out again."

"Nope, the day's over. Maybe tomorrow morning will be interesting."

"The honeymooning couple. Think it's some kind of confession?"

"To multiple murders? Unlikely. Milo's been wondering about Garrett as the high-IQ boyfriend but that's never felt right to me. Yes, he knows something about Poland, but in terms of direct involvement?" I shook my head. "If Amanda's visit to the condo is relevant, it backs that up. Garrett was in Italy so it wasn't him she came to see."

"Hmm," she said, cutting a small piece of lamb and chewing it.

I said, "What?"

"What if she was being sisterly and checking out his place for him while he was away? Watering plants, tidying up."

"Unless he's managed to conceal millions, he doesn't own a unit there. Plus Amanda doesn't come across as the tidying type."

"Your basic sloppy student?"

"I have no idea about her personal habits," I said. "She doesn't come across as other-directed."

"She wouldn't do a favor for her brother?"

"I guess anything's possible."

We ate some more.

She put down her fork. "So what **do** you think he wants, honey?"

"To pass on information he's been withholding about Poland," I said. "In the best of worlds he'll identify The Brain and clarify the link to Skiwski."

"Why step forward now?"

"Conscience? Fear? Who knows?"

Robin smiled. "Am I being annoyingly Socratic?"

"Not at all," I said. "I just don't have answers."

"Hopefully tomorrow will clear it all up."

"As Milo would say—"

"My mouth, God's ears."

"Your mouth, there'd be a good chance." I leaned over and kissed her hard.

"Whoa. I surprise-feed you, you get romantic, huh?"

"What, I'm all gastrointestinal tract?"

"Darling," she said. "You're a prince among men but you **do** have a Y chromosome. Please pass the carrots."

CHAPTER
40

Milo's seven a.m. text asked me to be at his office half an hour before the ten o'clock with Garrett and Brearely Burdette. I arrived at nine fifteen, found him hunched at his keyboard. He waved me to sit, kept typing.

An empty box from a West Hollywood baker and the crumbs that went with it littered his desktop. Ditto for a grease-splotched take-out carton from a pizza joint near the station. A mug filled with cold coffee sat perilously close to the edge. Toss in an unsmoked panatela, smudges under his eyes, black hair worked wild by nervous fingers, sweat stains in the armpits of his shirt, and a tie knot yanked down to mid-belly, and he'd been there for a while.

"Morning," he said. "For what that's worth. Went over the wedding list again, no overlap with the condo list. Doesn't eliminate anything with all those owners shielded by corporate bullshit, so I searched **those** to see if I could find a link to Academo. The geniuses at Google failed me."

He nudged the mug to safety, looked inside, shook his head. "You have breakfast?"

"I'm fine."

"You always are."

"When did you get here?"

"Six thirty but who's keeping tabs?" Wheeling his chair around to face me, he examined his Timex. "Forty minutes, let's strategize."

I said, "Nothing I say is going to teach you anything."

"Try me."

"Don't scare them away."

He nodded. "I called at eight to confirm. Garrett answered and said, 'Of course, sir,' but he did sound like someone with a gun to his head."

"Any indication why he got in touch?"

"Didn't ask. Tell you one thing, he stands me up, I'm going after him big-time. And his parents. They all know something and they're going to give it to me."

I said nothing.

He said, "Fine, I'm posturing. Apart from not freaking them out, what's the strategy?"

"Don't know that the concept's relevant."

"Why not?"

"Too many unknowns."

He rolled his shoulders, then his neck, a great ape chafed by a zoo cage. "I'll ask it this way: What if it was you doing the interviewing?"

Collecting crumbs, he sprinkled them into his wastebasket. Creating a delicate beige rain that he studied with weary but sharp eyes.

I said, "I'd treat it the same as meeting a new patient. Keep things friendly, do very little talking and a lot of listening."

"Psychological warfare."

"That's not exactly how I'd put it—"

"Fine, emotional manipulation. And if he tries to leave, I chain the goddamn door."

He'd returned with a cup of biohazard coffee from the big detective room downstairs when his desk phone rang.

"Really . . . be down in a sec."

Knotting his tie and smoothing his hair, he said, "Ten minutes early, ol' Garrett is eager."

I said, "Maybe you won't need the chain."

We walked up the hall where a couple of inter-view rooms sit.

He opened the door to the first, flipped the **Interview in Progress** switch. "Wait here, no sense overwhelming them with a welcome party." Winking. "Psychological **sensitivity** and all that."

I entered to find that he'd prearranged the furniture for The Soft Approach: table positioned in the center, rather than shoved into a corner to make an interviewee feel trapped. The chairs were also socially configured: three of them placed around three sides.

Like friends dining out, rather than two against one.

No equipment was visible but this room had been retrofitted last year with invisible audio sensors and video cameras. Flip the switch, it's a go.

I'd barely settled when Milo stepped in toting a fourth chair. Following him were Mr. and Mrs. Garrett Burdette.

The newlyweds were both adorned by subtle tans and stylish clothes. For the bride, a white silk blouse with billowing sleeves, black skinny jeans, and red crocodile stiletto pumps. I'd never seen the groom duded up but a few days in Italy had changed that: bright-blue linen shirt, white gabardine slacks, brown basket-weave loafers, no socks. An impressive dark stubble beard sparingly flecked with gray lent Garrett Burdette's face some grit and gravitas. So did black-framed Le Corbusier eyeglasses and a gold pinkie ring set with a tiny carved cameo.

A matching stone three times the size dangled from a gold chain nesting in the hollow of Brearely Burdette's smooth neck. Her lush, dark hair bore lighter tints than at the wedding. The hand not enhanced by a diamond ring led to an arm graced by half a dozen gold bangles.

Milo said, "You guys look great."

Objectively, the two of them did. But they hung

their heads as they shuffled in, gripping each other's hands, waiting passively as Milo arranged four chairs on four sides.

"Sit wherever, Mr. and Mrs. B. Make yourselves comfortable."

The look that passed between the couple said that was impossible, but they cater-cornered from each other and held hands atop the table.

"Coffee? Tea? Coke?"

"No, thanks," said Brearely Burdette. Hoarse voice, low volume. Slight redness around the sclera of her eyes suggested a tough morning. As she stroked the top of her husband's jumpy hand, his Adam's apple took an upward elevator ride before plummeting downward.

"Okay, then." Milo shut the door. As he sat near Garrett, Garrett sucked in his breath and looked at Brearely.

She said, "It's okay, honey. You know what to do."

As if she'd coached him. She probably had.

He blew out enough air to flutter his lips and turn them rubbery. Scratching his stubbly chin, he said, "All right . . . this is something I've been thinking about. I wasn't sure what to do so I waited to see if it would stay on my mind. It did. I told my wife. She convinced me."

"Sweetie-doll," said Brearely, "you would've done it anyway. You know what's right."

She gave his cheek a quick, light peck.

He said, "Thanks, babe—Lieutenant, I probably

should've come forward earlier. I guess I just—all the stress, who goes through something like what we did?"

Brearely nodded.

Milo said, "Unbelievable."

Garrett said, "So we **needed** to get away. Like I told you, a honeymoon now wasn't our original plan, we really were going to wait. But then things . . . piled up. My firm said okay. So."

Shrug.

Milo said, "Italy was good?"

Brearely said, "Amazing." To Garrett: "You chilled, you had time to think, you figured it out, here we are."

"More like you figured it out, babe. You gave me moral clarity."

"No, doll." She squeezed his hand. "I just listened. You knew. You **know**."

Her smile swung around, encompassing three sides of the table. Every man in the room graced with a share.

"I suppose," said Garrett. He pressed his wife's palm to his cheek.

She said, "You opened yourself up." The smile expanded. "And you also found out you've got a great beard. Look at my man's macho pelt, guys. Just a few days."

Milo said, "Impressive."

Garrett gave a mournful look. "Yeah, that's me, Mr. Macho. Sorry, Lieutenant, no sense delaying.

We're here because we might know something. I
might. About what happened. Or maybe not, you
be the judge."

Milo sat back and crossed his legs.

Garrett said, "What we said initially was true.
We don't know her . . . the victim."

"We even went over the invite list," said Brearely.
"Even though we knew she definitely wasn't on.
Then we remembered. Someone who almost was
going to be there. And when you said Poland."
Heaving chest. "Wow."

Garrett said, "We're talking about a friend of my
sister. Amanda, not Marilee. She asked us to add
him to the list. Last minute. It was annoying, a
hassle, we didn't want to do it but Amanda persisted
and got all . . ."

"Obnoxious," said Brearely.

Garrett bit his lip. "Amanda can get like that."

Milo said, "Persistent."

Brearely said, "Obnoxious and pushy. Who **does**
that at the last minute? The table plans took forever
to figure out, we used two separate computer pro-
grams. Then five days before, she comes up with
that?"

Milo said, "A friend of hers."

"Some kind of genius," said Garrett. "She called
him The Brain."

Brearely said, "You're obnoxious, who cares what
your IQ is?"

Milo said, "A friend."

"Or maybe more like a mentor," said Garrett. "An academic type."

I said, "Type?"

"She said she met him at the U., he was brilliant, had done endowed research"—deep inhalation—"in Poland. I said sounds like he's way older than you and she gave me one of her looks."

"The death-ray stink-eye," said Brearely. "We've all been on the receiving end. Especially Garrett, he's so nice to her, she thinks he's a sucker. But he's learning. It's like a learning **curve**."

Kissing Garrett's cheek again. She turned to us. "She's got anger issues, which she showed when we said no way, it's five days. Then his mom said couldn't we do one thing for Amanda, she has no friends." Sigh. "So we said okay and I had to go at the table charts again thinking OMG what the F am I going to do?"

Garrett said, "Amanda's different. Always has been. So when she said there was someone she wanted to invite, a guy, even though it was . . . a little late—I figured maybe she's turned a corner."

"Crazy late," said Brearely, eyes flashing. "A humong-o hassle. But you explained, doll, and what did I say?"

"You said okay, babe."

"I said **sure**. And **then** what happened?"

"Then I went to Amanda and said no problem, give me his name and address—"

Brearely broke in, "He goes to her, I'm working

on the chart, you're not going to believe this, guys, she says, hold on I have to ask him if he wants to come. I mean, think about it, now it's four days, she's made demands, pulled a hissy fit, and she hasn't even **asked** him? Now poor Garrett has to come and tell me, and yes I kind of freak out."

Garrett winced, remembering. "You were great, considering."

Brearely laughed. "I wasn't fine, I lost it. I mean I've been rearranging tables trying to fit some nerd in, he's probably going to come dressed all wrong, and now she's telling Gar we need to hold on? So, yeah, I pulled a monster freak."

Pouting at her husband. "I took it out on **you**, doll. I'm **sorry**."

"No big deal, babe."

"Because you're the sweetest." To us: "You know what it's like. You guys work with pressure. Don't you sometimes just say enough?"

Milo and I nodded.

Brearely turned back to her husband. "I was a total bee-**atch** and you didn't deserve it but water through the bridge." Back to us: "Then it got worse. **Tell** them, doll."

Garrett sighed. "I didn't hear from Amanda so two days before the wedding I texted her and asked what the story was."

"'Cause I was pressuring him," said Brearely. "'Cause my **mom** was pressuring **me**. Tell them what happened then, Gar."

"She didn't answer my text," said Garrett. Abashed, as if divulging a creepy family secret.

"Two days before," said Brearely.

"I tried calling," said Garrett, "got voicemail. Finally, I got hold of her and she made like it wasn't an issue anymore."

"No, no, tell them exactly what she said."

"She said he didn't want to come. The venue was too—it wasn't right for him."

"No, no, no, the exact words, Gar."

Garrett looked down at the table. "He said it sounded crass."

"Crass," said Brearely. "Try to do something a little different and you get ripped apart. He's a crass **ass**!"

Tears filled her eyes. "We wanted it to be special. Instead . . ."

Garrett said, "We made it work. In Rome. That trattoria. All the things we saw."

She sniffled. "Yes, we had a beautiful time. Our life is going to be beautiful forever." Shaking her head, she mouthed, **Crass.**

I said. "The guy sounds like a jerk."

"A jerk and an asshole and an effin' shitty-butt-wipe," said Brearely. "So now I've got to take him **out** of the table arrangement and move people around **again**. Like those Sudoku things Garrett does. One number doesn't fit, it effs up everything else."

Milo said, "You never got a name."

Dual head shakes.

Brearely: "We didn't think much about it. Then you guys came to see us at our apartment and you mentioned the Polish thing and I said, 'Isn't that weird, honey? Same as that guy your crazy bitch sister hassled us about.'"

She squeezed her husband's hand. "Then I saw your face. You got it right away, like you always do with that big brain of yours. You looked so freaked out, I had to give you my best shiatsu back rub."

Batting her lashes. Garrett blushed around his stubble.

Milo said, "Did Amanda give you any other details?"

Garrett said, "No, just what I told you."

I said, "An academic."

"She didn't use that word, I guess I assumed it because she met him at the U. and if he'd done endowed research I figured he had to be someone relatively accomplished. My sense is she was a little awed, which is why she tried to arrange it in the first place."

I said, "How'd she react to his turning her down?"

Garrett said, "She didn't react at all. But that's Amanda. Her . . . she's different."

"I'll say," said Brearely. "We're going nuts on the tables and she doesn't get it. Unbelievable. That girl is **all** about herself."

Garrett winced.

I said, "The Polish thing. Do your parents know?"

Brearely said, "They know because I told them. Her. Sandy. So she'd know what her daughter was putting me through. She wasn't very helpful."

Garrett said, "You know weddings, guys."

I said, "Supposed to be the happiest time, but."

Brearely said, "But some people act like butts, so it's anything but happy."

Garrett said, "What led you to the Poland thing?"

Milo said, "Can't get into it. So you talked to your parents about it."

"I called my mom right before we left for Italy. I figured they should know, in case Amanda was involved in something over her head. **I'm** more concerned about that now because since the wedding she's totally cut herself off from all of us. Not responding to my or my parents' texts or calls. My mom called the apartment where she lives and the manager says she's there, he sees her coming and going on her bike."

Something Bob Pena had chosen to withhold. Cherry tomatoes rolled along Milo's jawline. I began working my phone.

He said, "So that's a big change for Amanda?"

"Not really," said Brearely. "She's never even close to friendly."

Garrett said, "But normally, she would answer my parents. And me. Probably." Sigh. "She's a lot younger. Marilee and I were closer in age, we did things together. Amanda probably felt left out."

Brearely said, "It's not like you didn't try. She was always in her little cocoon."

No argument. Garrett looked ready to cry. "I'm just worried about her. That's why I wanted to come in and tell you everything. The Polish thing. I'm hoping it's nothing. I don't even know what it means to you."

Milo stood. "Thanks for coming in, you did exactly the right thing."

Brearely Burdette beamed. "Told you they'd appreciate it, doll."

Garrett Burdette rocked back and forth. "Great." Sagging with each movement like an inflatable sock-me doll wounded by a pinhole leak.

Milo said, "Anything else?"

Synchronized head shakes. When they rose, her arm looped around his waist and his rested atop her shoulders.

Milo held the door open and they exited, walking in step.

For all their differences and the horror that had marked the onset of their life together, they'd achieved the kind of mutual ease you see in long-term couples.

Out in the hallway, Garrett stopped and bit his lip. "I really am worried about Amanda. The way she's cutting herself off. And if this Polish guy is . . ."

Milo said, "Is what?"

"A bad influence. Trying to dominate her. I mean that could get bad. Right? Could you talk to her?"

Milo said, "We'll find her and have a chat."

"Thanks so much, sir. Thanks a **million**."

"Thanks even a google," said Brearely. "That's like a gazillion. I thought it was just a search engine." Nudging her new husband. "He **taught** me that."

CHAPTER
41

Back in Milo's office, he said, "Who'd you call in there?"

"I texted Maxine. No answer, yet."

"About what?"

"Amanda met The Brain at the U. Maybe so did Cassy Booker. The mentors of the DIY program weren't regular faculty. That could fit if we're talking about a psychopath."

"Why?"

"They're pretentious."

"He's claiming to be a prof but isn't?"

"Unlikely, that would be too easy to disprove. I'm thinking he's an also-ran who took a temp job and puffed up his credentials with impressionable students, maybe snowed them with verbiage—the world of ideas et cetera."

"Amanda and Cassy **and** Susie."

"She'd be especially vulnerable."

"But maybe not a total fake-out?" he said. "The endowed fellowship in Poland."

"Maybe it happened or maybe he was just a tourist in Warsaw who happened to come across Skiwski."

"Total bullshit artist."

"I'm not saying high-level psychopaths can't rise to the top. Look at politics. But this guy aims lower, picking off easy prey. Susie's learning problems made her feel stupid for most of her life. She found common ground with Peter Kramer and probably others like him. Then along comes The Brain. Maybe he watched her on stage and decided to snag her. However it happened, he made her feel bright and soon it's bye-bye Peter and she's bringing textbooks to clubs. In Amanda's case, the vulnerability came from being socially awkward and confronted with a new environment. Don't know enough about Cassy but that newspaper photo made her look timid and unsure."

"So not a professor," he said. "But if you call him one, he neither confirms nor denies."

"I could be wrong and he went all the way and got his Ph.D. More likely, if he began graduate studies, he didn't finish. He lacks the grit and thinks he knows everything anyway. Most important, if he lives in that tower, he's got money and can play armchair intellectual."

"Living on the Corridor," he said. "Psychopaths can also go far in business."

"That they can," I said. "But if he has time to take a gig at the U., he's not working full-time."

"Trust-fund baby."

"Some sort of passive wealth."

My phone pinged.

Maxine texting back: **In San Francisco for a conference. Believe it or not, that may work to your benefit.**

I typed: **Now I'm intrigued. A hint?**

The beauty of serendipity—oops—have to give a boring speech. Get back to you asap.

I showed Milo the texts.

He said, "Serendipity. Something came up by accident?" His fingers drummed his desktop. "Okay, now that we know Amanda's involved, I'm going looking for her. Starting with my own vulnerable prey. Pena, he's a total beta, right?"

We drove to Strathmore, parked near the cemetery, hurried to the complex. Milo stormed up to Building B, kept his finger on the bell.

A male voice said, "Stop pranking or I'll call the cops."

"This **is** the cops. It's Lieutenant Sturgis, Bob. Open up."

"Bob?"

Now it was obvious: deeper voice.

Milo said, "Open the door now. Please."

"This isn't a prank?"

"Come out and see for yourself."

Moments later a tall, athletically built black man wearing a brown polo shirt and khakis strode across the lobby. Younger than Pena—thirty-five or so.

Peering at Milo's badge through the glass, he opened the door.

"Sorry," he said. "I was told to expect pranks."

"By who?" said Milo.

"The management company."

"Academo."

"That's the owner. Management's through a subsidiary, High-Level Incorporated." A hand shot out. "Darius Cutter. How can I help you?"

"You're the new manager?"

"Since yesterday," said Cutter. "Still getting oriented."

"What happened to Bob Pena?"

"If he's the guy before me, what I was told was he quit. Today's my first full shift, haven't gone through any paperwork."

I said, "Mr. Pena made a sudden decision."

"Oh, yeah," said Darius Cutter. "Three days ago I was working at the facility in Sacramento. Human resources emails me to call, they incentivize me to come down here A-sap. So here I am."

Milo said, "When you say 'the facility,' we're talking another Academo setup?"

Cutter nodded. "I went to Sacramento State, got a degree in engineering, got hired by the physical plant on campus—alternative emergency hookups during brownouts, coordinating power feeds.

Couple of years ago, Academo built a place up there—bigger than this one—and made me an offer I couldn't refuse."

I said, "Good employer."

"Competitive salary, good benefits. But I grew up here, my mom lives in Mid-Wilshire, so moving back was fine."

"Good job, good benefits," said Milo. "Wonder why Pena would give that up."

"You'd have to ask him," said Darius Cutter. "Who knows why people do the things they do? Is there something I need to know about?"

"Not really."

"Not **really**? That sounds kind of worrisome."

"Let's leave it at Mr. Pena being a person of interest to us."

"The company never mentioned anything sketchy, just that he quit. Should I be worried about him?"

"Nah," said Milo. "He's a pussycat. Can we get his contact information?"

"If I can find it," said Cutter. "Come on in."

CHAPTER
42

We followed Cutter to the office Pena had occupied. No change to the furniture but the desk was barer. An Adidas athletic bag sat in a corner. Cutter said, "If I have time, I'm going to the Equinox in the Village. That's one thing Sacramento had that this place doesn't, a gym."

He opened a file drawer, rummaged awhile. "Nope . . . nope . . . nope . . . nope nothing." Same results with the next two drawers but the fourth produced a file tabbed **Management Personnel**.

Cutter shuffled, scanned, pulled out a sheet of paper. "Here you go."

Robert Edward Pena's vital stats included his Social Security number, driver's license, a home address in Culver City, a landline, and the cell he hadn't responded to.

Milo copied the info. "Thanks, Mr. Cutter. As

long as you've got that folder, is there anything on Peter Kramer?"

Cutter began shuffling. "Nope . . . nope . . . actually there's nothing in here but Pena. Who's Kramer?"

"Mr. Pena's former assistant."

Cutter frowned. "He had an assistant? They didn't give me one."

Cutter walked us back through the lobby. At the door, I said, "Your tenants are mostly students but you do have some faculty living here."

"That's also the way it was in Sacramento. But not a lot, mostly visiting faculty and some emeriti— old retired profs who wanted a cheap place close to campus. In terms of who's here, I have no idea, yet. Why?"

"Routine questions," said Milo.

"If you say so," said Cutter.

As we walked away, he remained at the entrance to B, arms folded across his chest.

Staring, but not at us. More like gazing out into nothing.

Milo said, "We provoked some thought in him, poor guy. Funny about Pena, huh? We talk to him about Kramer and he gives up his job."

"Or someone made the decision for him," I said. "Like they did for Kramer."

"Jesus. Don't even theorize about that."

A block later: "Let's check out Pena's house. You don't really think he got offed."

I shrugged.

"Don't do that. Not **that** way."

"What way is that?"

"Like I'm a patient and you're trying to nudge me to insight." He rubbed his face. Grunted. "Even though I basically am."

Culver City, west of Overland and south of Culver Boulevard. Well-kept pink bungalow on a quiet block of similar structures all painted in pastels.

Empty driveway, drapes drawn. No mail on the ground but that didn't mean much. The U.S. Postal Service had access to a lidded brass slot to the left of the door.

Milo lifted the lid and peered. "Too dark, can't see. No bad smells, at least not from here."

He checked out the property. On the right side of the house, a waist-high white wooden gate blocked access to the backyard. Locked but easy enough to get over.

He was contemplating his choices when the door to the baby-blue box next door opened and a woman stepped out holding a rolled-up newspaper.

White hair pinned high on her head, seventies, wearing a maroon sweater, mustard-colored slacks and brown boat shoes. Her free hand rested on her hip. Waiting for an explanation.

When none ensued, she said, "Can I help you?"

Milo walked toward her, flashing his badge.

She said, "The police? Bob and Marta? Something happened to them on the road?"

"I certainly hope not, Ms.—"

"Alicia Cervantes. Then why are you here?"

"Bob was involved in a case we're working on."

"Involved how?"

"As a source."

"Of what?"

"Information, ma'am. We're doing some follow-up."

"What kind of case?"

Milo smiled. "Sorry, can't say. So they went on a trip?"

Alicia Cervantes looked him up and down. "What kind of source could Bob be to the police?"

"I really can't get into it, ma'am."

"Huh."

"He's not in trouble if that's what you're asking."

The newspaper slapped against her other hip. "Well, I know **that.** They're good people. If you told me different I wouldn't believe you."

"When did they leave?"

"Yesterday evening. Packed up the van, I went out to say goodbye. They looked fine. Not like people involved with the police."

"Any idea where they were headed?"

"Why?" said Alicia Cervantes. "You want to follow them on the freeway or something?"

"No, ma'am. We're just trying to contact Bob."

"Follow-up? Whatever that means."

I said, "It was just the two of them traveling?"

My turn to be inspected. "Why all these questions, like they're spies or something? No, it wasn't just them. They took Paco and Luanne."

Milo said, "Their kids?"

Alicia Cervantes broke into laugher. "Paco's a black Lab, Luanne's a tabby cat."

I said, "Sounds like an extended trip."

"Why?"

"Taking the pets."

"Don't jump to conclusions," said Alicia Cervantes. "Whenever they travel, they take the animals. Would you leave yours? If you have any? Once they went to Desert Hot Springs and Luanne was sick so they asked me to watch her for a couple days and give her special food. Of course I said yes. Very nice cat, didn't try to bother Fernando, that's my lorikeet."

Milo said, "So no idea where they're headed."

"Nope."

"Okay, thanks, Ms. Cervantes."

When we'd walked a step, she said, "Maybe Sequoia, maybe another state park. They like the parks, if they can bring the animals. So you're not going to find them."

Like Darius Cutter, she stood there as we returned to the unmarked. Unlike Cutter, she focused squarely on us.

Milo muttered, "Community relations."

I said, "Maybe Pena looked scared and that's why she's protective."

He pulled away from the curb. "First ol' Bob takes sudden retirement, then he packs up the van and splits. Something to do with that building got to him." Smiling at me. "At least your morbid possibility wasn't borne out."

"Lucky Bob," I said. "Do you have that list of residents from the Wilshire tower here in the car?"

"It's in the murder book." He hooked a thumb toward the backseat.

I reached behind and retrieved the blue binder.

"I told you," he said. "Already went over it a bunch of times."

He'd asterisked the residents shielded by trusts and corporate entitities, making my life easy. I spotted what I'd hoped to find and showed it to him.

"High-Level, Inc.?" A nanosecond of confusion was replaced by clarity. His face turned chalky, highlighting acne pits and lumps; a lunar exploration module sweeping over the moon.

"The outfit that manages the place, shit."

I said, "Subsidiary of a subsidiary of a subdivision et cetera."

"Why the hell didn't I think of that?"

"It was just a guess."

He groaned. "Don't do that."

"What?"

"The aw-shucks modesty thing."

"I mean it—"

"Yeah, yeah." He smiled sourly. "It's like that old shampoo commercial, don't hate me 'cause I'm beautiful? I will **not** despise you because you're intellectually gifted."

He punched the steering wheel with the heel of a big hand. "The Brain has met his match!"

"Aw shucks."

Barking laughter, he swerved and parked, said, "Gimme that," and inspected the list. "Twenty-fourth-floor penthouse. Trust-fund **bastard**!"

CHAPTER

43

Back at his office, he chewed on an unlit cigar and dove into Academo's business records, sifting through layers of corporate camouflage.

High-Level, Inc., was a corporation duly registered in the state of Delaware.

Milo said, "Consider the wisecrack uttered."

Click; save; print. Soon a four-inch paper stack sat next to his screen. He read each sheet and passed it along.

Proposals, prospectuses, other business filings.

The kind of small-print, preposition-clogged legalese that inevitably crosses my eyes and numbs my brain. Party of the first, party of the second; the Marx Brothers collaborating with a desk-jockey churning out municipal regulations.

The gist was that High-Level, Inc., functioned as the maintenance arm of Columb-Tech, Inc., the parent company of five other corporations, including Academo, Inc.

Goodsprings, Inc., owned and operated drug rehab centers in five states.

Vista-Ventures, Inc., owned and operated industrial parks and office complexes in seven states.

Holly-Havenhurst, Inc., owned and operated senior-care facilities in nine states.

Hemi-Spherical, Inc., owned and operated residential complexes in eleven states.

At the helm of each, Founder, Chief Executive Officer, and President Anthony Nobach and Chief Operating Officer Marden Nobach.

Below the brothers' names, each company sported an impressive roster of legal counselors and board members. I'd barely unfogged my cerebral cortex when one name caught my eye.

Chief exploratory officer at High-Level, Inc.: Thurston Nobach, M.A.

A title I'd never heard of. Exploring what?

Then I realized if you compressed it to initials, you ended up with another version of **CEO.**

Exactly the kind of pretense I'd imagined for a psychopathic poseur.

I googled Thurston Nobach and scored on the first hit.

Full-color web page teeming with vertigo-inducing movement as holographic meshes furled, unfurled, and floated around the screen.

Then: utter blackness, followed by the oozing

materialization of a red **Enter** button and an invitation to **Traverse My World.**

Accepting the offer brought me to a high-def, close-up photo of a good-looking fox-faced man in his thirties sporting wavy, black, shoulder-length hair, a flap of which obscured one eye.

The visible iris was gray and piercing. Below Thurston Nobach's cleft chin, the silk collar of a peacock-blue shirt was visible, as was a silver chain around a bronze neck. A dyed-blond triangular soul patch shifted to the left by an off-kilter, thin-lipped smile and a left ear graced by a two-carat emerald stud filled out the picture.

Intense and not afraid to be noticed.

A **Continue** button led me to **Ideations, Strivings, Journeys.**

Thurston Anthony Nobach, M.A., ABD, thirty-seven years old, listed himself as an alumnus of Old Dominion Day School and The Pedagogic Preparatory Academy, both in Columbus, Ohio. Next came Brown University, where he'd earned a B.A., cum laude, in American studies, followed by Columbia University, where he'd earned a master's degree in linguistics.

Next screen: bright-red italics on a gray, faux-granite background:

Following all that formal—and formalized— education, I found myself assiduously assessing the relative benefits of intense auto-didacticism

versus classroom versus tutorial modes of trans-
mission, e.g. the classic scholarly conundrum
and, surprisingly, came to no facile conclusion.
Here I must confess to a bit of timidity. Given
no clear path, I opted to hazard a new journey,
albeit one rife with tendrils that coiled around
the conventionality of ancient avatars: e.g. pur-
suing doctoral studies at Columbia in the hopes
of probing ephemerally-transitory and quasi-
random patterns of post-cultural grammatology,
metaphysical presupposition, and figurative
semiology. In the end, I terminated my journey
with an ABD that inspired laudatory serenity.

Those initials I recognized: "All But Dissertation."
Cosmetic shorthand for Ph.D. students who'd
either changed their minds or flunked their orals.

After almost-graduation, Thurston Nobach's
intellectual curiosity had "propelled me to seek distant harbors." First was Maui, Hawaii, where "I
autonomously researched the Multi-Ethnic Vox,
e.g. the sometimes tenuous, sometimes tense, sometimes tensile kinship/autonomy/orthogonal flat-line
between Collective Concept and Voice."

Next: Auckland, New Zealand, "seeking an
antipodal awakening as I continued to decompress
after descending the depths of exploratory curiosity
in the bathysphere of the crushingly rodent-like
marathon masquerading as formal education."

I.e., doing nothing.

For two years in Florence, "I honed my visual observational skills and eventually reached a place where I could rationally contemplate a carefree swan-dive into the reflecting pool of visual arts. My Da Vinci dream phase, if you will."

That was memorialized by thumbnails of four pen-and-ink drawings. Broken lines, awkward composition, unclear subject matter.

"I traveled away from that world due to a near-Aortic constriction brought upon by a revelation regarding the ultimately futile process of rendering."

I.e., I don't know how to draw.

Nobach's last recorded overseas trip had taken place eight years ago.

"After finding myself immersed in the Bob Cratchett / Uriah Heep tanning vat of the so-called business world, I discovered that my axons and dendrites were atrophying and returned to the world of ideas."

I.e., an "endowed" year in Warsaw, Poland.

No university mentioned.

Financing courtesy a Holly-Havenhurst Liberal Arts Scholar's Award.

I googled the fellowship. No mention of anyone else ever receiving it.

The subsidiary that ran old-age homes.

I.e., siphoning money from Daddy.

I pictured Thurston Nobach drifting the streets of Warsaw buttressed by a fat allowance. All that leisure time leading him to come upon the monster who'd given his life new focus.

Milo was ahead of me, breathing hard, frantically flipping pages of the murder book. He stopped, wide-eyed, slapped a page, reversed the binder, and showed it to me.

The Polish newspaper article Basia Lopatinski had given us.

Ignacy Skiwski pretending to play guitar. Surrounded by a small group of young people. Milo jabbed a face. He didn't need to.

A figure sitting to Skiwski's left. Long legs suggested height. Sitting low suggested a high waist.

Over eight years, the changes in Thurston Nobach weren't radical. Back then his face had been a bit softer around the edges, the black hair even longer, bound by a leather headband. No yellow soul patch, diamond earring instead of an emerald, shabby-looking beige tunic in place of the bright-blue shirt.

John Lennon glasses perched atop a beak-like nose as he observed Ignacy Skiwski.

Just another Euro-hippie digging the street vibe.

Until you checked out the smile: razor-lipped, impatient. As if chafing for the opportunity to utter something clever.

And the eyes: hard, judgmental, challenging the camera. The only one of Skiwski's acolytes to look away from the guitar and face the camera.

Jackal among the sheep.

I said so.

Milo grunted and returned to the documents, working faster, shoulders bunched. I moved on to the final page of Nobach's website. **My Manifesto.**

KIND READER, PERMIT ME THE INDULGENCE OF SELECTIVE SELF-EXPRESSION. OR PERHAPS SHOULD WE SET UP A SYNOD, A CONCLAVE, A TED TALK—insert scoffing laughter—AND JOINTLY COME TO THE REASONABLE CONCLUSION THAT MY DARING TO OPINE IS NOTHING MORE THAN A BIT OF COGNITIVE-AFFECTIVE FLOTSAM MY POOR BENIGHTED CONSCIOUSNESS NEEDS TO FLING AWAY????

I.e., See? I'm a modest guy.

The real subtext: I know how to rein in my arrogance and summon up a Humble Brag when it suits me.

I began reading, bracing myself for another shit-storm of jabberwocky. Found, instead, a surprisingly brief exposition.

**The Nature of Consciousness
Submitted, hat-in-hand, by Thurston "Thirsty" Nobach, M.A., ABD, Eternal Searcher**

Really, sir? sez I to myself.

You're going to attempt to scale the alps of a meta-question? The answer: Yes, I will because meta is really mini. Because Nietzsche, Sartre, Caligula, et al., had no clue, histrionic egotists that they were, missing the final stop on the tram ride to oblivion.

There is no consciousness.

No self.

No personal boundaries, no rules impervious to exception, no individual existence that can be truncated from the cosmos, no greater meaning other than the transitory explanations with which we blanket ourselves during moments of weakness.

We are one with everything. We are everything.

More important: We are **nothing**.

Finis, no coda.
Au revoir.
Arrivederci.
Do widzenia.

I created a page link, emailed it to Milo's computer. It pinged arrival just as he put down the papers.

He rubbed his eyes and flexed his fingers. "How about you sum up?"

"Don't want to intrude on your consciousness."

"What?"

"Do yourself a favor and read."

When he was through, the cigar had been chewed to brown pulp. He tossed it, printed.

"Guy's nuts. Toss in his dad's dough and here comes the insanity defense."

"I promise to testify otherwise."

He laughed. "Least you didn't say cart before horse."

I said, "Notice his nickname?"

"Thirsty."

"Amanda had a sticker saying that on the back of her textbook. Bet you he prints them up and hands them out as goodies to the faithful."

"He's running a cult?"

"Or keeping it personal—mind-games one-on-one."

"Hmmph. Well, let's get into his personal space."

He pulled out his list of generally agreeable judges. No answer at the first two. The third, Giselle Boudreaux, first in her class at Tulane Law and the youngest sib of three New Orleans cops, said, "Now we're talking. See? All it took was some elbow grease."

"Doing my best, Your Honor."

"Everyone claims that. Lucky for you, in this case it's enough. Write up the address as a comprehensive and email it. I'll give you telephonic authorization soon as I receive it but you know the drill: Someone has to come by and retrieve actual paper."

"You bet," said Milo. "There are two addresses I need access to."

"Ah, the guy's rich," said Boudreaux. "What, something at the beach?"

"If only." Milo explained.

"A crib in a dorm? You know he's there for a fact?"

"It's likely."

"Sorry, then. Likely isn't actual. All I need is you're wrong and I've warranted a nonexistent location."

I fought the impulse to break in. **Ah, but there is no reality. No truth. No lies . . .**

Milo said, "If I'm wrong, nothing really lost."

"No? All I need is some bubblehead reporter having an orgasm over judicial overreach."

"How 'bout this, Your Honor: I find nothing, the paperwork vanishes."

"Hmm. I don't know . . . all right, but only because my family would yell at me if they find out I wimped out on a murder."

"Thanks a ton."

"You've also got to give me two separate applications."

"No prob."

"For you. I'm the one has to read your sparkling prose, it's my day off and I'm just about to tee off at Brentwood."

"I'll keep it simple—"

"Just funnin' with you," said Boudreaux. "This prick did what you say, I want to help fuck him up."

As he uploaded the warrant applications, I re-read Thurston Nobach's manifesto. "In terms of the raid, sooner the better."

He wheeled forty-five degrees from his desk and faced me. "Why?"

"This." I held out the page.

"Yeah, yeah, more gobbledygook, no good no bad. So what?"

"No self, no consciousness, no real death. I think there's a message here. He's making the case for suicide and tailoring it to depressed, impressionable victims like Cassy Booker. And now Amanda, riding her bike over to his place and sticking around. She's isolated, depressed, has trouble relating to everyone else but worships him. Nobach sniffs that out, ropes her in by appealing to her intellect, and when the time's right, he supplies the means—a little nip of an opioid cocktail—along with pseudo-intellectual encouragement."

"You think that's what happened with Susie?"

"Maybe that was Nobach's intention. He figured her for a stupid stripper but she was older and toughened by life and less compliant. That could be why Nobach terminated the relationship. Or even worse, she did. In either event, she defied him and earned a nasty death. Something was supposed to

happen at that wedding—a payoff, a fake reconcili-
ation, we may never know. The important thing
now is, he's focusing on Amanda, and what Garrett
just told us—shutting out her family—says he's
edging her closer to the end."

He rubbed his face. "What're you saying? I don't
wait for the warrant?"

"I'm just telling you the way I see it."

He speed-dialed Giselle Boudreaux, began ex-
plaining.

She said, "Life-threatening situation? What the
hell do you need me for, call it a welfare check."

"Thanks."

"For what?"

Starting with DMV, he ran a search on Thurston
Nobach. One vehicle, a silver, one-year-old BMW
M5. Copying the info, he stood, slipped his gun
into his hip holster. "Any psychological wisdom on
which place to try first?"

I said, "Why choose?"

CHAPTER

44

Ideally, approaching a violent offender is a carefully planned scheme. But no matter how well thought-out, fraught with anxiety.

I'd demolished that by urging fast action on Thirsty Nobach's premises. Complicated matters further by suggesting two simultaneous raids.

It churned my guts.

It made Milo serene.

As if some seldom-utilized bundle of nerve-fibers in his forebrain had been activated, he stretched, yawned, and reclined in his chair as he summoned Moe Reed, Sean Binchy, and Alicia Bogomil to the interview room where we'd talked to the newlyweds.

Three separate calls, talking to each detective in a smooth, silky tone I'd only heard when he finished a serious meal enhanced by alcohol.

Not what the kids were used to. Binchy and Bogomil paused before saying, "Okay."

Reed said, "You all right, L.T.?"

"Peachy."

He loped to the room, arms swinging, whistling an almost-tune, held the door open. "Go in, back in a sec."

While he was gone, the D's arrived.

I said, "He went to get something."

They looked at the four chairs, remained on their feet.

"Got to save one for him," said Binchy.

"He okay?" said Reed.

"Thinking mode," I said.

"That's always a good idea," said Bogomil, smiling wryly.

Heads turned as Milo charged in toting a whiteboard on an easel. "Class is in session, kids. Some lecture but mostly lab. Sit."

Three butts hit three chairs. I was fourth.

He walked up to the board. "Here's the deal."

Marker in hand, he summed up the evidence on Nobach and jotted down the basics. Three pairs of wide eyes.

"This just happened?" said Bogomil.

"Fresh off the griddle, Alicia. We've got one definite residence for the suspect and one likely—a unit in that dorm his daddy owns. Judge Boudreaux says no warrant is necessary because of overwhelming evidence Nobach intends harm to Amanda Burdette. Think of this as an emergency welfare check."

"Because of what he wrote on his website," said Reed.

"Because of Dr. Delaware's educated opinion about what he wrote. Onward: You and Alicia will be handling Strathmore after I set up entrance for you with the new manager. Do your best not to be noticed. In fact, wait in the car until I tell you. At best, the search will dud out. At worst, you'll encounter a murderous psychopath, so be careful. Once I get you in, I'm over to the condo where you'll go as soon as we're finished here, Sean. It'll take time to find side-street parking so you might not beat me by much. If you do get there early, take a stroll on Wilshire near the building but same rule: Don't get spotted. Especially by the doormen, one of whom is ex-Pacific Division. He may be righteous but after working with rich people he may not. Once I arrive, I'll deal with him. Next item."

He listed the tags and description of Thurston Nobach's M5. "All of you look out for it. You see him driving to or from one of his cribs, initiate a tail and let me know."

Clicking on three cellphones as the car data got copied.

"Any questions?"

Binchy looked at Bogomil, who looked at Reed.

Reed flexed massive arms and smiled. "One thing, Prof. Is this going to be on the final?"

◆

When we were all out in the hall, Binchy looked at me. "Doc going to be part of it, Loot?"

Milo said, "Protected and served by me."

Bogomil said, "Good. This piece of shit sounds whack."

CHAPTER

45

Milo lead-footed it to Westwood Village, drove around the corner from the Strathmore complex, and then drove an additional half block and parked. Once out of the car, he hitched his trousers, patted his holster, then patted a jacket pocket swelling just above the Glock.

I said, "Second gun?"

He said, "Once a Boy Scout, always prepared. I don't need to give you the drill, do I?"

"Hang back, stay safe, don't get in the way."

"Bet you were always a good student." Leaning into the breeze, he began walking.

Another prolonged push on the doorbell to Building B.

Darius Cutter said, "If this is some sort of—"

"It's Lieutenant Sturgis again, Mr. Cutter. We need to talk."

"You're kidding—hold on."

Cutter was at the door within seconds. Once it opened, Milo charged in, covering the lobby and stepping into Cutter's office.

Cutter turned to me. "He looks pissed. What's going on?"

"He'll fill you in."

"Great."

By the time we got to the office, Milo had positioned his bulk to the left of Cutter's desk, blocking access to the desk chair.

"Sit, Mr. Cutter."

Cutter stared. "It's kind of blocked?"

Milo stepped back, allowing Cutter just enough room to pass. When Cutter sat, he moved in closer.

Cutter looked up at him. "You're making me feel like I did something."

"God forbid." Wolf-teeth. "You're going to do something now: Tell me which unit is Thurston Nobach's."

"**He's** involved? Oh, God."

"Which unit?"

Cutter gulped. "He's the boss's son."

Milo got taller.

Cutter said, "He doesn't really live here, he just keeps a place for management. Not that he manages anything."

Milo leaned in, inches from Cutter's face, big hands flat on the desk, as if bracing for a leap. Cutter had tried to personalize the room. Blotter, iPad, a couple of framed photos. Milo lifted one of the frames. Cutter and an older woman. "Your mom? Looks like a nice lady. **What unit?**"

"This building," said Cutter. "Top floor. B-four-twenty-five. At the back."

"Is Nobach here now?"

"I haven't seen him."

"Since when?"

"Um . . . I guess yesterday? Around . . . I guess five p.m.?"

"Coming in or out?"

"Out."

"Any idea where he was going?"

Cutter shook his head. "He just wheeled his bike out of the elevator."

"He has a bike."

"Nice one."

"What color?"

"Silver. He left dirt tracks in the lobby. Like I'd complain."

"What way did he turn once he got outside?"

"Right."

"East."

"Um, yeah."

"When did you go off-shift?"

"Seven, I had stuff to do. Setting up—"

"He could've returned without your noticing."

Cutter nodded. "You can't tell me what—"

"What I can tell you is you're going to walk out of the building with us. Two other detectives will meet us and you're going to give them the key to B-four-twenty-five."

"This is some kind of a raid? You don't need a warrant?"

"Everyone asks that, too much TV," said Milo, clapping Cutter's shoulder. Cutter shuddered. "In fact, give **me** the key right now."

"All I have is a master, sir."

"Does it work for all three buildings?"

"Yes."

"Even better."

Cutter fished a jangling ring out of a desk drawer, removed a stainless-steel key, and handed it over. "You're sure this is okay?"

"Better than okay. Let's go, Mr. Cutter. Take a walk into the Village and get yourself a latte and don't return until I tell you."

"I'm on the job," said Cutter.

"Your job right now is staying safe and being discreet. That means no calls to anyone." Flicking the photo frame. "Even Mom. You seem like a good person. Don't get yourself involved."

"Oh, God," said Cutter.

Milo walked to the door, texting. Cutter sat there for a second, then followed him out.

◆

Reed and Bogomil met us outside the glass door.

Milo said, "This is Mr. Cutter. He manages the building and has furnished us a master key, which will get you access to Unit B-four-twenty-five. As well as to C-four-eighteen, where you-know-who lives."

Cutter said, "Who?"

Milo winked. "Mr. Cutter has been **super** cooperative and now he's going to get himself a latte."

Bogomil said, "Enjoy, sir."

Cutter said, "Actually, I'm a tea drinker."

Milo waited until Cutter was out of earshot. "No idea if Nobach is here, try his place first. Wait until the hallway's clear then knock, wait, knock, give him a chance. No response, go in armed but subtly—no big announcement. He's not there, try Amanda's, same deal. Once you've covered both places, call me."

"Got it," said Reed.

Bogomil nodded.

Milo said, "Stay safe."

Bogomil said, "I always try. Life is good."

CHAPTER
46

When it rains it pours: two parking spaces on Selby south of Wilshire. Milo's unmarked nosed in front of Binchy's current civilian drive, a grimy white Mustang courtesy the impound lot. The three of us walked toward the pink building, Milo patting both his gun bulges.

When we were a building away from the pink tower, Milo told us to wait and kept going. Striding past the condo, side-glancing, returning.

"Unfortunately, my boy Jeremy's not there, just Rudy Galloway, the ex-Pacific guy, and another valet. I'll take Rudy, you handle Other, Sean."

Binchy said, "Handle meaning . . ."

"Make sure he doesn't do anything heroic. Last time we were here, there was no one at the front desk and from what I could see, same thing now.

But there has to be someone in charge with the keys. Ready?"

Without waiting for an answer, he sped off.

Rudy Galloway knew a cop when he saw one. Yards before Milo reached the portly valet, he tensed up. By the time Milo reached him, he'd shifted to a broad, collegial smile.

Only two black Mercedeses in the porte cochere, no one waiting to come or go.

Binchy veered to corral the second valet. I caught up with Milo. Already returning Galloway's smile.

Galloway was saying, "West L.A., huh? Good deal, there. Rich folk, not a lot to do."

"Stuff happens," said Milo. "But yeah, I like it."

"I mean sure, stuff happens everywhere, but I was with Pacific for twenty years. The gang stuff south of Rose could shrink your nuts."

"So I've heard," said Milo.

"Definitely," said Galloway. "So what's the deal?"

"We're here for an emergency welfare check, Rudy. C'mere." Drawing Galloway to a far corner of the covered drive, he stopped next to the phone-booth-sized valet stand and underhanded a photo of Amanda Burdette.

"Who's that?"

"You've never seen her?"

For all his cop experience, Galloway couldn't control his eyes as they ping-ponged from left to right. He knew Milo knew. "Oh, yeah—you know, you're right, she has been here. She some sort of offender?"

"Why would you say that, Rudy?"

"You know," said Galloway. "College kids, always with the dope."

"She show signs of addiction when she comes to visit Mr. Nobach?"

Nobach's name made Galloway blink. Running a finger around his collar, he licked his lips. "Naw naw, just, you know. College brats. They're always playing around with the dope."

"She is a college student, Rudy. So how come she visits Nobach?"

Galloway licked his lips. "Couldn't tell you."

"How often does she visit Mr. Nobach?"

Galloway looked relieved. A question he could answer honestly. "Not a lot—maybe I seen her . . . five times."

"Over what time period?"

"Couldn't tell you." Resumption of eye-tennis. "It's not like a regular thing."

"Unlike this person."

Underhanding a photo of Susie Koster.

Galloway's mouth stayed shut but a gurgling noise rose from his gullet.

"Rudy?"

"Yeah, this one was regular. Kimbee. She lived here for a while. That's why I know her name. She'd drive a little Honda down there and use one of his spaces."

"Nobach's."

Nod. "What's going on?"

"When did Kimbee live here?"

Galloway rotated his head. Scratched the ample flesh under his chin. "Look, I don't wanna tell you something's not true."

"Best guess, Rudy. I won't hold you to it."

"A year ago? Three-quarters? They rode bikes together. That's how I know her name. From him talking to her—turn right, Kimbee, we'll go to Holmby. That kind of thing."

Galloway looked at the photo again. "She wore those tight shiny bike pants. Red." Raised eyebrows; crocodile smile.

"So she had her own card key."

"Yup," said Galloway. "Parked herself. When she wasn't biking. C'mon, pal, what's going **on?**"

"Like I said, a welfare check."

"On Nobach or the kid?"

"Maybe both."

"What, a dope thing? Shit, all I need. We've had them before, last year EMTs came for the grandson of one of the residents. Persian kid, maybe sixteen, friendly, you'd never know. Ambulance took him to the U." Galloway pointed to a phone in the valet stand. "I can save you trouble, call up there and see if they're okay."

"Don't," said Milo, staying Galloway's arm with his hand. Galloway's eyes widened.

Milo said, "So Nobach and this girl are both up there now."

"I couldn't say."

"You just said 'They're okay.'"

"I was just—you said you wanted to check both of 'em, so I said I'd call about both of them." He shrugged free of Milo's hand. Looked at his uniform sleeve as if it had been sullied. "What the **hell's** going on?"

"Rudy," said Milo, "once a pro, always a pro, right?"

Galloway's "Right" was more lip movement than sound.

"You been in situations. Now it's us in a situation. One you're **not** in. Okay?"

"Okay." Galloway looked over at Binchy, in the opposite corner of the driveway. Having an apparently friendly chat with the other valet. Both of them relaxed, the thin, sallow, sixtyish man tapping a foot. Probably a discussion of music, Binchy's favorite topic. His perfect record of never meeting a stranger unblemished.

Galloway said, "You brought three guys? There's gonna be trouble?"

"Not if we can help it, Rudy. When's the last time you saw Nobach?"

"Couldn't—okay, if you don't want exactly, I'll estimate."

"Do that, Rudy."

"Let's see." Pretending to calculate. "Maybe two hours ago? Could be three."

"He bike over?"

"No, came in his Bimmer."

"Anyone with him?"

"Couldn't tell you," said Galloway. "I focus on what's here. They drive in themselves and don't call us to retrieve, it's not my business. Also, he's got tinted windows. Even if I looked I couldn't see."

Milo studied him.

He said, "That is the total truth." Crossing himself.

"Wouldn't assume otherwise," said Milo. "So you're on board."

"With what?"

"Two things," said Milo. "First, keep out of it— not a word to anyone. Second, tell us how to get a key to Nobach's place without his knowing."

Another lip-lick. "Is there gonna be . . . noise? It's a big thing here. Someone's always bitching about noise."

"The quieter the better, Rudy. As long as you and your partner—what's his name?"

"Charlie," said Galloway, rolling his eyes. "Civilian. Been parking cars his whole life."

"Can Charlie be trusted?"

"Yeah, he does what I say. He's a little, you know." Tapping his temple. "No rocket scientist."

"Good. You take charge and make sure Charlie doesn't screw up."

Galloway frowned. "Basically, all you want is I do nothing."

"Yeah, but a really **professional** nothing," said Milo.

"Huh?"

Milo covered his eyes, ears, and mouth in rapid sequence.

"The monkey thing," said Galloway.

"The smart thing, Rudy. Now how do we get a key?"

"The head guy, sits at the front desk."

"Don't see anyone at the front desk."

"That's 'cause he's a lazy bastard, goes into his office, that door behind the desk, does who knows what, leaving all the crap to us. Luggage, packages, dog walking. Not in the job description. We're supposed to load and unload but once it goes inside, him and the other inside guys are supposed to handle it."

"Bunch of slackers, huh?"

"Wasn't perfect before but now it's worse," said Galloway. "They used to have four of them. Now it's that prick Petrie and one other and today Other's out sick." He laughed. "Petrie's nephew, like he's gonna give a shit."

"Same old story," said Milo.

"Same old same old," said Galloway.

Couple of old-timers united by the pleasure of their discontent. All that was missing was beer on tap and ESPN above the bar.

Milo said, "Okay, Rudy, we're ready to rock, appreciate your being on board." Motioning to Binchy, who shook Charlie's hand and ambled over.

Galloway said, "Sure, no prob. I'll take care of the genius." He pulled a pack of Kents and a lighter from his pant pocket, arched a thumb at the booth. "Not supposed to smoke in there, but screw it. It's like I'm back on the job. Doing my thing, screw civilians."

"There's the old team spirit, Rudy."

Binchy and I waited in front of a semicircular pink marble desk as Milo went behind and knocked on a rosewood door.

Laurence Petrie took a minute to emerge. Swallowing some sort of snack, wiping his mouth with the back of his hand. Forties, narrow-shouldered, and delicately built, Petrie had wispy peanut-butter-colored hair and a questionable beard the same color. His double-breasted blazer was well tailored and festooned with brass buttons. Gray slacks were pressed, a white-on-white shirt was starched and spotless.

All that nattiness ruined by a clip-on repp-stripe tie pretending to evoke memories of a prestigious school.

He looked us up and down and said, "Ye-es?" like one of those classical music radio hosts who talk like they stuff plum pits in their cheeks.

Milo vaulted into the hard-line approach: Compressing his eyes and mouth and advancing rapidly until he was three inches from Petrie's now-pale face. Talking softly but fast. Telling not asking. All the while, creating an expanding loom that dwarfed the one he'd inflicted on Darius Cutter.

Petrie said, "Law enforcement? No problem, let me call my bosses."

"Who's that?"

"The management company."

"No," said Milo. "No calls to anyone. In fact, you'll need to leave the building and surrender your cellphone."

"Why would I do that?" said Petrie. More question than defiance. As Milo had grown, he'd shrunk.

"Because there's a situation, here, Laurence."

"I understand, sir, but the building is my responsibility."

"I respect that, Laurence. Right now, your responsibility is to avoid getting caught up in something you don't understand."

"That's true, I don't understand," said Petrie. Relieved. A man whose loyalties ran shallow.

"Your phone, please," said Milo.

Petrie handed over an i6 in a black leather case. "Why not? They don't pay me enough to mess with you guys."

"Smart move, Laurence."

"Lance," said Petrie. "That's my nickname." The eager-to-please sociability of the newly conquered.

"Smart move, Lance." Milo switched off Petrie's

phone, pocketed it, and held out his hand. "The key to twenty-four hundred."

"Of course, Lieutenant. You'll actually need two. One for the elevator, one for the door. There's only two units on top. No hallway, just a vestibule. His is to the left."

"Who lives to the right?"

"Austrians," said Petrie. "They're away. You've got it all to yourself."

Milo held out his hand.

Petrie said, "Oh, sure, keys. All I've got are the masters."

"I promise to take good care of them."

"Can I ask how long will this take, sir?"

"Not a second longer than it needs to, Lance."

"Welfare check," said Petrie. "We've had them before. Old people. Sometimes they die." No emotion.

Opening a drawer. No jangly ring like in Cutter's desk, just two gold-plated keys on a black-and-gold plastic lanyard.

"My daughter made this," said Petrie, swinging the chain. "I'd like to get it back."

Milo guided Petrie to the motor court. Petrie walked past the valets and turned left.

Galloway watched and flashed a see-what-I-mean sneer. Smoking openly and flicking ashes perilously close to one of the Mercedeses. Off to the side,

Charlie stood looking unperturbed and still tapping his foot.

Milo and Binchy turned toward the elevator. Only one for a building this size. No easy escape but the chance of confronting Amanda or Nobach in a small space was a new factor.

He'd walked three steps when his cell vibrated his inside jacket pocket. He yanked it out, read a text, froze. Mouthed a silent obscenity.

Texting back, he showed the original message to Binchy and me.

From Alicia Bogomil: **negative at nobach's place but amanda's place her mother. Bound and gagged, head injury, breathing but not conscious. 911 on its way. We figure best to wait until she's taken care of before detail searching nobach place?? Maybe one of us should go to hospital??**

Milo's response: **right on both counts. She look fatal?**

Alicia: **Im no doc lt but at least her breathing's regular okay hear the siren. Over and out.**

Milo put his phone back and turned to me. "How do you see this?"

I said, "Sandy Burdette paid an unannounced visit to Amanda, wanting to talk to her about Nobach. She might've known something about him, had concerns about Amanda's attachment but hadn't wanted to make waves. Then Garrett came home and kicked up her anxiety. When she got to Amanda's room, Nobach was there. Words were exchanged, he attacked her from behind, tied her up, and brought Amanda here."

Binchy said, "Is Amanda a victim or a co-conspirator?"

"Only one way to know."

CHAPTER
47

The elevator arrived within seconds, rosewood doors gliding open with a whoosh. The car was paneled in the same wood. Stingy compartment, barely enough room for the three of us, filling with the odor of ripe sweat as the doors eased shut.

Milo inserted the smaller gold key into the slot next to 24 (P) and we sailed upward. Moments later, we were facing a massive Venetian mirror affixed to a white wall. The vestibule floors were white marble. Bad for noise suppression.

Milo unholstered his Glock and tiptoed out into the vestibule. Binchy armed himself and followed. Then me. Function unclear.

Long narrow vestibule, nothing but the mirror relieving the starkness. A white door to the left was designated PH1 by blocky, steel characters. Same for PH2 to the right, where an unopened package sat near the threshold.

Gun in hand, Milo tiptoed to the left, pressed his ear to the door, waited, pressed again, then made a zero-sign with thumb and forefinger. Looking down at his gun for a moment, he breathed in and slid the larger key into the bolt, turning slowly.

Slight creak, then silence.

He waited, shoulders bunched, before toeing the door open an inch, waited some more before peering through. His eyebrows arced as he nudged the gap another couple of inches. Another brief inspection. Head shake. Half a dozen more inches. Finally, he created enough space to slip through, gun-arm extended.

Binchy followed, motioning me to hang back.

I stood there until he stuck his head out and nodded. Joined the two of them in a vacant ten-by-ten foyer.

The same white marble flooring, noise mercifully cushioned by a high-pile, black-and-gold Chinese rug.

Snarling dragons and chimeras, fanged mouths agape, serpentine tails intertwined.

Beyond the foyer was five hundred square feet of space meant to be a living room.

No living here; not a stick of furniture, no windows, just three walls of floor-to-ceiling ebony bookshelves. Every inch filled with volumes but for a scarlet door notched into the broad rear unit.

Thousands of books. Not the bland-jacketed texts Susie Koster had hoarded. Every one of these was covered in gilt-trimmed, tooled leather, the bookbinder's art displayed in a riot of colors and textures.

I stepped closer and read a few spines.

WORDHAM'S MUSINGS ON THEOSOPHY.
   VOLUMES I THROUGH IX
The Collected Verse of Mrs. Aphra Sleete
Price & Worthington's Annual Autumnal Survey
   of Sedges and Other Marsh Vegetations
Von Boffingmuell: The Man, The Plan
Yorkshire Fancies, Possibilities, and Various
   Other Indulgences

Milo and Binchy were reading, too. Milo looked angry, Binchy puzzled.

Milo edged over to the scarlet door. More leather, pebbled; oval red-lacquer doorknob.

No key-slot, no bolt.

He repeated the ear-press, retreated several steps, and repeated again, footsteps on the cushy rug no more than puffs.

I became aware of the utter lack of sound.

Not a serene silence. This was cold, blank, negative air, rife with bad possibilities. The kind of clogged silence that promises malignant surprise.

Milo placed his hand on the red knob. Rotated. Sprang back.

The scarlet door swung out smoothly on hidden hinges. Milo inched forward, allowing his Glock to lead the way.

He hazarded a peek. Then a longer look.

Nodding, he stepped through.

Same drill: Binchy leaving me to wait, followed by the go-ahead.

Now we stood in an even larger space, this one floored in black granite as glossy as an oil spill.

To the left was a white kitchen that looked as if it had never been used.

Finally the taming of the silence: a faint hum, courtesy the electronic veins, arteries, and capillaries that run through every high-end building.

Good insulation, those books.

In this room, two walls of glass offered jaw-loosening western and northern views. Dead-center on the granite, a pair of black leather Eames chairs flanked a silver six-foot cube aspiring to be a coffee table.

Atop the cube: a plastic packet of orange-tipped hypodermic syringes and a small baggie empty but for bits of white grit toward the bottom.

Behind the cube, an open doorway.

No sound but the electronic hum.

Sidling as far from the opening as possible, Milo advanced, Binchy close behind.

No permission for me to enter but I followed. Heard music rising above the hum, faint but unmistakable.

Lilting, trebly, reedy—some sort of flute, a chiffon of notes rising in pitch then returning to base.

The same arpeggio, over and over.

The kind of New Agey stuff looped in strip-mall day spas, designed to relax.

It stiffened both detectives' gun-hands and prickled the short hairs on the nape of my neck.

They advanced. Again, neither of them held me back so I walked through the opening after they did.

Dim bedroom. Sparse but massive, likely created by combining two sleeping chambers.

This floor was cushioned by a snowdrift of white flokati rug. A black leather base held a bed wider than a king, draped tautly in silver silk. Pillows in hues that recalled the books out front were scattered on the bed and the rug. A doorless entry to the right revealed a slate, walnut, and smoked-glass bathroom.

Milo pointed to the wall facing the bed.

Covered by gray flannel drapes except where it wasn't.

An eight-foot gap revealed the handle of a sliding glass door that led to a marble-floored balcony.

The southern view, barely encumbered by a waist-high glass railing aiming for invisibility.

I imagined what would be seen. Planes landing at LAX. Miles of the neighborhoods avoided by people who lived in the Wilshire Corridor.

From this high, everything would be beautiful.

Today it wasn't.

At the rightmost periphery of the window was a

hint of brown wicker and orange cushion. High-end, weather-resistant outdoor furniture.

Resting near the edge of the cushion was a bare foot.

Small, white. Inert.

Milo charged.

We burst onto the balcony, three sets of eyes camera-clicking.

Amanda Burdette, prone on her back, on a stylish brown wicker chaise.

Face as gray as her shapeless dress.

The hem of the dress riding up, legs white as the marble floor where they weren't encased by a black body shaper.

On the floor, a coil of rubber tubing and a used syringe.

Ruby dot in the crook of her left arm.

Thurston Nobach, in a white, hooded caftan that trailed onto the floor, had been standing with his back to her, enjoying the view. Behind him, a pulsating tide of sound, the beeps, chitters, and burps of the city. Muted by altitude but not vanquished.

Milo's and Binchy's "Police! Freeze!" duet caused him to wheel. His lower jaw dropped like a dump-truck scoop.

Staring at us. Long hair ponied, the tail flopping against his shoulder. Harder, rougher face than in his website photo. Thirty-seven but I'd have guessed ten years older.

I've seen that in psychopaths: oozing through life apparently glib. But their bodies know different and their cells die in rebellion.

Nobach's mouth slammed shut, surprise giving way to rage.

As the photo from Warsaw had suggested, tall man, just below Milo's six-three. High-waisted, broad-shouldered, hints of muscularity beneath the billowing caftan.

He said, "What the fuck gives you the right?" Looked at Milo's gun, then Sean's, and added his own roar to the city sonata.

Fisting his hands and bracing his body. Arrogant enough to dare warfare?

Milo sidestepped him, offering Binchy direct access to Nobach. That confused me until I saw him reach for the secondary bulge in his pocket—what I'd assumed to be a second weapon.

He drew out a squat white plastic cone with a clear plastic spout at the bottom and a clear plastic push-button at the top.

Naloxone nasal spray. LAPD patrol officers carry it now, and so do county sheriffs. Not so much detectives. This Boy Scout had come prepared.

As he bent over Amanda and inserted the cone into her nostril, Thurston Nobach shoved Sean aside and hurled himself at the chaise.

Sean body-blocked him. Nobach roared again, louder, and clamped his hands around Sean's neck.

Sean's one of those habitual optimists who

mainline good cheer. Despite years as a cop, that had worked out just fine. Now it threw him off.

Unprepared.

He struggled to free his gun-arm but Nobach had pressed against him so close that the limb was immobilized.

Nobach's large hands blanched as they pressed harder. Sean's eyes rolled and he gave up on the weapon, gasped, and flailed at Nobach's grip with his free arm.

Milo was just starting to turn away from Amanda when Nobach planted his feet wide and swung Sean toward the waist-high glass barrier.

Sean's gun clattered to the floor as he fought to resist. Nobach's rage won out and Sean's upper body tilted over the glass.

I dove forward, taking hold of Sean's shirt and pulling him back. Nobach struck out at my face with one hand, missed as he tried to push Sean over with the other.

For less than a second, Nobach and I played tug-of-war with Sean's body. Then he said, "Fuck this," let go, and swung at me.

What could've been a bone-crusher grazed my right cheek as I feinted to the left and concentrated on pulling Sean to safety.

Sean, gasping, saw his gun on the floor and went for it.

Milo moved on Nobach.

Nobach weighed his options.

I shouted, "ABD pretentious asshole."

Nobach's eyes went blank. He round-housed his fist toward me. I stood there as if ready to take it, then moved to the left just before he reached me.

Forward inertia murdered his balance. Staggering, fighting for stability, he tried to plant his feet but got caught up in the puddling hem of his caftan.

He kicked at the cloth violently.

Tripped and pitched forward.

Long-legged and high-waisted. The wrong center of gravity when you were fighting a thirty-two-inch railing.

Arms aloft, mouth a black O, he went over.

Binchy watched him, saucer-eyed. I rubbed my left cheek. Heating up and swelling. Maybe more than a graze but nothing felt broken.

Stirring from the chaise drew me away from the pain. A series of gurgles, coughs, and mewls as Amanda Burdette came to.

Milo said, "There you go, kid," and lightly slapped her face.

She looked up at him, groggily.

"You're okay, kid."

Cloudy eyes flinched, shut, opened.

It took a few moments for anything close to lucidity to appear.

"There you go, kid," said Milo.

"Go away," she said. "I don't like people."

CHAPTER
48

Even a high-end building needs somewhere to put garbage. The pink tower's refuse-storage facility consisted of eight industrial dumpsters tucked into a caged square at the rear of the structure.

Directly below the south-facing units, but no reason to look down when up was so beautiful.

Thurston Nobach landed atop the left-most bin.

Postmortem photos didn't reveal much in the way of humanity. More like a clotted stain, which Milo termed "Beyond apropos."

Once Nobach's parents were notified of his death, they reacted the way people used to getting their way do: mustering a battalion of lawyers to draft a demand letter, ordering immediate release of all information and material related to the cruel, callous, negligent police behavior leading to the death of an innocent young man in the privacy of his own home. Page two announced intention to file criminal charges against the perpetrators of said behavior, to be named. The final page tacked on a civil suit for damages related to . . .

Multiple copies were couriered simultaneously to the mayor, the D.A., several state and federal legislators, the local office of the FBI, and the city councilwoman and county supervisor whose districts encompassed the Wilshire Corridor.

That died quickly when the lawyers had a look at the contents of evidence obtained at Thirsty Nobach's condo and a unit in the building he "managed."

Radio silence. New goal: damage control.

Futile goal. Six hours after Nobach went over the glass, Maxine Driver called me at home. I was in the kitchen, ice pack pushed to my face, Robin and Blanche trying not to look upset.

"Sorry," she said. "I got caught up in convention nonsense—serving on an inane committee but you know how it is. Anyway, the serendipity I mentioned was a historian from Emory on the same committee—maybe kismet, huh? Turns out his much younger wife was here as an R.A. and she interviewed to be an advisor for that program. She didn't get it, Alex, but she knows who did—"

"Thurston Nobach."

Silence. "You got there without me."

"No big deal, Maxine."

"We're still pals?"

"You bet."

"When the time's right you'll tell me the story?"

"Got a few minutes right now?"

With Maxine in the loop, everyone on campus knew by morning. By noon the following day, lurid details, some of them true, quite a bit not, spread to social media.

As Thurston Nobach became the fiend of the moment, the people who'd created him withdrew from public life.

No attempt to achieve accuracy. That's the way it is, nowadays: facts, lies, the stuff in between.

CHAPTER

49

I got to read the material soon after Milo.

LAPD Document 18-4326-187D: Materials seized from two units at Academo-Strathmore Student Residences, Westwood Village.

Unit C-418

1. One socket wrench yielding blood, hair, and cranial bone matching that of assault victim Sandra Burdette, the handle additionally yielding latent fingerprints consistent with those of suspect T. Nobach.
2. Additional latent fingerprints consistent with those of suspect T. Nobach on the edge of a dresser and a bathroom counter

in Unit C-418, the latter admixed with blood from victim Burdette.

A. Supplementary data: eyewitness identification of suspect T. Nobach by victim Burdette as the man who assaulted her from behind when she attempted to leave an argument she'd had regarding his relationship with her daughter, attempted homicide victim Amanda Burdette.

B. Related supplementary data obtained at 12345 Wilshire Boulevard, Unit 24, PH1, former primary residence of suspect T. Nobach: latent fingerprints from a used hypodermic syringe containing traces of heroin and fentanyl matching Suspect T. Nobach's fingerprints and found near the unconscious form of attempted homicide victim A. Burdette, subsequently revived by LAPD Lieutenant Detective Milo Bernard Sturgis.

Unit B-425

1. Two glassine envelopes containing heroin laced with fentanyl. The proportion of fentanyl consistent with that found in the system of homicide victims Susan Koster and Michael Lotz and attempted homicide victim Amanda Burdette.

2. Three glassine envelopes containing powdered cocaine.

3. A bottle containing five benzodiazepam tablets, the label authorizing prescription of 50 tablets issued to Michael Lotz, prescribing physician Manuel Licht, M.D., The East Venice Community Clinic.

4. An acoustic guitar labeled King-Tone internally, manufactured seven years ago in South Korea. Five of six metal strings intact, the A-string missing and consistent with a ligature used in the homicide of victim Susan Koster.

5. One roll of 200 adhesive-backed decal-type stickers with the word "Thirsty" printed in black ink. Match to similar decals found on twelve textbooks belonging to attempted homicide victim A. Burdette.

6. Four color photographs of what appears to be a young deceased white female, subsequently identified as Cassandra Booker, manner of death previously registered as undetermined and subsequently altered to homicide. The images placed in an envelope embossed with suspect Nobach's name on the flap, along with a page of handwritten doggerel credited to suspect Nobach by himself, the cursive writing subsequently matched to samples from suspect Nobach's checkbook. **The young pass quickly. But never slickly. Dully naïve, they take their leave. Leaving no mark but a tiny little prick-ly.**

7. Four color photographs of what appears to be a middle-aged, deceased white male, subsequently identified as homicide victim Michael Lotz. Similar envelope to Booker, another page of doggerel. **He lives in a hole, the humanoid mole. No more than a prole, a step above the dole. Was there even a soul?**

8. Four color photographs of what appears to be a deceased young woman, subsequently identified as homicide victim Susan Koster. Similar envelope to Booker and Lotz. More extensive doggerel.

   Ooh, the shape. The curves, the swoops. The nape. She swings she prances. Pretends she dances. Playing a role. Riding the pole. Ceding her hole. Without resistance. Though there was assistance! Ah, the allure of the page. Believing she was sage. Not filth in a cage.

9. Four color photographs of what appears to be a deceased young woman, thin, long blond hair, as yet unidentified. Placed in an unmarked envelope along with a postcard depicting the Honolulu Hilton, Oahu, Hawaii.

10. Four color photographs of what appears to be a deceased young woman, thin, short brunette hair, as yet unidentified. Placed in an unmarked envelope along with a post-

card depicting the Lord Byron Hotel, Rome, Italy.

I finished reading, poured myself a double Chivas, sat back, and thought.

For all the probative value of the drugs, the prints, the guitar, and the bad verse, the piece of evidence I found most interesting had never made it to the murder book.

A collection of correspondence, including room measurement charts and bills of sale, exchanged over a two-year period between "Dr. Thurston Nobach, Esq.," and Smythe-Sheetley Booksellers, 65 Cambria Lane, London SW2V 5PS.

The company's motto:

"DECORATIVE, VINTAGE VOLUMES PURVEYED BY THE METRE."

CHAPTER

50

Within ten days, the swelling that had ballooned my left cheek subsided. Three days after that, I got a call from Brearely Burdette.

"I heard you got socked in the jaw, Dr. Delaware. Are you okay?"

"I'm fine, thanks. How's everyone doing?"

"Sandy's still in the hospital. She's got three skull fractures and will probably have headaches for a while but they say she'll be basically okay. They think. Amanda . . . you know, she's Amanda. Will told me he asked you to treat her but you said you couldn't and referred her to another therapist. That was probably a good idea. I wouldn't want her for a patient."

No sense getting into ethics. I said, "That's true." I'd just heard from the psychologist I recommended, Michelle Tessler. ("Obviously not a short-termer,

Alex. At least she's honest. You might say to a fault, but that beats digging through layers of bullshit.")

"Anyway," said Brearely, "I'm glad you're okay and I'm calling to invite you to lunch with me and Garrett. To express our thanks."

"That's lovely but unnecessary."

"That's exactly what Lieutenant Sturgis said—though he said 'kind' not 'lovely.' But I convinced him and he convinced Detective Binchy. So I said he should convince you, too, but he said you're your own person, he's got no influence."

"You're meeting with them?"

She laughed. "Not a meeting, we're having **lunch** with them and we'd **really** like you to be there."

I hesitated.

"Puh-**leeze,** Dr. Delaware? It would mean **so so** much."

"When and where, Brearely?"

"Tomorrow, The Shack in Malibu. Do you know it?"

"I do."

"Great! One o'clock, I hope that's not too short notice, if it is we'll change it."

I checked my calendar. "It's fine."

"Awesome. I **knew** I could pull it off!"

Gorgeous day in Malibu. When isn't it? Excepting fires, sewage leaks, fatal accidents, and other human assaults on Divine Intention.

The Shack was twenty-eight miles north of

Sunset on the land side of PCH. I'd passed it but had never been there.

A quick turn off the highway took the Seville up a dirt mound to a clearing. Weathered redwood picnic tables were scattered in front of a white clapboard former bait stand.

I'd gotten stuck in a traffic snarl just south of the Colony—from the length of the SUV motorcade, a politician coming to rattle a tin cup at celebrities—and by the time I arrived Milo had finished two of four cardboard containers of fried shrimp, each with a side of curly fries. Sean sat next to him, working on an oversized soft-tortilla mahi-mahi taco.

Facing them sat the newlyweds, holding hands behind paper plates of barely touched grilled snapper and steamed vegetables. Overdressed for the setting: Garrett, still stubble-bearded, in a vanilla-colored linen suit and a black T-shirt, the woman once known as Baby in a flowing red silk dress that exposed just a hint of cleavage.

The red was a couple of tones deeper than the scarlet sheath Susie Koster had worn to her death. As far as I recalled, bride and groom had never seen a full shot of her. At the most a ribbon of red at the bottom of the headshot.

So no sense interpreting.

On the other hand, maybe Brearely **had** caught enough color to start thinking. Or just feeling.

When it came to the human urge to process

horror by undoing, redoing, distorting, or simply pretending, you never knew.

Everyone greeted me.

Milo said, "Order at the counter."

Brearely said, "Oh, I'll do that for you, Doctor. What do you want?"

I said, "It's fine," and climbed to the shack. A sunburned couple in front of me took a while to decode their lunch desires before the kid behind the counter yelled, "Next!"

I ordered a taco like Sean's and an iced-tea. A sign said, **Pay Here,** so I held out cash.

The kid shook his head. "Dude in the suit took care of it, got his plastic numbers. Fill your own drink. When the grub's ready, someone'll bring it to you."

I returned to the table with a number on a metal stand and the tea.

"What'd you get?" said Milo, drawing carton number three near.

I pointed to Sean's plate.

Sean smiled and flashed the V-sign. Not his usual everything's-great grin; a shallow, obligatory uplift of lips. He was back on the job, doing desk work. Still talking in a rasp and wearing turtlenecks, today's bright green.

I sat to his left, at the short end of the table. He reached over and squeezed my hand. Held on, finally let go. Eventually, we'd talk about what happened.

"So," said Garrett. "We're really glad you all agreed to come. We really want to thank you. Not that the other detectives weren't great, but you were at . . . you were there when it happened."

Brearely said, "We **had** to thank you. For saving our wedding."

Milo and Sean and I stared at her.

"I don't mean literally, guys. Spiritually, that's more important." Touching her heart. "You did your wonderful detective work and proved it had nothing to do with us. That we didn't do anything wrong, none of our friends did. Even though some people said we did."

Milo said, "Who?"

Garrett said, "Idiot trolls on Facebook and Twitter."

"They trolled us because of the theme," said Brearely. "Saints and Sinners. What did they call it, honey?"

"They accused us of minimalizing sin, reducing it to a joke," said Garrett. "As if trying to lighten things up was some sort of moral failing."

His wife looked up at him lovingly.

I said, "That's pretty stupid, not to mention tacky."

"Anonymous makes it easy," rasped Sean.

Milo said, "Want us to track them down and slam 'em in jail?"

Brearely's eyes widened.

"He's kidding," said Garrett. "Right?"

Milo said, "Well . . . yeah, just fooling. Sorry if it scared you, Brearely."

"Don't be," said Brearely. "You have a right to joke. Your job, it's so serious, I don't know how you do it. That's why we wanted to do something nice for you. Even though it's just lunch. But we figured getting away from all the horrible stuff you see and coming out here would be like . . . healing."

Milo said, "I rarely pair 'just' with lunch."

Brearely said, "Huh?"

Garrett cued her with a laugh.

"Oh. Ha—look, here's your food, Doctor."

We ate and listened, for a while, to the meld of the ocean across the highway and roaring traffic before Garrett said, "We feel as if you vindicated us. That's helped clear our heads and allowed us to move forward and for that we'll always be grateful. We're also inviting you to next year. On our anniversary, we're going to throw a party. Nothing like the wedding. Just a party. If we can afford it, maybe someplace near here, Brears loves the ocean."

Brearely said, "I do and my mom knows places." She turned to her husband and cuffed his arm lightly. "I **hope** it's nothing like the wedding. Just **kid**ding."

Garrett gave a well-practiced smile. With luck, he'd be doing it for years. "So, if you can make it, around a year from now."

Brearely said, "We'll send you all e-vites. Way before, so you can arrange. Okay?"

Sean looked at Milo. Milo looked at me.

I said, "Sounds like fun."

"Great!" said Brearely, springing up and going around the table kissing each of us on the cheek. Sean blushed. Milo worked hard not to smile.

"So that's it," said Garrett, standing. "You guys eat, it's all paid for. We weren't really hungry, we just wanted to make sure you got good lunches."

Before we could thank him, he took his wife's hand and led her down the dirt mound. The two of them kept going until they reached the shoulder of the highway, then stopped and looked both ways.

Sean rasped, "They're going to try to cross?"

Milo rested his brow in his hand. "That's all we need, a real sad ending."

Fretting the way parents do when risks present themselves. Doing nothing because the kids were old enough and at some point, they just had to find their own way.

These two did. Watching patiently as vehicles roared pass. Finding a lull in the northbound traffic and running for the median.

They stood there for a while until the southern route cleared. Ran across the three remaining lanes and made it to the beach.

Garrett peeled off his suit jacket, managed to remove his shoes while standing. But he went no farther.

Standing in the sand, watching as his life partner

ran coltishly toward the breakers. Lifting up the hem of her red dress, luxuriant hair fanning.

She reached the water's edge, bent and scooped. Splashed like a toddler.

Too far to hear her, her slender back to me. But I knew she was laughing.

About the Author

JONATHAN KELLERMAN is the #1 **New York Times** bestselling author of more than forty crime novels, including the Alex Delaware series, **The Butcher's Theater, Billy Straight, The Conspiracy Club, Twisted, True Detectives,** and **The Murderer's Daughter.** With his wife, bestselling novelist Faye Kellerman, he co-authored **Double Homicide** and **Capital Crimes.** With his son, bestselling novelist Jesse Kellerman, he co-authored **A Measure of Darkness, Crime Scene, The Golem of Hollywood,** and **The Golem of Paris.** He is also the author of two children's books and numerous nonfiction works, including **Savage Spawn: Reflections on Violent Children** and **With Strings Attached: The Art and Beauty of Vintage Guitars.** He has won the Goldwyn, Edgar, and Anthony awards and the Lifetime Achievement Award from the American Psychological Association, and has been nominated for a Shamus Award. Jonathan and Faye Kellerman live in California, New Mexico, and New York.

jonathankellerman.com
Facebook.com/JonathanKellerman

LIKE WHAT YOU'VE READ?

Try these titles by Jonathan Kellerman,
also available in large print:

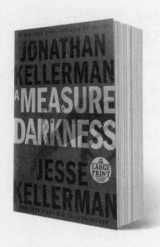

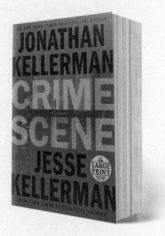

Night Moves
ISBN 9780525590361

A Measure of Darkness
ISBN 9780525637479

Crime Scene
ISBN 9780525524977

For more information on large print titles, visit
www.penguinrandomhouse.com/large-print-format-books